Where THE BOYS COME TO *die*

Other Books by Porscha Sterling

Addicted to You

Where THE BOYS COME TO die

PORSCHA STERLING

Kensington Publishing Corp.
kensingtonbooks.com

DAFINA BOOKS are published by

Kensington Publishing Corp.
900 Third Avenue
New York, NY 10022

All Kensington titles, imprints, and distributed lines are available at special quantity discounts for bulk purchases for sales promotion, premiums, fund-raising, and educational or institutional use. Special book excerpts or customized printings can also be created to fit specific needs. For details, write or phone the office of the Kensington Sales Manager: Kensington Publishing Corp., 900 Third Avenue, New York, NY 10022. Attn. Sales Department. Phone: 1-800-221-2647.

ISBN: 978-1-4967-4197-4
First Trade Paperback Edition: March 2026

ISBN: 978-1-4967-4203-2 (e-book)

10 9 8 7 6 5 4 3 2 1

Printed in the United States of America

The authorized representative in the EU for product safety and compliance
is eucomply OU, Parnu mnt 139b-14, Apt 123
Tallinn, Berlin 11317, hello@eucompliancepartner.com

Where THE BOYS COME TO *die*

Prologue

"Damn shame I gotta put a bullet through your forehead. You got such a pretty face."

Sincere squeezed her eyes closed, gritting her teeth as Lorde pressed the barrel of his gun against her skull. The hard, cold kiss of steel sent a shiver down her spine. Fear gripped her soul and clawed at the loose fragments of her mind, rendering her unable to even think a single sensible thought.

The world around her blurred, but the terror she felt was inescapable. The rough texture of the pavement biting into her knees, the muted scuff of boots stomping against concrete, and the faint drone of a streetlight above them only added to the eerie atmosphere.

And then there was Lorde's voice.

Low. Smooth. Clearly amused.

A stream of warm urine ran down her leg, pooling at her knees, now bruised and aching after she was forced to kneel on the concrete. Laughter erupted from behind her, sharp and mocking. The Saints, Lorde's followers, were there watching the spectacle as if it were entertainment. They reveled in her humiliation. Sincere clenched her jaw, swallowing back the acid rising in her throat. She wanted this moment to be over, but Lorde wasn't done playing with his food.

"You said the reason I ain't never seen you around is 'cause you don't be out like that," he mused, his voice dripping with condescension. "Always at home . . . readin' and writin' your little songs."

He snorted, shaking his head like the idea alone was laughable.

More laughter from his men was heard.

"Childish shit," Lorde sneered. "I bet you wish your little nerdy ass would've just stayed home tonight."

A sharp pang stabbed through her chest. *Yes. Yes, I do.* She wanted to scream it. If only it meant that she could turn back time. Because even now with a gun to her head and death grinning in her face, she refused to give him the power of knowing how desperate she was in that moment.

Instead, her mind drifted, clinging to the last remnants of normalcy. Of the hours before this. Before this moment, before Lorde's men forced her into this alleyway. Back when she was doing the one thing that she loved the most. Before she answered Aaliyah's call.

She should've let it ring. Should've stayed curled up in bed, pencil in hand, trying to force creativity to strike. Desperately trying to finish the song that had been tormenting her for weeks. But she didn't. Because whenever Aaliyah called, Sincere followed. She always did.

Now, because of that loyalty, she would die in the dirt, a bullet tearing through her skull, while her mother sat in her night class, believing her daughter was safe at home.

She wouldn't even know.

A fresh wave of nausea clawed at Sincere's insides.

Lorde cocked his head, watching her misery with dark amusement. He looked so evil, almost satanic, in his gaiety. "What? Cat got your tongue?"

Silence.

Sincere inhaled slowly, her bottom lip trembling with fear.

She lifted her gaze as she accepted her fate, locking onto his with everything she had left inside her.

She wouldn't beg. She wouldn't plead. She would not die a coward.

Lorde's eyes flickered, something unreadable passing over his face. And then . . . he smirked.

Click.

The metallic snap of the safety being released sliced through the air and Sincere thought she would release her bowels. Her pulse pounded in her ears. Her mind raced, reaching for something that could make this moment stop.

But there was no way out. No escape. No way to rewrite the past.

Because the story of how she got here had already been written . . .

A few hours earlier . . .

The streets of New Orleans throbbed with a pulse of its own at night. The air was filled with lust and dripping in sin. The sultry sounds of jazz music was the soundtrack of the night. And the intoxicating scent of fried catfish and powdered-sugar-kissed beignets clung to the Louisiana heat like a slow, lingering kiss.

This was everything that Sincere loved about home. She didn't have to go anywhere else to know this would always be her favorite city.

The All-Saints Festival was already in motion by the time they arrived. It was a feast for the living and the dead. A place where spirits danced in the air, their whispers threading through the laughter, the murmured prayers, and the banging of glass as people lined bottles against the wall to honor their departed loved ones.

But tonight, as they approached, something felt different.

As Aaliyah stopped to observe the crowd, finding a place for them to begin, Sincere stood on the corner, watching, feeling all the energy around pressing against her skin like a second layer of flesh. Her hands trembled at her sides, but she wasn't sure if it was from the energy of the city or of the night itself. Something was coming. She could feel it, creeping up her spine like a slow, knowing touch.

She wasn't supposed to be here. She knew it like an intuitive hit or some sort of premonition. In that moment, as Sincere stood observing the activity around her, she knew deep down inside that whatever her mother's reasons were for keeping her distance from this were for a good cause.

"Sincere, stop looking so scared. You look like somebody's lost puppy."

Aaliyah's voice snapped her out of her thoughts, and Sincere turned, catching her best friend's cocky grin and the dangerous sparkle in her eye. Aaliyah thrived in places like this—where trouble was an inevitability, not a possibility.

"I shouldn't have come," Sincere muttered, tucking her hands into the pockets of her denim shorts. "If my mom finds out—"

"She won't." Aaliyah rolled her eyes, linking arms with her. "Besides, we're here to have fun. And maybe . . ." She shot Sincere a knowing look. "Maybe get close to a few Saints."

Sincere's stomach flipped. "The Saints?"

"As in *the* Saints. The only reason we're even here." Aaliyah grinned, her perfectly glossed lips stretching over pearly white teeth. "New Orleans royalty, baby. And we're about to meet them."

Aaliyah had always been reckless. Sincere loved her for it, but tonight, something felt *different.*

The air had shifted around them.

The night had eyes.

And they were watching.

Aaliyah had the kind of personality that was contagious. Her energy was always so high that it was hard to not join in. She was the type of person who could make a snail race fun. That said, it didn't take long for Sincere to fall right in line. Less than half an hour later, she had a belly full of beignets from Café Beignet as Aaliyah finished up the last drops of her daiquiri, or—as the residents of NOLA called it—"purple drank."

"Ooh, a psychic! I want to get my fortune read!" Sincere said, spotting a lone tarot reader perched at a table, her eyes shadowed beneath a wide-brimmed hat.

Aaliyah raised a brow. "How much is it?"

The old woman sat in the shadows, her fingers tattered and thin as she shuffled her cards.

Sincere hesitated as Aaliyah pushed her toward the small table.

"Twenty-five dollars," the woman murmured.

Her accent was thick and she delivered her words slowly, like molasses dripping from her tongue. Both girls froze at her response, exchanging wide-eyed glances.

"How did she hear me over all this noise?" Aaliyah whispered, clutching Sincere's arm.

"I don't know," Sincere muttered.

"Crazy," Aaliyah said, recovering with a shrug. "Here. This is my thank-you for coming out with me. Go ahead, get your future read or whatever."

Sincere barely noticed Aaliyah press the money into the woman's palm before she felt those dark, unblinking eyes settle on her like a storm cloud.

Aaliyah bumped her hip playfully. "Girl, go! What you scared for? It's just a card."

"I ain't scared," Sincere muttered, though her voice betrayed her nerves.

"Mm-hmm." Aaliyah was clearly unconvinced, but not about to let her back out.

Taking a deep breath, Sincere walked toward the table, each step feeling heavier than the last. The woman didn't look up, her eyes focused on the worn deck of cards she shuffled with slow, deliberate movements. Her hands were thin, almost skeletal, and her skin stretched tight over knuckles that looked like they'd seen more years than most.

"Pick one."

Sincere's fingers hovered, shaking, before finally grasping a card. She turned it over.

Death.

Aaliyah sucked in a breath beside her.

Sincere felt ice drip into her veins.

The old woman tilted her head, studying the card with the patience of someone who already knew the answer.

"An ending," she murmured. "But also, a beginning."

Sincere's heart pounded. "What does that mean?"

The woman didn't answer. She just smiled.

Sincere tried to find her voice, but it felt like it had been snatched right out of her throat. Her eyes darted to Aaliyah, who was standing off to the side, her arms crossed and her face twisted into an expression that was half concern, half disbelief.

"What's it say?" Aaliyah asked, stepping closer and squinting at the card.

"Death," Sincere managed to get out. The words tasted foreign on her tongue. "It says . . . death."

"Girl, no it don't," Aaliyah said quickly, shaking her head as if the force of her denial could change the meaning of the card. "It don't mean that. It means change or transformation or something like that, right?"

She glanced at the woman for confirmation, but the old psychic said nothing, her lips pressed into a thin, unreadable line.

Aaliyah looped an arm around Sincere's shoulder and guided her away from the table, muttering under her breath about "spooky old women" and "bad energy." But Sincere couldn't shake the feeling that something had shifted, not just in the air around them, but in her. The card felt like a warning, a message she couldn't yet understand, but knew she couldn't ignore.

Aaliyah was quiet as they moved through the crowded street, her gaze darting around like she was searching for something—or someone. Sincere couldn't tell if she was spooked by the reading or just caught up in the energy of the festival, but her usual confidence seemed to be back in full force by the time they reached a corner where the crowd had thinned.

Aaliyah spotted it first. A gold chain lay discarded in the street, the fleur-de-lis pendant catching the glow of the streetlights. It looked expensive. Way too expensive to belong to just anybody.

"Somebody lost this," Aaliyah said, scooping it up, her grin widening.

Suddenly, Sincere felt the chill again. Her eyes narrowed as she stared at the emblem more clearly. It looked official, almost like a crest, and something about it felt . . . dangerous. "This doesn't look like just some random chain. You think it belongs to somebody important?"

"Probably a Saint," Aaliyah said with a shrug, tucking it back into her purse. "But they won't miss it. They got enough money to buy ten more just like it."

The mention of the Saints made Sincere's chest tighten. She'd heard enough stories to know they weren't the kind of people you wanted to cross, and the idea of her best friend holding onto something that might belong to them made her stomach flip.

"What are you gonna do with it?" Sincere asked, her voice low, almost cautious.

Aaliyah grinned, her confidence unwavering. "Pawn it, obviously. I need the money."

"I don't think that's a good idea," Sincere said quickly, her brows knitting together. "If it belongs to a Saint and they find out—"

"They won't," Aaliyah cut her off with a dismissive tone. "Stop worrying so much, Sincere. Nobody's gonna care about one little chain."

But Sincere wasn't so sure.

"You should put that back," she whispered.

Aaliyah laughed and waved her off. She wasn't trying to hear that. The rule was "finders keepers, losers weepers" and she was on the better end of the deal.

Sincere's stomach twisted. Something about that chain felt wrong.

It felt like a trap.

She opened her mouth to argue, but before she could, the hairs on the back of her neck stood on end. It was a strange feeling, like the air around her had thickened, pressing down on her chest and making it hard to breathe.

And then—

She felt him before she saw him.

A presence.

Watching.

She turned her head slowly, her eyes scanning the crowd.

He was leaning against a lamppost, his hazel eyes dark with unreadable intent. He didn't move, didn't speak. He just watched.

"Sincere? What's wrong?" Aaliyah's voice pulled her back, but Sincere couldn't tear her eyes away from him.

"I think he's staring at me," she whispered, her voice barely audible.

Aaliyah followed her line of sight, her expression shifting instantly when she spotted him. A slow, knowing smile spread across her face. "Oh, he's not just staring at you, baby. He's looking at you like you're the prize in a raffle."

Sincere's breath hitched. "Who is he?"

"That's Lorde," Aaliyah said, her tone dropping like she was sharing a secret. "He's one of the top dogs in the Saints."

Sincere's stomach churned. She'd heard his name before. Whispers about him floated through the streets like an urban legend. He wasn't just a member of the Saints, he was their future. Although he wasn't in the top spot yet, everyone knew that one day Lorde would be their leader.

"Which makes him dangerous, doesn't it?" Sincere asked, her voice trembling.

"Dangerous is the point. It's a show of power," Aaliyah said with a sly grin. "He's the kind of man who could change your whole life if you let him."

Sincere swallowed hard, her chest tightening as she turned back to look at him. Lorde hadn't moved, but the intensity in his gaze made her feel like he'd already taken a step into her world.

"I don't want my life changed," she murmured, more to herself than to Aaliyah. "It's fine the way it is."

"Don't be so sure," Aaliyah said with a wink. "Sometimes a little danger is exactly what you need."

Sincere didn't answer. She couldn't. Her gaze was still locked on Lorde, and the look in his eyes told her everything she needed to know. He wasn't just watching her. He was claiming her. And somehow, she knew this was only the beginning.

The thing about men like Lorde was that they didn't ask for permission. They didn't hover or linger in the corner. They walked into a space, claimed it, and dared anyone to challenge their right to be there. Lorde was no different.

One moment, Sincere's feet were rooted to the cobblestone street, her pulse loud enough in her ears to drown out the festival's music. The next, he was moving toward her, slow and deliberate, like a lion stalking prey that didn't even realize it had been spotted.

"Sincere, come on!" Aaliyah hissed, tugging her arm, but she couldn't move. Her feet felt like they'd been cemented to the ground.

She wasn't sure what it was—fear, curiosity, or the pull of something she didn't have a name for—but she couldn't look away. His eyes, sharp and focused, were locked onto hers, and the intensity in his gaze made her feel like he could see right through her. By the time he was standing in front of her, the world around them had dimmed into the background, as though the festival itself had bent to his will and quieted just for him.

"Evenin' baby," he said, his voice smooth and low, laced with an accent as rich with culture as the city itself. He didn't look at Aaliyah, didn't even acknowledge her presence. His focus was all on Sincere, as though she were the only person in the world worth noticing. It wasn't the kind of attention that made her feel flattered. It was the kind that made her feel exposed.

Aaliyah was undeterred. She stepped forward, wedging herself between Sincere and Lorde with a confidence only she could muster.

"I know you. You're Lorde," she said, her voice dripping with charm. "I guess by the way my girl's looking at you, I'd say you've made quite the impression."

Lorde didn't blink. His lips curled into a faint smirk, but his eyes stayed fixed on Sincere.

"Oh yeah? Well, what's your girl's name?" he asked, his tone casual, like he wasn't demanding an answer, but simply expecting one.

Before Aaliyah could reply, Sincere finally found her voice, though it was shakier than she would've liked. "It's Sincere."

"Sincere," he repeated, letting the name roll over his tongue like licorice. "I like that."

His smile widened slightly, and for a moment, she thought he might've been handsome if it weren't for the way he looked at her—like an object that he owned. As if she had no choice in the matter at all. Maybe that was attractive to some women, but Sincere hadn't been raised to think of herself as powerless.

"Thanks," she murmured, shifting uncomfortably under his gaze.

Aaliyah, clearly irritated by being ignored, laughed loudly, drawing his focus to her for the first time.

"Tell me, what's up? Are you gonna just flirt with my girl and not even ask me for my name?"

His eyes cut to Aaliyah briefly, his expression unreadable. "I don't need your name," he said simply before turning his attention back to Sincere.

Aaliyah's laugh faltered, her smile tightening, but she recovered quickly.

"Well, excuse me," she said, stepping closer to Sincere and looping her arm through hers. "But if you're trying to get at my girl, you're going to have to try a little harder."

Sincere could feel Aaliyah's nails digging into her arm, and for the first time, she realized her friend wasn't just annoyed. She was nervous.

"You don't like my style?" Lorde asked, his smirk returning as he cocked his head slightly to the side.

There was something playful about his tone, but at the same time, it didn't seem playful at all. Aaliyah, to her credit, didn't back down.

"I mean, you can't really try to talk to a woman and ignore her friend," she shot back, her voice steady.

Lorde didn't respond immediately. Instead, he took a slow step closer to Sincere, his gaze dropping to the curve of her lips before rising again to meet her eyes.

"What about you, Sincere?" he asked, his voice low enough that his question felt like a secret between them. "You don't like my style either? Or do you see me as a man who goes after what he wants?"

Her breath hitched, her chest tightening as the air around her seemed to grow heavier. Unlike Aaliyah, Sincere didn't have a problem with entertaining boys her age. She preferred to swim in the shallow end of the pool rather than plunge into the deep end. Lorde's forwardness left her unable to find a response.

"I—I don't know," she stammered, her voice barely above a whisper.

His expression sharpened, his mouth curving in a way that felt more like a warning than a smile. "Well, I guess I'll have to stick around and find out."

Before she could respond, before her brain could even process the weight of his words, Aaliyah stepped in again, her tone sharper this time.

"All right, Lorde—well, nice to meet you, but we've got places to be." She grabbed Sincere's hand and started to pull her away, but not before Lorde leaned in just close enough for his breath to brush against Sincere's ear.

"I'll see you around, baby," he murmured, his voice like velvet laced with iron.

Sincere barely sat down on the seats when Aaliyah cranked the engine, the loud rumble blending into the music and chaos of the festival behind them. She sank back onto the headrest, still trying to shake the image of Lorde's intense gaze following her through the crowd. Her palms were clammy, her chest tight, and some unseen force was pressing down on her like she couldn't take a full breath.

"Sorry, I snatched you away like that, but did you see that tattoo on his arm?" She waited for Sincere to respond, but it took a moment for her to catch her breath.

"No." She shook her head. "I couldn't see nothing but his eyes."

"Well, if you had seen it, you would know that it matched this." Aaliyah pulled out the chain from her pocket and pointed at the thick diamond and gold fleur-de-lis charm dangling in the end.

Sincere's eyes widened. "Are you saying you think it's his?"

Aaliyah dropped the chain in the space between them and sighed, allowing her body to drop back into her seat.

"Yeah," she replied in a small voice. "I can't keep it. I have to give it back. I don't want no smoke with Lorde."

"Yeah," Sincere agreed. "I wouldn't either."

She couldn't explain it, but Lorde unsettled her in a way that was hard to describe. He wasn't like the boys she'd dealt with before, not the sweet-talking types who made promises they had no intention of keeping. Lorde didn't need to promise anything. His presence alone demanded attention.

"Girl, you okay?" Aaliyah asked, snapping her fingers in front of Sincere's face as she backed the car into the street.

"I'm fine," Sincere said quickly, though the slight tremor in her voice betrayed her.

Aaliyah raised a brow but didn't press. "Look, I know he's intense," she said, her tone softening, "but don't let him get in your head. He's just a man. A man with a reputation, sure, but still just a man."

Sincere nodded absently, her thoughts too tangled to untangle. But before she could respond, she saw him again. He was standing in the street, hands in his pockets, his expression calm but unreadable. The dim streetlights overhead cast menacing shadows across his face, and Sincere's stomach dropped when Aaliyah slowed the car, muttering under her breath.

"What the hell does he want now?" Aaliyah hissed, her knuckles tightening on the steering wheel.

Before Sincere could stop her, Aaliyah rolled down the window. Lorde stepped closer, his movements unhurried, deliberate. The tension in the car was palpable as he leaned into the driver's-side window, his sharp hazel eyes cutting straight to Sincere.

"You leaving already?" he asked, his voice low, smooth, like he had all the time in the world to talk them out of their skin.

Sincere swallowed hard, trying to steady her breathing. "We were just—" She stopped mid-sentence when his eyes flicked down, catching on something in the middle console of the car. The chain. The one Aaliyah had showed her earlier, the golden links catching the light like they were begging to be noticed.

Sincere's blood ran cold as she watched his expression shift, the easy smirk disappearing as his lips pressed into a hard line. His eyes darkened, the calm in his demeanor evaporating like smoke.

"Where'd you get that?" he asked, his tone low and dangerous.

"What?" Aaliyah asked, her voice too casual as she tried to follow his gaze.

"That," Lorde said sharply, pointing to the chain. "That's mine."

Aaliyah froze for a split second, and then she did the worst possible thing she could have done. She laughed.

"Oh, this?" she said, her voice tight. "It was on the road. We didn't know it was yours."

Lorde's eyes snapped back to hers, and Sincere could feel the temperature in the car drop.

"You didn't know," he repeated, his voice as calm as it was cutting. "This is my territory. Everybody in the Deep knows that chain is mine."

Sincere's eyes traced back to Aaliyah and her expression only confirmed his statement.

"We were gonna give it back," Aaliyah added quickly, her grip tightening on the wheel. "It's not that deep."

For a moment, the air was thick with a silence so strong, it made Sincere want to scream just to break it. Then Lorde leaned further into the car, his gaze returning to Sincere.

"You knew about this?" he asked, his voice dangerously soft. "You was in on it?"

"I . . . I didn't—" Sincere started, her words tripping over themselves, but she didn't get a chance to finish.

Aaliyah hit the gas. The car lurched forward, the sudden motion jerking Sincere back against her seat as the engine roared. Lorde stumbled back, catching himself before falling backwards, and for one terrifying moment, Sincere thought they'd run him over.

"Are you crazy?" Sincere screamed, gripping the sides of her seat as Aaliyah swerved onto the main road.

"He was about to do something, Sincere!" Aaliyah yelled, her voice high and panicked. "You saw the way he was looking at us!"

"He's definitely about to do something now!" Sincere shot back, glancing over her shoulder just in time to see headlights flash behind them.

"Shit."

Aaliyah's voice was tight as she gripped the steering wheel, her fingers trembling.

Lorde's black Escalade was following them.

Gaining on them.

Sincere's stomach sank. "He's following us," she whispered.

Aaliyah didn't respond. Her jaw was set, her eyes locked on the road ahead as she pushed the car faster, the tires screeching around every corner. The first gunshot came out of nowhere, shattering the back windshield with a sharp, deafening crack.

Sincere screamed, ducking instinctively as glass rained down around her. "Oh my God, he's shooting at us!"

"No shit, Sherlock!" Aaliyah snapped, swerving hard to the

left as another shot rang out, this one slamming into the back tire.

The car jerked violently, the steering wheel shaking in Aaliyah's hands as the engine sputtered. Sincere clutched the dashboard, her heart pounding so hard she thought it might break through her chest.

"We have to stop!" she cried, her voice cracking with panic. "You're going to crash. We need to stop *now*!"

"No, we don't!" Aaliyah yelled back, her knuckles white as she fought to keep the car steady. "I can lose him!"

But the car trailing them wasn't letting up. Another shot came, blowing out the other back tire and sending them skidding sideways before it slammed into the curb. Sincere's head snapped forward, the seat belt digging into her chest as the car shuddered to a halt.

Metal crunched and glass rained down all around them. For a moment, there was nothing but the sound of the engine sputtering and the uneven rasp of her breathing. Then came the footsteps.

Deliberate and slow.

Sincere's blood turned to ice. She turned her head just in time to see the driver's-side door ripped open, one of Lorde's men yanking Aaliyah out and slamming her against the car.

"Don't do this!" Sincere screamed, her voice hoarse from desperation. "Please, don't—"

"Shut up!" another one of the men snapped, kicking her hard enough in the ribs to knock the air out of her lungs.

This wasn't over. Not even close. Her hands started scraping against the rough concrete as she tried to scramble to her feet.

"Stay down," a voice snarled above her, and a boot pressed against her back, pinning her to the ground.

The world spun around her, the sounds of shouting and laughter blended into a chaotic blur. And then he was there.

Lorde.

He stepped into her line of vision, his presence commanding even in the chaos. His eyes locked onto hers glowing like embers of fire in the dark, and for a moment, everything else disappeared.

"This," he said, holding up the chain in front of Aaliyah. "This was your first mistake."

"No . . . no, no, no!" Sincere sobbed, her voice cracking as she struggled against the weight holding her down. "Please! She's—she's sorry! She didn't mean—"

The boot lifted from her back, and she barely had time to push herself up on trembling hands before another pair of hands grabbed her, yanking her to her feet. She swayed, unsteady, her breath coming in short, panicked bursts as she found herself face-to-face with him.

He stood in front of her, the chain dangling from his hand like a trophy, his hazel eyes burning with an intensity that made her knees weak. There was a black mark on the side of his shoe where Aaliyah's tire had nearly clipped him, but his face was calm, eerily calm, as though none of this had affected him at all.

Sincere's stomach churned as his hazel eyes swept over them, cold and calculating. He moved slowly, the chain dangling from his hand, its golden links catching the faint glow of the streetlights.

"Which one of you took it?" he asked, his voice quiet, but sharp enough to cut through the silence.

Neither of them answered.

Lorde tilted his head slightly, his gaze slicing between the two of them. His lips curved into something that might've been a smile if it wasn't so void of humor. "Don't play dumb with me," he said, his tone hardening. He turned to Aaliyah, whose chest was rising and falling rapidly as she avoided his gaze. "Was it you? It was you, wasn't it?"

Aaliyah didn't say a word. Her hands shook at her sides, her lips parting like she wanted to speak but couldn't find the courage.

Sincere saw it then. The fear in her friend's eyes, the way her confidence had crumbled under Lorde's intense gaze. Realizing Aaliyah couldn't handle this, she did the only thing she could.

"It was me," Sincere blurted out, her voice trembling as she stepped forward. "I took it. I'm sorry."

The words hung in the air, and for a moment, no one moved. The men exchanged glances, their expressions a mixture of confusion and amusement.

Lorde's gaze shifted to Sincere, his hazel eyes narrowing as he studied her. He stepped closer, his head tilting as he took her in, from the valiant lift of her chin to the way her hands trembled at her sides.

"You're lying," he said finally, his voice calm but firm.

Sincere's breath caught, her heart sinking. "No, I'm not. I—"

"Don't insult me," he interrupted, his tone sharper now. He gestured to Aaliyah with the chain. "Her shitty reputation speaks for itself. I know who she is. And you . . ." He stared down at Sincere, eyes narrowing slightly. "You don't have the guts."

Sincere's lips parted, but she couldn't force any words out. Her throat felt like it was closing up, her pulse thundering in her ears.

Lorde turned to his men, his expression hardening. "Separate them," he ordered, motioning toward an alley on the other side of the street. "Take them down there. Separate ends. I'll decide what happens to them."

Sincere's chest tightened as the men moved in. "Wait, please!" she cried, but her words fell on deaf ears.

Rough hands grabbed her, pulling her away from Aaliyah, who was dragged in the opposite direction.

"Sincere!" Aaliyah screamed, her voice cracking as she struggled against her captors.

Sincere fought back too, but it was no use. She was shoved into the dirt of the alley, her knees scraping against the ground as two men pinned her down, their grips bruising. Tears streamed down her face as she struggled, her cries muffled by the sound of her own sobs.

"Please," she whimpered, her voice barely audible. "Please, don't hurt her."

She squeezed her eyes shut, her body trembling as she prayed silently. But then the gunshot came. It was loud and sharp, echoing through the alley like a thunderclap. Sincere froze, her heart lurching in her chest as terror gripped her. She felt like the ground had dropped out from under her, her stomach twisting painfully as the realization hit her.

Aaliyah.

"No!" she screamed, her voice raw and broken. She sobbed hysterically, her shoulders shaking as the men held her down, forcing her to her knees. The cold, rough ground scraped against her skin, and she barely noticed the damp warmth spreading beneath her. She'd wet herself, but she didn't care.

Her mind was spinning, her thoughts a chaotic blur of panic and grief. The only thing she knew to do in that moment was the one thing that her grandmother had told her to do in times like this. She started to pray. She prayed so hard, she didn't even realize Lorde was standing in front of her until his voice cut through the fog.

"Quiet," he said, his tone cold and sharp.

Sincere's sobs stifled to a whimper as she looked up at him, her tear-streaked face pale and trembling. His expression was calm. *Too* calm. And the sight of it made her stomach churn.

He crouched down in front of her, the gun still in his hand, its barrel glinting faintly in the dim light. "You prayed for her, didn't you?" he asked, his voice soft, but laced with something cruel.

Sincere nodded weakly, her breath hitching as more tears spilled from her eyes.

"And what about you?" he continued, tilting his head slightly. "You gonna pray for yourself now?"

Her lips trembled, but she couldn't answer.

"She's not dead . . . yet. But let's see how your prayers work out for you."

He raised the gun, the barrel pointed directly at her forehead. Sincere's breath hitched, her chest heaving as fresh tears poured down her face.

"Please," she whispered, the word barely audible. "I . . . *we* didn't know."

Lorde smirked, his gaze dropping to the wet stain on her dress. "You pissed yourself," he said, his voice low and mocking.

The men behind her chuckled, their laughter cold and hollow, but Sincere didn't care. All she could think about was the gun, the weight of it aimed at her head, and the fact that she wasn't ready to die.

Lorde's finger hovered over the trigger, and for a moment, she thought he was going to do it. But then he lowered the gun. "You won't die tonight," he said, his voice soft. He leaned in close, his breath warm against her ear as he whispered. "I'll let you live. But, someday, when you least expect it, I will come for you. And when I do, you'll be mine."

Sincere's chest tightened, her tears blurring her vision as he straightened, the chain still clutched in his hand.

"Let her go," he said to his men as he left them to follow his orders.

The hands holding her down released her roughly, and she stumbled forward, her knees hitting the ground again.

As she scrambled to her feet, one of the men grabbed her arm, his hand brushing against her side before shoving her toward the street. Another grabbed her backside, laughing as he groped her as if finding comedy in the way Sincere recoiled.

"Get outta here," one of them snarled, and she didn't need to be told twice.

She ran away as fast as she could. Her legs burned, her lungs screamed, but she didn't stop. As she passed the alley where Aaliyah had been taken, her steps faltered, and her stomach dropped when she saw Lorde standing in front of her.

And then—

The sound of a gunshot sliced through the air. It was loud and sharp, echoing through the alley like a thunderclap.

Sincere froze, her heart lurching in her chest as terror gripped her. She felt like the ground had dropped out from under her, her stomach twisting painfully as the realization hit her. She knew it then. Didn't need to see a body for the confirmation.

Her best friend was dead.

Chapter 1

Sahara: The Artist Formerly Known as Sincere

Five Years Later

The house was still. Still in a way that pressed against the walls like a long-held breath. Sahara had learned to live with silence, even pretended to love it. But the truth was, silence had never been her friend. Because silence bred loneliness, and loneliness was something she never invited, yet it followed her everywhere. It wrapped itself around her like a second skin. Settled deep into the polished hardwood floors, stretched up to the high ceilings, clung to the designer furniture like an invisible force. It was the worst kind of company, because it reminded her of what she'd lost. Of *whom* she'd lost.

Aaliyah.

Her mother.

Everyone who meant everything to her.

Her mother wasn't dead, but she hadn't spoken to her in years, so she might as well have been. Of the two, Aaliyah's presence was what Sincere missed the most. She was the loud one, the bold one, the kind of girl who could light up a room with nothing more than a look. She was *everything* Sahara wasn't. Confident and untouchable, like the sun was in her orbit, while Sahara was the quiet, thoughtful one, merely happy to exist in her shadow and reap the rewards that came with her presence.

But now Aaliyah was gone.

And suddenly, the shadow that had once been comforting became suffocating. Suddenly, she wasn't *Sincere* anymore.

She couldn't be.

Lorde hadn't killed her that night, but he might as well have, because she died alongside Aaliyah.

To survive, she reinvented herself.

And now she was Sahara.

She was no longer the scared, naive girl from the past, but the multiplatinum, award-winning artist—the *phenomenon*. Sahara had become the vocalist with the voice that moved crowds, the woman whose name trended worldwide. A star whose face was plastered on billboards and magazine covers.

It had only taken a few years for her to fully transform. She had manifested it, sacrificed for it, *earned* it. By all accounts, life was perfect. Or, at least, it *should* have been.

But nobody had ever told her the ugly truth about success: That no amount of money could erase what happened to Aaliyah. And no amount of security could protect her from the terror that tortured her from the inside.

Sahara's house was as breathtaking as the world expected it to be. Her estate was grand and immaculate—a fortress disguised as a home. Although she hadn't heard a peep about Lorde since that tragic night years ago, like so many decisions she made in her life, she picked it based on her fear of him. Even though she tried to ignore his threat, it lived somewhere in the back of her mind, subconsciously engineering most of her life decisions.

Her estate was hidden behind high black iron gates and tucked away in the quietest part of Atlanta, with two large bullmastiffs she purchased, not as pets, but to roam the land and deter intruders. It was the kind of place people dreamed about. A home that whispered *I made it* without her ever having to say a word.

But to her, it wasn't a home.

It was just another stage.

Sahara leaned against the cool marble of her kitchen island, silk robe tied loosely at her waist, staring at the digital clock on the stove—*11:48 p.m.* Her company wasn't due until midnight. She still had time.

Sahara glanced toward the fridge, where an unopened bottle of Moët waited, untouched. She didn't drink. Never had. But she liked knowing it was there. It made her feel like she had a choice. At the end of the day, that's all life ever really came down to: choices. She had learned that choices could make or break a person.

Or worse . . . They could turn you into someone you never wanted to be.

The knock came at exactly 11:50, breaking the silence.

Sahara didn't rush to answer. She never rushed to do anything for a man. Instead, she padded barefoot to the front door, imported hardwood floors supporting her pretty pink manicured toes. She stopped by the half bathroom to take a moment and spray a touch of Baccarat Rouge on the inside of both of her thighs. Something about the scent drove a man crazy.

She continued to the front and tied the robe tighter around her waist, her curls still damp from the shower, pausing just long enough for the anticipation to build on the other side of the door. The knock came again, sharper this time, and a small smile tugged at the corners of her lips. Men were always impatient when it came to her. Always gracious for whatever crumb she was willing to give.

When she opened the door, Clay stood there, his frame filling the doorway. He had the look of a man who'd just walked out of a gym catalog: clean-cut, broad-shouldered, with the kind of arrogance that made women look twice. His grin widened when he saw her, boyish and confident, like a contestant on a game show who had just been shown his prize.

"You're late," Sahara said, her voice smooth and a touch playful.

"Traffic," he replied, holding up a white bakery bag and a bottle of champagne.

She barely reacted to the sight of it. All this time and he still hadn't realized that every glass he ever poured for her went untouched. His grin didn't falter as he stepped inside, brushing past her like he belonged there. Sahara let the door close softly behind him, watching as he placed the bag and bottle on the counter with practiced ease. He always brought something, but she let him think it mattered.

"Hungry?" he asked, turning to face her.

Her lips curved into a faint smile as she leaned against the counter, letting the silk robe slip just enough to show a sliver of skin. "Not for food."

Clay's grin widened, and she saw it—that flicker of anticipation that came right before men lost themselves. He stepped closer, his cologne filling the space between them. It was warm and earthy. A scent that lingered long after a man left. Thankfully, she had plenty of candles and incense to deal with that.

"You ready for the show tomorrow?" he asked, his voice low now, soft.

The question made her stomach twist. Everyone wanted to

know if she was ready. The fans, the press, the bloggers who dissected every move she made. Six months off the radar had turned her into a mystery they couldn't stop trying to solve. Rehab wasn't the kind of answer they wanted, so they made up their own. Cloning conspiracies. Secret pregnancies. Rumors that she'd died and been replaced by a look-alike.

The whole world was waiting for her comeback. Six months of rehab, media silence, and unanswered questions. They didn't know about the pills, or the nights she'd spent staring at the ceiling, wondering how the hell she'd ended up like this. They only knew the image. The star. Sahara.

She didn't care what they believed. Sahara had learned long ago that the world never cared about the truth, only the spectacle. It was way more interesting to come up with stories as to why she'd disappeared than the reality that she was an addict.

"I'm always ready," she said, her voice light, easy. She reached up to straighten his collar, her fingers brushing his neck. "But I don't want to talk about that."

Clay's grin widened, his body relaxing as he stepped closer to her. "What do you want to talk about, then?"

"Nothing," she said, slipping her arms around his neck and pulling him closer. "The only thing I'm ready for . . . is you to shut up and give me some dick." Sahara batted her lust-filled eyes.

Reaching down, she wrapped her hands around Clay's meat and squeezed it between her fist. "Mmm," she moaned, tossing her head back as she stroked him seductively and slowly, loving the feel of his strength growing in her hand.

He was so thick and juicy. So big. She felt his heart beating through the bulging vein that traveled all the way down the shaft and through the head. It made her mouth water.

"Ohh, Sahara." He squeezed his eyes tightly together, relishing in the pleasure. "I love you."

"I love you too, daddy," she moaned into his ear, whispering sweet lies. It was sex talk. Nobody really meant it. It was about the moment.

His legs got weak, so he moved backward, guiding her to move with him until he lowered down onto her suede sectional.

"Sahara, pleeeeasssse. Don't stop."

There was nothing sexier than hearing a man moan her name. Giving pleasure was so empowering. She opened her eyes and looked into his. They were so clouded with emotion. So full of desire and want. The moment he saw how well she could please one of the smallest muscles on his body, she had complete control of him.

"How about I give you something even better?"

Sahara hovered her hips over the top of him, jerking him back and forth until the moment when she pushed him in, her pink folds spreading to swallow him whole. She never used protection, even though she knew that she should. Every time she had sex it was like playing Russian roulette with a penis. That was her reckless side. The part of her that didn't care if she lived or died.

Taking control, she directed him by grabbing his hands and cupping them around her ass cheeks. She didn't need him to tell her how to move. She just knew that feeling that ass twerk from the inside and outside made a man lose his shit.

Although Clay had the kind of body that made you think he spent most of his time in the gym, his movements were uncoordinated, fumbling almost. Sahara made up for it, guiding him with her hands and her body, showing him exactly how to please her while making him think it was his idea.

She moved like she was conducting a symphony, her hips rising and falling to the rhythm she set. His breaths came in short, sharp bursts, his hands gripping her thighs like they were the only thing giving him life.

"Damn, baby," he groaned, his voice thick with awe. "You're something else."

Sahara smiled faintly, leaning down to press her lips against his ear. "You bring it out of me," she lied, her tone sweet and soft. She didn't have to mean it. He'd believe her anyway.

He gripped her tighter, his head tilting back as he let out a low, guttural sound that made her feel powerful. She reveled in it. A man's pleasure became her weapon. She moved faster, her body arching as her hands braced against his chest. His heartbeat was wild beneath her palms, and she could feel the tension coiling in his muscles as he came.

When the moment was over, he collapsed against the pillows, his chest rising and falling as he tried to catch his breath. Sahara slid off of him gracefully, reaching for her robe and pulling it back on. He felt weak and she felt powerful, meaning her job was done.

She didn't cuddle him after . . . it wasn't her style. She liked the space it gave her, the quiet reminder that no matter how close someone got, she was always the one who left first. Everything moved how she willed it to.

"That was . . ." Clay started, his voice trailing off as he searched for the words. "I don't even know what to say. It was . . . damn."

He looked at her with this mix of awe and longing that always made her uncomfortable. Like he thought he'd unlocked some hidden part of her.

He hadn't.

Didn't even make her cum.

When she wanted that to happen, she did that for herself. She never wanted a man to think he was responsible for her pleasure.

Unable to figure out his next words, Clay lay back on the bed, breathing heavily, trying to recuperate from the best sex of his life. Sahara was the kind of woman he'd never met before. She knew what she wanted and wasn't afraid to take it. She was bold, confident, and made no apologies. It was hard as hell not to find that sexy.

On top of all that, every time they fucked, she did it like it could be their last time. She put her all into it, getting off on finding ways to provide him pleasure. She was a one-of-a-kind woman and his only regret was that he hadn't found her *before* he got married.

"You need to go home," Sahara said as she rolled off the side of the bed and stood to her feet. "I have to get showered and get my mind ready for the show. And you need to go home to your wife. Maybe then, she'll stop blowing up my phone."

She stretched her arms to the sky, elongating her perfect, naked body, showing off curves that were evidence of a childhood spent eating jambalaya and gumbo. She was BBL-free and thick in all the right places. She wore her weight with a confidence that came from being the baddest in the room. The woman so many men wanted, but none had the skills to tame. So many wanted to have her, but Sahara refused to be kept. And that just made them want her even more.

"Why do you do that?" Clay asked, using his elbows to lean up on the bed. His brows set into a deep frown, though his dick was standing straight on end, clearly wanting more.

"Why do I do what?" Sahara pretended to be dumb as she headed to the shower. When she heard Clay rise from the bed, she inwardly groaned.

"Why do you always try to dismiss me as soon as we're done? You act like you don't want me here."

"I *did* want you here," she clarified to him. "If I didn't, I wouldn't have let you in."

She tried to close the bathroom door to force space between them, but Clay put out his hand to stop it.

"Sahara, don't play dumb with me." His voice lowered to a

tone that was supposed to be serious, more threatening. "Is it just sex? Is that all there is between us?"

Sahara had to bite her lip to stop from laughing. "What else could there be?" She threw her hands in the air, clueless. "Clay, you're married. And not just to anyone . . . you're married to my manager. This was always just about sex. We knew it wasn't going anywhere."

Rolling her eyes, she turned to start the shower, but there was something about Clay's sudden silence that set off the alarms in her head. Her intuition picked up on the vibe immediately. This was a familiar place. One she'd been many times before. It was the moment when she got the signal that it was time to go.

"But . . . what if something has changed. What if I *want* there to be more?"

Turning slowly, Sahara let out a deep exhale, hating that this moment had come so fast. Clay was a rare find. He was a man married to a woman who didn't care where he was or who he was with because, for her, work always came first. On top of that, he had a huge dick. Of all the many men flowing in and out of her life, this one was going to be a hard one to give up.

"Clay, listen to me." She placed her hands on either side of his face, forcing him to look her in the eyes. "It's not you. It's me. Please, don't take this personal. I just don't want anything else. You're a great guy, but it's only ever been about the sex for me. And that's all."

She saw it the moment it happened. The moment when everything inside of Clay seemed to deflate, as if he were imploding in on himself. He took a few steps backward until the back of his legs hit the bed and then they folded, as if he collapsed onto it rather than taking a seat.

"But . . . I thought you loved me," he said.

Sahara's eyes shot through the bathroom door and over to him. *He thought . . . what?*

"Clay . . . I've only ever said that during sex. It was part of the experience." She squinted at him. "You thought I *meant* it?"

He didn't even open his mouth, but the droop in his shoulders said everything.

"You need to go," she said gently, tying her robe around her waist. "I have to get some sleep before tomorrow."

Clay sat up, his brows furrowing as he watched her move to the bathroom. "Why do you always do that?"

"Do what?" she asked, glancing over her shoulder.

"Act like I don't mean anything to you," he said, his voice quieter now, almost wounded.

Sahara's blank expression didn't falter, but her chest tightened. She hated this part. "You mean something to me," she said softly. "But you know what this is, Clay. You knew from the start."

His shoulders slumped and she could see the disappointment in his eyes.

"Yeah," he muttered, standing and grabbing his clothes. "I guess I did. I'll just get my things and get out."

He said the words as if he were seeking pity. Like he was hoping for her to yell out and stop him, tell him that he didn't have to go. She wouldn't.

She didn't say anything as he dressed, didn't stop him as he left. When the door clicked shut behind him, the house was quiet again, and she felt the weight of it settle over her. She hated being alone, but she hated having her peace disturbed even more. She moved to the couch, curling up with her knees to her chest as she stared at the darkened TV screen.

This was who she was now. Sahara. The woman no one could keep, no one could touch. Men thought they loved her, but they didn't. They loved the illusion she gave them, the version of herself she let them see. If they ever saw the truth, if they ever met the broken girl she kept hidden, they'd be the first to leave.

She exhaled and rested her head against the back of the couch, closing her eyes. And that's when she heard it. Somewhere in the back of her mind, a voice whispered, soft and familiar. It didn't occur often, but it still happened. Every time there was silence, especially when she was alone.

Someday, when you least expect it, I will come for you.

Sahara opened her eyes, her chest tightening as the memory began to fade. She shook her head, pushing the thought away. Lorde was gone. He wasn't coming back. At least, that's what she told herself. Instead of letting her mind linger on him, she forced herself to focus on her current situation with Clay. He was a present and real concern. She had no time to sit around worrying about a ghost.

Why does this always happen? I was so careful with him.

It was like it didn't matter what she did. How careful she was. How upfront or how clear. How much she communicated her boundaries. None of it mattered, because they always fell in love with the fantasy in the end.

Because the reality was, Sahara was no good for anyone.

Maybe it all changed that one night years ago; when being desired by a man changed her entire life. It was that moment that transformed her into a black widow. The tarot card was right: Death and transformation were imminent in more ways than one. Aaliyah had died, but so had Sincere's innocence.

And now, she was poison placed on the tip of licorice—sweet to taste, yet toxic and deadly. Where love gave life, all she had to give was heartbreak and sorrow.

She was the place where the boys came to die.

Chapter 2

"I *told* you that you were gonna rock that shit. And that's exactly what the hell you did! You got on that stage like you never even left it. Straight *fire*! I'm so proud of you!"

The air inside the room was filled with the scent of vanilla-scented body oil and the faint traces of the blunt that Lena had sparked earlier. The bass from the party outside rumbled beneath them, vibrating through the floors. Which was why Sahara was taking her time leaving the room. She was enjoying the quiet before she stepped into Rocco's chaos.

Rocco was her boyfriend. Not by choice—it was just something he decided. No discussion. No question. Just one day, the title was his, and that was that.

As an independent rapper who had just secured a major-label deal, Rocco was on the rise, making moves that kept his name hot in the industry. Sahara's manager saw the opportunity before she did. Being with him meant visibility, connections, and, most importantly, protection. In an industry where power dictated everything, a woman without the right affiliations was easy prey.

Sahara hadn't objected. Sometimes survival meant playing the game.

"I'm glad you said that because I was so nervous," Sahara

replied, running a hand through her curls to smooth them down over her head. "There were so many people in the crowd just watching. Trying to see if I would crack. Hell, *I* thought I would crack. I mean, it was the first show I've ever done sober."

"Exactly. And you *did* that. Which only proves that you can do whatever you want to do. No limits!"

Leaning over, Lena wrapped her arms around Sahara's neck, pulling her into a tight hug while jumping up and down. In true Lena-style, she was overly excited and amped up. Everything about her was always on ten. That was one of the main things that drew Sahara to her. She was the type of person who naturally elevated the mood with her presence, which reminded her so much of Aaliyah.

"Thanks, Lee." Sahara grinned, giving her girl a hug back.

Being honest, she was surprised herself. After six months away from the stage, mixed with the fact that she'd never performed sober before, she was on edge up to the second that she stepped out in front of the crowd.

"The fans gave me energy. It was a high like nothing I'd ever experienced before. Probably because I've always been too numb to feel it," she added as an afterthought. "I hope I never get back on that shit."

Lena didn't respond and once Sahara picked up on her silence, it became clear why. Although she'd stopped popping pills before shows and parties, Lena was still deep in the party life. She didn't need much of a push; she used any and every opportunity to get high.

"We need to finish getting ready so we can get out of here. You hear the way that music is thumping? I know it's live out there right now. Rocco never disappoints when it comes to throwing a party."

Scoffing, Sahara rolled her eyes. "Yeah and based off the long line of half-dressed women that I saw strolling up in here earlier, I'm sure my presence isn't being missed."

"Girl, don't worry about them bitches," Lena said as she sat down at the makeup counter in Sahara's bathroom to fix her hair. "Rocco would be stupid to play you for somebody whose only talent is how well they can swallow a dick."

She made a face to place extra emphasis on how ridiculous an idea that was before picking up a mascara wand to place some finishing touches on her lashes. Truthfully, she didn't need any extra primping. Lena was gorgeous. With smooth umber skin, auburn hair, and striking hazel eyes, she was a true goddess to anyone with eyes. On top of that, she had a natural body with curves that she didn't need to go to the doctor to make or the gym to maintain. She was one of the lucky ones: a woman who could do and eat what she wanted without dealing with any of the consequences.

"That's what you might think, but someone may need to tell Rocco that," Sahara whispered to herself, as she slid into the bandage dress selected by her personal stylist.

Rocco and Sahara were the kind of couple who looked good on paper. Both of them were independent artists who created a following on their own. It made sense for them to be together, but outside of being in the music industry, they couldn't be more different.

Rocco was the type of artist who built a name off of being something he wasn't. He was a gangster rapper, always rhyming about hood shit and gang life without ever having lived it. He made so much noise in the industry, but went the extra mile to make sure no one knew about his upbringing or family. He was a pretender; someone who grew up privileged, but acted like he didn't in order to fit in. It worked for him. His money and privilege were exactly the thing that got him seen and known as a rapper.

Sahara sat in front of the vanity, running a delicate hand over her braids as she checked her reflection. Not a flaw in sight.

Face beat, curves cinched, aura untouchable. A bad bitch in every sense of the word. But beneath the surface, she felt . . . *nothing.*

Lena, perched on the arm of the chaise lounge, flashed a sly smile through the mirror, arms crossed over her chest. "So, you gonna tell me or I gotta drag it out of you?"

Sahara arched a brow, playing innocent. "Tell you what?"

Lena rolled her eyes. "Don't act dumb, ho. I know somebody was in your bed last night, and it damn sure wasn't just you."

Amused, Sahara turned in her seat. "Oh, so now you a psychic?"

"Nah, but I *am* your best friend. And your ass wasn't answering my texts after midnight, which means one thing . . . *somebody* was putting it down."

Sahara let out a soft chuckle, reaching for her lip gloss and gliding it across her full lips. "Maybe I was just sleeping."

"Girl, *please*," Lena scoffed. "You ain't been to sleep before three a.m. since I met you. Who was it?"

Sahara hesitated just long enough for Lena's curiosity to sharpen.

"Oh, this is gonna be good," Lena said, leaning forward. "Spill."

Sahara sighed, stretching her arms behind her head. "Clay."

Lena's eyes widened before she threw her head back in laughter.

"*Clay?*" she repeated, shaking her head. "Not your manager's *husband*, Clay? *Stacy's* Clay?"

"The one and only."

Lena let out a low whistle, clearly impressed. "Sahara, you ain't got no damn sense."

Sahara's lips formed a thin smile. "Not really."

"Whew," Lena fanned herself. "You *are* on demon time. I mean, I get it. Stacy is a bitch. Horrible energy, always trying to boss you around like you ain't the reason she got a job. I mean, I respect the revenge. But damn. You *really* had to fuck her husband?"

Sahara turned back toward the mirror, running her fingers over the gold necklace resting against her collarbone. "It wasn't about her."

Lena gave her a knowing look. "Mmm. You sure about that?"

Sahara met her gaze through the reflection. "Honestly? Maybe a little."

Lena chuckled. "Petty."

Sahara shrugged. "It's not like she cares. She doesn't even *like* him. Their marriage is a business arrangement. All about convenience. She's got her own side pieces. Trust."

Lena nodded, crossing one leg over the other. "That still don't mean *he* don't care. You do realize that, right?"

Sahara sighed, rubbing her temple. "Yeah. And that's the problem."

Lena's smile softened, curiosity shifting to amusement. "Wait. Don't tell me he's catching feelings?"

"*Hard.*"

Lena let out a loud, dramatic laugh. "Damn. What did you do to that man?"

Sahara leaned back in her chair, staring at the ceiling. "Gave him what his wife don't. Attention. A soft touch. A little bit of a fantasy." She exhaled. "And now? He's texting too much. Showing up unannounced. Talking about feelings."

Lena shook her head, her grin widening. "You really flipped the whole game on these niggas, huh?"

Sahara arched a brow. "What do you mean?"

Lena leaned forward, her eyes gleaming with admiration. "You know how they gas us up, love-bomb us, say *all* the right shit—then disappear when we start catching feelings? You flipped it. You *are* the player now. You think like a man and these fools don't even know what to do with it."

Sahara tilted her head, contemplating Lena's words. "Maybe."

"Nah," Lena countered. "Not *maybe*. Definitely. You out here playing the game better than them."

Sahara didn't respond, but the truth twisted inside her like a blade. She wasn't playing. This wasn't a game to her. This was survival. She didn't know how to operate any other way.

But Lena didn't know that.

To the world, Sahara was the woman who couldn't be touched. The woman who controlled her life, her body, her choices. The woman other women envied, praised even. But the truth?

She was *empty* inside.

None of those decisions was based on what she wanted. They were based on fear. She was scared to let go enough to allow a man to have any control over her. Sahara reached for the glass of water sitting on the counter, taking a slow sip before speaking. "I have to cut him off."

Lena groaned. "Damn. You really gonna do him like that?"

"What else can I do?" Sahara asked. "He's getting attached. And the second a man gets attached, he starts expecting. Expecting me to be soft. Expecting me to be *his*. And I'm nobody's."

Lena grinned. "That's what makes you a legend."

Sahara let out a soft laugh, shaking her head.

"I appreciate that."

"Just remember." Lena waved a dismissive hand. "Playing with fire is fun. Just don't get burned."

Sahara's smile faltered, just for a second. But she covered it well, turning her attention back to the mirror, back to the illusion she had mastered.

Lena stood, grabbing her purse. "All right, Ms. Boss Bitch. Let's get out there before the party ends. You ready?"

Sahara took one last look at herself in the mirror.

Flawless and perfect.

She stood, smoothing out her dress. "Yeah," she said, steeling her expression. "Let's go."

And just like that, the mask was back on.

By the time they made it to Rocco's backyard, the party was jumping. Music thumped through the speakers, vibrating the ground beneath Sahara's heels as she made her way through the sea of bodies. The scent of coconut rum, hookah smoke, and heavy cologne clung to the air.

She spotted Rocco way before he did her. He was laid back on a suede sectional near the pool, with his arms draped around two women who looked like they stepped straight out of the Instagram Explore page. His diamond chains shined brighter than the sparkling water glowing from the lights in the pool. When one of the girls whispered something in his ear, his lips spread into a wide grin, and he flashed his diamond-covered teeth.

Sahara barely blinked.

But her "friends" sure did.

"Straight up, which one of them hos I gotta slap for you? Sahara! Do you *see* this shit? Rocco is straight up *trying* you!"

"Mm-hmm," the other four women standing around replied in response to Jahzara, who, as usual, didn't wait a single second before doing her best to instigate drama.

Rolling her eyes dramatically before tossing her long, Brazilian Remy tresses over her shoulder, Jahzara acted like she was sincerely appalled to see Rocco with his arms wrapped around two barely covered beauties. Truthfully, she couldn't be happier at the fact that Rocco was shamelessly flirting with other women right in front of her so-called friend. As much as

Jahzara tried to hide it, she was jealous of Sahara to the point that it was toxic.

The other four sitting around Sahara—Glen, Ramiya, Tasha, and Kyla—were all watching the same show and probably felt the exact same way about it. They were other artists in the industry, which meant that even though things seemed friendly among each other, everything was really a competition. The only person Sahara really trusted was Lena.

"*Oh hell no.* He's practically tonguing that ho down!" Jahzara practically sang, flipping her long, honey-blond curls over one shoulder. "Sahara, do you *see* this shit? Rocco is straight up trying you *right* now."

Her voice was loud—intentionally so. Loud enough for nearby partygoers to hear the alleged disrespect, loud enough to stir the pot and keep the drama bubbling. It was the kind of energy she lived for.

Mm-hmm's and dramatic gasps followed instantly from the circle of women surrounding Sahara. Glen shook her head like she was personally offended, Ramiya let out a fake *tsk-tsk* under her breath, and Kyla widened her eyes like she couldn't believe the audacity.

Sahara leaned back in her chair, tracing the rim of her cocktail glass with one finger. Power radiated from her calm as she murmured, completely unbothered, "Is that what we're doing tonight?"

"Girl," Jahzara pressed, her tone teetering between amusement and instigation, "ain't no *we* in this. This is *him* disrespecting *you*."

Lena let out an exaggerated sigh and leaned closer to Sahara's ear. "They're so damn predictable," she muttered.

A low, knowing confidence rolled off Sahara as she replied, "Aren't they?"

"Oh, so you just gonna sit here and let him make a fool outta you?" Glen cut in, her glossy lips pursing as she took a sip of her champagne. "Girl, you are way more liberal than me, because my man could never!"

"What man?" Lena said, tilting her head to give Glen a sideways glance. "Because last I checked, you ain't got one."

Glen rolled her eyes, immediately catching an attitude. "Bitch, neither do you. Don't try me like that."

"You tried yourself by trying to throw shade at my girl when you spend your nights in that lonely-ass bed, clutching a pillow."

Glen's expression twisted instantly. "And since when do I need a man? Unlike some people, I don't need to be somebody's arm candy to be relevant."

Lena gave her an unimpressed look. "Baby, you could *never* be arm candy. You built like a pack of Now and Laters."

The group *oooh'ed*, Ramiya even letting out a cackle before disguising it with a sip of her drink. Glen's jaw tightened, but she didn't want to go too far and risk looking *too* pressed.

"You ain't gotta do us like that," Jahzara shot in, speaking up for Glen. "She's not the only one who is questioning why Sahara is acting like she's okay with this." She motioned over to where Rocco was now whispering in one of the girls' ear while she giggled obnoxiously. "We just trying to see what's up with our friend."

"Friend?" Lena frowned. "Where were all you hos a couple months ago when she stopped doing shows?"

"Don't try that," Ramiya said. "I would've been here the second I got a call. You know we weren't being funny, right? Don't you, Sahara?"

Until that moment, she was barely paying attention to the conversation, because something else had caught her eye. A man, one who drew her attention for the very reason that it seemed like he was trying to avoid being seen, was the subject of her focus.

"Yeah, I know y'all ain't mean nothing by it. I didn't take it personal," she replied to Ramiya, without really thinking about it. It didn't really matter one way or another that they didn't check in with her when she disappeared. Lena was the only person bothered by it.

"Well, speak for yourself, because I took it all personal," Lena let it be known. "It's so funny how I didn't hear a peep from none of you hos, but as soon as Rocco announced this party, her phone was ringing off the hook."

A spark of mischief lit Jahzara's face as she watched the exchange like it was free entertainment.

"Well, clearly, we needed to be here because you just gonna let your man be hugged up with other women like that?"

Sahara took a slow sip of her drink, letting the liquor burn down her throat before answering. "He's not my property," she said simply. "If he wants to flirt and have fun, he can do what he likes."

Jahzara's perfectly arched brow lifted in mock surprise. "Oh, so you don't care. Is that what you're saying?"

"I don't."

Glen leaned in, curiosity gleaming behind her shaded contacts. "Like *at all*?"

"Nope."

Ramiya clicked her tongue. "Damn. You real mature, girl. 'Cause if that was *me*, I'd be flipping tables."

"Or throwing drinks," Kyla added.

"Or both," Glen said with a laugh.

"Well, *you* might," Lena cut in, her voice laced with sarcasm. "But Sahara doesn't need to do all that. If she wanted to make a statement, she'd just replace him."

Sahara tilted her head, her composure sharpening to a blade's edge. "Exactly."

That made the group shift. A subtle flicker of envy passed between them before Jahzara covered it with a fake pout.

"Damn, girl, I wish I had your level of chill. Teach me how to be unbothered."

Sahara swirled her drink, giving her a slow once-over. "You can't teach what's natural."

The group *ooh'd* again, Glen biting back a laugh as Ramiya pressed a hand over her mouth. Jahzara gasped in mock offense. Even she had to laugh, holding up her hands in surrender.

"Damn. Just drag me then."

Across from where they sat, on a circular sectional near Rocco's infinity pool, the man who Sahara had noticed earlier was standing near the firepit, keeping warm as he scrolled through his phone. He was definitely representing one of the labels. That much was clear from his professional attire and serious vibe. It was obvious that he wasn't there to party, being that he was drinking water and his only reaction to the blaring music was a subtle nod of his head every now and then.

Leaning over to Lena, Sahara kept her eyes on him. "Lee, which labels are here?"

Although she kept her voice low, the others, being artists themselves, had ears trained to pick up on any information that could be used for their benefit. And, of course, Lena noticed it.

"Um, let's walk over here and talk to Stacy about it," she replied, referring to the head of Sahara's management team.

Sahara didn't hesitate. "Lead the way."

Grabbing her by the arm, Lena led her away to a high-top table that put her right in the line of sight of the man she had been staring at to begin with.

The group's eyes followed them as they left, their laughter lowering to hushed whispers the second Sahara was out of earshot. But she didn't need to hear them.

She already knew she was the topic of conversation.

"Sit here and I'll go find Stacy. There was no way I was going to give you all that information in front of Jahzara and them. I don't trust them hos. They're opportunists, and the only reason they're even at Rocco's party is because you wanted them here."

"They are my only friends in the industry, Lena," Sahara reminded her. "I couldn't *not* invite them."

Lena frowned. " 'Friends' is a strong word."

Things like this used to be fun, or at least entertaining enough to distract her from the parts of her life she wanted to ignore. But, these days, being on the scene wasn't fulfilling anymore. Neither was being surrounded by people who faked friendship in order to gain access to the things they wanted. Atlanta wasn't Beverly Hills, but the people were just as fake.

Sahara leaned against the high-top table, keeping her posture relaxed, controlled. Always in control.

Lena, however, was not. "You need to cut them hos off," she said, nodding toward the group Sahara had just walked away from. "They're not your friends. I don't even know why you entertain 'em."

Sahara let out a quiet chuckle, tapping the side of her glass. "Because you don't let your enemies *know* they're your enemies, Lee. You play the game."

Lena rolled her eyes. "I hate that game."

"You hate losing," Sahara corrected, cool confidence threading through her tone. "And you hate waiting for people to show their hand. Me? I like to watch. They'll overplay their position eventually."

Lena scoffed. "Yeah? And in the meantime, they'll be smiling in your face, drinking your liquor, trying to get into every room you open up for them. You don't owe them, Sah."

Sahara tilted her head, watching her friend's expression carefully. Lena was always quick to call shit out, quick to move on emotion. That was the difference between them. Lena felt everything too deeply, too fast. Sahara had spent too many years teaching herself not to feel anything at all.

"They don't have to know what I think of them to be useful," Sahara murmured. "That's the difference between you and me."

Lena's mouth tightened. "Nah, the difference is I say how I feel and I *mean* it. If I don't like a bitch, I *don't like a bitch*. Ain't no smiling in their face. You? You let 'em think they winning."

Sahara smiled, slow and unbothered. "That's because they always lose in the end."

"Always playing the long game." Lena groaned dramatically, throwing her hands up. "Girl, you are *exhausting*."

Sahara laughed softly, but her focus had already drifted. She felt him before she saw him. An unfamiliar presence pressed against her senses, a new energy in a space filled with predictable ones. When she turned her head, her gaze landed on him.

He stood midway between her and where Rocco was entertaining his groupies, posture relaxed, but with an unmistakable presence. A tailored suit, crisp, dark, and highlighted by the soft glow of the flames. He wasn't drinking or surrounded by women vying for attention. He wasn't here for them.

And he was watching her. But . . . not like most men did. There was no hungry glint in his eye, no quick glance at her body before trailing back up to meet her face. His stare was measured, unwavering, weighted with something she couldn't place. He held her gaze without hesitation, without apology.

Interesting.

Sahara took a slow sip of her drink, tilting her head slightly, assessing him.

Lena followed her line of sight and immediately frowned. "Who is that?"

Sahara's gaze narrowed with interest. "That's what I'm about to find out."

Lena narrowed her eyes. "He doesn't look like he belongs here. Doesn't even seem like he wants to be."

"Neither do I," Sahara murmured, already stepping forward. "He's probably representing a label."

Lena turned up her nose. "Which one? I've never seen him anywhere."

Sahara shrugged. "Doesn't mean anything. He doesn't look like the type who wants to be seen."

Lena paused for a moment before sighing dramatically. "Let me go find your manager before you end up giving a record deal to a scam artist."

Sahara barely heard her because she had already decided that it was time to make her move. She wanted to know who he was and she wasn't the type of woman who sat around waiting for anything.

"I don't think I've seen you at one of these before," she stated, once she was standing by his side.

The man played it cool, acting like he didn't even know she was there until she opened her mouth to say something. Truthfully, he was debating whether or not he wanted to entertain a conversation. He was there for a reason and casual chitchat wasn't part of it.

He looked at her fully now, eyes flicking over her face, but his expression remained unreadable as he replied. "That's because I've never been."

Yeah . . . that tracks, Sahara thought.

She studied him with a faint tilt of her head. "Oh? Not a fan of the music?" Her tone was laced with dry amusement, the slight sarcasm curling the edges of her voice. Because this man? He didn't look like he had a single Rocco song in his playlist.

His lips twitched—just barely. "I wouldn't say that."

"But you wouldn't *not* say that either."

He exhaled a quiet chuckle. "Rocco isn't exactly my vibe."

Sahara nodded approvingly. "Smart man."

That pulled a genuine grin from him. "What's *your* vibe?"

She took a slow sip of her drink, letting his question sit between them for a moment. "Anything with soul. I don't do industry garbage."

His gaze flickered with something unreadable. "You don't consider yourself industry?"

Sahara arched a brow. "That a trick question?"

"No." His eyes stayed locked on hers. "But I can tell you don't see yourself the way the world sees you."

That made her pause. "Enlighten me," she said smoothly. "How does the world see me?"

His voice was calm, certain. "As a woman who knows what she wants and gets it. Someone who isn't afraid of anything. But you are afraid of something."

"And what is that?" She was waiting with bated breath for his answer.

His gaze held hers. "You're afraid of not being in control."

Her fingers tightened slightly around her glass.

He wasn't wrong.

She let out a soft breath, shifting the conversation. "If Rocco's not your vibe, what are you doing here?"

Sahara masked the satisfaction she felt as he noted the way she shifted the conversation. A subtle tactic to regain control and keep things on her terms. He let her have it, though.

Leaning back slightly, he slid his hands into his pockets. "Business."

Sahara's lips parted slightly. *Ah. There it was.*

"And what business is that?"

His expression didn't change. "I represent a label that's looking to make some acquisitions."

Sahara tilted her head, intrigued now. "And let me guess . . . I'm on the menu."

A slow nod. "Among a few others."

She turned slightly, tapping her nails against her glass. "Would I have creative control?"

He didn't hesitate. "Depends on what you're willing to fight for."

She narrowed her eyes slightly. "Would I have control over my image?"

"That's up to you," he said plainly. "The industry will try to mold you. It's *your* job to make sure they don't succeed. At the end of the day, everyone is looking out for their own interests."

Sahara studied him carefully. He wasn't sugarcoating. He wasn't selling her a dream. And she respected that. She opened her mouth to say something else, but before she could, a voice cut in. A very annoying, intrusive voice.

"Well, well. Sahara, so you *do* know how to network."

Sahara didn't even have to turn around to know who it was.

Stacy.

Her manager's presence loomed beside her, her polished voice dripping with passive- aggression.

Sahara's grip on her glass tightened slightly, but she kept her expression smooth as she turned. The only reason Stacy still had a job was that she was good at what she did. Besides that, Sahara couldn't stand her. She was a constant thorn on her side and Stacy made it clear that the feeling was very much mutual.

Stacy's sharp gaze flicked between Sahara and the man. She lingered on him, sizing him up. "And who might *you* be?"

For the first time, Sahara saw a glint of something sharp in his gaze. He still hadn't told her his name and something about his hesitation made her feel like it was intentional. Like he had something to hide. Which intensified her need to want to know more.

He didn't rush to answer. Instead, he let Stacy's question settle, let the weight of it fill the space between them. He was patient—too patient for a man being pressed for information. A man with nothing to hide would have already rattled off his name, his label, the rehearsed pitch.

But he wasn't just any man.

And he was definitely hiding something.

Sahara watched him carefully, her grip tightening slightly around her glass. He was unreadable in a way that made her curious.

Finally, he exhaled out a slow and measured breath. "Quentin." He said his name smoothly. "I'm representing Crown Records."

Sahara's fingers twitched. That was a downright lie. She didn't know how she knew, or which part of what he said was a lie. She just did. It was in the way he said it, too careful, too even. The way his jaw flexed subtly after, like he was testing out a name that didn't belong to him. Clearly, lying wasn't something that came natural to him.

Stacy raised an unimpressed brow. "Never heard of it."

Supreme didn't blink. "You will."

The sheer confidence in his tone made Sahara's stomach tighten, just slightly. She tilted her head, watching the way he barely acknowledged Stacy, like she was just another voice in the room. But his focus was all on Sahara.

That was new.

Stacy scoffed. "Is that right? And who else is on this . . . Crown Records?"

His gaze stayed on Sahara. "She would be our first major artist."

Sahara's eyes narrowed with a quiet, knowing humor, but she didn't speak, watching as Stacy's eyebrows shot up like she was trying to hold in laughter.

Stacy let out a *tsk* before shaking her head. "Wait. Wait. Let me get this straight. You're trying to sign *Sahara*—a multiplatinum award-winning artist—onto a no-name label with zero known talent?"

Supreme didn't react. He barely even looked at Stacy. Instead, he studied Sahara. "I think that would be a great thing for her. It means that she can call the shots."

The weight of his gaze felt intentional. It wasn't like the way other men looked at her, hungry and entitled. No, his was steady. Unshaken. Like he was *already certain* of her answer.

"Plus, we have backing," he said simply, adding it like an afterthought.

Stacy sucked her teeth. "Yeah? From who?"

"The kind of people who don't put their names on things," Supreme replied smoothly. "But they have money. And they're willing to put it behind the right talent."

He let that last part hang, his voice dropping just slightly, like it wasn't just about business.

Sahara exhaled, tilting her head slightly. "And you think *I'm* the right talent?"

His gaze flicked lower for just a second. Too quick to be anything, but slow enough for her to feel it. "I don't think," he murmured. "I know."

Something in Sahara's chest tightened. Just slightly. He was too sure of himself. Too sure of her.

Stacy laughed dryly, waving a dismissive hand. "Yeah, yeah. Go ahead and send the offer over. We'll review it."

Supreme nodded once. "I'll be in touch."

Then, without another word, he turned and walked away.

No drawn-out pleasantries. No lingering *call me*'s. He just . . . left.

Sahara watched him go, taking in the way he moved. Purposeful. Every step was deliberate, not a single one wasted. His suit was expensive, but not loud. His cologne lingered in the air between them, faint but clean, sharp.

She had spent years around men who needed to be seen, men who thrived off attention, validation, power plays. But he wasn't looking to be the loudest in the room. He was looking to own it. That realization sent something hot rolling through her stomach. She didn't know what to make of him yet.

"Bye, then," she murmured under her breath.

"Sahara," Stacy snapped, pulling her out of her thoughts. "You're not actually considering this, are you?"

Sahara lifted her glass, taking a slow sip before answering. "I consider everything."

Stacy rolled her eyes before stalking off.

Lena slid in beside her, watching Stacy disappear before turning back to Sahara. "All right, what the hell was *that* about?"

Sahara shrugged. "He said he represents a label."

Lena frowned. "Which one?"

"Crown Records."

Lena's face twisted. "Crown what?"

Sahara's voice carried a sly edge. "Exactly."

Lena sucked her teeth. "You're really *considering* this shit?"

"I don't know. He said they were backed by big money. He seemed like he could submit an offer to me that I can't refuse."

Lena's brows furrowed. "And what kind of offer would be one you *can't* refuse?"

Sahara blinked.

For once, she didn't have an answer.

But she had a feeling she was about to find out.

Chapter 3

"I can tell by the look on your face that I'm getting on your nerves, but I'm only doing this for your own good."

Stacy's voice rattled through the speakers of Sahara's phone. There was a blend of urgency and control in her tone that frustrated Sahara to the core. She rolled her eyes so hard they nearly got stuck.

"Look, Sahara," Stacy pressed, her face tight with irritation as she spoke on FaceTime. "This is the moment we've been waiting for. Do you even realize how many people would kill for these offers? Atlantic is ready to finalize, RCA is willing to pivot your entire brand into a global movement, and Sony's throwing the biggest check. So . . . what are *we* doing?"

We?

Sahara took a slow sip of her water to avoid having to bite her tongue.

Lena, lounging across the dressing room couch with a mimosa in hand, made a loud, exaggerated gagging sound as she listened. Sahara had to press her lips together to keep from laughing.

"I need you to take this seriously," Stacy continued, oblivious to Lena's theatrics. "No slipping up, no sarcasm, no off-brand commentary. You are walking a tightrope right now and one wrong step could—"

"Have me flat on my ass," Sahara finished dryly. "Yeah, yeah, I know. You've said it about five times now."

Lena snorted, raising her glass in an exaggerated toast. "Cheers to you finally telling that bitch like it is."

"Well, I'm sorry if my overly-cautious state is bothering you." Stacy's nostrils flared, her already too-tight ponytail pulling at her temples. "But you have to remember what's at stake right now. You can't just *float* through this, Sahara."

Sahara leaned back in her chair, steady and unbothered. She didn't float through anything. She just didn't let herself be pressured into moves that didn't sit right.

"These labels are making power plays. You don't have that kind of time," Stacy pressed. "You need to choose before they move on."

Sahara tapped her nails against the armrest. "I still have time."

"Barely," Stacy huffed. "You're really waiting for that no-name indie label?"

Lena perked up at that, arching a brow as she set her drink down. "Oop. This about that fine-ass dude from the party?"

Sahara ignored her.

Stacy didn't. "It's not about him," she snapped. "It's about her holding out for something that doesn't exist."

Lena made a *tsk* sound, shaking her head. "Let my girl explore her options, damn."

"This isn't about exploring, this is about securing the bag before it's gone."

Sahara sighed, shifting in her chair. "I just want to see what the offer looks like before making a decision. That's all."

Stacy countered back. "You don't even know what you're waiting for."

Sahara didn't reply. It wasn't just Supreme. It was the feeling she got from him. He was different—calculated. The type of man who didn't talk just to talk, who wasn't pressed to be liked. She'd spent her career navigating men who thought they were slick. Men who fed her lines and dressed up false promises as golden opportunities she couldn't pass up.

Supreme didn't play those games.

That's what intrigued her.

But Stacy wasn't trying to hear that.

"You need to stop wasting time," Stacy said, pinching the bridge of her nose like Sahara was giving her an actual migraine. "If that contract isn't in my inbox by the time you leave this interview, we're moving forward."

She held Stacy's gaze; her defiance coiled around a single word. "We?"

Stacy's expression didn't change. "Yes, *we*. Because I'm not about to let you fumble your future because you want to chase a pipe dream."

Lena made a dramatic choking sound in the background. "Not her whole career being a 'pipe dream'."

Sahara bit back a laugh, clearing her throat. "We'll talk after the interview."

Stacy exhaled sharply. "That's the only time you've got left."

Seated just outside of the frame, Lena was mouthing words dramatically, mocking Stacy's voice as Sahara sat through yet another overly prepped, unnecessary pep talk on FaceTime.

"And remember, keep it *light*," Stacy's sharp voice rang through the phone, snapping Sahara's attention back. "We're in negotiations, Sahara. No controversial statements. No 'I do what I want' bullshit. Stay polished."

She angled her head just so, her gaze steady, tone edged with defiance. "Me? Controversial?"

Stacy's sigh was long and exasperated. "Sahara, I swear to God—"

"I got it, Stace."

Lena exaggerated a silent scream before grabbing a pretend gun, mimicking blowing her brains out. Sahara stifled a laugh, biting the inside of her cheek.

"Are you even listening to me?" Stacy barked.

Sahara straightened her face instantly, her voice honeyed but firm. "Every word, boss lady."

Stacy studied her through the screen, not buying it, but too pressed for time to argue. "Just . . . don't say anything I'll have to clean up later."

Click.

Call ended.

Lena let out a loud, dramatic groan. "I'm sorry, but I have to say it. That bitch is insufferable."

Sahara shook her head, laughing. "She's strategic."

"She's an opportunist and you know it. That woman stays breathing down your neck. I don't know how you do it."

Sahara stretched her arms above her head, letting out a slow exhale. "By reminding myself that she works for me, not the other way around."

Lena grinned, lifting her mimosa again. "Period."

Sahara leaned forward in her chair, staring at her reflection in the massive vanity mirror. Flawless, as always—skin glowing, lips painted the deepest shade of red, hair swept up in a soft, but intricate updo. She looked like she had the whole world in her hands. At the same time, she felt like she was balancing on the edge of a knife.

Behind her, Lena sprawled across the couch, scrolling through her phone. "Be real, are you really holding out for this mystery label?"

Her tone carried a quiet defiance. "I'm considering all my options."

Lena scoffed. "Mm-hmm. And how much of this consideration has to do with that man from the party?"

Sahara shot her a look. "I don't make business decisions based on men."

Lena arched a brow. "Maybe. But you do make decisions based on vibes. And you've been acting really curious since you met him."

Sahara rolled her eyes, but didn't deny it.

Lena sat up, tossing her phone on the table. "What does he have to offer that would actually make you say yes?"

Sahara tapped her nails against her knee, thinking. Money didn't move her. Freedom did. Control did. She had spent years making sure no man, no one, ever dictated her life again. But there was something about Supreme. Something about his certainty, his calm, the way he looked at her like he already knew something she didn't.

And that . . . was dangerous. She had to know more.

Lena watched her closely. "You don't know, do you?"

Sahara exhaled, shaking her head. "It has to be more than just money."

Lena nodded, standing up and stretching. "Well, whatever it is, you better figure it out quick. Because time's running out."

Sahara glanced down at her phone one last time.

Fifty-eight minutes.

Still nothing.

She set her phone down, squared her shoulders, and stood. "Let's get this interview over with."

"ATL, we got the one and only Sahara in the building tonight!"

The ON AIR light flicked red and the energy in the studio surged.

Sahara leaned into the mic, her posture regal, her presence commanding. The silk of her dress kissed her curves, her golden skin catching the soft glow of the studio lights. She looked exactly like the woman everyone expected her to be.

Big Reese's booming voice filled the room, signaling the start of the interview. "ATL, let's get into it! We got Sahara with us tonight! Let's give her a warm welcome!"

The applause track played as the show's hype energy filled the space. Sahara leaned into the mic, her presence radiating effortless confidence.

"Damn, Reese, you tryna make a girl feel special."

"You don't need me for that, baby girl. The people been waiting for you!"

Sahara crossed her legs, exuding the kind of confidence that made men want her and women want to be her.

"Tell me something," Reese leaned in, grinning, "after that six-month hiatus, you came back like you never left. How does it feel to be Sahara again?"

Sahara's smile didn't falter, but something in her chest tightened. She had never stopped being Sahara. That was the problem. She shrugged, her expression smooth, voice carrying the ease everyone expected. "Feels like I never left."

Big Reese chuckled. "That's what I like to hear! But let's talk about what everybody really wanna know. What happened? Where did you go?"

The energy in the room shifted. Not in a bad way, but in a way that let Sahara know this was the moment. She could either give them the polished industry answer . . . or let a little truth slip through.

Her throat felt tight.

She could say what Stacy wanted her to say. Some generic, uninspired speech about growth, creativity, or balance.

Or she could be honest.

She took a breath, twirling her ring around her finger. "The truth is . . . going from being someone who just made a few songs for a few people who followed me, to becoming someone who had songs that people all over the world knew it . . . started to get to me."

Big Reese's brows jumped. "Oh, so you had to step back before you pulled a Doja Cat and started going in on your fans and stuff like that?"

Sahara shook her head, barely stifling a laugh. "No, it wasn't going to get that far. I would never go off on my supporters. It just took a while for me to get used to the lack of privacy. Balancing that with my actual life."

"Now, I gotta ask. There was no secret pregnancy, no clone or anything like that?"

Sahara giggled at the thought of it all. "No, nothing like that. I just needed to center myself again. Find my inspiration. Or rather, remember the person who inspired me to make my songs public to begin with."

Big Reese nodded. "That's one thing I've wanted to ask you for a while. You're such a unique artist. You have your own style, own sound. It's almost hard to figure out where to place you because you're so versatile. Where do you get your inspiration from?"

"My inspiration comes from a friend," she said, her voice softer now. "She was the kind of person who lived life on her own terms. Didn't take no for an answer. She believed in me before I even knew what I was capable of."

The words hung heavy between them.

Big Reese leaned forward slightly, sensing the weight behind them. "Sounds like she meant a lot to you."

"She did." Sahara's voice almost cracked, but she swallowed it down. She kept her eyes trained on the mic, not letting herself drift into that night. The memories still felt like razor blades in the dark.

"Well, what happened to her?" Big Reese asked. "If I might ask."

She swallowed once again, trying to force down the lump

that felt lodged in her throat. Big Reese leaned in, seeing the emotion welling in Sahara's eyes, but as a true journalist, she was more than eager to exploit it for ratings if it came down to it.

"She was murd—" Sahara caught herself. Blinked. "—she passed."

Big Reese nodded solemnly. "Losing people you love . . . that's the kind of pain that don't never leave, huh?"

Sahara steadied herself. "Not really." The energy was thick, her chest tight, but she had made it through.

"How about we switch gears right now because a lot of people have been waiting on the line to share some love with the independent queen, the one only Sahara. But, before we get to that, I have to ask . . . How did you come up with the name Sahara? Is it because you stay leaving these niggas out here thirsty for more?"

Sahara couldn't bite back a laugh. "Not at all. Honestly, I went through a dry spell for a long time where I couldn't write anything. Didn't want to write. I was too afraid of expressing the heavy feelings that I felt at the time after my friend died." Her throat got tight and she paused. "I renamed myself Sahara to kind of play on that moment once I began writing again. To be a constant reminder of why I do what I do. I never want to be that person who is afraid of feeling . . . ever again. The name that was given to me at birth is Sincere."

Big Reese nodded, the wide grin spreading across her face. "That's dope. I gotta respect it. And I know you would come up with something deep, because that's what you do. Now for our first caller. Who is this and what you got to say?"

And just like that, the mood shifted.

"Sahara! Oh my God, it's really you! I'm not gonna cry—I swear I'm not gonna cry!"

Sahara grinned instantly, relaxing into her seat.

"Awww, baby, don't cry! What's your name?"

"It's Tiffany! Oh my God, girl, I have been riding with you since the 'Remember When' days! Do you hear me? Since back when you was still going by Sincere!"

Sahara laughed, genuinely touched. "Damn, you really a day one! 'Remember When'? Girl, you just aged me."

Tiffany squealed. "I don't even care! You got me through some real shit! 'Cry Over You'—oh my God! That song got me through my *first* heartbreak! And 'Never Going Back.' Girl, I sent that to my ex and blocked his number right after!"

Big Reese chuckled. "Damn! Not you inspiring breakups, Sahara."

Sahara laughed, but there was real warmth in it. "Listen, I'm all for letting go of what don't serve you, baby."

Tiffany gasped dramatically. "That's why I love you! Sahara, you just give bad bitch energy, but like . . . with realness. Like, you ain't one of these celebrities who acts brand-new once you get on! You still one of us!"

Sahara felt something in her chest loosen up. Because that right there was the point. She never wanted to be out of reach. She never wanted to be some plastic, industry puppet. She just wanted to be her.

"Thank you, baby," Sahara said, genuinely touched. "That means the world to me."

"*No, thank you!*" Tiffany shouted. "All right, I'ma stop hogging the line. But I love you, girl! And if you ever tour again, I'm front row!"

"Don't worry, Tiffany, I got you," Sahara promised, still smiling as the call ended.

She was still feeling the warmth of the moment when the next caller came in. And just like that, the warmth vanished.

"Yo, Sahara! I love you! Been rocking with you since day one, ya heard me? And I mean, *the real* day one, baby."

This person had a thick New Orleans accent, something that

Sahara had worked very hard for many years to erase from her speech pattern. She forced a smile, even as her heartbeat quickened. "Thank you, mama. I appreciate that."

"Yeah, um, I also wanted to say that . . . I remember your friend. She was good peoples. I'll never forget what happened to her."

The air stilled and Sahara's mouth went dry. The static from the phone line buzzed faintly in the background.

Big Reese grinned, oblivious. "Oh yeah? You from her hood?"

"Fasho! Listen, we love you out here, Sahara. Why you don't never come back home? The city is so proud of you! Your friend would be too."

By this time, Sahara's reality was spiraling. She looked completely dumbfounded as she sat in her seat, frozen in space, unable to think, speak or move. Big Reese, sensing that something was up, decided to take over the call.

"Oh, you go way back with Sahara for real then! You knew her friend?"

The caller hesitated. "I do. Her name was Aaliyah, wasn't it? I remember the night she was killed."

Sahara felt all the air leave her body. It was one of those moments where everything tilts. The kind of moment where the entire world narrows into a single, sharp-edged truth. She hadn't said Aaliyah's name. She hadn't even hinted at it. Which meant . . . this person really knew her. In all of her attempts to escape her past, cover it up and become someone else, it all was catching up to her.

Suddenly, the studio felt too small, the mic too close, the air too thick to breathe. Her ears rang, her vision blurred, her heart pounded like it was trapped inside of her body and fighting for release. She couldn't do this anymore.

Lena's voice cut through the panic like a lifeline. "Ayo, let's take a break real quick," she announced, reaching across the table to cut the mic feed before Sahara could completely spiral.

Big Reese blinked in surprise. "Uh—yeah, yeah, we'll be back in a few, y'all. Stay tuned."

The ON AIR light flicked off.

Sahara barely felt herself being pulled up, barely registered Lena guiding her toward the bathroom.

All she could hear was—*Her name was Aaliyah, wasn't it?*

The sound of the door locking behind them was barely a whisper beneath the pounding bass outside, but to Sahara, it was a gunshot in her ears. The panic in her chest swelled—sharp, fast, like a vise tightening around her ribs. She braced herself against the counter, fingers gripping the edge so tight her knuckles went white.

Breathe.

In.

Out.

She could hear Lena's voice, but it sounded far away, underwater, like her ears had sealed themselves shut against reality. The name Aaliyah still echoed in her head. Not just the name, but the voice that spoke it, the recognition in it.

Somebody knew.

Somebody remembered.

Somebody from New Orleans had been able to reach her—and just like that, the fragile illusion of her carefully constructed life cracked.

Lena's reflection appeared behind her in the mirror, her face pinched with concern as she reached out. "Sah? What the hell was that about?"

Sahara blinked rapidly, shaking her head, trying to pull herself back to the present. "Nothing. Just . . . I just need a second."

"Bullshit." Lena wasn't having it. She folded her arms,

weight shifted to one hip, watching Sahara like she was trying to solve a puzzle she'd been working on for years. "Who was that? What did they say that got you lookin' like you just saw a ghost?"

Sahara let out a shaky breath, willing herself to be normal, to be unaffected—to be the version of herself the world believed her to be. Cool. Untouchable. Always in control.

"It's nothing," she said again, but it was too damn late for that.

Lena's eyes narrowed. "You're lying."

"I'm not."

"You are."

Sahara groaned, pressing her fingers against her temple. "Lena, please—"

"Nah." Lena cut her off, stepping closer, her voice dropping into something lower, sharper—frustrated. "I'm not lettin' this go, Sah. You do this every time. You shut down, pretend like nothin' fazes you, but I ain't stupid. That call rocked you. And I wanna know why."

Sahara avoided her gaze, her heart hammering too fast, too loud.

"What are you hiding?" Lena pressed, her voice softer now, but still insistent. "You won't even tell people where you from. You always playin' off this 'secretive' thing and it worked when you were a small fish, but now that you blowin' up . . . how long you think that's gonna last?"

Sahara swallowed, her throat dry as hell. She had always known this conversation would come sooner or later. Lena wasn't wrong. She had dodged the question about her past for years, let people assume what they wanted. Some thought she was from Atlanta, others swore up and down she was an LA girl. She never confirmed nor denied. She let the mystery become part of her brand—the "enigmatic" Sahara, the woman who gave the world her music, but never her story.

It was fine when she was underground.

It was fine when she had control.

But Lena was right. The bigger she got, the less power she had over her own narrative.

". . . I'm just not ready yet," Sahara finally admitted, her voice barely above a whisper.

Lena sighed, shaking her head, but she didn't look surprised. "Is that why you so scared to sign with a major?" she asked. "You tryna protect yourself from your past comin' out?"

Sahara's silence was the only answer Lena needed. The air between them was thick with unspoken truths, too many questions and not enough answers. Sahara could see it on Lena's face—the exhaustion of always being the one left out. The frustration of being loyal to someone who wouldn't let her all the way in.

"Damn, Sah," Lena finally muttered, rubbing a hand down her face. "That's heavy."

Sahara forced calmness to mask the turmoil beneath it. "It's life."

Lena didn't laugh. She just stared at her for a long second before finally exhaling. "You know you can tell me, right? Whenever you ready."

Sahara nodded, but they both knew it was empty. She didn't know if she'd ever be ready.

A beat of silence passed between them before Lena glanced down at Sahara's phone. The screen still lit up with notifications. A frown crossed her face as she swiped it open, scrolling through the latest messages. Then, suddenly, her jaw dropped.

"Hey," Lena murmured. "Looks like your man came through."

Sahara blinked, confused for a split second before Lena turned the phone around to show her the text on the screen.

Stacy: *Got the offer from Crown. Call ASAP.*

"Whoa," Lena breathed. "It must be good."

Sahara stared at the text, her pulse still uneven, but for a different reason now.

Supreme had kept his word.

And now . . . she was about to find out just how good his deal really was.

Chapter 4

"Let me get this straight, girlfriend. You just signed a deal better than you ever thought you could get. With more freedom over your music and image than anyone I've ever heard of in this industry, but you're second-guessing it because of location? You're overthinking this shit, Sah. For real."

Sahara tilted her head back against the headrest, phone pressed to her ear, barely listening to Lena's voice as it crackled through the speakers. "I'm not overthinking it," she muttered, rubbing her temple. "I just . . . don't wanna be in New Orleans."

Lena let out an exasperated sigh. "And why the hell not? You from there. Ain't like it's some foreign-ass country where you don't know nobody."

Sahara exhaled sharply, pressing her fingers into her eyes. She was too tired for this conversation. Too tired for any of it. "That's the problem. I'm from there," she murmured. "I don't want to be anywhere near it."

Lena was silent for a beat and Sahara thought—for one second—that maybe she'd let it go. But, of course, that wasn't part of her plans. "You ain't even gotta live there, bitch!" Lena snapped, proving once again that she never let shit go. "You travel there, handle your shit, then bounce. Simple."

Sahara rolled her eyes. "It's never that simple."

"Oh my God, yes it is!" Lena groaned. "They gave you everything you wanted! Complete creative autonomy. Your own marketing team. Your own brand specialists. Your music, your way. That's unheard of! And the only catch is that the headquarters is in New Orleans? Be for real, Sahara."

Sahara drummed her fingers against the steering wheel, staring at her reflection in the rearview mirror. She knew Lena was right. She'd fought hard for this deal, this moment—full control, no strings. A new kind of noose was being formed around her neck. One she couldn't quite see, but felt all the same.

Returning to that city, even for business, felt like something else. Like stepping back into a past she had no business revisiting. Like giving something, or someone, the opportunity to pull her back in. But she wasn't that girl anymore. Right?

"You done?" Sahara finally muttered.

"No. Because you still on that bullshit," Lena snapped. "Listen, if you don't want the house they're giving you, don't stay in the house. If you don't wanna be in New Orleans, don't stay in New Orleans. But take the damn deal, Sincere."

Sahara's breath caught.

Lena never called her Sincere. She hadn't heard anyone call her by her name in so long that it sounded foreign, like something that belonged to another person entirely. Sincere was who she was before. Before fame. Before the lights. Before she became Sahara—the untouchable, the fearless, the woman who took whatever the fuck she wanted and never looked back.

But for one small second, Lena had stripped all of that away. Suddenly, it felt like she wasn't the powerhouse artist she'd created as an alter ego. Being called Sincere left her bare and exposed. Turned her back into the little girl from New Orleans, standing at a crossroads.

Sahara swallowed, staring out the windshield, forcing her voice to stay even. "I already took the deal."

Silence.

Then Lena shrieked, "*Bitch! What the fuck!* Why you just now telling me?"

Sahara winced, pulling the phone away from her ear as Lena lost her mind on the other end of the line.

"You let me sit up here going on and on and you already signed?! Oh, you ain't shit!"

She chuckled under her breath, affection lacing her words. "I like to let you rant. You get so passionate."

"Girl, I am sick of you!" Lena huffed. Then, as if remembering the actual point, her voice dipped into a sultry purr. "Okay, signed-ass superstar. What we doin' to celebrate?"

Sahara exhaled, tilting her head back. "Nothing. I'm tired."

Lena gasped dramatically. "Oh, so you Hollywood now? That's crazy. Ain't take your ass long to change."

Sahara laughed. "Never that. One thing you can count on is me staying exactly the same. No matter what, I'll always be exactly who I've been."

"I hope so," Lena replied. "Don't need you getting *famous* famous and changing on me."

Sahara shook her head at that, though Lena couldn't see it. "If anything, this will just let me really show the world who I am. I can make decisions with the backing of major money. Hopefully that'll even keep Stacy off my ass." She chuckled. "I know it's a good thing, Lee. I just want to make sure I'm being smart about what I do. Got a lot riding on this and I don't want to make the wrong move. I know you want to celebrate, but I just really need to think about how I'm going to go about this."

Lena sighed on the other end of the line, the energy in her voice shifting. "I get it," she murmured. "This is big. You gotta sit with it first."

Sahara appreciated that about Lena. For all her theatrics, she knew when to back off.

A beat of silence passed before Lena added, "But don't sit too long. Your toxic trait is that you overthink shit, and I refuse to let you talk yourself out of a blessing."

Sahara arched a brow, tone wry. "I already signed, remember?"

"Yeah, but that don't mean your ass won't find some reason to self-sabotage."

Sahara rolled her eyes but didn't argue.

Lena hummed, clearly satisfied with the lack of protest. "A'ight, well, I'ma let you process your emotions or whatever. But if you change your mind and decide to celebrate, hit me up. I'll be outside."

Sahara chuckled. "Go harass someone else, please."

"I'm on my way to do just that." Lena's grin was evident in her voice. "But I love you, bitch."

"Love you too, ho."

The call disconnected, leaving Sahara in silence. She tossed the phone onto the passenger seat and tapped her fingers against the wheel, exhaling slowly. She should feel excited. This was what she wanted—what she had fought for. The right deal. The right team. Full control over her artistry. So why the hell did she feel like she had just signed away something more? Like she had just invited something dangerous back into her life.

Sahara shook off the thought as she pulled into her driveway. And that's when she saw it: The first warning sign of bullshit pending was in the form of an obnoxiously loud, flaming orange Lamborghini sitting in her driveway like it belonged there.

The second sign was the fact Sahara was hit with the urge to just keep driving, right past her own house as if she didn't even know who lived there. Especially since she was currently on a high and didn't want to come down. She had just signed the contract with Crown Records, finalizing the deal. They'd agreed to all of her terms and now she was officially a signed artist. Her days of being indie were gone. It was a bittersweet moment; she was excited and thrilled, but also nervous.

Any other day she could stomach Rocco enough to keep the facade of their relationship going. He didn't require much. His personality was about as deep as a kiddie pool, so it didn't take much to satisfy him. All he wanted was a woman around to stroke his ego. Sahara's presence alone did that.

After pulling in next to his car, she continued to sit there, unmoving. Still wondering if she should just leave, she gripped the steering wheel, tapping her nails against the leather as she stared at the mess she regretted still being connected with. Not that being with Rocco was *all* bad. He served a purpose. Besides being good for business, keeping Rocco around helped keep the other men she dealt with from pressing for more. At least, at first.

The problem was Rocco's time was up a long time ago. They'd only been together for six months and that was about three and a half months longer than she was used to keeping men around. His presence felt like a permanent smudge on glass. One that refused to wipe clean no matter how hard she tried. It didn't matter how many times she attempted to push him to the edges of her life, he always found his way back to the center, clawing for her attention like a spoiled child.

She exhaled sharply, rubbing her temple. She should've never given him a key. But Rocco wasn't the type to take "no" well. And every time he felt her slipping from his grasp, he threw a new stunt. Whether it was ghosting her for days just to see if she'd chase him. Or popping up on blogs with random women, their arms looped through his as he grinned for the cameras. Or pouting, sulking, throwing tantrums about how she never showed him she cared. Attention was all he ever wanted. But Sahara never gave it.

Rolling her eyes, she finally shoved the car door open, stepping out. The second she hit the walkway, she spotted it, the third and final warning sign. Her living room, visible through the floor-to-ceiling windows, was a fucking floral massacre. Balloons floated aimlessly near the ceiling, while red, pink, and white roses sprawled across every available surface. There was a massive gold-foil banner stretched over the entranceway: CELEBRATING THE QUEEN

Sahara deadpanned.

Oh, this nigga is extra.

She hadn't even stepped inside before Rocco's voice boomed through the house.

"*Happy birthday, baby!*"

She didn't blink.

She stared at him as he stood proudly in the middle of her living room, arms outstretched like he expected her to fall into them. Instead, she folded her arms, her mood flat and completely unmoved.

"It's not my birthday, Rocco."

His grin faltered slightly.

"What? Yeah, it is." His brows furrowed. He glanced down, pulling out his cell phone from his pocket to take a peek at the screen. "It's October eighteenth."

Sahara tilted her head. "And my birthday is tomorrow. The nineteenth."

Silence.

She watched as he blinked once . . . twice . . . like she just told him she had a twin he never met.

Then, after an awkward pause, he threw up his hands, grinning again like it was nothing. "Ohhh . . . well, shit." He waved it off. "*Happy early birthday, baby!*"

Sahara rubbed her temples. She was so over this. Stacy and Lena begged her all the time to delay breaking up with him until after she got a solid footing in the industry. Now that she was officially signed to a label, that time should be now. Maybe she could go ahead and put an end to all of this now.

Her phone chimed. Again. She checked the screen. It was Clay with yet another message. Despite the fact that it should've been obvious that he was being ignored.

Yo, I heard about the deal. Let me pull up on you.

And above it was the message she'd ignored before that:

I'm proud of you, ma. Let's celebrate.

And before that:

I know you probably at the house. Open the gate for me.

Sahara?

She locked her screen, exhaling sharply. Clay was getting too attached. Too comfortable. He wasn't like Rocco, who was all about performative affection and power moves. Clay felt real.

Felt too emotionally present. Felt like a problem waiting to happen. And that was why she had to cut him off.

Rocco was still watching her, but for once, he wasn't the one blowing up her phone.

He shifted, shoving his hands in his pockets. "What you tryna do tonight, birthday girl?"

Sahara dragged a hand through her hair. "Honestly? I kinda wanna just be alone, maybe read a book or something."

Rocco's whole face shifted. Like someone just put him in a choke hold. "A book?" He blinked. "On your birthday?"

"Early birthday."

"Same thing."

Sahara saw the exact moment he checked out. His eyes glazed over, his jaw set tight, his whole body language screaming disappointment. She could tell what he wanted to hear: Something like, "Let's throw a party," or "Let's hit Miami," or "Fly me to Dubai."

But she wasn't that girl. Not for him. Not for *anyone.*

She let him off the hook with a small, dismissive wave. "It's cool, Rocco. You can go. I know this ain't really your vibe."

She saw the way relief flashed across his face before he tried to mask it. "You sure?" he asked, pretending like he wasn't about to speedwalk out the door.

She nodded. "Yeah."

"Bet."

He was already halfway to the door, phone in hand, probably texting his next move for the night. Then, as an afterthought, he turned back. "Oh, right," he muttered, digging into his pocket.

When his hand emerged, he was holding a small black box. He opened it. Inside, was a platinum, diamond-encrusted chain: big, flashy, gaudy as hell. Definitely not her style. "Here," he said, stepping forward and placing it in her palm. "For you, baby."

Sahara lifted it, feeling the weight of the diamonds. She already knew what was coming before he even said it.

"Make sure you tag ya boy when you post it on the 'Gram."

Ah. There it was. The *real* gift was not for her. It was for him.

Sahara's smile was tight and practiced as she dropped the box onto the counter. "Thanks."

He gave her one last cocky grin, then stepped out. Gone without a second thought. The moment the front door shut, she let out a slow exhale, tilting her head back, staring at the ceiling.

It always ended like this.

Men swarmed her, convinced she was something they could hold onto. Something to possess, to tame, to win. Yet, every single one of them left feeling hollow because she didn't belong to anyone. Not Rocco. Not Clay. Not anyone. She built this life to be free.

So why did it feel like she was still in a cage?

A few hours had passed and the silence in the house felt too still. Too unchallenged.

Sahara lay stretched across her couch, a half-read book resting against her stomach, her fingers idly tapping against the cover. The words blurred together on the page; her mind was elsewhere.

This was the thing about sobriety. When she was high, the mundane became cinematic. Even a random thought could spiral into a full-blown adventure. Lying on the couch and getting lost in her own thoughts could feel like a whole-ass experience.

But now that she was sober, everything felt like nothing.

She exhaled sharply and grabbed her phone, ordering some food just to fill the space. At least she still had one addiction left—food. If she was gonna feed the void, might as well do it properly.

When the doorbell rang, she barely looked up as she got the bag from the delivery driver, muttered a quick thanks, and retreated back into her solitude. She set the bag down, opened the takeout box, and pulled her phone into her lap. Scrolling through social media was a mindless escape, a distraction from the gnawing restlessness creeping up her spine.

Everyone's lives were loud, chaotic, over-the-top. Club appearances, expensive-ass vacations, engagement announcements, birth reveals, petty beefs. Shit, even the ones faking happiness were at least doing something. Sahara was doing nothing. And that "nothing" was sitting on her chest like a weight.

Then, her phone chimed. She glanced at the screen, her thumb swiping up lazily before her eyes focused. A text from Stacy.

Signed, sealed, delivered! I have the final contract in your inbox and the paper version on the way to your house. Congratulations! Don't party too hard!

Sahara's lips tugged into a small, private smile.

It was official.

She had signed earlier today, but now they had countersigned too. She was officially no longer an indie artist. The thought excited her. It also terrified her. Being social media famous was one thing. She had always hovered just under the radar, famous enough to make millions, to have die-hard fans, but still able to move without constant eyes on her. But international fame was a different beast entirely.

She'd spent years building walls, staying semiprivate, keeping her personal life just out of reach. Would this deal strip that away? Would she still be able to live freely? Her stomach tensed as an old fear crept into her mind. What if this brought him back? What if someone from her past came looking? But then, she exhaled and shook her head. That was crazy. There was no way Lorde was still checking for her. It had been five years. Hell, for all she knew, he wasn't even alive. Men like him didn't have long life expectancies.

The thought was cold, but she didn't let herself feel anything for it. Just as she was settling back into silence, her phone buzzed again. This time, it was Lena.

Sahara answered, laughing before Lena even got a word out. "Damn," she said, shaking her head. "The ink is barely dry on the paperwork and you already know what's going on. Stacy must've texted me and then immediately hit you."

Lena's voice came bubbling through the speaker, full of energy, high off excitement. "Actually, bitch, I been blowing Stacy up all damn day," she admitted with zero shame. "I needed to make sure everything was locked in, dot the i's, cross the t's. This is history, baby! I gotta celebrate our deal!"

Sahara chuckled. "Ours, Lena?"

"Exactly," Lena shot back. "Our deal. Because who was on your ass all year about signing with the right people? Me. Who's been handling shit behind the scenes? Me. Who's making sure you not out here playing yourself in bad business deals? Me, me, and *me*. That said, yeah, we celebrating our deal."

Sahara rolled her eyes playfully. "You're so dramatic."

"I'm so right is what I am," Lena quipped. "And speaking of right, I know you wanna go out. Stop playing."

Sahara leaned back against the couch, shifting slightly. "I might later in the week. Right now, I just wanna chill."

Lena groaned dramatically. "Girl, you sound so boring. What happened to you? You used to be fun."

Sahara laughed. "I still am fun. I just . . . I don't wanna be around all that tonight."

Lena sucked her teeth. "All what? Fine-ass men and free bottles?"

"You mean disappointment?" Sahara corrected. "Loud-ass clubs, fake-ass people, and dudes who think buying a section means they own you for the night?"

Lena gasped like she was personally offended. "Excuse me, but I happen to like my men rich, ignorant, and bottle-service adjacent. That's the soft life, baby."

Sahara didn't miss a beat. "You mean the sponsored life."

"Same thing." Lena didn't even deny it. "Listen, God bless the men who keep my rent paid and my nails fresh. If that makes me a villain, so be it."

Sahara shook her head, amused. This was why she loved Lena. She was both shameless and unapologetic.

"Who you trying to catch tonight?" Sahara asked, stretching her legs across the couch.

Lena let out a devilish little laugh. "Girl . . . let's just say he owns a few nightclubs, a car dealership, and a trucking company. Real boss shit."

Sahara snorted. "Whoa, you did your research."

"You damn right. If I'm gon' play the game, I need to know who's worth playing with."

"And what exactly is your game plan?"

Lena's voice dropped to a sultry purr. "Give him just enough attention to let him know I see him. Let him flex a little. Let him feel like he's the one hunting me."

Sahara laughed. "Oh, so you *are* the game."

Lena giggled. "Bitch, duh!"

They chatted for a few more minutes, Lena filling her in on some messy industry drama, who was beefing with who, which rapper's baby mama got into a fight at a strip club last night.

Sahara listened, laughing here and there, but the whole time, she felt that creeping boredom settling back in. Even with Lena's high-energy storytelling, she still felt removed. Life was feeling like she was watching a movie she wasn't really invested in.

Eventually, the conversation wound down and Sahara exhaled. "Go catch your baller. I'll hit you up later this week."

Lena sighed dramatically. "Fine. But if you change your mind, I'll send a car."

Sahara smiled. "Not happening."

"Your loss, bitch."

"Goodnight, ho."

They both laughed before ending the call.

Silence fell again. Sahara popped a piece of sushi into her mouth, chewing slowly as she scrolled. The silence was too much. She needed something to pull her out of this nothingness.

Sex. That's what she needed.

The thought carried her outside, stepping onto her balcony, inhaling the thick Atlanta night air. The summer heat clung to her skin. She looked up at the obsidian sky, loving the peace she felt as she stood beneath it. And then, as she brought her eyes down . . . That's when she noticed her neighbor had company. Sahara leaned against the railing, eyes trailing down.

By the pool, legs spread, shoulders broad, sitting like he owned the space—a chocolate masterpiece. A well-built man with a thick, athletic build, long legs sprawled comfortably, a Red Stripe in one hand, an iPad in the other.

Her brow arched.

Jamaican?

Curiosity sparked, curving her lips into a slow grin.

She had heard stories. People said that island men were passionate and possessive lovers. The kind who knew how to take control in bed. That wasn't a bad way to spend the night. Sahara tilted her head, thinking it through. She didn't usually fuck this close to home. It was too messy and risky. But, hell, it was almost her birthday. After dodging Clay and enduring Rocco, she owed it to herself.

She thought for a moment about her neighbor. She was an attorney. A smart, no-nonsense Black woman who was successful by anyone's standards. She was married to the job, which meant that her man spent a lot of lonely nights at home. Not someone Sahara would be friends with, but not someone she disliked either.

Sahara thought about what she was considering for a moment. Was she really about to do this? The answer came almost immediately.

Yes.

It was just sex.

It didn't mean anything.

Men cheated regardless.

Better he do it with her, a woman who wouldn't be calling, stalking, trying to take him.

She wasn't interested in keeping anyone.

She just needed a few hours of pleasure.

That's it.

Decision made, Sahara walked back inside. She turned the

music up loud enough to travel and lure him in. Then, with practiced ease, she stepped out onto the balcony, her skin glowing beneath the dim lighting. She let her hair down, running her fingers through it. Tousled it just right and then, slowly, smoothly, she pulled her top over her head. Her exposed chest was hard for anyone, man or woman, to ignore. Bouncy, round melons, completely unaffected by the effect of gravity. Perky nipples practically begging for attention.

It wasn't long before she could feel his attention shift.

The iPad lowered.

His head tilted up.

His gaze stayed.

Hook. Line. Sinker.

She leaned over the balcony, shooting him a slow, knowing smile. "You busy?" she asked, voice smooth as honey.

Interest lit his face. He shook his head, eyes never leaving hers.

Bingo.

"Wanna come over for a bit?"

The way he stood immediately, the way his muscles shifted as he sat the beer down and straightened his shirt—she already had her answer.

And just like that, her boring night had just gotten a lot more interesting.

By the time he left her bed, it was too late in the night to be made right with any reasonable explanation. The glow of his phone had been a steady pulse in the background for hours. First, it had buzzed persistently on the kitchen counter while she was bent over the marble island. Round ass positioned high on the air, her fingers gripping the cold surface as he drove into her with a hunger that made the world disappear.

It vibrated again, flashing in the dim light, when they moved to the living room couch. She heard it, vaguely, beneath the sound of his heavy breathing in her ear, beneath the whispered filth that poured from his mouth as he took her exactly how she wanted.

Then, they reached the bedroom. By then, his phone no longer existed. Whatever desperate texts, missed calls, or frantic voicemails his girl was sending him didn't matter, because he didn't see them.

That had been hours ago. Now, he was gone, and his problems weren't hers to worry about. As long as he didn't include her in whatever story he spun to clean up his mess, she was fine. He would definitely figure something out. Men like him always had a story.

Sahara stretched lazily, satisfied, and walked into her luxurious master bathroom, already anticipating the slow, indulgent soak she was about to take. She filled the deep, oversized Jacuzzi tub with warm water, oils, and bath salts that made the water shimmer like crystals were in it. The scent of lavender and jasmine curled into the air, mixing with the scent of the flickering candles positioned around the room.

Sliding in, she let the heat sink into her skin, her head tipping back onto the edge of the tub. She let a sigh escape her lips. This was the perfect night. And yet, there was still one person lingering in her mind.

Quentin.

That's when she realized that everything she did with the guy who had just left was only to erase his face. But here he was, back again. Sahara cursed silently. She closed her eyes, but his stare found her there too. The way he looked at her at the party. The way he never broke eye contact, never let himself be pulled into the orbit of men who worshipped her like a goddess.

There was something about him. For the first time in years, she had curiosity about a man. And it had nothing to do with sex. In her opinion, love didn't exist. Not *real*, romantic love from a man. Men only wanted to conquer. They wanted what they couldn't have. She had learned that the day Aaliyah died.

And the worst part about it was that Aaliyah's death was her fault. If she had just given Lorde what he wanted, Aaliyah would still be here. If she had given him a little attention or some small show of interest, he would have gotten bored eventually.

Who knows, he might have even been generous. Given her money. Bought her some shit. She could've played him like she did every other man and Aaliyah would still be breathing. Sex was the easiest thing to give. But a life couldn't be replaced.

Instead, she let pride, fear, morals—whatever the fuck it was—get in the way. In the end, it was her best friend who paid the price. *That* was the lesson: Men would always take what they felt belonged to them. That was the reason she vowed never to allow anyone to think that she belonged to them.

Sahara squeezed her eyes shut, forcing the memory away. She let out a slow breath, sinking lower into the water. The heat began to lull her into something close to peace.

Then she heard it.

A bump.

A thump.

Some sort of sound.

She wasn't quite sure, but it was definitely something that didn't belong. Her body stiffened and her breath stilled. She sat up slightly, listening. But she didn't hear anything. Maybe it was nothing. Her phone was nearby, so she reached for it, thumb moving fast as she pulled up her security cameras. Every entry point was locked. Every monitor showed emptiness.

Sahara exhaled, shaking her head. She needed to relax.

Maybe Lena was right. She needed a dog inside the house as well as outside of it. She hated dogs, though, so she wouldn't even consider it. Sahara was more of a cat person. But, as Lena always reminded her, a cat wasn't gonna do shit if someone ever tried to break in.

Sahara let out a soft, dry laugh, running a hand through her damp curls as she thought about it. Then she heard it again. Another bump. This one was much louder.

And then . . . footsteps.

Her heart slammed into her ribs.

She grabbed a towel and wrapped it around herself, standing slowly. She didn't know why her first thought was that maybe the guy from earlier came back—or worse—his girlfriend, pissed and ready to cause a scene.

As she moved through the house, something felt off. The air felt wrong. The house was silent. She crept through the hallway, her bare feet light on the floor, her pulse loud in her ears. That's when she saw it—a light—one that she definitely had not turned on. Her guest room door was slightly ajar.

Sahara froze.

No one had been in there since Lena slept over weeks ago.

The slow, icy creep of dread slid down her spine.

She swallowed hard, her fingers tightening around the knot in her towel as she moved closer. She reached out, pushing the door open inch by inch.

Then—

Hands.

On her.

A palm slammed over her mouth before she could scream. A thick, muscular arm wrapped around her waist, locking her in place. Sahara fought. She kicked, scratched, twisted, her body thrashing in a desperate attempt to break free. But whoever it was, they were strong.

She felt something tighten around her throat. Her body jerked, breath cutting off, eyes wide. Then there was a sharp prick. A needle sank into her arm. The world tilted. Her lungs burned. Her limbs lost strength. Her vision blurred. And then . . .

Everything went black.

Chapter 5

Sahara's head was pounding before she even opened her eyes. A dull, metrical throb in her skull mirrored the frantic beat of her heart as she drifted back to consciousness. She was alive. Wasn't hurt but something was wrong.

Her arms and legs were bound.

Her mouth—gagged.

The realization sent a surge of panic through her veins, her body jerking instinctively against the tight ropes digging into her wrists. A muffled whimper fought its way past the cloth pressed between her lips as she struggled, the raw burn of friction searing her skin. Darkness cloaked her vision, the fabric wrapped around her eyes making her feel like she was trapped in a nightmare she couldn't wake up from.

Where am I?

Her last memory played in broken, incomplete fragments as she struggled to make sense of her reality. She remembered the warm bath. The candles. A sound, followed by the slight unease she brushed off as paranoia. And then, the noise. The hand over her mouth. And, lastly, the sharp sting of something piercing her skin before the world collapsed into nothingness.

Now, she was here. Now, she was . . . Well, she had no idea *where* she was.

The sound of a door creaking open made her straighten her spine.

Oh shit, she thought. Her heart began to drum.

Footsteps, terrifyingly slow, echoed through the space, each one sending another wave of terror rippling through her chest. She forced herself to be still, inhaling shallow breaths through her nose, straining to listen.

A chair scraped against the floor, the sound harsh against the eerie silence. Then, fingers—warm and firm to the touch—grasped her chin.

"Wake up, baby."

That voice.

Her stomach plummeted.

Lorde.

Although she hadn't heard his voice in years, it was one she would never forget. It was a core memory that left a permanent stain in her mind. A sob tried to claw its way up her throat, but she swallowed it down, refusing to give him the satisfaction. His grip tightened slightly before he chuckled, his breath hot against her skin.

"I told you, didn't I?" he murmured, his tone dripping with amusement. "Didn't I tell you I'd come for you?"

Before she could answer, the blindfold was yanked away. Light slashed across her vision, blinding her for a moment before she adjusted, blinking rapidly as her surroundings came into focus. The room was unfamiliar and empty. The walls were bare, only dim lighting illuminating them.

In the center, there was a single table with papers spread across it. It resembled an interrogation room. But it was what sat beside the table that made the blood curdle in her veins.

Her stomach twisted.

"You know him, right?" Lorde asked with a grin on his face. "My right-hand man, Supreme."

The man from the party was working with Lorde. Quentin,

or whatever his name really was. The one who had captivated her in that moment with his unreadable eyes and quiet confidence. He had deceived her.

She inhaled sharply, her chest rising and falling in sharp movements as her gaze darted between the two men. Lorde, lounging like a king, his satisfaction radiating as he watched her squirm. Quentin, or actually *Supreme*, standing near the wall, arms crossed, his face blank but his body tense.

He wouldn't look at her.

"What's wrong, baby?" Lorde taunted. "Not happy to see me?"

Sahara willed herself not to react, not to show the sheer terror flooding her veins, but Lorde had always been good at reading people and that skill had only gotten better over time.

"You're the fuckin' devil. Why would I be happy to see you?" she spat.

He laughed softly, shaking his head.

"You think you're better than me?" His tone sharpened, his grin stretching wider as he gestured toward the papers on the table. "Thought you was smart, huh? Thought this little music shit was gonna keep you safe? Nah, baby. It led you right to me."

Her brows furrowed as her gaze shot to the documents.

No.

Her heart dropped. It was worse than she thought. Supreme hadn't just led her to Lorde. He *sold* her to him.

No. No. No.

Lorde tapped the papers with a lazy finger. "Your career? Yeah, I bought that." His eyes gleamed with satisfaction. "So now, I own you."

A shudder tore through her. This wasn't real. This couldn't be real.

"See, you was so busy out here thinking you had all this freedom, all this control." Lorde leaned closer, his voice dropping into something intimate and venomous. "Now, look at you. Somehow you came right back to me. Right back where you belong."

Sahara's breath came in sharp, ragged gasps. Her pulse pounded against her skull, panic clutching at her insides, but she refused to let it spill over. Not in front of him.

Lorde saw it anyway and he fed off it. He reached into his pocket, pulling out her phone. "Since I'm feeling generous, I figured I'd let you handle one last bit of business before we get down to real work." He smugly tapped the screen before holding it out.

Rocco's name flashed across the display.

Sahara stiffened.

"Go on," Lorde urged. "Tell him it's over. We both know you don't really like him no way."

She said nothing, her nails biting into her palms as she clenched her fists.

Lorde arched a brow. "Oh, you wanna play stubborn now? Cool." He answered the call, putting it on speaker.

"Sahara? Baby, where you at? I've been looking for you all—"

"She got something to tell you," Lorde cut in smoothly, amusement lacing his voice.

There was a beat of silence as Rocco registered what was going on.

"Yo, who the fuck is this?" His voice was edged with sharp defensiveness.

Sahara hesitated, but Lorde's eyes darkened, his patience thinning. She swallowed hard.

"It's over, Rocco."

There was another pause before he managed to choke out a word. "What?"

She closed her eyes. "We're done."

"Wh—what?" He stuttered. "What you mean? Why you doing me like this?"

Lorde flashed her a shit-eating grin. "Ain't no need to be sad. She ain't done. Tell him what you been doing while he was out here thinking you was his."

She didn't speak, but she didn't have to. Lorde did it for her.

"Yo, my guy," he laughed, shaking his head. "You really thought she was just sitting at home, waiting on you? Man, she been fucking other niggas left and right under your nose."

It took Rocco a minute to process.

"The fu—Is that true, Sahara?"

She couldn't say anything. Coming face-to-face with her actions was much harder than she'd expected. But Lorde wasn't done.

"That ain't all, though," he added, tilting the phone slightly. "I took the liberty of sending you some receipts from her latest activities."

A dull vibration could be heard and then some shuffling on the other line.

"Wait . . . Is that *Clay*? Are these photos of you fucking Clay?"

Sahara's stomach dropped. Shame burned hot in her chest as she closed her eyes, bracing herself. Within the next couple hours, everything she'd done right under Stacy's nose would come to light. There was no way Rocco would keep this secret to himself.

Rocco was silent for a long moment as he scrolled through the photos Lorde sent him. Then, his voice, raw and trembling with rage.

"You a lying-ass bitch, Sahara."

Lorde chuckled, ending the call before tossing the phone onto the table.

"He'll get over it."

Sahara exhaled shakily. She barely cared about Rocco, but the situation—the way Lorde peeled away every bit of control she thought she had. In a matter of moments, he had managed to totally derail a life that took years for her to create, using power that she didn't even know she'd given him. It made her sick.

"You evil motherfucker. What gives you the right to come and fuck up my life?"

Lorde studied her, amusement flickering in his gaze before his expression hardened.

"See, this is what I don't like. You act all high-and-mighty. Like you ain't just as dirty as the rest of us."

She snorted derisively. "You're delusional."

"Delusional?" He leaned in, his voice a murmur against her ear. "At least I own my bullshit. I'm a straight shooter." His fingers trailed down her jaw, his touch burning her skin. "But you? You like to pretend you a good girl while you hide your bullshit. You're afraid to be judged. Scared motherfuckers won't accept you when you don't even accept yourself. Just fake as fuck."

His breath was hot against her skin as he whispered it.

Her body remained still, but her pulse was slamming out a rhythm she could feel in her throat.

He pulled back, dark amusement dimming his eyes. "Don't worry, though. I'ma fix that. By the time I'm done with you, you gon' know exactly who you are."

Sahara clenched her teeth, glaring at him right in the eyes, unwilling to show any hint of weakness.

"Don't fight the process, Rah Rah." His voice dipped lower, more intimate. "You my equal, baby. And when you finally stop fighting me, I'ma make you a queen."

A cold shiver ran through her as his words settled into her psyche.

"Why?" She just had to ask, stopping him just as he turned to walk away. "Why is it such a big deal that you make me your queen when I don't even want to be? You can have anyone."

Lorde turned around to face her, his eyes sharp and focused. His expression deadpanned.

"Because that's just it," he said. "I can have anyone I want. And, even after having them, I still want you."

Lorde let her go, rising to his feet. "Leave her here for now," he told Supreme. "And go ahead and take off the zip ties. She ain't going nowhere until I say she can."

The door shut behind them.

And Sahara sat there, staring at the papers in front of her, while swallowing the scream threatening to tear out of her throat.

She was trapped . . . and she had no idea how to get out.

She was in Lorde's world now.

No more Sahara.

And Sahara became Sincere . . . again.

Chapter 6

The lights are low, the vibe is cold,
I'm sinking into the blue . . .
Don't make a deal with the devil . . .
Because someday, he'll come for you.

Sincere woke up to the absence of sound. None of the expected noises of the city. *Where am I?*

Her breath caught in her throat. Her body felt sluggish, heavy—like she was waking from anesthesia. She shifted, silk sheets sliding against her bare skin. The mattress beneath her was far too soft, plush in a way that felt almost obscene, like sinking into a cloud. The luxury around her was suffocating, like a trap disguised as comfort.

Her eyes fluttered open, the dim glow of morning light stretching long shadows across the walls. The room was stunning. The furniture, the art on the walls—it all screamed money, power, and control.

Her stomach twisted. Something felt wrong. She sat up slowly, muscles sluggish, head foggy, like she was drugged. Panic flickered, but settled just beneath the surface, waiting to strike. She swallowed hard, forcing herself to stay still.

Think. Don't react.

Her fingers clenched the sheets, grounding herself as she

scanned the room. Massive. Expensive. Clearly, a showpiece, not a home.

She swung her legs over the side of the bed, pressing her bare feet to the floor. Instead of cold marble, polished hardwood met her skin, warm from the morning sun filtering in through floor-to-ceiling windows. The sensation jolted her awake, sharpening the fog in her brain.

Slowly, she rose to her feet, heartbeat drumming in her ears. She moved toward the glass, her fingers shaking slightly as she pulled the curtain back—and froze.

Her breath left her in a sharp exhale. She knew exactly where she was.

The Mississippi River stretched wide in the distance, like shining crystals under the first light of morning. Skyscrapers towered around her. She was in one of them; a luxury high-rise, looking down at the city from the highest floor. Below her, the streets of New Orleans were already alive, cars weaving through the tight grid of the city streets.

She pressed a hand to the window.

She was in the center of the city—the Central Business District.

Her pulse pounded as she took it all in. She was home. The one place she'd tried so hard to escape. Lorde brought her here. Her fingers curled into fists. This wasn't just a penthouse. This was a prison. The walls around her didn't have bars, but she could feel them just the same.

She steadied her breathing, forcing herself to think instead of react.

There had to be a way out. But first, she needed information. Sincere moved toward the bedroom door, hesitating just a second before turning the handle. It gave easily. No locks or resistance. That didn't make her feel any better.

The hallway was just as grand as the bedroom. The luxury decor continued with high ceilings, full floor-to-ceiling windows, and crystal chandeliers. But something about it felt . . . wrong. Too perfect. Too untouched. Like a place staged for a showing, not a home where someone actually lived.

Her breathing was controlled, even, but her mind raced as she moved through the space. She ran her hands along sleek wooden surfaces, opening drawers, rifling through cabinets. Nothing. No keys, no mail, no signs of life.

She checked the bookshelves in a room that looked like an office combined with a mini- library. It housed bookshelves lined with leather-bound classics that looked unread, placed more for aesthetics than use. She walked through the living room, then through a formal dining room, a designer kitchen with appliances that had never been used.

A place this size should've had staff, security—somebody. But there was no movement, no noise, no trace of another person.

Her skin tingled.

She turned back toward the bedroom, heart knocking against her ribs. She felt like she was moving through a dream, floating but hyperaware. And then she saw it.

The closet.

She had walked past it earlier without really looking. But now . . . she stepped forward, pressing her fingers to the handle before pulling it open.

Her breath hitched.

Everything inside was *hers*.

She stepped in slowly, trailing her fingers over the clothes. Designer pieces, delicate silks, expensive leathers. Her handbags lined the shelves. Her red-bottom heels neatly arranged like a showroom.

Someone had packed up her entire life and brought it here. Suddenly, she felt violated in a way that she couldn't explain. Who had gone through all of her things? Who had searched through her entire life without her permission? How long did she have to be unconscious for all this to happen?

A lump formed in her throat, but she refused to acknowledge it. She wasn't a child. She wasn't weak. She wasn't going to cry. Her suitcase sat neatly in the corner, along with her favorite makeup case. Everything perfectly placed as if she had arranged it herself.

And then she saw another thing on the nightstand: her journal.

Her chest squeezed. She picked it up, fingers grazing the worn leather cover. The last place she had left this was in her home in Atlanta. She turned, her gaze shifting to a small cabinet near the bed. She pulled it open—rows of identical blank journals lined neatly inside. The exact kind that she liked, along with matching pens from her favorite brand.

A whole collection. Ready for her.

Her pulse roared in her ears.

This was too much.

This wasn't just abduction. This wasn't just control. This was obsession to the highest degree. Someone had studied her for a long time, preparing for this exact moment. Sincere was particular about everything and someone had watched her long enough to know this about her.

She forced herself to exhale, gripping the journal in one hand, the other pressing against her temple.

Focus. Think.

She wasn't staying here. That was nonnegotiable. She wasn't anyone's prisoner. Sincere moved with purpose, heading for the front door. She didn't even care where it led. She just needed out.

She yanked it open—and froze.

Two men were stationed right outside—both massive. Dressed in all black, they were broad-shouldered, built like statues guarding the gates of hell. They stood at attention, not even flinching at her sudden appearance.

Her spine straightened, her expression shifting into one of cool indifference, masking the fire burning inside her. When she tried to step out, one of them shifted a little, using his body to subtly block her.

"Move," she ordered. "I'm leaving."

"That's fine." The taller one barely blinked. "We'll take you wherever you want to go, as long as it's approved by Lorde."

Her stomach flipped. Once his words really settled in, her jaw clenched.

"You're fucking kidding me."

Neither of them reacted.

She took a step forward, but they didn't move. She squared her shoulders, exuding control even as her pulse threatened to race.

"This is kidnapping," she said, her voice low, steady.

The shorter one tilted his head slightly. "Not kidnapping, miss. You're free to go anywhere you'd like. Within reason."

Control. Control. Don't let them see your frustration.

Sincere nodded once. Then she moved fast. She lunged, trying to shove past them. It was a fake out, a sharp movement meant to catch them off guard. But the shorter guard sidestepped effortlessly, blocking her path like he had already anticipated the move.

Her frustration sharpened.

"Miss, don't make this difficult."

That was it.

The tight leash she had on her composure instantly snapped. She lashed out, her fist aiming for the taller one's face. But he moved with eerily smooth precision, shifting just enough that her knuckles only hit air.

She swung again, kicking this time, but they were trained to anticipate and counter without striking back. Blocking every move like she was a child throwing a tantrum.

Fury boiled in her chest. "I am *not* staying here!" she screamed.

They remained silent. Unmoving. Like they knew she wasn't going anywhere. That realization made something deep inside her crack.

Breathing hard, she stepped back, regaining control. She wasn't going to keep fighting like a caged animal. She would think her way out of this. They wanted her to break. She wouldn't give them the satisfaction.

Slowly, she lifted her chin, and turned back into the house. Her steps steady and unhurried. She slammed the door behind her. But the fire inside was still there. It wasn't going anywhere. Lorde would regret underestimating her.

Sincere paced the length of the grand foyer, her hands clenched at her sides. The adrenaline from her failed escape attempt still surged through her bloodstream, every nerve in her body on high alert. She had fought, she had clawed, she had screamed. And yet, the guards hadn't even flinched.

They knew she wasn't getting out and they fully expected for her to cause a scene. Which meant all of this had been thought out. Lorde had prepared for this moment long in advance. She wouldn't be able to make it out without a plan.

The thought alone sent a fresh wave of anger slicing through her. She inhaled deeply, forcing herself to focus. *Think, don't react.* This was Lorde's game. He wanted her off balance, emotional, so consumed with rage that she wouldn't think rationally.

Her eyes flicked around the room, assessing every detail she hadn't noticed before. The house was a masterpiece of subtle control. No visible security cameras, but she didn't doubt that they were there. She was stuck inside a fucking dollhouse. And Lorde wanted to pull the strings that forced her to react as if she were a puppet.

Her jaw tightened.

She needed to regroup. And she needed to find her phone.

Sincere retraced her steps back toward the bedroom, her pulse still beating steady. If she was going to play this game, she was going to play it smart.

When she entered, her gaze went straight to the nightstand. She hadn't paid it much attention before, but something about the way it sat—almost too neatly beside her journal—felt . . . intentional.

She approached cautiously, pulling the drawer open.

And there it was.

A phone that looked exactly like hers, same case and all. The only difference being that everything about this one looked brand-new.

Her stomach twisted.

Sincere's fingertips hovered over the device before she snatched it up, pressing the side button. The screen lit up. It was already set up to mirror hers . . . except that it *wasn't* hers.

She moved through it and saw that all of her contacts were already loaded into it. But there was one major difference: Every man she'd ever dealt with was gone. Scrubbed. Erased.

Her breath came slow and even, but inside, she burned. Her lips parted, about to curse into the quiet, when the phone suddenly vibrated.

A text.

She stared at it, jaw tightening as she read the words on the screen.

I only want what's best for you. And that's me. You'll see.

It came from a number saved under the name "Daddy."

Sincere's fingers curled around the device so tightly she could feel her nails digging into her palm.

And then, another message popped up.

You'll thank me one day.

She pressed down her anger, burying it under a steady and calm composure.

Sincere wanted to smash it into the wall. But she wouldn't. He wanted a reaction. He wanted her furious, spiraling, cursing his name like a helpless little thing. Instead, she forced herself to relax, rolling her shoulders back as she typed her response.

You're delusional.

She hit *send*, tossed the phone onto the bed, and turned back toward the nightstand . . . only for another text to vibrate against the sheets.

I left you a gift. Check the small bag on the nightstand.

A cold chill traced its way down her spine. Sincere slowly turned back toward the drawer, swallowing down her distaste as she pulled it fully open.

Her stomach dropped. Inside, neatly placed, was a small, clear bag of pills.

Sincere's fingers hovered over it. Her heart slammed against her ribs as she felt the pull of her addiction calling out to her.

The way it used to make her feel.

The way it used to help her escape.

She gritted her teeth and slammed the drawer shut—only to freeze.

Her thoughts merged. Though her pride screamed at her to walk away, her willpower was waning. With a sharp breath, she yanked the drawer open again and her fingers closed around the bag before she could think twice. She didn't want to take them, but she couldn't force away the need to have an emergency hatch. A way to drown out everything around her if it came to that.

Sincere ran her tongue along her teeth, pushing through the nausea curling in her gut. She needed to get out of here. She grabbed her purse, threw on a fresh pair of jeans, a fitted top, and sleek sandals. When she stepped back out into the hallway, she kept her expression neutral, her energy controlled. She refused to let them see any sign of weakness.

The guards were still at their post when she reappeared.

"I want to leave," she said smoothly.

The taller one tilted his head slightly. "Where to?"

She kept her voice even. "A spa."

A pause. Then, a short nod. "We'll arrange it."

That easy.

But of course, nothing with Lorde was ever truly easy. She followed them to the private elevator that led to an alternate route in and out of the building. One specifically available for her and her alone. Something probably meant to be an extra layer of security for residents, but in this case, Lorde used it to keep her under his control.

As the black SUV pulled up outside, Sincere kept her breathing steady. She needed to be strategic and calm. She slid into the back seat, folding her legs gracefully beneath her as the doors locked automatically. The tinted windows gave her almost no view of the outside world, and she forced herself not to fidget. A few minutes was all she needed. In a few minutes, she'd have a plan.

The SUV rolled smoothly through the streets, the purr of the engine a steady, almost hypnotic presence. Sincere kept her posture relaxed, her expression unreadable as she gazed out of the tinted window. She didn't recognize the route, but she didn't need to. The moment they hit the French Quarter, her stomach twisted.

She had spent years avoiding this city, distancing herself from the ghosts it carried. Now, she was back—dragged here against her will, like a pawn moved across a chessboard. Sincere forced her breathing to stay even, forced her hands to remain loose in her lap. She needed to be calculated. She needed a lifeline.

The spa's ambiance tried to encourage a calmness that she couldn't feel. Soft instrumental music played overhead, mingling with the gentle splash of water from a decorative fountain in the lobby. The scent of eucalyptus and lavender filled the air, meant to be calming, but it did nothing to settle her nerves.

She slipped into the locker room, scanning the area. A few women lounged in plush white robes, sipping cucumber water, chatting about weekend plans, oblivious to the fact that one of them was in the middle of a hostage situation.

She spotted an older woman placing her phone on a bench as she adjusted her robe.

Perfect.

"Hi, do you mind if I use your phone to call my sister? I accidentally left mine at home."

"Of course!" The woman smiled and quickly handed it over.

Moving swiftly, Sincere grabbed it and dialed the only person who could give her answers.

Lena picked up on the second ring, her voice bubbling with excitement. "Sincere! Bitch, where you been?"

Sincere's chest tightened at the sound of a voice that felt normal, familiar, and safe. For a brief second, she could almost pretend none of this was happening.

"Lena, I'm in New Orleans and . . . I shouldn't be here," Sincere said, keeping her tone even, controlled. "I don't even know how I got here. Someone took me from my home a few nights ago."

There was a pause as Sincere waited for a response.

"What?" Lena let out a short laugh. "Girl, are you playing a game with me? We are all in New Orleans. You approved the move here . . . what do you mean you don't know how you got here?"

"This guy, Lorde, he—"

"Yessss, girl! I met Lorde and he is sexy as hell! Why you ain't tell me that you had a man like him sitting on the bench?"

"Because I don't!" Sincere said with more force than she intended. Looking around, she backed away from the other visitors and lowered her voice. "I'm trying to tell you, Lena. He forced me to come here."

"What do you mean? It was in the contract. Stacy sent it over to me on your birthday. I tried to call you about it, but you texted and said you wanted time alone to celebrate with your new boo."

Sincere frowned. *I never said that*, she thought. *How long has Lorde been talking for me?*

"What else did I say?"

"Um . . ." Lena seemed hesitant. "Just that you would hit me when you got settled in your place."

Sincere was speechless. She could barely wrap her mind around what she was hearing.

"Sis . . . is everything okay?" Lena finally said, as if just realizing this wasn't a joyful moment.

Sincere's fingers tightened around the phone. "Wait . . ." Sincere exhaled, keeping her tone measured. "Stacy's here too?"

Lena scoffed. "Girl, yeah! Everybody who wanted to move came down here. Office and everything relocated. All of us were paid to move to New Orleans and given a stipend to decorate. I've been online all day buying all kinds of shit that I don't need. You really didn't know?"

She hadn't known because she hadn't agreed to any of this.

Lorde had set all of this in motion without her knowledge, shifting her entire life as if she were a doll in his carefully curated playhouse. She swallowed down the bitter taste of rage. Now wasn't the time to unravel.

"I need you to come get me," Sincere said smoothly. "I'm going to send you the location from this phone. Don't call it back, though. It's not mine."

Lena didn't even hesitate. "I got you, boo. Give me fifteen minutes."

Sincere let out a quiet breath of relief, handed the phone back with a quick, grateful nod, and stepped toward the mirror.

Her reflection was unreadable, but beneath the surface, she was boiling.

Fifteen minutes.

She just had to hold it together for fifteen minutes.

Sincere pulled the hoodie lower over her face as she slid into the passenger seat of Lena's luxury SUV, her entire body jittery with nerves.

Lena took one look at her, then burst into laughter. "Girl, what is this? You running from *TMZ* or something?" she teased, eyeing Sincere's hunched posture and the way she tugged her hoodie tight around her head.

Sincere exhaled sharply, pressing back against the seat, feeling her muscles unclench for the first time in hours. She knew Lena meant no harm. That was just her personality. She was always lighthearted, always quick with a joke.

For a second, she just closed her eyes, absorbing the peace of being with someone who made her feel safe.

"And what are you wearing? That is not couture. It looks more like . . . thrift shop." She took a few sniffs. "And smells like it."

"I took it from someone in the spa."

Lena's nose curled up. "Ew! Why?"

"Because I was trying not to be seen. That's why I told you to pull around the back," Sincere explained. "I told you. I'm here against my will. I didn't come here because I wanted to. Lorde *forced* me."

Lena paused, a frown tugging her eyebrows as the words sunk in. "So . . . you were serious."

"Yes!" Sincere snapped, overexcited that Lena was finally getting it. "That's what I've been saying!"

"Well, you need to start from the beginning. I need to know everything."

Sincere shook her head. "No, we need to go to the police. Right now."

The look on Lena's face looked like she'd seen a ghost. "We can't do that. If we go to the police saying any of this, it'll be on the news. Then *TMZ*! You just came back and you are right at the point where your career can really take off. Do you really want to jeopardize it by accusing your label of kidnapping you?"

Silence passed as the heaviness of it all settled in. Tears welled up in Sincere's eyes. She felt trapped.

"I'm not saying you are stuck," Lena told her. "I'm just saying we gotta handle this the smart way. We need to move slow and think through it. Not act off emotion."

"I need a drink," Sincere muttered.

"Oh, now you talking." Lena brightened, seizing the moment. "That's something I can help you with. My place it is."

Sincere expected something nice—Lena always had good taste—but when they pulled into the private gated community, her brows lifted.

Damn.

Lena parked in front of a modern, all-white luxury town house, floor-to-ceiling windows giving way to an impeccably decorated interior. It was a minimalist dream—clean lines, muted colors, and statement pieces that screamed of luxury.

Sincere followed her inside, glancing around as Lena tossed her keys on the counter and grabbed a bottle of Veuve Clicquot from a built-in wine fridge. "Champagne? We celebrating something?" Sincere asked, sliding onto one of the plush barstools.

Lena gave her a look as she popped the cork. "Yeah, bitch. You living the high life and we are going to figure out how to keep it that way. What else?"

Sincere's lips pressed together. Lena really thought this was a win. She stayed silent as Lena poured the drinks, taking in the ambiance of the place. It was different from what she was used to—Lena had always been about city living, but this was some full-on suburban rich wife shit.

Lena set a glass in front of her. "Okay. Spill."

Sincere wrapped her fingers around the stem of the glass, but she didn't drink. Instead, she met Lena's gaze and told her everything. Starting all the way at the beginning.

"So now . . . here we are years later. I thought none of it was true until the night of the day I signed the contract. When Lorde kidnapped me." The words landed heavy, sucking the air out of the room.

Lena blinked. Then snorted. "Bitch, be serious. Tell me you're playing with me."

"I *am* serious, Lena," Sincere snapped, voice edged with frustration. "He took me. I woke up in a fucking house I've never seen before, with my whole life packed up like I agreed to it. I saw two men standing at the door, I have no control over where I go, and I don't even know if I can trust this phone he gave me."

Lena leaned back, expression shifting from amusement to mild concern. "Hold up. You mean . . . he really just moved you down here? Like, without saying shit?"

Sincere exhaled sharply. "Yes. And you, *and* Stacy. You really didn't find that weird after I was just saying I didn't want to go back?"

Lena sipped her champagne, brows drawing together. "I

mean . . . yeah, it was a little sudden, but girl, I just thought you came to your senses! Especially when Lorde cut that check! I mean, it's not like you're in the desert, it's just New Orleans!"

Sincere's fingers tightened around the glass. She wasn't getting it. "This isn't about where we are, Lena. It's about the fact that I didn't have a choice."

Lena set her glass down. "Okay, okay. I hear you. That's wild, it really is. But look . . . he didn't hurt you, did he?"

Sincere hesitated. Because technically, no. Lorde hadn't physically hurt her. However, that wasn't the point.

Before she could respond, Lena leaned in. "You sure this isn't just . . . Lorde being a man with money? 'Cause, let's be real. You got men who can barely pay rent thinking they got ownership over the women they deal with. A nigga like Lorde is just taking that shit to another level. But it makes sense because he's literally on another level!"

Sincere rolled her shoulders back, grounding herself. "That's not what this is. He's not just some man with money. He's from my past, he hurt my friend, and I don't trust him."

Lena pursed her lips. "Okay. Well, what you wanna do? You tryna run? Get out of town? 'Cause I'm just saying, his money is long *and* he is in charge of your career. It ain't gon' be easy."

That was the first real thing Lena had said all night. Sincere knew that. She knew disappearing wasn't as simple as hopping on a flight and switching her number. But she couldn't stay trapped.

She sighed, rubbing her temples. "I don't know. I just . . . I needed to talk to someone about it. Someone I trust."

Lena softened at that, reaching out and squeezing Sincere's hand. "Bitch, I always got you. You know that."

Deep down, Sincere knew that, but Lena's understanding of the situation was too casual. It was like she didn't see the danger in it. She saw nothing wrong with Lorde controlling everything because of what everyone was getting out of it.

Sincere forced a small smile. "Yeah. I know."

Lena chuckled, filling their glasses again. "By the way, I'm not trying to be funny, but I've seen him. And if that man kidnapped me? Chile! It'd be an episode of *Beauty and the Beast*, for real."

Sincere sighed, feeling completely exasperated as Lena laughed at her own joke.

This wasn't gonna be easy at all.

"He's been watching me for a while," Sincere said as she fell back on cushions behind her. The more she spoke, the more stressed she got. "I didn't even go public about rehab, but he must've known about it."

Lena shook her head as she sipped from her glass. "There is no way. That wasn't made public."

"That's what I'm saying. He's been watching me. He gave me pills. He left them in my room for me, saying they were a gift."

Lena leaned back against the plush couch, swirling her champagne. "Did you try it?"

"Of course not." Sincere's stomach turned. "Even if I wanted to, I don't trust him. It could be laced with anything."

Lena snorted. "Girl, please. Lorde ain't gon' spend all that money on you and your team just to have you overdosing off some weak shit."

Before Sincere could argue, Lena held out a hand. "Lemme see it."

Sincere hesitated. Then, reluctantly, she reached into her bag and placed the small bag of pills in Lena's palm.

Lena examined it, nodding in approval. "Oh yeah. This the good shit."

And then, before Sincere could stop her, she pulled out a

small mirror from her purse and crushed a pill on the glass. Before Sincere could react, she tapped out a small line, leaned down, and took a hit. Then she let out a slow, satisfied exhale.

Lena grinned. "Whew. Bitch, you trippin'. This is the *real* deal."

Sincere stared at the bag on her lap, feeling the beginning of a war waging inside her. She wanted to stay clean, but everything in her life felt so out of control. She needed to feel something that wasn't fear. Hesitant but craving, Sincere finally gave in. Only moments after her first hit, the feeling began to set in. And just like that . . . the tension eased.

For the first time since her life started spiraling out of control, she felt light. She would get back to balance when there wasn't so much pressure. Right now, all she wanted to do was float.

Chapter 7

Smells like money is being made, Supreme thought as he walked into the casino.

The scent of tobacco and whiskey told him that the patrons were having a good time. The sound of shuffling poker chips meant they were spending money. Happy people spent money more freely. It was a rule of the economy.

Supreme leaned back in his chair, swirling the dark liquid in his glass, watching the room like he always did, silent, observing, and taking in the small details. He wasn't here for fun. This was business.

The poker lounge was one of the Saints' high-end businesses. It was one of the few that had nothing to do with the streets—nothing illegal. No bricks being moved, no backroom deals with cartel niggas. This was different. This was money on paper, clean money, the kind that gave the Saints legitimacy.

And that's where Supreme thrived. While Lorde ran the squad, he made sure their money was clean. The goal was to only deal in legitimate deals one day. But things like that took time. People got nervous if you tried to flip the script overnight. They had to move gradually.

Supreme's phone vibrated on the table. One glance at the screen and his patience wore thin. It was Lorde. He should've let it ring, but if there was one thing Supreme knew about his cousin, it was that he didn't like being ignored.

With a sigh, he picked up the call and lifted the phone to his ear. "Yeah."

Lorde's voice came through casually. "What you up to?"

Supreme took a slow sip of his drink. "Handling business. What you want?"

In the background, he heard something shuffling like women talking, laughter, and the faint tap of nails against something hard. Then Lorde spoke. "Tell her I want my cuticles rounded. I don't want that square-looking shit."

Supreme let out a low laugh. "You deadass getting a manicure? Bro, you trippin'."

"Nigga, women don't like no rough-ass palms. You gotta take care of your shit. That's why you ain't got no wife yet."

Supreme ignored that. "Man, what you want?"

Lorde let a small pause stretch between them before answering, voice shifting into something sharper. "Need you to sit with Sincere today."

The irritation hit Supreme's chest instantly. "Nah. I'm done dealin' with that. The contract been signed. It's done."

"You got something confused, cuz." Lorde chuckled. "That wasn't a request."

Supreme ran a hand over his beard, already annoyed. "I ain't no damn babysitter. Find someone else."

Lorde sighed, but it wasn't frustration. It was amusement. "Nigga, you act like I'm asking you to change diapers. Just make sure she don't get stupid. I'll be back later."

"I don't even know what the fuck your thing is with her. You move the whole world for this girl, and for what? Some moment y'all had years ago? Shit don't make sense."

Lorde went quiet for a second. When he spoke again, his tone was low, dangerous. "That moment changed my life. You don't gotta get it, just respect it."

Supreme didn't argue. Family was family. And he respected Lorde, even when he thought he was crazy as hell.

He let out a long breath, giving in. "This the last time I'm doing this."

Lorde snorted. "Nigga, save that shit. I ain't trying to hear it."

Then the line went dead.

Supreme shook his head and finished off his drink before rising from his seat.

This was gonna be a long-ass day.

The drive over was silent. Supreme wasn't in the mood for music or thinking too hard about what he was about to step into. By the time he pulled up to the high-rise building, he already knew Sincere was going to be a problem. He didn't know how, but he did know that he didn't feel like dealing with it.

He stepped out of the car, adjusting his watch, moving with that quiet, effortless confidence he always carried. He didn't hesitate, never second-guessed. After taking the private elevator to Sincere's floor, he unlocked the door and walked inside like he owned the place.

And there she was.

Sitting on the far end of the plush sectional in the oversized living room, legs crossed, posture stiff, face unreadable. She looked completely calm, but her eyes burned with something wild.

It wasn't fear. Wasn't even anger, which he expected. It looked more like determination.

Supreme took a second to study her.

She was beautiful, that much was obvious. She had the kind of face that made men dumb, made them think with everything but their brains. But Supreme wasn't most men. And beauty didn't impress him as much as power did.

But she had that too.

Even in her cage, she carried herself like a queen. That was intriguing to him. As he waited for her to be the first to speak, she looked him up and down, eyes sharp.

"Interesting . . . I just didn't think you were the type."

Supreme lifted a brow. "Type for what?"

She tilted her head slightly. "The type to follow a man like Lorde. You don't strike me as someone who does well with taking orders."

His mouth curved, more from curiosity than amusement. "That so?"

"It's so." She leaned forward, her gaze never leaving his. "So why do you?"

He could've brushed her off and given her some vague, dismissive answer. But he didn't.

Instead, he took a step closer, lowering himself onto the leather armchair across from her, stretching his arms along the rests like he had all the time in the world.

"Let me ask you something. You ever played chess?"

She blinked, slightly thrown off by the shift in conversation. "What?"

"Chess. You ever play it?"

She hesitated. "Yeah. A little."

He nodded. "Then you should know this. The king don't move much. He stays put, lets everybody else handle shit. The pawns get sacrificed first. But the knight?" He leaned in slightly. "The knight moves differently. He got options. That's me. I move how I need to, but I ain't no pawn."

She stared at him, her expression unreadable. "And Lorde . . . What is he?"

Supreme easily caught her rookie move. "I guess you can call him a king."

If she was looking for something to bruise his ego, she was going to have to search harder than that. Her lips curled slightly, but there was no amusement in her expression. "That sounds like an excuse for following a man who doesn't deserve your loyalty."

Supreme exhaled, shaking his head. "You don't know shit about what he deserves."

"I know enough."

There was that sharpness again. He leaned back, watching her, waiting for her to crack, but she didn't.

Instead, she studied him, eyes calculating. "You think you're unreadable. That no one can figure you out."

He tilted his head slightly. "Am I wrong?"

"You are." Her slow knowing confidence settled in her words. "Because I already did."

That made Supreme pause for half a second.

She leaned forward, voice softer, but more cutting. "You hate being here as much as I do. You're just better at hiding it."

That got to him. Just a little. He let the silence stretch, let her think she had won something. Then, finally, he spoke. "You need to learn how to control your anger, Sincere."

Her brows drew in, forming the slightest crease.

He lifted his chin with a subtle show of defiance. "When you can make a person angry, you can control them."

For the first time, she didn't have a response.

And for the first time, Supreme saw exactly why Lorde couldn't let her go. Supreme leaned back, arms folded across his broad chest, watching her too carefully, like a man sizing up a problem he hadn't yet decided how to solve. His face didn't give much away, but Sincere could feel his scrutiny.

She ignored it. At least, outwardly. She wasn't new to men like him. Men who studied before they struck, who watched for weaknesses the way a predator watched for the first limp in its prey. The only thing was that she wasn't prey. And she sure as hell wasn't about to start acting like one.

She kept her posture relaxed, her face unreadable as she focused on something simple. Like picking at the polish on her fingernails, as if this entire situation was nothing more than an inconvenience.

But Supreme didn't miss the details.

He saw how she positioned herself. Not fully facing him, but angled just enough that she could see every exit. He noticed how she kept her breathing steady, her fingers eagerly scratching off the glossy lacquer. She wasn't panicking. She was thinking. Calculating.

She was *too* much like him. It unsettled him in a way he didn't want to admit. That was the thing about women like her. They made you think you were in control, but really, they were the ones pulling the strings.

Lorde might think he was the puppeteer in this situation, but Supreme was starting to see the truth. Sincere wasn't as weak as he thought she was. She had a way of baiting men. Not in an obvious way. Not in a way that clearly said she was trying to manipulate him into anything specific. But she was keeping her cool and that made her more dangerous than if she had screamed, cried, or begged.

Sincere glanced up at Supreme just once, long enough to see the thought behind his eyes. He was putting pieces together.

Good.

She wanted him to think. She wanted him to start questioning why a man like him was being told to play babysitter. She wanted him to wonder why Lorde couldn't just let her go.

Because when men like Supreme started questioning the things they were blindly following, that's when the cracks started to form.

And all she needed was a crack so that she could wiggle in.

She let the silence stretch between them just long enough to make it heavy. Let him think she had given up on trying to crack him, that she had settled into quiet acceptance.

Then she struck.

"You were at Rocco's party that night," she said, her voice casual. "You weren't just there to enjoy the party, though."

Supreme didn't move, didn't react. But she caught the way his gaze darkened. Just the slightest shift, like a twitch he wished he could take back.

"You were playing me," she continued, leaning back into the couch, feigning relaxation. "Scoping me out for Lorde. Being his pawn. How long have you been doing that?"

He said nothing. Had absolutely no reaction, not even a blink. It irritated her.

"You don't have an answer to that?" she pressed.

Supreme leaned forward, allowing the weight of his silence to speak first as he rested his elbows on his knees. He finally looked her dead in the eye. "I don't have anything to explain to you."

"Convenient."

"That's reality."

Sincere tilted her head slightly, studying him like he was an equation she was on the verge of solving. "I pegged you for an honest man," she mused, her voice dipping into something softer, smoother. "One with a moral compass."

A shadow of a grin touched his lips, but his eyes stayed cold. "That's where you fucked up. Assuming."

She laughed under her breath, but there wasn't an ounce of amusement in it. "No," she said, shaking her head. "See, I don't assume. I observe." She paused, letting her gaze drag over him. "And you don't move like the rest of them. You don't talk like them. Even now, you look uncomfortable being here, like this ain't even what you signed up for."

She saw it again. That flash of something real in his eyes.

He huffed out a breath, sat back against the couch, and folded his arms. "You done psychoanalyzing me?"

"Not even close," she shot back, smiling sweetly.

A flicker of reluctant admiration crossed his face. He wasn't amused, but he was impressed.

"I just want to know why you're so loyal to him," she said, her voice level, despite the bitter taste in her mouth.

"Because I am."

She studied him, trying to pick apart the layers of that answer. It had to be more than that. He didn't seem like the type to go for blind loyalty. There had to be something else. Something deeper.

"So that's it? You just do whatever Lorde says, no matter what?"

He stared at her, unreadable. "I don't follow nobody," he repeated, his voice lower this time. "But I respect my family."

Sincere's lips parted slightly in realization. "Family," she murmured. "You're related."

"Yes." Supreme nodded. "First cousins. Might as well be brothers."

The pieces were coming together now. It made sense. This was the unspoken bond. But something else was very clear. Lorde might have been Supreme's family, but he was still not someone Supreme fully agreed with.

She saw it in the way his jaw ticked, in the tightness that crept into his posture when she pushed certain buttons. He wasn't just uncomfortable. He was conflicted. That was something she could use.

She folded her arms. "I never would've thought you were a Saint," she mused, shifting the conversation just enough to watch him react. "Didn't even pick up on the New Orleans accent," she added, watching his face closely.

He didn't reply.

Sincere's lips curled slightly.

"I guess you hid it," she said, tilting her head slightly. "Like how I do."

Supreme's gaze darkened slightly. That got his attention.

"It seems we have a lot in common."

He stared at her, expression blank, but eyes searching. He didn't like that. He hated the way she spoke like she knew him, like she could pick him apart. What pissed him off even more was the fact that she wasn't exactly wrong.

They were similar. Both running from something. Both pretending to be something they weren't. Both playing roles to survive. The difference was that Supreme had made peace with it, while Sincere still wanted a way out.

He let a silence stretch before shaking his head, a hint of a smile betraying him. "You talk too much."

Sincere smiled. "Some may say that."

Supreme exhaled a short laugh, looking away for the first time.

She was the kind of woman who was dangerous in a way that snuck up on you—like a slow poison. It was a power that women like her had to ruin men.

He had seen it before.

Back when he was just a kid, he remembered sitting in the back room of his mama's house in the Lower Ninth, listening to her read his daddy's letters from prison. His mother was a powerhouse of a woman, but she had loved a man who couldn't be tamed. In the end, she had paid the price for it.

Supreme had watched that love destroy her. He watched her wait on letters that barely came. She bore the silence like a scar that would never heal. *That* was what love did. It left people waiting and wanting. But Supreme promised himself a long time ago that he would never be that man. He never wanted the obsession with love to blind him to reality.

Sincere wasn't just some woman caught in the middle of a game she didn't understand. She understood too much. She had this way of pulling things out of people, seeing things she wasn't supposed to see. It made sense now, why Lorde was so obsessed with her. She wasn't just a woman. She was a mirror. One that reflected the shit people tried to keep buried deep inside. She pulled it out without even being aware of what she was doing, placing it in front of them and forcing them to deal with it.

He could feel her watching him now, her eyes sharp, analyzing him the way she had been from the moment they sat down. For the first time, Supreme was starting to see that maybe that was why Lorde couldn't let her go.

"I have to say this, you were good," she admitted, her head tilting slightly. "You had me thinking you were a sexy man who happened to be interested in me."

He let out a low chuckle. "And that was the problem?"

"The problem," she said, voice cooling, "was that you weren't real. You knew exactly who I was, but I didn't know a damn thing about you."

"Right." Supreme shook his head dismissively. "You still don't."

She studied him for a second, then smiled.

"Yeah, but I'm getting there."

Chapter 8

One of Lorde's favorite things was the purr of his Maybach as he cruised down the scenic streets of Baton Rouge. This was his version of relaxation, down the streets he'd run down barefoot as a child. He leaned back against the smooth leather, exhaling slowly as his fingers drummed a tune against his knee.

Baton Rouge was different from New Orleans, less rhythm, less soul, and a bit less history, but it was still his. It was a place where power was dictated by who people feared most. And Lorde had built his name on being *that* motherfucker.

A small gris-gris bag, tied tightly with twine, hung from the rearview mirror, filled with crushed bones, herbs, and a few secrets only he and his priestess knew. A bundle of dried sage rested near the armrest; the scent subtle but strong. He didn't play when it came to protection, spiritual or physical. These were the objects that gave him comfort despite being a person who a lot of people probably wanted dead.

Lorde tapped his fingers against the armrest pensively before pulling out his phone, pressing a number. The call connected with a *click*.

"Yo," came the voice on the other end. It was Monk, one of his most trusted lieutenants.

Lorde didn't waste time. "Checking in with you 'cause I'm

meeting with Silvan. Wanted to make sure you would be on point when I do."

There was a pause as Monk downloaded the full meaning of what Lorde was saying. And then, finally, he spoke. "Supreme know 'bout it?"

Lorde clenched his jaw, grinding his teeth together. He could feel his patience thinning as his grip tightened around the phone. Supreme's name was the last thing he wanted to hear right now.

"You just heard me say Silvan's name, and that's the first question you ask?" His voice dropped a few octaves, laced with irritation. "Ain't no way in hell Supreme would cosign this. Plus, I don't need his approval to make moves, so why the fuck would I run it by him?"

There was a pause on the other end of the line. Monk knew better than to push, but Lorde could still hear the hesitation in his breath, the subtle shift in his energy. It annoyed him.

"Look, you know I respect you, Lorde," Monk started, his voice careful, deliberate. "But Supreme—"

Lorde cut him off. "Supreme ain't me."

Silence.

Lorde let that sit, let the weight of his words sink in before he continued. "I don't need his permission to run my own operation. I don't need his blessing to do what needs to be done. Supreme don't like getting his hands dirty. He still got one foot in the past, still worried about what the old heads think, like we not out here tryna build something bigger than they could ever come up with."

"That's why it don't sit right with me," Monk admitted, voice low and full of conflict.

The ease drained from Lorde's face. His fingers flexed against the armrest, irritation thrumming under his skin. "I don't need it to sit right with you," Lorde said coolly.

Monk sighed, "What's next? You bringin' Silvan in?"

"I'm bringin' in money."

Lorde let the words settle. He didn't have to spell it out. Monk knew exactly what kind of money Silvan dealt in. It was bigger than drugs. Bigger than weapons. And Supreme, along with the rest of the old heads, would never approve.

"The elders?" Monk finally asked.

Lorde scoffed, rolling his neck. "What about 'em?"

"They ain't gon' like this."

"They ain't gotta like it." His tone was sharp, dismissive. "They outdated, Monk. Always talkin' 'bout honor and legacy. What legacy, huh? Where the millions at? The Saints should be on top, but we out here still livin' off street code like this some ancient manuscript. Fuck that."

Monk was silent. He didn't agree, but he wouldn't argue either. That's what Lorde liked about him. He knew his place.

"Besides," Lorde continued, his voice laced with condescension, "you know Supreme stay up under them. That's what really got you hesitatin'."

Monk didn't deny it.

Lorde let the moment stretch before speaking again, his tone dipping into something dangerously smooth.

"Aye . . . you still my nigga, right?"

A beat. Then, "Always."

"Good." Lorde's voice was like silk over a blade. Both sharp and deadly in the same breath. "Now, make sure the drop from Miami goes smooth. I ain't tryna deal with no bullshit on top of everything else."

"I got it," Monk assured.

Lorde hung up without another word, tossing his phone onto the seat beside him.

The old ways were dead. He was just the only one with the balls to bury them.

Lorde's jaw flexed as he pulled his phone back into his palm, clicking over to his security app. Sincere's feed came up first. She was sitting in the doorway of her room, absently picking at a plate of food. The overhead light cast long shadows over her face, making her look . . .small.

Not weak but contained. Something about that sent a slow ripple of satisfaction through his chest. He flicked the feed to the next screen.

Supreme flashed on the screen. His cousin sat nearby, scrolling through his phone like he wasn't in the middle of a job. As if he wasn't babysitting the woman Lorde had spent years thinking about.

What really fucked him up was that she was *talking* to him. Not ignoring him like the others. It was subtle, barely even noticeable. The way her eyes cut in Supreme's direction, the slight tilt of her head, the way her lips barely moved. Lorde felt a burning sensation in his chest.

He clicked the screen off.

He had two problems: Sincere and Supreme. And he didn't trust either one of them. But . . . not in the same way. Supreme's loyalty was unquestionable. He was honorable. *Too* fuckin' honorable, in Lorde's opinion.

Supreme was a man who saw the world in black-and-white when Lorde knew damn well it was made of shades of gray and blood-red. But even if Supreme didn't always agree with Lorde's methods, he'd never outright betray him. Loyalty, in their world, was the only real currency. And Supreme had proven time and time again that when it came down to it, he would always choose family.

But in order to do what he needed to do with Silvan, he had to keep Supreme preoccupied so he didn't find out about it. Which is why he chose him to watch Sincere . . . which led to his other problem.

Sincere was a different kind of problem. She was the kind of woman who made men stupid. She could do it when she wasn't even trying, and that was what made her dangerous.

Lorde had seen plenty of bad bitches in his lifetime. Women who knew how to work a room, how to bend a man's will with a flick of their wrist or the curve of their lips. Sincere wasn't like them. She didn't play at seduction. She didn't have to. Her power wasn't in her beauty, though she had that in abundance. It was deeper than that. It was woven into her energy. It was the very fabric of who she was.

She was a *mystère*: A woman with the ability to pull men into her orbit without them realizing they'd been caught in her gravity.

A siren without a song.

A trap disguised as an open door.

A woman like that couldn't be trusted, because she wasn't just a weakness. She was a weapon. A powerful one that he could use once he forced her into submission.

Lorde didn't believe in love. He never let his guard down, never let any woman get too close. To him, love was a curse, a sickness. He'd much rather rely on control, but Sincere was a little bit better at it.

The insane part was he wasn't even sure if she knew it. She didn't come across like some master manipulator, weaving grand schemes to take men down one by one. She moved through life oblivious to the wreckage she left in her wake. She thought she was just *surviving*. Thought she was just doing what she had to do.

She didn't see what he saw. The way men bent and broke around her, trying to get her attention, fighting to be her exception. He'd felt it too. That pull. That energy that whispered to him even after all these years, still beckoning him.

Lorde flicked his lighter open and shut, the metallic *click-click* filling the car's quiet interior as he stared at the black screen of his phone, mind running a mile a minute.

Supreme had always been the golden boy. Even when they were kids, when their pops were running the Saints and setting up what would become the empire Lorde now controlled, Supreme had been the one everyone loved. Even now, he was the one they respected. He was the one who played by the rules. The one who listened to the old heads, learned the game the right way.

Initially, he was being groomed to be the next in line to be leader, but he never wanted that power the way Lorde did. He wasn't built to burn everything down and rebuild it in his image. That was Lorde's role. He was the wrecker, the one who brought change through chaos. Supreme was the balance.

When Lorde wanted to move recklessly, Supreme was the one who made sure he did it right. When Lorde wanted to body a nigga for disrespect, Supreme made sure it was calculated so it wouldn't fall back on him. He wasn't a soft man, not by a long shot. He was principled. And in a world where men changed loyalties like they did shoes, Lorde could always count on one thing. Supreme had never switched up on him. Not once. That *meant* something.

Which was exactly why it pissed him off so much that Sincere was talking to Supreme like she could figure him out when she barely said two words to him. He was the one who was supposed to call the shots, and she was the one who was supposed to follow the rules. The sooner she understood that he was the one who ran her world, the one who *had* been running it for longer than she even knew, the better things would be.

Which was why, once he got to his meeting with Silvan, he was going to do exactly what needed to be done. Because no one was about to fuck up what he built.

Not Supreme.

And sure as hell not Sincere.

The black Escalade rolled to a slow stop outside Dooky Chase's, a legendary Creole restaurant in the heart of New Orleans. It wasn't just a place to eat, which was why it was one of Lorde's preferred spots. It was also a place to be seen, to hold court, to make moves among the jazz music and the scent of hot grease and spices clinging to the air.

But Lorde wasn't walking in yet. He *never* stepped into a building without protection. Not just the kind that came with armed shooters stationed outside. Spiritual protection. The kind that ensured no ill-intentioned spirits, no evil eyes, and no curses followed him through those doors.

In Lorde's life, too much had happened for him not to believe there was some power or entity outside of what he could see that was guiding and protecting him throughout every moment of his life. As the grandson of a hoodoo practitioner, he relied heavily on her teachings. She was his personal *mambo* and she accompanied him during every meeting.

Clothilde was the only woman in the world he truly trusted. *Maman Clo*, as Lorde called her, wasn't just any hoodoo priestess—she was his grandmother, his blood, and the foundation of everything he believed in. She fully raised him and even partially raised Supreme, teaching them the ways of their ancestors, the art of protection, and the power of unseen forces that moved through the world carrying out the orders whispered during a believer's prayers.

Maman Clo stood beside him now, small only in stature, wrapped in deep indigo robes embroidered with protective *veves*, and her silver locks of wisdom hidden beneath a dark head-wrap. Her presence alone commanded reverence. In one hand, she held a small vial filled with blue liquid and in the other, a bundle of herbs that still burned at the edges, releasing a thick, curling smoke that carried the scent of anise, myrrh, and sage, among other things.

Lorde stood still as she moved around him, murmuring low, rhythmic prayers in Creole, her voice a steady whisper that calmed him instantly. It didn't matter how high he climbed, how many enemies he buried, how much power he accumulated. If Maman Clo didn't say he was good, he wasn't stepping foot inside that building.

She traced a symbol in the air before pressing two fingers, damp with the cooling blue liquid, against his forehead. A mark of protection. "*Gade kò ou, ti gason mwen*," she murmured.

Guard yourself, my boy.

The tightness in Lorde's body loosened as the final words of the ritual settled over him. When she finished, she kissed her fingertips, pressing them lightly against his forehead.

"I got it, Maman Clo," he muttered, adjusting the cuffs of his black button-up. "*Ou pa fini ankò, maman?*" he asked, meaning, "You're not done yet, Mama?"

Maman Clo scoffed, tucking the vial away into the folds of her robe. "You stay thinkin' my work is for me. It's for you. Always been for you."

"Okay, Ma."

Lorde didn't argue with her. He never did.

"You good now, *ma cher*. No bad spirits gon' follow you in. But I still don't like this meeting. This place is full of history. Not good history for our family. And, remember this . . . history don't forget."

"Come on, Maman Clo." Lorde grinned, pulling a thick wad of cash from his pocket and tucking it into the folds of her robe. "You act like I'm superstitious or somethin'," he joked with a smile. "But I understand."

She made a sound low in her throat, stepping back as his security detail opened the restaurant door.

"Watch your back, Lorde. Silvan don't sit with men unless he plannin' to own them. Don't let your guard down."

Lorde chuckled, shaking his head.

He didn't *get* owned. *He* owned.

Instead of responding back, he nodded at the men stationed

outside. They held their composure, keeping their postures stiff, weapons concealed, but ready. With a final glance at Maman Clo, Lorde pushed the doors open and stepped inside.

The scent hit him first, reminding him of all the reasons he loved this place. Garlic, butter, smoked sausage, and the rich scent of gumbo filled his nostrils, making him feel right at home. Silvan was already there, seated in a curved leather booth at the back, sipping on something dark, expensive, and probably older than both of them combined. He didn't look up immediately. Just swirled his glass, watching the liquid, before finally dragging his gaze up to meet Lorde's.

"You late," Silvan said, voice syrup-smooth. A hint of amusement flickered in his eyes.

"Nah. You early," Lorde countered. He slid into the booth with an easy confidence, arms stretched across the backrest like he owned the place. His gaze ran over Silvan, observing the gold chains shining against his dark skin to the slight swell in his stomach. Business was good for him, that was for sure.

"You been eatin' good," Lorde mused, tilting his head. "Stomach lookin' a lil' heavy, my guy."

Silvan's lips curled into a slow grin, his teeth shining under the restaurant's dim lighting.

"And you still out here lookin' like a starved Ethiopian. You gotta eat more, lil' brother. Don't want niggas out here thinkin' you weak."

Lorde rolled his tongue over the inside of his cheek, holding back the irritation simmering beneath his skin. Silvan had a way of throwing little jabs that sounded playful, but always carried an undercurrent of condescension. Lorde knew the game, though. He played it better. "I eat just fine," he said coolly. "Just like them Ethiopians you talkin' shit about."

He let the moment settle, his fingers tapping lightly against the table as he let his eyes drift over the restaurant. A waitress approached, setting a glass of whiskey in front of Lorde without him having to ask. He didn't drink much—never trusted a mind that wasn't sharp—but appearances mattered. A glass in front of him made him look at ease, unbothered, like this meeting was nothing more than a friendly sit-down between businessmen.

He picked it up, swirled the amber liquid once, then set it back down untouched. "You know why I'm here," Lorde finally said, his voice smooth, but laced with authority. "Let's get to it."

Silvan sighed, rubbing a slow hand down his beard before leaning back into the booth. "Yeah, I know why you here. But the real question is . . . why Supreme ain't?"

"Because he's not." Lorde's grip on his glass tightened for a second before he relaxed, cocking his head. "And why would that matter to you?"

Silvan's grin stretched wider, lazy and knowing. "Just an observation. Your right-hand man, who handles most of your business, the man that was standing beside you before you even had a seat at the table . . . ain't here for the biggest move you about to make?"

Lorde didn't say anything. He just let Silvan keep talking.

"That mean he don't know, huh?" Silvan tilted his head, feigning curiosity. "Or do it mean that you don't trust him to know?"

Lorde held Silvan's gaze. "Whoever ain't here is irrelevant. I'm here for the money. I'm here for expansion. Legacy. You think the Saints can keep riding off what the elders built forever? This ain't the nineties, and these old niggas still out here actin' like we at war over street corners."

Silvan tapped a single gold ring against his glass. He watched Lorde the way a snake watched a man step just close enough to strike.

"What's it gonna be? You bringin' me in?"

Lorde leaned back, delivering cool arrogance. "I'm bringing in money."

The weight of his words settled between them, unspoken but clear. Silvan knew exactly what kind of money Lorde was talking about. And he also knew that Supreme would never approve.

"The elders?" Silvan asked.

Lorde scoffed, rolling his neck like the mere mention of them was enough to piss him off. "What about 'em?"

Silvan shrugged. "They ain't gon' like this."

"They ain't gotta like it." Lorde's voice was sharp, dismissive. "They outdated. Always talkin' 'bout doing things with honor to create legacy. For what? Where the millions at? The Saints should be on top, but we out here still livin' off street code. Protecting folks who don't want to be protected at our own expense. Fuck that."

Silvan watched him for a moment, his expression unreadable. But inside, he was pleased. Lorde's arrogance was exactly what he needed. A crack in the foundation of the Saints, a man young and hungry enough to believe he could do better than the ones who came before him. That was the kind of man who was easy to steer and manipulate. His only problem would be Supreme. But Silvan would cross that bridge when he had to.

Silvan set his glass down, rubbing his jaw. "Tell me, Lorde . . . what happens when Supreme don't like what you doing? You know how he is. He ain't gon' be loud about it. He ain't gon' argue. He's steady, but he's always watching. Always thinking."

Lorde's jaw flexed.

Silvan smiled. He could see the wheels turning, Lorde's mind shifting gears.

"You got a plan for handlin' that?" Silvan pressed. "The last thing you want is for a third party to come in and mess up everything we're building."

Lorde's fingers drummed against the table. "I ain't worried about Supreme."

Silvan chuckled, lifting his glass. "That right? Then how you gon' make sure he ain't runnin' to the elders to undo shit once he finds out what you up to?"

Lorde didn't respond right away. Because that was a question worth considering. He thought back to the way Supreme always moved. He was careful, methodical, and loyal. But loyal to who? Him? Or the old heads that still thought the Saints should be run like some community outreach program? Ignoring him would be a mistake and Lorde wasn't stupid. He needed to keep his eyes everywhere.

His gaze shot to a figure hovering near the entrance. Dre was a new recruit, which meant he was young, hungry, and eager to please. A kid in his early twenties who still thought being a Saint was about power instead of responsibility. He had a lot of potential, which was one of the reasons Supreme took him under his wing a long time ago. That made him the perfect choice to do Lorde's bidding.

Lorde leaned back against the plush leather of the booth, his fingers drumming lightly on the table. His eyes returned over to the edge of the restaurant, where Dre stood just out of earshot, waiting for orders like a good soldier.

"Dre," Lorde called smoothly, not bothering to look up as he swirled the drink in his hand.

The young man straightened, stepping closer. His posture was sharp, but there was uncertainty in his eyes. He knew better than to hesitate, but something about the way Lorde's voice carried sent a chill through him.

"Yeah, boss?"

Lorde exhaled slowly, tapping his ring against the side of his glass. "I'm changing your assignment."

Dre's brows furrowed slightly, but he didn't speak. He just waited.

"From now on, you're on Supreme," Lorde continued, his voice as silky as the shadows pooling in the corners of the room. "Whatever business he's on every day, you need to be there. You're his shadow." Lorde finally met his eyes, letting the weight of his words settle between them. "But you work for me."

Dre tensed for a moment. And then, his throat bobbed as he swallowed.

"I—" He hesitated, turning his gaze toward Silvan, then back to Lorde. "I mean, Supreme don't—"

Lorde's eyes narrowed, pupils darkening. "What?" he asked, his voice low, quiet. His silence made people even more nervous than when he spoke.

Dre straightened his back to stand tall. "I'm just sayin' . . . he don't do no sideways shit. He solid. If you worried about him—"

"I didn't say I was worried," Lorde cut in smoothly, cocking his head to the side. "I said I want to know what he's up to. And I want you to report on that for me."

Dre nodded slowly, but there was a tightness to it, like he wasn't fully convinced, but wasn't willing to push back either. His loyalty to Supreme was clear, and Lorde could see the conflict swimming behind his eyes.

Lorde took another slow sip of his drink before setting the glass down, the sound a soft but deliberate *clink* against the table. Then, with a voice dipped in that signature charisma that had made men follow him blindly for years, he began to speak again.

"Look, this ain't what you think it is. You know I respect Supreme. He my blood. But even the best men got blind spots. I need you to be his insurance."

Dre frowned, processing.

Lorde leaned forward slightly, letting his words sink in, like he was doing Dre a favor instead of twisting the knife into something deeper. "I'm just makin' sure nobody around him is tryna play him dirty. You feel me?" Lorde said, lowering his tone like this was some important business that he was entrusting him with. "I ain't askin' you to set him up. Just . . . let me know if anything seems off. That's it. And keep it between me and you. You can do that?"

Dre's jaw worked like he wanted to say something, but instead, he nodded.

"I got you," he murmured. "Got you covered for real. No worries."

Lorde smiled, slow and satisfied.

"Yeah, I know ain't no worries," he said, the bite in his tone returning. Then his gaze turned just a shade darker. "Because if I find out something ain't right . . . If I find out you held somethin' back, you know what that mean, right?"

He let the sentence hang in the thick, humid air.

Dre stiffened, but he didn't need the threat spelled out for him. "Understood," Dre said, voice clipped, shoulders locked.

Silvan chuckled from across the booth, swirling his drink like he was watching an entertaining show. He waited until Dre had returned to his post to comment on everything that he'd just saw unfold.

"You always was a paranoid motherfucker, Lorde," Silvan mused, shaking his head with amusement.

Lorde leaned back in his seat, fingers lightly tapping against the rim of his glass. "And that's why I'm still here," he replied, flashing a grin that looked more like he was baring his teeth than anything else.

But what he didn't realize was that, across from him, Silvan was thinking the exact same thing.

Chapter 9

"You know how it is, man." Rocco's voice oozed through the speakers of the luxury SUV. His fake humility barely concealed his bitterness. "I ain't mad. I just think people need to know the truth."

Sincere froze, her stomach twisting into a tight, suffocating knot.

No, he wasn't about to tell the truth. He was about to tell *his* truth. On *The Morning Vibe*, with millions of listeners tuning in ready to eat up every word.

Trey Johnson, one of the hosts, snorted. "The truth? You sure you wanna go that route, Rocco? 'Cause I'ma be real, bruh. You got a history. And it ain't exactly squeaky-clean."

Trey's co-host, D-Lo, chuckled, jumping in. "Yeah, man. You tryna sit up here and act like you some victim, but you was outside. We all seen the receipts. You had, what? Three? Four different women caught up while you was with her?"

Rocco let out a dry laugh, but there was an edge to it, a bit of irritation that hadn't been there before. "Man, that's different. Y'all know how it is. Women throw themselves at a man in my position. Sometimes you get caught up. But that ain't what we talkin' about right now."

His tone shifted, becoming more calculated, performative,

steeped in practiced self-righteousness. "Sahara did me dirty," he said. "That's all I'ma say. She ain't who y'all think she is. She cold. Ain't got no loyalty in her."

The silence in the car was thick, almost suffocating as Sincere sat in the back of the Cadillac SUV with Lorde and Supreme, all of them listening.

Reclined with ease, Lorde absorbed the bullshit spilling from Rocco's mouth. The corners of his lips were lifted with smug satisfaction. At first, he found it amusing. How desperate this nigga sounded, how obvious it was he was licking his wounds in public like a pathetic, scorned lover.

Lorde had seen it a million times before: Men who lost control of their women always went out like this. Always. But, then, he glanced to his right. Sincere was too quiet. Her posture was too stiff, her jaw clenched a little too tightly.

Lorde watched her for a moment as his arrogance began to fade. He didn't like it. Didn't like the way Rocco's words had settled under her skin, how they burrowed into her like they had the right to do that.

He rubbed his chin, then flicked his wrist lazily. "Aye, turn that shit off."

The driver didn't hesitate. One tap and Rocco's voice disappeared.

Silence filled the space again, but the tension stayed. Sincere let out a slow, measured breath, her eyes locked on the blurred cityscape outside the window. She wasn't gonna let him see. But Lorde already did.

He leaned back, stretching his arm along the seat, voice casual, but his words sharp with meaning. "Rocco's a clown," he muttered. "You knew that when you was with him. And you know it now."

Still, no response.

Lorde watched her a second longer before shaking his head. "Let me tell you somethin'," he continued, his tone smoother now, more controlled. "Niggas like that never know what they got 'til they lose it. Then they gotta spin the story so they don't look weak. It's a game and anybody with a brain can see right through it."

Sincere blinked. For a fraction of a second, she let his words settle. In a way, they provided her with a little comfort. She hated that there was a part of her wanting to let them in. She hated that there was something comforting in hearing it, even if it was coming from him.

She shifted in her seat, forcing a thin smile. "You done with your inspirational speech?"

Lorde arched a brow, amused now, but not pushing. "For now."

Sincere turned back to the window. She wouldn't let him get in her head. She wouldn't let any of them get in her head.

Not Rocco *or* Lorde.

The BET Awards were moments away. She had to prepare her mind to deal with the flashing lights of cameras in her face, and the swarming press. All of the questions about her personal life, thanks to Rocco's many interviews that day.

He did this shit on purpose to take the attention off my performance, she thought.

Tonight was supposed to be her moment. But Rocco wasn't the only one capitalizing on it. So was Lorde. He decided that tonight he'd make his debut as the man in her life. The man who *owned* her. That realization made her sick.

Lorde stretched out in his seat, exuding the kind of power that didn't need to be spoken, draped in dark silk, gold glinting against his wrists and fingers. His signature scent, the richness of oud, warm leather, and a hint of dark amber, clung to the air between them. Even his smell wrapped around her senses with an arrogant permanence, forcing an impression whether you wanted it or not.

Sincere adjusted the diamond cuff on her wrist, her gaze

turning to the tinted window as they approached the building. She could already see the chaos—fans screaming, journalists swarming. They were waiting.

Her stomach twisted.

Sincere didn't want Lorde here as her date. She didn't want to cement the rumors that had already started swirling . . . that he was the real reason she and Rocco ended, that she had "traded up," and was moving from one power player to the next. She had always been secretive about everything, but this time she wanted everyone to know the truth. This wasn't about what she wanted, because Lorde owned her. Not just in the figurative sense, but legally. Her music. Her brand. The very name Sahara. It was all under his control now, wrapped up in the contract she had signed without knowing the full truth about who she was making the deal with.

But she couldn't say a thing, because the dirt would fall back on her as well. For the first time in a long while, she felt completely powerless. She hated that feeling and herself for not knowing how to fix it.

"You look good, ma," Lorde finally said, breaking the silence. His voice was smooth, deep. Almost soothing, if you didn't know better.

She forced a polite smile, refusing to give him anything real. "I know."

Lorde chuckled, low and knowing. "That mouth on you. Vicious."

Supreme, who had been silent all night, scoffed from across the car, shaking his head as he scrolled through his phone.

"What's that?" Sincere spoke up. "You don't think I look good, Supreme?"

He paused for so long that she initially thought he wouldn't say anything. "Yeah . . . you look all right." There was nothing flirtatious in his response. He said it like a matter of observation, but the air still shifted.

Sincere didn't miss the shift. The subtle tension that settled in Lorde's jaw before he forced it smooth again.

"Course she does," Lorde said, his tone easy, but his eyes weren't.

Sincere tilted her head slightly, watching Supreme. He'd been off all night. Silent. Brooding. Like something had been sitting too heavy on his chest. Maybe it was none of her business, but she noticed. "You good?" she asked before she could stop herself.

Supreme flashed his eyes up to her, then back down to his phone. "Yeah."

Lorde let out a slow exhale, rubbing his chin. "You sure? 'Cause you look like you wanna fight somebody."

"I don't," Supreme said, but the way his fingers tapped against his knee said otherwise.

Lorde nodded slowly, his expression unconvinced. "That what you tellin' yourself?"

Supreme shot him a look, and for the first time all night something passed between them.

Sincere didn't know what it was, but she could see it. Their eyes were talking. Before she could say anything further, the car slowed to a stop. Moments later, the door opened. And suddenly, the world was watching.

Los Angeles felt different tonight.

Something other than the usual glitz and glamour was in the air. It was the kind of atmosphere that made your skin prickle like something unseen was pressing in around you. Sincere had felt it the second they stepped off Lorde's private plane that morning, but it was even thicker tonight.

The streets outside the Peacock Theater were chaos. But that was a normal occurrence when Black Hollywood showed up. Limousines and luxury SUVs lined the curb and security flanked every entrance.

But it was the fans, the ones packed behind metal barricades, who made the night feel real.

They screamed out names, their hands outstretched, cameras flashing in rapid succession. The sound of their excitement mixed with the deep bass thumping from inside the venue, shook the pavement beneath Sincere's heels.

The carpet itself was an ocean of Black excellence, bodies wrapped in silk, diamonds, and ego. Familiar faces moved through the space, some with purpose, others lingering in carefully curated conversations, their voices dripping with false warmth and ulterior motives.

And she was the center of it all.

Sincere had walked red carpets before. She knew how to work the lights, how to position herself so her angles hit just right. She knew how to let the cameras eat her up without giving them too much, how to keep her eyes soft enough to appear inviting, but unreadable enough to remain untouchable.

She had perfected the art of being seen.

But tonight wasn't about her. Not really. Because Lorde was at her side and now, everything was different. Tonight was the BET Awards and she wasn't just walking a carpet. She was being presented.

Lorde's hand rested low on her waist, fingers firm, a reminder that he was in control. This was his way of delivering a silent, unspoken announcement to everyone watching that she belonged to him. The heat of his palm burned through the fabric of her gown. It applied constant pressure against her skin, one that made her stomach twist into itself.

She kept her posture poised, her head high, her face smooth with the ease of someone used to performing. Everything about her relationship with Lorde was a performance.

The press surrounded them like hungry wolves, microphones stretching forward, cameras snapping at every angle.

"Sahara! Over here!"

"Sahara, you look *stunning* tonight!"

"Lorde! Sahara! Power couple of the year?"

That last one had her teeth clenching behind a carefully composed smile.

Lorde let out a soft, knowing chuckle, and before she could move, he leaned in, his lips brushing against the curve of her jaw like they shared some inside joke. "Smile, ma. You don't wanna look ungrateful."

She resisted the urge to shove him away. Instead, she shifted, angling herself slightly, forcing distance that he would close again anyway.

The industry saw what they wanted to see: a love story.

They didn't see the bars of the cage.

As they moved down the carpet, she felt the weight of every whispered conversation trailing behind them. The energy was thick with speculation. Rocco had barely finished his little PR tour about their breakup and now here she was, standing beside another man. A *more powerful* man. The press smelled scandal. And Lorde thrived on it.

The murmurs rippled like an undercurrent through the crowd.

"Oh, this is about to be some drama."

"First Rocco, now Lorde? Damn."

"She upgraded."

"Or she didn't have a choice."

That last one nearly made her miss a step. Her stomach churned. She knew what this looked like. She knew what they were thinking. What they'd be saying online in the morning.

Sahara finally found her real boss. Sahara needed a man like Lorde to control her. Sahara was never the boss, just the face.

And she hated that it was starting to feel like they were right.

The second Supreme stepped on the scene, she felt him there. He had such a big presence, solid and unwavering. Being around him didn't feel oppressive like it did with Lorde. He was a few feet away, dressed in black-on-black, tailored to fit his frame perfectly, exuding that effortless, quiet authority that made people look twice. He wasn't flashy the way Lorde was. He didn't need to be. Supreme didn't demand attention. It just found him.

When their eyes met, something passed between them. A question. A hesitation. Or, maybe a warning.

Then, Lorde noticed.

"Damn, cuz. You gonna stand over there looking like security, or you gonna come let the people see you?"

There was an edge of amusement in Lorde's voice, but Sincere wasn't blind. This was a test.

Supreme's jaw flexed, but he didn't react right away. Instead, his gaze slid back to Sincere. His stare was quick, assessing, and unreadable. Then, slowly, he stepped beside them.

The photographers went crazy taking shots. Sincere was too aware of the optics of it as she stood wedged between Lorde and Supreme. They were the kingpin, the pop star, and the enforcer. Lorde was carefully creating an image, laying the foundation for his ultimate goal of being the new power couple of the entertainment world, ruling everything.

The picture they took told a thousand stories without a single word being spoken. And none of them were the truth.

"Sahara! Can we get a shot of you with the ladies?"

Sincere turned her head just in time to see Lena strutting up in gold Balmain, hair sleek, lips glossy, waist snatched, absolutely glowing under the lights. If the moment hadn't been so suffocating, she might have laughed. Lena was living her best life. Her best friend grabbed her hand, giving it a quick squeeze, and before Sincere could refuse, she was being pulled into another frame.

That's when she saw Stacy walking with Clay beside her and, suddenly, the air changed. Unlike Lena, she wasn't smiling. Lena could fake it with the best of them, but Stacy's displeasure was written all over her face.

Her posture was stiff. The way she avoided direct eye contact, and her fingers curled slightly against Clay's arm like she was chained to him told it all.

Sincere's pulse kicked up as she saw them approach. But Clay looked straight ahead. He didn't glance at her or acknowledge her presence. She didn't know why that hurt. But it did. It *shouldn't* have.

And, then, Lorde laughed. His low, amused chuckle felt like it scraped against her skin. "Damn, look at you, baby. You pulled the whole squad out tonight."

The comment was light, seemingly casual, but also mocking. Sincere kept her expression neutral. "You know I didn't invite them."

Lorde leaned in, dropping his voice just for her. "You ain't gotta invite 'em, ma. You a whole event by yourself. Of course, your team gotta be here."

She hated that she could still feel his breath against her skin and that he knew exactly how to unnerve her. The camera flashes kept exploding, so Sincere tried her hardest to keep it together, forcing herself not to reveal too much through her expressions.

Though she may have been faking it good for the cameras, from where Supreme stood, he saw everything. He noticed every stiffened movement, every forced smile. Every moment Lorde tightened his grip on her waist just to remind her who was in control.

Sincere hid it well, better than most. She knew how to pose, how to tilt her chin just so, how to let the cameras capture only what she wanted them to see. But Supreme had spent years learning how to read people. And Sincere's body was practically screaming bloody murder.

He tracked it all. From the slight way her fingers curled into a fist before smoothing out against her dress, to the way her shoulders locked whenever Lorde pulled her in closer, to the rigidness in her spine even when she leaned into him for the cameras. Her discomfort was clear, but Lorde was eating it up.

He was smooth, talking to the press with that easy, confident charm that made people fall in line without questioning why. He looked damn near presidential, playing the role of the powerful man claiming his queen.

But Supreme wasn't buying it, because none of it made sense. He'd been there when Lorde first mentioned getting into the music business. He'd sat in on the meetings, had made the calls, had helped finalize the paperwork to lock in Sincere's deal.

At the time, it made sense. Sincere was a rising star: young, hungry, talented as hell. A smart investment. But Lorde's obsession with her hadn't been disclosed when he was discussing his plans.

Supreme didn't get why Lorde was so pressed over a woman who clearly wanted nothing to do with him. It wasn't about money. That much was obvious. Sincere's contract was airtight, sure, but Lorde wasn't taking a significant cut from her profits. If anything, most of the revenue was being funneled right back into her career: her promotions, her marketing, her music. Lorde wasn't starving for her money. He didn't need it.

So why was he doing this? Why drag her out here and parade her around like some trophy? And more importantly . . . Supreme couldn't understand why *the fuck* did he care?

Lorde didn't move like this over women. Ever.

Supreme had known him his whole life. He'd grown up with

him, had seen him cycle through damn near every kind of woman imaginable. Women loved Lorde. He didn't chase because he never had to.

So why was this different? Why was *she* different?

Supreme didn't have the answer. Because despite the fact he had helped set this deal up and had been in the room for every conversation about her contract, he didn't actually know what the hell was going on. Because Lorde hadn't told him *shit*. That was the part that made Supreme's gut tighten. He didn't like feeling like he was playing a part in something without knowing all of the details. Lorde was playing some long game he hadn't been let in on and that raised his suspicions. Mainly, because he knew his cousin and if Lorde was hiding something, that meant he was covering up some foul shit.

He also knew how Lorde moved and from the look of it all, whatever was going on had nothing to do with business. Everything about it said this was personal. And if there was one thing Supreme had learned over the years, it was when Lorde took something personal, it never ended well. For anyone.

His eyes glimpsed back in Sincere's direction and paused to really observe her closely.

She wasn't just uncomfortable. She looked like someone trapped in a prison that she couldn't get out of.

As Sincere sat in her seat watching the performances, she made sure to keep her posture composed and her expression poised, but her nerves were scraping her insides. The stage loomed ahead, a massive, glowing behemoth that she'd soon have to stand on. She was a nervous wreck. She wasn't new to this. She'd performed on plenty of stages before. But tonight, under all these watchful eyes, knowing the whispers swirling around her name with Lorde right beside her, made it feel different.

Lorde was seated to her left, his presence impossible to ignore. He was relaxed, one arm draped over the back of her chair, gold glinting against his fingers as he scrolled lazily through his phone like none of this fazed him.

To her right, Lena was leaned in close, grinning and giggling in conversation with Milo, the man she'd been wrapped up with all night.

Lena doesn't even know what she's gotten herself into.

Milo was a Saint, meaning he was deep in the same world they were all trapped in. And yet, Lena was clueless about it all. She looked happy and carefree. Like she'd finally found her true love.

Then, a voice interrupted her thoughts.

"Sahara?"

She turned her head just as one of the BET Awards handlers approached, headset clipped to her ear, a clipboard in hand. "It's time for you to head backstage and start getting ready," the woman said with a polite, but firm, smile.

Sincere inhaled slowly, giving a small nod. "Right."

Lena immediately perked up. "I'm going with her."

Lorde appeared unmoved. "Course you are," he replied as if he owned the moment.

Sincere didn't acknowledge him. She just stood, adjusting the fabric of her dress as Lena followed her lead.

As they turned, she noticed movement from the corner of her eye. Stacy had gotten up as well. "I'll meet you at the dressing room," Stacy said, her tone brisk, professional. "I'm not going in with you. I'll be outside."

Lena didn't seem to notice the tension, but Sincere did. And honestly, she was too drained to care. They moved through the halls backstage, security and production crew running around them in a rush of last-minute preparations. The deeper they went, the more reality started closing in around Sincere. Her heart pounded a little harder, her throat tightening, hands clenching at her sides.

Her dressing room was waiting. The moment she stepped inside, the lights were too bright. The air felt suffocatingly still. Once they walked in, Lena locked the door behind them. Sincere exhaled sharply, pressing her hands against the vanity, eyes locked on her reflection. She looked good, but she didn't feel good. She felt on the verge of ruin.

Lena moved beside her, lowering her voice. "You're nervous."

Sincere scoffed. "No shit."

Lena gave a knowing smile, then turned, walking over to the small table stocked with complimentary champagne and fruit. She poured a glass, then grabbed her purse. "You know I always come prepared. You need something to take the edge off?"

Sincere stiffened slightly. The question hung between them for a moment, her pulse hammering. She shouldn't. She knew she shouldn't. But the nerves were gnawing at her. She exhaled, forcing herself to relax, then turned toward Lena.

Without a word, Lena pressed a small, white pill into her palm.

Sincere stared at it.

"It's nothing crazy," Lena assured her, voice soft. "It's one of the ones Lorde gave you. Just enough to take the edge off. You got this."

Sincere swallowed hard.

Her fingers curled around the pill.

Then, before she could talk herself out of it, she popped it into her mouth, tilting her head back as she dry-swallowed it down.

"Don't think too much about it." Lena smiled, watching her. "You're human, Sincere. We all need a little help sometimes."

Sincere closed her eyes for a second, letting out a slow breath.

Lena stepped closer, squeezing her hands. "Now," she said, her voice light, reassuring. "Let's get you ready for this show."

And just like that, Sincere let herself slip back into performance mode. There was no turning back now.

The only thing she heard was the sound of her own breathing. It was loud in her ears as she stood in the complete darkness. Watching. Waiting.

The arena plunged into darkness. A single breath of silence stretched through the air. The anticipation in her belly was thick enough to choke on.

And then . . .

Boom.

The beat dropped, pulsing like a heartbeat through the walls, rattling rib cages, vibrating through her bones. She felt it deep. A sharp snare hit, sending electric through her veins. The crisp against the bass, and then . . . there was light.

A golden glow washed over the stage, illuminating Sincere's nearly-naked silhouette in slow, teasing increments, showing nothing but bare, beautiful skin. Sincere stood in the center of the stage, bathed in warm, honeyed radiance. The shimmer of her totally sheer gown clung to her curves like liquid gold, showing off her bare skin underneath, leaving almost nothing to the imagination. It hugged her hips, moving with her as she rolled her shoulders back, her breathing steady, her pulse beating in time with the music.

And then—she sang.

Boy, you make me feel like fire.
Slow burn, take me higher.

Every touch, I fall deeper.
Don't stop, be my keeper.

Her voice was silky sweet, smooth and commanding. Her words curled around the melody with effortless sensuality. The music swelled, deep bass trembling beneath her bare feet as she moved, slow at first, hips swaying, arms lifting, the heat of the lights kissing her skin. She belly-danced for the crowd, winding her body like a snake. Pure kundalini awakening.

The drug had settled into her bloodstream now and she felt its warmth unfurling inside her. Every nerve tingled. Every inch of her body vibrated with energy. She felt alive in a way she hadn't felt in so, so long.

Your hands, your lips, your everything.
Pull me close, let me sink right in.
I lose my mind when you take control.
Boy, you got me, body and soul.

She let it take her. Let herself drown in the euphoria. The weightlessness of it felt like freedom. Her body moved like water. She wasn't thinking anymore. She was just *feeling.*

And the crowd felt it too.

They roared in approval. Their voices blended into a single, pulsing wave of excitement. She locked eyes with the cameras, with the thousands of people watching, but it wasn't enough. She felt ready to test her limits. Her gaze drifted past the flashing lights and the screaming fans.

And then, she found *him.*

Lorde.

Seated right where she left him, leaned back in his seat like a king surveying his kingdom. Eyes hooded, he watched her with a certainty that didn't need to be explained with words. Owning her with just his stare. And she let him.

Her hands slid over her own body, teasing, tormenting, fingers gliding over her curves in a way that was just shy of indecent. Her lips parted, breathless, eyes still locked on his as she purred into the mic.

Love me wrong, love me right.
Just keep me up all night.
Give me heaven, give me sin.
As long as I can feel you again.

She tilted her head, running her fingers through her hair before dragging her palm slowly down the length of her throat, past her collarbone, lower, and lower until she reached the seat of her passion.

The crowd lost their *minds.*

Lorde flexed his fingers against the armrest of his seat, his body completely still, but his presence stretched toward her.

Sincere felt it. Felt *him.*

The pill, the music, the moment: It all fused into something intoxicating. She let the pleasure of it wrap around her like silk. She let the heat of Lorde's gaze push her higher, let the energy of the crowd fuel her movements.

She was *alive.*

For the first time in forever, she felt unstoppable.

The bridge hit, softening into a hypnotic, ethereal hum as she dropped to her knees, back arching, fingers tracing the stage beneath her as if she could pull the energy in the room straight into her bloodstream.

The audience was *eating it up.*

And Lorde hadn't taken his eyes off her for a second. Something about it made her feel so sexy.

His fingers tapped against his knee now, his jaw tightening

for the briefest moment as she writhed on the stage. She *gave herself* to the music. The performance built into its final crescendo until finally, the last note rang out. She ironed like a siren, letting it hang in the air like a lover's whisper.

Then . . . lights out. Silence.

For one perfect moment, there was nothing but the sound of her own breathing, her chest rising and falling, sweat glistening against her skin, her body reveling in the euphoria.

And then there was chaos.

The audience erupted. Sincere stayed there, on her knees, head bowed, lips parted. Her adrenaline was still pulsing and the high still stretching. Then she looked up and found him again.

Lorde didn't clap or stand. But his face shined with pride. Like she had done exactly what he wanted. And in that moment, as she stared at him through the haze of flashing lights and pulsing blood, she didn't even have it in her to fight it.

Because right now, it felt *too good.*

As soon as Sincere stepped off the stage, Lena practically tackled her.

"Bitch! That was *everything!*" Lena screamed, wrapping her arms around Sincere and shaking her like a rag doll. "Do you even know how crazy that was? The internet is gonna be on *fire!* You just *ate* that. Oh my God!"

Sincere let out a breathy laugh. Her skin tingled, her heartbeat was erratic, and she felt light. Practically weightless, like she was floating. The high hadn't worn off. Not even close.

She smiled, shy but glowing, as Lena pulled back to look at her. "You think so?"

"I *know* so," Lena shot back, grabbing her hand and pulling her toward the dressing room. "Come on, let's get you out of this dress before you melt into a puddle of pure sex appeal right here in the hallway."

Sincere let herself be led, her body still buzzing from the

performance, from the power of it all. She had the audience in the palm of her hand and the world wrapped around her little finger.

And Lorde . . .

The way he watched her from the VIP section, the way his gaze had branded her made her feel like she belonged to him . . . She swallowed, shaking it off as they reached the dressing room.

Lena pushed open the door, laughing as she fanned herself dramatically. "Whew, girl. You really put your whole *soul* into that one."

But then Lena stopped short, because they weren't alone.

Lorde was there.

Leaning back against the couch, arms stretched along the top of it, his suit still pristine and wrinkle-free. He was watching them, with his eyes dark and hooded.

"Shit," Lena breathed, but she was grinning. "I'll, uh . . . I'll give y'all a minute."

Sincere's stomach tightened, her pulse tripping over itself.

Lena winked at her before slipping out, closing the door behind her, leaving them alone.

The silence thickened.

Lorde's gaze raked over her slowly, like he was savoring every inch of her. His smile widened. "Damn, ma. I knew you had it in you, but *that?*" He exhaled, shaking his head. "That was something else."

Sincere's breath hitched.

She was still high. Still floating.

The world felt warm and fuzzy around the edges, like everything had been dipped in gold, smoothed out, softened.

And Lorde . . .

She really looked at him. The sharp angles of his jaw, the deep brown of his skin, the way his suit clung to his body just right. The way he smelled. The rich and intoxicating, dark oud and leather and power.

Something inside her stirred. It felt primal and hungry. Her mind fought it—*no, not him, not like this*—but the battle was already slipping through her fingers, crumbling like sand.

Lorde tilted his head, amusement flickering in his eyes. "What's wrong, baby? Still feeling that high?"

She was.

And she was so starved for something, anything—she didn't know if it was comfort, control, or the simplest, most animalistic need for touch. But whatever it was, she couldn't stop herself. Before she knew what she was doing, she was *on him.* Her hands were in his shirt, pushing the fabric apart, fingers pressing against his hard chest.

His expression didn't waver. His hands found her waist, gripping, pulling her onto his lap like he had been waiting for this moment all night.

"You sure about this, ma?" he murmured, but his voice was thick, his breath uneven.

She wasn't sure about *anything*, but right now, she didn't care.

Her lips crashed against his. It was all heat and desperation, his fingers digging into her waist as she kissed him harder, deeper, her body moving instinctively, grinding against him in a slow, torturous rhythm.

Lorde groaned against her mouth, his hands slipping lower, gripping her ass, pulling her even closer.

Her mind was screaming at her to stop, to think, to not let this happen—but her body wasn't listening. She wanted this. And for the first time in a long time, it felt good to just let go.

Lorde's lips trailed down her jaw, his hands sliding up her back, tracing the zipper of her gown, teasing, and then, suddenly—

He pulled away.

Sincere blinked, dazed, her lips swollen, her breath ragged.

Lorde's eyes were darker now, his jaw tight with restraint. "Damn," he muttered, shaking his head. "We gotta save this for later."

Sincere stared at him, her entire body aching, her head still spinning. "What?"

Lorde chuckled, gripping her waist firmly, lifting her off his lap with ease before standing. He leaned in, his lips brushing her ear as he whispered. "The world is waiting for their queen."

Her stomach flipped.

She barely processed it as he turned, straightened his suit, and strolled toward the door.

He didn't look back. Didn't give her the chance to drag him back. When the door clicked shut behind him, she let out a breath she hadn't realized she was holding.

Her body was burning. Her mind was racing. And for the first time in forever, she felt alive. Maybe this was her reality now. Maybe the best thing to do was just . . . get used to it and make the best of it.

Enjoy it.

Because, really . . . is something controlling you if you actually want it?

Sincere adjusted the hem of her dress, exhaling as she stepped out into the humid Los Angeles night. Into the aftermath of an evening where everyone had been *somebody*—or, at least, wanted to be.

Lena was on her phone a few steps ahead, giggling at something Milo had said, her wrist flicking as she gestured animatedly. Supreme stood off to the side, scrolling through his own phone, posture relaxed, but eyes always scanning. He was on autopilot, always watching, always ready for something.

The SUV was waiting at the curb, the back door already open. Lorde stepped up beside Sincere, not touching her, but close enough that his presence alone made her stomach tighten. She wasn't sure if it was from anticipation or something else entirely.

Lorde slid a hand into his pocket, glancing toward Supreme. "I need you to ride with Lena so we can be alone. We'll meet y'all at the after-party."

What he said wasn't a question, but a command. He had plans for Sincere and didn't want Supreme and his "all-seeing and all-judging" eyes in the middle of them.

Supreme's head lifted slightly, eyes narrowing just a fraction. He didn't move right away, just held Lorde's gaze for a second longer than necessary before slipping his phone into his pocket. "That right?"

Lorde tilted his head slightly. "Yeah. That's right."

Supreme nodded once, slow and deliberate. "Aight." Then he walked away with no further protests or questions.

Lorde didn't bother watching him go. His attention was already back on Sincere. "Get in, ma," he murmured, voice smooth, amused.

Sincere hesitated—there was something uneasy curling in her gut—but she ignored it. She slid inside. The moment the door shut behind them, sealing them into the world of black leather and tinted windows, Lorde poured her a glass of champagne, his smile stretching wider.

"Toast to that performance," he said, holding his glass up.

Sincere took hers, clinking the rim against his before taking a slow sip. The warmth of the alcohol slid down her throat, but it wasn't enough. She wanted more.

Lorde seemed to sense it before she even had to say anything. His hand dipped into his pocket and a second later, he held up a small plastic baggie between two fingers.

"You tryna keep that high goin'?"

Sincere hesitated. The edges of her buzz were already dulling, reality creeping in too fast, too sharp. She reached for the baggie.

Lorde grinned. "That's my girl."

Less than ten minutes later, the champagne was flowing as they headed up to the hills to party with other members of the elite. The music was low, vibrating through the speakers.

Sincere felt light. Warm. Unstoppable.

The champagne was hitting just right. The pill was dissolving into her bloodstream, sending a warm, delicious fog through her limbs. And Lorde was right there. She felt him watching her, the heat of his gaze dragging over her body like a touch.

Sincere turned her head slightly, her lashes lowering as she studied him. The sharp lines of his jaw, the full, dark mouth, the lazy dominance in his posture. She shouldn't have wanted him, but she did. Something in her snapped and before she could think twice about it, she was on him. Her fingers curled into the silk of his shirt, her lips finding his, the heat of her body pressing into him like she was trying to climb inside his skin.

Lorde groaned, one hand locking around her waist, the other threading through her hair, tugging just hard enough to make her gasp against his mouth. "Damn," he muttered, his breath warm against her lips. "You tryna start somethin'?"

Sincere's answer was the roll of her hips against his lap, the friction sending a bolt of heat straight to her core.

Lorde let out a low chuckle, his grip tightening. He kissed her again, slower this time, dragging it out. Teasing her.

Her body moved before her mind caught up. Her hands slid

up his chest, fingers curling into the silk of his shirt, her lips colliding with his in a way that felt *reckless*.

Lorde groaned against her mouth, gripping her hips, pulling her closer. "Finally," he muttered, voice thick with hunger. "Been waitin' all night to have you like this."

Sincere moaned softly, rolling her hips against him, the friction sending heat rushing through her veins.

Lorde let out a low chuckle, dragging his teeth along her jaw before leaning toward the driver. "Skip the after-party," he ordered. "Take us to the hotel."

Sincere barely heard it.

She was too far gone.

Time blurred, one moment fading in and then out into the next. They got to the hotel before Sincere had a chance to really process where they were. She was so high and so light as she stood up in the back seat, waving her arms outside of the sunroof of the SUV. Smiling with her eyes closed, feeling as if she were dreaming, she danced under the night sky. She had no idea what was in that pill Lorde gave her, but it had her on another level.

"We're here," he told her once the SUV had come to a stop.

It was only then that Sincere realized they were no longer moving. For her, the world was still revolving. In fact, it was revolving around *her*.

Scooping her into his arms, Lorde carried her through the entry of the hotel, not setting her on her feet until they were inside the lobby. She had the most luxurious room in the building, something Lorde made sure of. Everywhere she stayed needed to be fit for a queen. Sincere hadn't appreciated the sentiment when he said it, but now . . . she was starting to look at him in a different light.

The door clicked shut behind them once they entered the room and that's when things went into overdrive. Lorde had her against the wall before she could take a breath. His hands were everywhere—pulling, gripping, and squeezing her close. His lips crashed against hers, messy and desperate, his breath warm against her skin.

"You feelin' me now, huh?" he murmured, sliding her dress down her shoulders. "You ain't gotta fight it, ma. You mine now."

Sincere gasped as his hands roamed lower, as he guided her back toward the bed.

And then, something shifted.

Lorde's grip tightened. His movements changed. He turned her around, pushed her down roughly. "Spread 'em," he ordered.

Her body obeyed before her brain could catch up. His hands were rough. His touch didn't feel like it was about pleasing her. It was about making her obey.

"Open your mouth," he said once he'd pushed her onto her knees. He gripped the sides of her jaw as he waited for her to react.

She barely had time before he was forcing himself into her mouth, his fingers gripping the back of her head, guiding her, demanding.

Sincere gagged, tried to pull back, but he didn't let her.

"Nah," he muttered, his tone dark, commanding. "You wanted this, right? Take it."

Her stomach twisted as he had his way with her, pushing her into whatever position he wanted her in. She let it happen because she was shocked, or maybe too afraid to move. She didn't know what to do, so she did nothing.

When he was done, he pulled out, flipped her over and spilled his seed all over her bare back. He exhaled heavily, running a hand over his head before grabbing the bottom of her dress and wiping himself clean.

Like she was nothing.

Lorde chuckled under his breath. "Damn," he muttered. "Thanks for the pussy. Just as good as I thought that shit would be." He didn't kiss her. Didn't hold her. Just adjusted his pants, buttoned his cuffs, and left.

"In an hour we go to the airport to head back home. Be ready." That was the last thing he said before he walked out the door.

Sincere lay there, silent and staring at the ceiling. Her mind was racing. *Is this how Clay had felt?*

She thought it would feel better than this. She thought that she could change how she felt about him. Feel safer and more in control.

But it didn't.

Chapter 10

Sweat and liquor clung to the air like a ghost that refused to leave. Sincere's penthouse looked like it had been the setting of a house party. Glasses still littered the tables, half-melted candle wax pooled near untouched dinner plates. Somebody wasn't eating, but they were doing a hell of a lot of drinking.

Supreme stood at the edge of the balcony, his weight shifted onto one arm as he rolled a blunt between his fingers. The slow crackle of burning paper and weed filled the space between his thoughts. He exhaled slowly, watching as the smoke curled into the thick, humid morning air.

He normally didn't smoke like this, but life had him stressed in ways he couldn't explain. Sincere had him facing his own demons and she didn't even know it. His eyes cut toward her bedroom. He couldn't see her, but his mind's eye remembered what she looked like the last time he peeked in.

Sincere lay sprawled across the king-sized bed, one arm draped over her forehead, the dress she wore when she partied with Lena the night before still clinging to the curves of her body. The silk fabric was bunched up at her thighs, the hem barely covering her ass.

After a night of partying, drinking, and pill-popping, she came home exhausted. She hadn't even changed. Her breathing was deep, steady, but not peaceful. The way her fingers twitched in her sleep, the restless parting of her lips, the faint crease in her brows all told a different story.

Addicts never really rested. Sleep, maybe, but never rest.

His mother's words rang in his head, echoing louder than he wanted them to. *A mind that isn't sober is a mind that can't be trusted.* He took another slow drag, letting the smoke settle in his lungs before exhaling through his nose.

Sincere was a lot of things: beautiful, talented, fucking mesmerizing when she wanted to be. But she wasn't in control. And people who weren't in control were dangerous, to themselves and to anybody who gave a damn about them.

He'd seen it before. His grip tightened around the blunt as his mind dragged him back to a memory he never liked revisiting. His brother's face. He always had such focused, determined eyes. He was always looking at the world like he could outsmart it. First came the pills. Then the deals. Next the recklessness. And finally, Silvan's drugs laced with fentanyl that took him out.

A slow coil of anger wrapped itself around Supreme's ribs, squeezing tight. Silvan built his empire off people just like Sincere. These were girls with talent, beauty, and something to offer, but having no protection. The only difference between them and her was the man pulling the strings.

Setting his blunt on the table outside, he walked back in and checked on Sincere. She stirred in bed, her body shifting beneath the sheets, her lips parting as if murmuring something in the depths of a dream she couldn't wake from.

Supreme exhaled sharply, rolling his shoulders back before pulling his phone from his pocket. The unease settled in his bones like an itch he couldn't scratch, an unanswered question that wouldn't stop gnawing at him. He scrolled through his contacts, hitting Dre's line.

Two rings.

"Yo."

His voice was rough with sleep, but Supreme caught something else in the undertones, a slight hesitance.

"When Lorde and Sincere get in from LA the other night?" he asked, his voice neutral, controlled.

"They ain't fly in together," Dre informed him.

Supreme frowned, pushing off the balcony railing. "What?"

"Yeah, uh—Lorde came straight back after the awards. Sincere landed this morning. Around four. You ain't know?"

His jaw flexed. "Nah, I took my own flight back. Wanted some time alone." Something was *off*. The feeling in his gut sharpened, the unease spreading through his chest. He let the information sit for a second before switching gears. "Where you at?"

Dre hesitated before answering. "In the car," he said, too casually.

Supreme caught that. "Why?"

"Headed your way," Dre said. "Lorde told me to check in. Help you with Sincere."

Supreme's frown deepened. "Ain't much to do. She's sleeping."

"Yeah, but, uh—figured I'd still come through."

Dre wasn't a morning person. Hell, he wasn't even a before-noon person. Getting up voluntarily at this hour—nah. This wasn't *his* idea. Supreme didn't respond right away.

Dre was young, but he wasn't stupid. He knew Supreme could sniff out a lie like blood in the water. And right now, he was lying.

"Lorde put you up to that?"

Dre cleared his throat. "Nah."

Supreme's jaw tightened. His mind moved fast, putting the pieces together. Lorde was moving chess pieces. And Dre was the pawn. Supreme exhaled slowly, flexing his fingers as he pushed down the irritation crawling up his spine. "Aight," he said. "Hit me when you are outside."

Dre let out a breath, like he was relieved the conversation was over.

The call disconnected.

Supreme stared at the phone for a long second before slipping it back into his pocket. Lorde was setting things in motion and he didn't like being in the dark. Not about *shit* like this. He cracked his neck, exhaled again, and left the room. It was time to meet Dre in the garage and see just how deep this rabbit hole went.

The parking garage was silent except for the distant hum of traffic above. The underground lot was dimly lit, the fluorescent bulbs overhead casting a dull glow against the concrete. The air was thick, damp, carrying the scent of gasoline and something faintly metallic.

Dre was leaning against his car, hood up, eyes locked on his phone, scrolling. He looked too focused, like he was trying too hard to look busy. Supreme didn't announce himself because he didn't have to. Dre tensed the second he felt him near, his fingers pausing over the screen before he slipped the phone into his pocket and straightened up.

"You need somethin'?"

Supreme studied his unreadable expression. "What did he have you do the other night?"

Dre hesitated.

Supreme didn't repeat himself.

Dre shifted, running a hand over his braids. "I didn't do anything, man. Just drove him to a spot, that's all."

Supreme's patience was wearing thin. "Don't play with me, Dre. You're a bad liar."

Dre's jaw clenched. His gaze flicked around the garage, like he was checking for cameras, before he let out a breath.

"Look," he muttered. "I wasn't in the room. I just took him to a meeting."

"With who?"

Dre looked like he wanted to run away as fast as he could. "With . . . Silvan."

The name dropped like a deadweight in Supreme's chest. A slow, ice-cold rage wrapped itself around his ribs.

Lorde was dealing with Silvan. "It's just business," Dre rushed to say. "That's it."

Supreme couldn't accept that. Working with Silvan wasn't just business.

It was *betrayal.*

Supreme's fingers curled into fists at his sides, his breath slowing as he absorbed what Dre had just said. Lorde and Silvan's names had no business being in the same fucking sentence. His blood ran cold. He forced himself to keep his expression neutral and his voice steady, even though everything inside him was telling him to react.

"Why didn't you say something sooner?"

Dre's shoulders were tense, his posture stiff like he was waiting for Supreme to snap. "Because it's not my place, man," he muttered, running a hand over his jaw. "I don't know what you want me to do. He's the boss."

Feeling uncomfortable with the silence between them, Dre shifted on his feet, glancing away. "Look, I ain't reporting nothing back to him, but I'm just supposed to be following you around so you don't figure out what's happening with Silvan. That's it. That's why I ain't wanna tell you. Ain't shit you can do about it anyway."

Supreme's jaw flexed. His mind was racing now, piecing together shit he should've seen earlier. The way Lorde had been moving, the plays he'd been setting up, the power moves that seemed random at first, but were starting to make too much sense now.

He kept his voice calm. "You did the right thing, Dre. Don't let him drag you down with him."

Dre let out a dry laugh, shaking his head. "You sure this is the right move? Going against him?"

Supreme's eyes narrowed. "I didn't say I was going against him," he said smoothly. "I'm just keeping my eyes open. You should do the same."

Dre nodded slowly. Understanding passed between them, but Supreme knew better. Lorde didn't *trust* anybody and if Dre slipped up, he was done.

Finally, Dre exhaled, shaking his head. "Look, man . . . I ain't tryna get caught up in whatever this is. But if he sent me to watch you, that means he's watching me too. You get what I'm saying?"

Supreme knew Dre was a small pawn in this.

"You in deep now," Dre muttered, rubbing his neck. "I know you and Lorde go way back, but this ain't like before. I dunno what he's on, but it's different."

"Keep your head down," Supreme said to him.

Dre nodded, then glanced around before pushing off his car. "I gotta roll. If I stay too long, he's gonna start asking questions."

Supreme gave him a slight chin lift in understanding. Dre hesitated for another second, then pulled his phone from his pocket and tapped the screen a few times before locking it and shoving it back in his hoodie.

Then he was gone.

Supreme stood in the garage for a long moment after, hands on his hips, head tilted slightly as he processed all of it. His pulse was steady, but the tension in his muscles was impossible to ignore. He'd spent years standing next to Lorde, handling business, making moves, making sure they both came out on top. Lorde had always been calculated, always played the long game, but this was something else.

He was working with Silvan.

The same Silvan who had his brother murdered, Lorde's cousin. And Lorde had willingly *aligned* himself with that? Lorde had crossed a line and it was one that Supreme wasn't sure he could ignore. Now, he had a decision to make. He could either stay blind or stay loyal.

The walk back up to Sincere's penthouse was quiet. Supreme couldn't ease his mind and the thoughts sat like heavy weights on his shoulders. He barely touched his phone, ignoring the few missed calls and texts that had come through since he'd been in the garage.

When he stepped back inside, the place was still eerily silent. Sincere hadn't moved. She was still sprawled out on the bed, in the same dress, still out cold from the night before. She was deep in it now, hooked like the addict she was trying not to be again. And Lorde was keeping her that way on purpose.

His stomach turned at the thought. He walked toward the bed, stopping at the edge as he looked down at her. She looked so . . . small and fragile. He reached out, brushing a loose curl from her face, watching as she shifted slightly, but didn't wake up.

A mind that isn't sober is a mind that can't be trusted. His mother's voice echoed again, louder this time.

Supreme leaned against the doorway, arms crossed, eyes locked on her sleeping form, wondering if she even wanted to wake up. His mind was moving too fast, running through the time since he'd met her. He pieced together every red flag, every moment he'd ignored, every time he'd let shit slide because Lorde was Lorde and that was just how he moved. Now, it felt different because Lorde wasn't just keeping Sincere. He was owning her, trying to break her down. This was personal and Supreme needed to know why.

Chapter 11

The knock at the door was sharp, cutting through the quiet of the morning like the edge of a blade. Sincere's stomach twisted on instinct, her pulse jumping just enough for her to feel the subtle shift in her body. She had been curled up on the couch for the past hour, staring blankly at the muted television, her silk robe draped loosely over her shoulders, the fabric pooling at her thighs as she sat cross-legged, trying to pretend she wasn't waiting for something—*for someone.*

The horror of the night she spent with Lorde still clung to her skin. The phantom touch of Lorde's hands lingered in her mind longer than she wanted to admit. Her body ached in places she hadn't realized until she moved, but it wasn't the satisfying soreness she was used to after a night spent tangled in the sheets with a man she wanted. No, this was different. This felt hollow.

Sincere heard another knock, more impatient this time. She hesitated, her fingers tightening around the edge of the robe, pulling it closer as if it could shield her from whatever was waiting on the other side of that door. She already knew who it was. And the truth was, she wasn't ready for this.

But she got up anyway, padding barefoot across the cool floor, the silk of her robe brushing against her thighs with each step. When she reached the door, she took a slow breath, exhaled just as slowly, and then unlocked it. The moment the door swung open, she was met with the unyielding presence of . . . Stacy.

She stood there, poised and unreadable, her presence as sharp and precise as the way she carried herself. A cream-colored blazer hugged her frame, the crispness of it practically daring a wrinkle to form, paired with tailored slacks that made her look every bit the composed, no-nonsense woman she had always been. Her hair was slicked back into a flawless bun, not a single strand out of place, and her lips were pressed into a firm, professional line.

The only thing that betrayed her otherwise perfect exterior was the way her eyes locked onto Sincere's with an intensity that made it clear she wasn't here for pleasantries.

Sincere swallowed. "Stacy."

She didn't smile or acknowledge her beyond a curt nod before stepping inside, her heels clicking against the floor with a confidence that only came from a woman who knew exactly where she stood and what she was walking into.

Sincere turned, shutting the door, watching as Stacy placed a crisp white folder on the marble kitchen counter with precision.

"Business," Stacy said flatly. "Lorde asked me to drop off the finalized contracts for your next release."

Sincere pressed her lips into a thin line. Right. Business.

There was nothing personal about this. Stacy was here because Lorde had *sent* her, because despite everything, despite how much Sincere had ruined, this was still moving. Stacy was simply the one making sure the machine kept running smoothly.

Sincere crossed her arms loosely over her chest, eyeing the folder on the counter before glancing back at Stacy. "He could've sent someone else."

Stacy lifted an unimpressed brow, the smallest glimpse of

something dark in her gaze. "He wanted me to bring it personally."

The words made something uneasy settle in Sincere's gut. Of course, he did. This was a calculated play in a game she hadn't even realized she was a part of until it was too late. She should let Stacy leave. But she couldn't. She had to say something or at least try.

"I'm sorry," she blurted out, the words tumbling from her lips before she could stop them.

Stacy tilted her head slightly, her eyes narrowing. "For what, exactly?" she asked, her voice cool, deliberate.

Sincere licked her lips, suddenly feeling more self-conscious than she had in a long time. "For . . . everything," she admitted, shifting her weight from one foot to the other. "For what happened with Clay. For—"

"Save it." The words were clipped, emotionless. Stacy took a step forward, closing the distance between them with an ease that felt almost predatory, her eyes never leaving Sincere's face.

"You think I'm *heartbroken*?" Stacy asked, her voice carrying the heaviness of something unspoken.

Sincere felt her throat tighten. "I—"

Stacy let out a quiet, humorless chuckle. "Sincere, you are not important enough to break my heart."

The words hit harder than they should have. Sincere didn't know why she had expected something else. Why she had thought for even a second that Stacy would allow her to see the damage she had caused.

She tried again. "I still hurt you. And I'm sorry."

Stacy scoffed, folding her arms over her chest, her expression cool and detached. "You wanna know what hurts?" she asked, voice quieter now, but even more deadly. "That people like you *always* get away with this shit."

Sincere's breath caught in her throat.

Stacy took another slow, measured step forward. "You get

to be selfish. You get to be reckless. You get to ruin lives because people are so damn *fascinated* with watching you spiral."

Sincere's stomach churned, her fingers tightening into the fabric of her robe.

Stacy's lips curled, but there was no warmth in it. "You've built a whole brand around being the modern woman, right? The *sexually liberated* star who doesn't give a fuck about anybody else's feelings."

Sincere swallowed hard, but Stacy wasn't done.

"But I know the truth," she murmured, her voice softening just enough to make the words sting. "I see you."

"And what do you see?" Sincere forced the words pass the lump in her throat.

Stacy tilted her head slightly. "I see a broken girl who's been begging for attention her whole damn life."

Sincere's chest ached, a lump forming in her throat.

Stacy took another step, closing the distance between them until they were only a few feet apart. "You don't know how to *get* love," Stacy said quietly. "You've decided to *collect* it . . . by playing the role of a cum bucket instead."

Sincere flinched, her breath catching in her throat. And then . . . *whap!* The sharp crack of her palm against Stacy's face echoed through the room like a gunshot. For a moment, everything stilled.

Sincere's chest rose and fell rapidly, her hand still tingling from the impact, her nails curled inward like she was ready to strike again if necessary. She hadn't planned to do it, but the words—that filthy, degrading phrase had left Stacy's lips like venom, and before she knew it, she had lashed out.

Stacy didn't stagger or stumble. She stood firm, her face turning only slightly from the force of the blow before she shifted back, dark eyes locking onto Sincere with a simmering rage that burned hotter than anything she had ever seen in her before. For once, Stacy's mask of cool, untouchable composure cracked.

Sincere took a step forward, her own anger a live wire beneath her skin. "I get that you're mad. I get that you feel like I did you dirty, but I *pay* you. *You* work for *me.* Don't you ever forget your place again."

Stacy's jaw tensed.

Sincere tilted her head slightly, voice lower now, laced with something sharp. "You don't talk to me like that. If you can't stop yourself from doing it, then quit."

The words hung heavy between them. Sincere knew the power she held. She knew that, no matter how much Stacy hated her in this moment, she was still her boss. And if she really wanted to? She could replace her with a snap of her fingers.

Stacy knew it too. For a second, it seemed like she might lash out. But then, with a deep inhale, she bit her tongue. *Literally.*

Sincere saw the way her jaw flexed, the way her lips pressed into a thin line before she finally turned on her heel. Without saying another word, Stacy simply snatched the folder off the counter, strode toward the door, and walked out.

Sincere exhaled, rubbing a hand over her face as she stood there in the now-quiet space, her heart still racing, her emotions still tangled up in everything Stacy had just thrown at her.

A cum bucket.

Stacy's words played over and over in her mind, eating at the edges of everything she had built her identity on. She wasn't a fool. She knew how men like Rocco, Clay, and every other disposable man she had tossed aside saw her. But what about real men? Men like Supreme?

A lump formed in her throat. She pushed the thought away before it could take root. She had other things to focus on . . .

like the faint noise echoing through her penthouse. Her entire body stiffened. A slow, creeping sensation crawled up her spine, a whisper of fear that wrapped around her chest like a vise.

It sounded like music.

What the hell?

She turned slowly, her pulse picking up again, her mind immediately flashing back to when she had been kidnapped before. The last time she had heard something off in her own home, it had led to her to being dragged into a nightmare she was still trying to fight her way out of. Her breaths came a little shorter as she moved. She forced herself to walk toward the sound instead of freezing up. She stepped lightly, her bare feet soundless against the floor, her fingers tightening around her robe.

The sound grew louder the closer she got to a room at the end of the hall. She picked up on a familiar beat. *Is that a video game?* Her brows furrowed in confusion. And then, finally, she reached the slightly cracked door and pushed it open. What she saw made her freeze.

Supreme . . . comfortable as hell, laid back in *her* space. His long frame was sprawled across the couch, PlayStation controller in hand, completely absorbed in the football game playing out on the massive screen in front of him. The Saints vs. the Chiefs. He barely acknowledged her, his gaze locked on the screen, his fingers tapping buttons with effortless precision.

Sincere just stared at him. For a moment, the sheer absurdity of it almost made her laugh. Instead, she tightened her grip on her robe and stepped further into the room, her brows lifting in disbelief.

"Aren't you supposed to be outside?" she asked. "I told Lorde that if he was gonna have people babysit me, they could do it from *outside* the building."

Supreme didn't even flinch. Didn't so much as glance in her direction. "Yeah," he muttered, still playing, "he told me you said that."

Her brows *jumped.* "Well?" she pressed, crossing her arms. "So why the hell are you in *here*?"

Her patience was wearing thin as she glared at him, waiting for an answer that would justify why he was sitting in *her* house, in *her* room, on *her* couch, playing a game like he lived there.

This time, he *did* glance at her. Just briefly. Then, with the same lazy, unbothered energy, he leaned back a little, controller still in hand. "Because I can't play my game outside," Supreme said, his tone matter-of-fact, as if that was supposed to be a perfectly acceptable reason for his intrusion.

Sincere's mouth nearly dropped. She expected him to be smug, maybe even slightly amused at her irritation. But the way he casually dismissed her demands like she had no authority at all had her standing there, blinking, thrown off balance.

Supreme didn't give her a second glance. He kept his eyes on the screen, fingers pressing buttons with an ease that said he was deep into the game. "Plus," he added, a smile tugging at his lips. "This room must be good luck. Since I started playing in here, my boys been beating Mahomes's ass."

Something about that made Sincere's irritation wane just a little. She had never seen Supreme so casual before. No scowl. No tension. No air of superiority. Just a man kicking back, completely at ease, talking about football like the rest of the world wasn't complicated as hell.

That alone made her pause. Her gaze flicked to the screen, watching as the animated version of a Saints player stiff-armed a Chief and took off down the field. "You a football fan?" she asked, tilting her head slightly.

"Nah," Supreme muttered, still focused. "I'm a Saints fan."

Sincere let out a short laugh. "They'll never beat the Chiefs in real life."

Supreme's head snapped toward her so fast it was almost comical. His lips parted like she had just told him the world was flat. "Yo, why would you put that energy out there?" He shook his head and turned back to the screen. "See, this is exactly why we can't have nice things."

Sincere grinned, folding her arms as she watched him. "Ohh, so you one of those types, huh?"

"What types?"

"The ones who think everything in the world happens based on vibes and energy," she teased.

Supreme scoffed, eyes never leaving the screen as he made another play. "Yeah, ain't you?"

She shrugged. "Not really. I don't do the religious thing. Don't do the spiritual thing either."

That got his attention. He glanced at her, brows raised slightly, before turning back to the game. "What you believe in then?"

Sincere sighed, rolling a shoulder. "I just believe shit happens."

Supreme let out a short chuckle, shaking his head. "Dangerous way to live."

There was something about the way he said it—low, almost to himself—that made her pause. Before she could question it, he leaned forward, fingers flying over the controller, his focus shifting once again. "You gotta get ready," he said casually, his tone almost an afterthought. "We leavin' in about thirty."

Sincere frowned. "Leaving for what?"

He didn't even blink. "Stacy was supposed to tell you about the board meeting you got this morning."

Sincere's arms tightened across her chest. "She didn't tell me anything."

Supreme let out a low hum, barely paying attention as he kicked a field goal. “Probably didn’t wanna after you slapped the shit out of her.”

Sincere froze. A sharp, unsettling chill crept up her spine. She hadn’t realized he heard that. Her breath caught, the conversation with Stacy flashing through her mind—the venom, the slap, the things that were said that she wasn’t proud of. She stared at him, trying to gauge just how much he had heard.

Supreme kept playing, acting as if the pause in her breath, the tension suddenly crackling in the air, wasn’t there. But after a long stretch of silence, he finally dragged his gaze to her.

“You need to go get ready,” he repeated, ignoring the stricken look on her face.

Sincere clenched her jaw and turned sharply, stalking toward her room.

Supreme barely heard the sound of her door closing. His focus remained on the game, but his mind was on her. He knew she was spiraling. That confrontation with Stacy had shaken her, and now she was probably up there trying to decide if he saw her the way Stacy did.

Like she was weak. Shameful. A woman with no control.

He exhaled, shifting slightly on the couch as he thought about it. He didn’t. That was the funny part.

Stacy had the audacity to come into Sincere’s house, making money off her name, and still had the nerve to talk to her like that? Nah. Regardless of what had happened between them, Stacy deserved that slap. Sincere needed to stop bringing bullshit so close to home.

When she returned, she was dressed, but something about her still seemed off. She sat down on the couch, adjusting the cuff of her sleeve, avoiding looking at him directly.

Supreme sighed, dropping the controller onto the table before sitting back against the cushions. “I heard everything.”

Sincere's body stiffened slightly.

His voice wasn't teasing or condemning. "I ain't sayin' what you did with Clay was right," he added, his tone level, "but Stacy was outta line." He tilted his head slightly, his dark eyes locking onto hers. "And if she still plannin' on workin' with you, she need to be reminded of that."

Sincere inhaled slowly, digesting his words. It was unexpected, the validation. For the past twelve hours, she had been drowning in self-doubt, questioning everything about herself, everything she had believed in. But Supreme didn't see her as weak. That gave her the smallest bit of confidence back.

She exhaled, shaking her head slightly. "Lesson learned. Business and pleasure shouldn't mix. Ever."

Supreme's lips curved slightly. But there was something else in his gaze. "Really?" He leaned forward slightly, his fingers tapping against his knee. "What's the deal with you and Lorde?"

Her entire body locked up. That wasn't a conversation she expected to have with him. She sat up straighter, lips pressing together as she debated how to answer. Instead, she decided to flip it. "What do you think the deal is?" she asked, her voice even.

Supreme watched her for a moment before shrugging slightly. "Lorde told me you made a deal with him, and it was time to collect."

Sincere let out a dry, humorless chuckle. "You think it was about money?"

Supreme's expression didn't change. "Wasn't it?"

Sincere shook her head. "Nah. It never had to do with money."

That had his full attention now.

She exhaled, resting her elbows on her knees. She had been holding this in for too long. Maybe it was time someone else knew the truth. She lifted her gaze to meet his, inhaling deeply before she said, "You wanna know why I'm really here?"

Supreme nodded once, slow and deliberate.

Sincere exhaled again, running a hand through her hair before she finally spoke. And then, she told him everything.

"Do you realize your following is up twenty percent since the awards? They loving the new Sahara with her new boo!"

The moment the words left Ava Chen's mouth, Sincere felt her entire body tense up. She sat at the head of the sleek, modern conference table, her posture flawless, her hands resting lightly on the cool surface. Around her, the team of executives Lorde had hired, her new team, were practically squealing as they flipped through reports and analytics like they were reading scripture.

Quiet among the chaos, Stacy sat a few seats down, sharp as ever, her face unreadable. She hadn't said much yet, but she was watching Sincere carefully, waiting for her reaction. After working with her for so many years, she knew that she wouldn't like anything about what was coming next.

Across from Sincere, Carter Ellis, one of the company's lead strategists, grinned as he slid a tablet across the table toward her. "They're eating this up. Look at the headline here. LORDE AND SAHARA: POWER COUPLE OF THE YEAR," he repeated.

Sincere barely glanced at the screen, where a slideshow of metrics and social media analytics flashed in front of her. The numbers were staggering. There were millions of engagements, retweets, shares, comments, and fans dissecting every moment of her awards-night appearance with Lorde. They were in love with the idea of them.

She resisted the urge to close her eyes, to breathe through the nausea that curled low in her stomach. Instead, she reached for her water, taking a slow sip before responding. "So, what?" Her voice was cool, unreadable. "Because people are talking, I should build my brand around a man?"

The room fell quiet for half a second before Carter chuckled. "Come on now, you know that's not what we're saying."

Across the table, Michelle LaRue, dressed in a sharp white pantsuit, leaned forward, her manicured fingers tapping lightly against her iPad. "It's about image, Sahara. Strategy. We have to take advantage of what's happening organically. This isn't something we forced. This is what the public wants. And in this industry, the public's perception is everything."

Sincere tilted her head slightly, her expression neutral. "And what exactly is their perception?"

At the far end of the table, Malcolm Greene, the older Black man with salt-and-pepper hair and a heavy Rolex on his wrist, jumped in smoothly. "That you and Lorde together is electric." He leaned back, spreading his hands. "That you're unstoppable. That you're powerful. The industry hasn't seen a real hip-hop power couple in years. You two bring a level of mystique, of danger, that makes people hungry for more. You can't buy that kind of chemistry."

Sincere resisted the urge to scoff. These people didn't have a clue. She folded her hands in her lap. "That's funny, because for the last decade, I've built my brand on the opposite of that. My music, my presence . . . everything has been about empowerment and embracing the courage to be soft and feminine, but also powerful. It's been about owning my voice and not shrinking under someone else's shadow."

Michelle smiled, as if she had been waiting for that response. "Who says anything about shrinking? There is nothing wrong with a strong woman being with a strong man," Michelle continued smoothly. "It makes a statement. If anything, you're showing your fan base that it's possible to be all that and have love. That's a huge thing in a world where people are saying the only way a Black woman can find love is to reduce herself to make a man comfortable. You're showing that we don't need to do that."

The words landed. Sincere stayed silent, absorbing them. The way she had been raised, love and power had always been at odds. Her mother had taught her that you couldn't have both—not as a woman. You could either be adored, or you could be in control. But this was a different perspective.

That said, she liked it. She just didn't like the idea of Lorde being the man she made that statement with. The thought of him, his grip on her, his voice, the control he already had over her life, made her stomach turn.

And then, Carter's voice cut in. "You know what would really solidify this?" His eyes gleamed with excitement. "Something collaborative. A duet, maybe?"

Before she could even open her mouth, the others jumped in, feeding off the energy, throwing out idea after idea.

"You two together on a track? It'd be massive. I mean, I don't even know if Lorde raps, but he has to, right?" David Rojas, head of marketing, looked around at the others for help. "Why else would he invest so much into the music industry? I figured he did all this because he went this route after deciding not to be an artist."

"I don't know . . . I've never heard him rap before. But he is sexy," Michelle said, smiling. "What about a music video? Something cinematic, something with heat."

"A joint interview. Something raw, intimate."

"Hell, even a *Vogue* spread would go crazy."

The voices layered over each other, excitement rising, filling the space like static.

Sincere felt herself disconnecting, floating outside of her own body, watching as they built a reality around her that she had no control over. They didn't care about her—not really. All she was to them was a headline.

Nausea crept up her throat and her breathing became shallow. She could still feel Lorde's hands on her from that night. Her grip on her water glass tightened.

And then, finally, Stacy spoke. "Sahara?" Her voice was smooth, professional, but there was something knowing in it. "What do you think of all these . . . ideas?"

Sincere swallowed thickly, forcing herself to snap back into the moment. "I think . . . I need to use the restroom," she said abruptly, pushing her chair back.

Sincere stood before anyone could argue and before they could see the cracks forming in her composure. She walked out, her heels clicking against the floor, ignoring the way Stacy's gaze lingered on her as she left.

Supreme had been sitting outside the boardroom, leaned back in one of the oversized leather chairs in the waiting area, phone in hand, listening. He wasn't trying to eavesdrop. But he didn't have to. Voices carried in places like this, especially when people were excited. And, from what he had heard, they were all damn near foaming at the mouth to keep Lorde's name tied to hers.

He shook his head, exhaling slowly. He wasn't surprised. Sincere wasn't just talented and famous. She was powerful, and people in power were either used or destroyed.

That's why Lorde had made sure she was his before anyone else could take her. That's why he was watching her this closely. When he saw her leave the boardroom in a rush, her back too straight, her movements too stiff, he knew. He stood, slipping his phone into his pocket, and followed.

Sincere braced her hands against the cool marble counter, her fingers pressing into the hard surface as she stared at her reflection in the pristine bathroom mirror. She looked fine—perfect, even. The stylists had done their job. Her hair was laid to perfection, sleek and glossy, her makeup flawless—subtle, but powerful, accentuating her high cheekbones and sharp jawline. The fitted black suit hugged her body in all the right places, structured shoulders giving her an air of authority, the deep-cut neckline daring, but sophisticated. Every inch of her exuded control.

But her eyes told the truth. She was breaking. Her lashes fluttered as she inhaled deeply, pressing the tips of her fingers against her temples, trying to push back the dull ache forming in her skull. *Keep it together. Keep it together.* Her stomach twisted and the pressure in her chest tightened. She gritted her teeth, pushing away the nausea climbing up her throat.

Then, the door swung open.

Sincere jumped, twisting around, hands flying up in disbelief. "Seriously?"

She gaped as Supreme strolled into the women's restroom like he belonged there, calm, unbothered. He didn't even pretend like he was in the wrong. He just closed the door behind him and leaned lazily against it, arms folded over his chest, like this was just another conversation in another place.

Her mouth fell open. "First my house, now the damn bathroom?"

Supreme lifted a shoulder in a half-assed shrug. "You looked like you needed some air."

She narrowed her eyes. "And you figured the best way to help me breathe was by busting into the ladies' room?"

Another shrug. "Didn't matter before."

Sincere stared at him. Then, despite herself, she let out a short, dry laugh. "This is an actual public building, Supreme. There's security. You can't just go wherever you want like you own the place."

"Ain't nobody stopping me," he said simply. "Might as well."

Her irritation flared, but only for a second. It wasn't that Supreme didn't listen. He did that just fine. He didn't care when it came to shit like this. He did what he wanted, moved how he pleased, and if anyone had a problem with it . . . well, that was their problem.

She huffed, running a hand down her face. "One day, you're gonna pull this shit in the wrong place and get tackled by security."

"Doubt it," he said easily. "People like me."

She scoffed, folding her arms. "No, they don't."

He tilted his head slightly. "You do."

Sincere opened her mouth, then closed it.

He was chuckled, fully aware he had caught her slipping.

She rolled her eyes. "You're ridiculous."

"That a no?" He lifted an eyebrow. "You don't like me?"

Her jaw clenched. "I tolerate you."

"Mm-hmm." Supreme dragged out the sound, clearly not believing a word.

Sincere exhaled sharply, some of the tension easing from her shoulders. *Damn him.*

He was watching her now, his sharp gaze scanning her face, reading every inch of her like a book he had already memorized.

"Hey . . . you good?"

And that's when she realized . . . he knew. He saw the tears she had been holding back. Her stomach clenched. "I'm fine," she muttered, turning away.

Supreme didn't move. Didn't blink. "Sure." His voice was low, smooth, but laced with something she couldn't ignore.

Sincere reached for her purse, needing something to do, something to focus on. And then she saw the pills peeking out of the open bag. Her breath hitched.

Shit.

Her hand darted forward, shoving the bottle deeper into her purse, but it was too late.

Supreme's whole demeanor shifted. He unfolded his arms and his gaze sharpened. The air in the room grew heavy. "What the fuck is that?" His tone was calm, but there was a razor-sharp edge beneath it, one that made the hairs on her arms rise.

Sincere's heart jumped. "They're not mine."

Supreme's eyes didn't move from hers.

She gripped the purse tighter, swallowing hard. "Lena must've left them in my bag at the awards. I was gonna give them back to her when I saw her."

Supreme's expression didn't shift, but she knew he didn't believe her. "She know you tryin' to stay sober?"

Sincere pressed her lips together, hesitating. "She was just trying to help," she said quickly.

Supreme shook his head. "Helping you get high ain't help, Sincere. She's trying to make you relapse."

Her jaw clenched. "She's not like that."

He studied her before tilting his head slightly. "You sure?"

She hesitated. Her chest felt tight. Lena was all she had. The only one who had been through everything with her. Supreme . . . he didn't get that.

"She wouldn't do that to me," she said firmly.

Supreme didn't argue. His jaw tightened, but he let it go. "You should get back in there," he muttered.

Sincere let out a breath, rolling her shoulders back, forcing herself to straighten. She nodded once. "Yeah." Her hand brushed against her purse again—just slightly. She ignored the conflicting thoughts in her head, swallowed hard, and walked out.

Supreme stayed behind. The low whir of the air vents filled the quiet space, but he barely noticed it. The scent of Sincere's perfume still lingered in the air. His arms folded tightly across his chest, his jaw locked, his gaze still fixed on the door she had just walked through.

He should've been relieved that she was back in that boardroom, handling business, doing what she needed to do. But his gut was screaming at him. Something was wrong. She was fighting herself. The one person she trusted most was Lena. And she wasn't helping her win that fight. She was keeping her trapped in it. And that shit hit too close to home.

Supreme rolled his shoulders back as tension knotted tight between them. His fingers tapped against his bicep as his arms remained crossed, his mind running in circles around the same thought. He had seen this before. He'd actually lived it.

The memory crept up on him, uninvited. A hospital waiting room. His mother's voice, raw and broken. His own hands, balled into fists. A doctor saying something about too late and organ failure and nothing we can do now. The rage and the guilt. It was an overwhelming, unbearable loss. Another chance to make right all the things that had gone wrong with his brother. That's what he had begged for. To do something different. To save him, instead of walking the other direction when he should've been fighting for him the hardest.

His throat tightened because God never brought his brother back. And yet, maybe, in some crazy way, this was his chance to save someone he cared about. His eyes lingered on the door one last time before he let out a slow breath, because whether she wanted him to or not, he wasn't gonna let her drown.

Supreme reached into his pocket and pulled out his phone. His jaw was tight as he unlocked the screen with a quick swipe, scrolling through his recent calls until he landed on Dre's name. The kid had been parked outside since they arrived—posted up in the lot, waiting for the moment Supreme gave the signal that they were leaving. But they weren't leaving.

The phone rang twice before Dre picked up, his voice casual, but laced with that same youthful cockiness that he always carried. "Yo."

Supreme leaned against the counter, gripping the phone a little tighter. "You know Lena? The chick who was with Milo at the BET Awards the other night?"

"Yeah. I know who she is." The hesitation in Dre's voice wasn't long, but it was there—a brief pause, barely noticeable to most. But Supreme caught it.

That was the thing about Dre: He wasn't good at hiding shit. Even when he thought he was playing it cool, his voice always gave him away. And right now that slight shift in tone told Supreme everything he needed to know. Dre knew more than just who she was.

Supreme's grip on the phone tightened as he pushed off the counter, his voice dropping just a little. "Tell me about her."

Dre wasn't stupid. He knew Supreme didn't ask shit just to ask it. If he was inquiring about Lena, it meant something was up. And now, Dre had to figure out how much he wanted to say.

Supreme could almost hear the gears turning in Dre's head, that slight shuffle of movement through the receiver like he was shifting in his seat, deciding whether he should play dumb or be straight up.

Finally, Dre exhaled. "What you tryna know?"

Supreme's jaw ticked. "Everything."

And from the silence that followed, he knew—

Dre had a lot to say.

Chapter 12

Lorde sat comfortably in the high-back leather chair, his legs spread wide, his wrist lazily resting on the armrest as he swirled the amber liquid in his glass. Across from him, Lena knelt on the floor, her gaze flicking up to him, filled with something that almost looked like worship.

She was still catching her breath, lips swollen, eyes searching his face for approval like a starving dog waiting for scraps. She wanted more. More than just the pieces he gave her when it suited him.

But Lorde never gave more than necessary. He let his fingers brush over her cheek, a light touch, deceptively gentle. "You're her friend, aren't you?" His voice was smooth, slow, deliberate. He dragged his thumb over her bottom lip, watching as she shivered under his attention. "Then act like one."

Lena swallowed. "I am. I do."

Lorde attempted a smile, but there was no warmth in it. "Then do more."

Her lips parted slightly, like she wanted to argue, but she didn't dare. She knew better than to test him.

Lorde's touch dropped away and just like that, the moment was over. He sat up, adjusting his cuffs, smoothing down his shirt like she wasn't still on her knees for him. He took his time standing, rolling his shoulders before reaching for his glass. The moment he brought up Sincere, he caught the whisper of irritation in Lena's face.

Jealousy.

She tried to hide it, but Lorde had spent too much time shaping her to miss the signs. "She's . . . fine," Lena said, hesitating just enough to amuse him. "I think she's starting to come around."

Lorde grinned, taking a slow sip.

Good.

Sincere was his most valuable asset. The key to everything.

He turned his gaze back to Lena, watching her carefully. "You know she's the key to us having the life we want, right?" His voice was soft, almost hypnotic, the way it always was when he needed her to fall back in line.

Lena chewed her lip, nodding. "Yeah . . . but you've been saying that for years. Since you made me start working with her."

Lorde's lips spread wider. There it was. A tiny glimpse of resistance and doubt. She still thought she had a choice in any of this. He took another slow sip, letting the silence stretch between them. Lena had no idea how deep she was in. How from the moment he found her, she had been nothing more than a pawn in his game.

He had studied Sincere before she even knew his name. He knew her weaknesses, her patterns, her desperate need to cling to something familiar. Lena had been built for this role. The same background. The same look. The same raw, broken energy.

Just like Aaliyah.

Sincere had been waiting for another Aaliyah and Lorde had given her one in Lena. She just didn't know that her new best friend was a gift from him.

Lorde tilted his head, letting out a small chuckle. "You're really questioning me now?"

Lena shifted uncomfortably. "I just don't get why we still need her. You have everything you need already."

His smile didn't falter, but there was a new weight behind it. He moved closer, brushing a loose strand of hair from her face, his touch deceptively affectionate. "This music thing?" he murmured. "It's gonna be my legitimate business. Once I expand the management company and start my own label, the feds won't be able to touch us. Then, we won't need her anymore."

Lena stared up at him, hope flickering in her wide, brown eyes. She believed him. She always did. She was pathetic . . . but useful.

For a second, Lena hesitated before speaking. "I don't know . . ." Her voice was softer now, almost uncertain. "Sincere's my only friend."

Lorde's expression immediately darkened. "She's not your friend."

The words were quiet, sharp. Like a blade slipping between her ribs, cutting her deep. Lena flinched. Regardless to how their friendship started, Lorde's constant reminder that it was fake hurt her deeply.

"I keep telling you this. She keeps you around for her. You make her feel good about herself." His voice was easy, his eyes locked onto hers, stripping her bare. "You support her dumb decisions and it makes her feel better about being a mess. You think she cares about you? She doesn't even know you."

Lena looked down, her breath unsteady, because deep down she knew he was right. Sincere didn't know the real her. Sincere knew the version of Lena she had been sent in to play. The version Lorde had built for her. And Lorde was the only one who knew everything. And he still wanted her.

Her lips trembled slightly as she nodded, her fingers curling into fists.

Lorde nodded. "Good girl." He leaned down, pressing a

slow, gentle kiss against her temple, savoring the way she leaned into him like he was all she had left. She was pathetic to him, but so, so useful. He reached into his pocket and pulled out a small, plastic bag, tossing it onto the bed beside her.

Her breath hitched. It was just enough of what she needed to keep her coming back.

"Keep being good to Daddy," he murmured, his voice mockingly soft, like he was speaking to a child. "And Daddy will keep being good to you."

He turned without another word, his steps slow and intentional as he grabbed his jacket and walked toward the door.

Lena stayed on the floor, eyes locked onto the bag beside her, her fingers twitching at her sides.

The door clicked shut behind him.

And she didn't move.

The bass bumped so loud in Lorde's nightclub that it rattled the streets outside. This place was one of his prime moneymakers, a front to wash his money, but to the outside world, it was just another high-end spot catering to New Orleans' elite.

The flashing neon lights, the VIP booths filled with celebrities and businessmen, the endless flow of champagne and high-priced cocktails—it was all for show. The real money moved behind the scenes, in the back rooms where cash got cleaned, product got moved, and power shifted with a shake of a hand.

Lorde walked in like he owned the world. In this space, he did. His lieutenant, Milo, was already waiting for him in the private lounge, nursing a whiskey on the rocks. The man stood as Lorde approached, offering a nod of respect before they clasped hands in a firm shake.

"Everything's moving steady. No hiccups," Milo reported smoothly.

Lorde slid into the booth across from him, stretching out

like a man with no worries. He took his time, pulling out a cigar, letting the silence sit between them before lighting it. He liked to make people wait. It reminded them who was in control. Finally, he exhaled a slow stream of smoke, his sharp gaze cutting through the dim lighting.

"Good," he said. "Keep it that way. I don't like surprises."

Milo nodded. "The new shipment came in last night, no problems at the port. Everything was clean. Numbers are up too. About twenty percent higher than last quarter."

Lorde hummed his approval. Twenty percent meant expansion. Growth. Power. "And the new routes?"

"Running smooth. I got our guys in Houston handling that side. Miami's still a little shaky, but nothing we can't fix."

Lorde took another pull from his cigar, nodding. Miami was always shaky. Too many greedy motherfuckers trying to play both sides, thinking they could cut him out. They'd learn soon enough. He leaned back, tapping ash into the crystal tray beside him, his mind working through every angle. This wasn't just about profit. It was about control.

You keep the machine running, you keep everyone in line.

That's how he built his empire. By making sure every piece moved exactly where he wanted it. He was good at what he did, which is why he was the youngest leader ever to run the Saints organization.

Milo leaned forward slightly, lowering his voice. "I meant to ask you—Lena said you wanted to bring her in more. Get her running things on the legit side?"

Lorde's reply came slow but packed with certainty. "Yeah. She's good for it. Smart. Knows how to move."

Milo nodded, sipping his drink. "She been good to me, man. Solid."

Lorde almost laughed.

Poor bastard.

He had no idea that the woman he was claiming was on her

knees for another man every other night. Still, Lorde didn't correct him. He let him believe it. It kept Milo motivated to think he had something valuable, something worth protecting. Lorde didn't care what people believed, as long as they stayed useful. If Milo wanted to believe he could turn a ho into a housewife, so be it.

His phone vibrated on the table, disrupting the moment. He glanced at the screen.

Unknown Caller.

Again.

The old heads were trying to figure out what he was up to. Lorde's jaw flexed, irritation flickering across his face. They had been calling all night. Checking in. Asking questions. Poking their old-ass noses into shit that didn't concern them.

He ignored it. Milo noticed, but didn't comment. They got back to business, running through the ledger, cross-checking shipment reports, securing the next moves. But the phone kept buzzing every few minutes. When the elders wanted to stick their nose in shit, they were persistent as hell.

Finally, Lorde dragged his fingers down his face and picked up the call, his voice cool, but sharp as a blade.

"Talk."

The voice on the other end was gravelly, old but sharp, one of the Saints' oldest members—Bishop.

"Well, good evening to you too, son," Bishop began, a dry chuckle escaping through his lips. "Hope I'm not bothering you with all the calls, but I had to get confirmation on some things I've been hearing. Word is, you been meeting with Silvan. Trying to do business with him."

Lorde's jaw tightened, but he kept his voice calm. "Where'd you hear that?"

"Does it matter?" Bishop's tone was even, unreadable. "What matters is whether it's true."

Lorde tapped ash from his cigar, taking a slow pull, stalling just enough to make them doubt themselves. Then, smoothly, he said, "Y'all worry too much."

There was a pause, then another voice joined the call. It was Dawson, another OG.

"Ain't about worry, Laurent," he said, using Lorde's government as a power play. "It's about the Saints' legacy. We built this shit to be more than street corner hustle. We got real businesses now, real power. We're making money without getting our hands dirty. You out here entertaining conversations with a nigga like Silvan? That shit don't sit right. We not trying to go back into the past. We need to step into the future."

Lorde clenched his jaw. These old niggas really thought they were building a dynasty. Thought they could erase the dirt they built their foundation on. Old as they were, they were naive and weak.

He adjusted his watch, his tone smooth as silk. "Y'all act like I'm making deals with the devil."

"Ain't you?"

"No." A perfect lie. "I'm making alliances. Expanding our reach. That's what y'all wanted, right? Growth? The more we negotiate, the more we eliminate threats. Without looking over our shoulders, it'll be easier for us to go legit. Basic business shit."

Bishop wasn't convinced. "Silvan's poison, Lorde. The kind that can't be cleaned up. You don't negotiate with snakes. You *kill* them."

Lorde's patience thinned. "Y'all been in the game long enough to know you don't turn down an opportunity just because of what a man used to be." He let his voice drop slightly, letting the edge of authority cut through. "I'm running things now. If I say there's value in working with him, then there's value.

"Your father wanted—"

"My father tried to do things y'all way and he got killed for it," Lorde spoke up, interrupting Dawson from going further. "And it wasn't no enemy that did it either. It was his own fuckin' friend. I'm not making the same mistakes he did. Y'all chose me to run this and I'm going to run it the way I see fit."

Bishop's long sigh could be heard from the other line, but he didn't say anything to that.

After a short while, Dawson finally spoke again. "We're watching you."

Lorde's smile widened. "Ain't nothing to watch, so don't waste your life watching me. You ain't got much of it left."

And with that, he ended the call.

He sat back, exhaling a long breath, rolling his neck as frustration coiled in his chest.

Fucking dinosaurs.

They didn't understand how things were now. The world moved at the whim of the powerful and Lorde aimed to be the most powerful of them all.

Milo had been watching during the call, sipping his drink, his expression unreadable. "Everything good?"

Of course," Lorde replied with a simple nod.

Milo nodded slowly, swirling the whiskey in his glass. "You know they won't stop. They don't like you fucking with Silvan."

Lorde's eyes darkened. "I don't need their permission."

Milo studied him for a second, then gave a short nod. "Just be careful. Old heads got long memories. Sometimes it's good to listen."

Lorde chuckled low, leaning in just enough to make his presence feel heavier. "They got long memories, but I got long reach. Ain't no sense in living in the fuckin' past."

Milo met his gaze, then nodded again. The conversation was over.

Lorde grabbed his cigar, stood, and smoothed down his suit. "I'll check back in soon." He turned toward the exit, satisfied that he had everything under control. Everything was in motion and soon, the whole city would be his.

The suburban streets were so much different from the fast pace of the city, nothing like what he was used to. It was a world away from the chaos of his empire, from the weight of his name and everything it carried. Here, in this little pocket of normal, no one knew who he was. No one whispered his name in fear or admiration. No one knew that the blacked-out Range Rover cruising down the manicured streets belonged to a kingpin. And that's exactly how Lorde liked it.

He pulled up to the modest two-story house, the porch light on even though the sun had barely started to set. The curtains in the front window shifted, a small shadow moving fast. He barely had time to cut the engine before the front door flew open.

"Daddy!"

Marcus barreled down the steps, a flash of untied sneakers and wild curls bouncing with each hurried step. Before Lorde could even react, his son flung himself into his arms, wrapping around his neck like he'd been waiting for this moment forever.

Lorde caught him effortlessly, his arms locking tight around his little boy's small frame. For a second, everything else disappeared. "Damn, lil' man. You tryna knock me over?" Lorde smiled, ruffling Marcus's curls as the boy laughed against his shoulder.

"I missed you!" Marcus's voice was pure, untainted, and Lorde felt something deep in his chest tighten at the sound of it.

"Missed you too, champ."

And that wasn't a lie. If he could, he would spend every moment of every day with Marcus. He would do just like his father did with him, ride through the streets, handling business with his son permanently glued to his side. But even though he was deep in the street life, he didn't want Marcus following the path that he walked. He did as much as he could to protect him from it. To give his son the option to do something different.

The separation also worked in his favor. Every time he took a trip up to see Marcus, it was like escaping to go live another life, one where he didn't hold the weight and pressure of unspoken expectations on his shoulders.

As soon as he stepped out and scooped Marcus into his arms, he felt a lighthearted emotion that he couldn't explain and he didn't want it to go away. The moment he stepped inside the house, though, the warmth in the air around made a drastic shift.

Lorde barely had time to take in the familiar scent of vanilla and clean linen before he saw Nia. She was standing in the kitchen, staring directly at him with her arms crossed as she waited.

Her face was unreadable, but Lorde knew that look well. She'd been holding something in, waiting for the moment she could finally let it out. Judging by the tension in her shoulders, that moment was now.

"Marcus, go wash up for dinner," Nia said, her voice smooth but firm.

Marcus pouted, but obeyed, running toward the bathroom without argument. As soon as he was out of sight, her gaze snapped back to Lorde.

"You think I don't see what's going on?"

Lorde sighed, already tired. "Nia, what the fu—"

"No," she cut him off, stepping closer. "I've been watching you out there playing house with Sahara while I'm in here raising your son. Everybody saw you at that awards show with her! All my family and friends! Do you know how humiliating that is?"

Lorde exhaled slowly, adjusting the cuffs of his tailored black button-up like he wasn't the least bit fazed. "You know how this works, Nia." His voice was low, patient. "The less the public knows about you, the safer you and Marcus are. You're my priority and I gotta protect you. You know that."

Nia let out a short, bitter laugh. "Really? 'Cause I don't feel like your priority when I'm waking up to pictures of you and her all over the internet! You got the world thinking she's your woman while I'm supposed to just—what? Stay quiet? Pretend I don't exist?"

Lorde took a slow step forward. "You do exist." His voice was smooth, dangerous. "And you exist safely. That's because of me. That's because of the way that I separate this life"—he rotated his index finger between their two bodies "—from that one." He pointed outside.

Nia's jaw clenched. He could tell she wanted to argue, wanted to keep pushing. But she didn't. She was an emotional woman, but her love for him ran deep. Plus, she loved the life that he gave her. It was the life of her dreams. She wasn't going anywhere.

Instead, she shook her head, swallowing her pride. "Marcus deserves better than this."

Lorde softened. Not much, but just enough to soothe her fears. "Marcus has everything he needs. A good home. A good mother. A future." He lifted a hand, tracing his fingers gently down her jawline, his voice dipping lower. "And so do you. But for me to do that, I gotta keep you here and you gotta let me do the things that I need to do."

Nia's breath hitched, her body betraying her even as her mind fought against it.

Lorde leaned in, pressing a slow, lingering kiss to her lips.

Knowing her body so well was a weapon and he knew it, because no matter how angry she was, Lorde was her weakness.

Nia was his security. As much as she hated what he did, Nia

was too deep in it to leave. Too smart, too involved. And her photographic memory was his greatest asset. She memorized codes, shipment details, contacts—everything that mattered when it came to his business. There was no paper trail, no evidence linking him to the things he did under the radar . . . only her mind. The elders would never be able to prove what he was up to. As long as he made sure she stayed loyal to him, she would never give him up.

Lorde watched her carefully, his fingers tracing the edge of her waist.

She knows too much. That's why she stays on my payroll.

Because as long as she was comfortable and well-kept, as long as she felt like Marcus needed him, and as long as she believed in his lies . . . she would never turn on him.

Lorde pulled back slightly, his lips still close enough to feel the warmth of her breath. "You're the one I trust, Nia. The only one who's always been there for me."

Nia closed her eyes, exhaling slowly. "Lorde . . ."

"I'm serious. Don't let this media circus mess with your head." His tone was smooth, laced with reassurance. "I'm doing all of this for us. For Marcus. You gotta do your part too."

Her lips parted slightly, hesitation flickering across her face. She wanted to believe him. She always did. "I will, but you need to tell me the truth," she whispered. "Is she really just a pawn in all this?"

Lorde didn't blink. "I told you before. She's nothing to me. We both came up with this plan together. I'm just putting the plan in place."

The lie came effortlessly, rolling off his tongue like a practiced script. The truth was that *he* came up with the plan and convinced Nia that it was for her benefit.

Nia studied him, searching his face, waiting for some telltale crack in his demeanor. Lorde was too good for that. He wasn't new to this. He was true to this.

Finally, she sighed. "I don't like this, Lorde."

"You don't have to."

His words were final and so was her silence.

Marcus ran back into the room then, beaming. "Daddy, can we play before you leave?"

Lorde glanced at the clock. He had business to handle, meetings to run. Empires to build. But instead, he crouched down, holding out his arms. "What you wanna play, champ?"

Marcus grinned, pulling out his basketball. And for the next hour, Lorde was just a father. A real one. No empire. No schemes. Just his son's laughter echoing through the quiet house, the one sound that still made him feel human. Even if he knew it was only temporary. Because at the end of the night, Lorde wasn't a father. He was a king. And kings didn't get to be soft.

Not for long.

The streets blurred past as Lorde gripped the wheel, his knuckles pressing into the smooth leather, the quiet murmur of the engine barely filling the silence in his head. Nia's neighborhood had always felt like a different world, a place so far removed from the empire he ran from the blood and money that kept it moving. Out here, there were no soldiers, no whispers of betrayal, no constant power plays. Just a quiet house with a woman who still loved him despite knowing exactly who he was. Just a boy who looked at him like he was a hero, when the world knew better. It was a lie he had spent years perfecting. And yet, it was the only thing in his life that felt real.

His fingers tapped against the gearshift, his mind already moving past Nia, past Marcus, past the life he had no choice but to keep at arm's length. Because while she was worried about Sincere, Lorde was thinking about something else. Something that had been nagging at him for days now.

Sincere was proving to be more resilient than he expected. Most people bent fast. A little pressure, a little reminder of who held the power, and they folded like paper, but she fought it. She fought him. It was subtle. Small moments of defiance, the way she still looked him in the eye like he wasn't the one who owned her. The way she still acted like she had a choice.

He hated that. But at the same time, he liked it. He needed her to fight back—just enough to keep things interesting. Because the truth was, breaking someone completely was never the goal. You had to leave just enough for them to still believe they were choosing you. If you crushed them all at once, there was nothing left to control.

No, he needed her to struggle, to resist. Because when she finally gave in and realized she belonged to him, *that* was when he'd really have her.

Part of what he told Nia was true—Sincere *was* just a means to an end. She had the potential to get him something that he wanted, but had never been able to achieve himself: the kind of power that came with *fame*.

Money was nice, but having the attention of the world? A lot came with that. With Sincere's talent and demeanor, she had a way of making people love her. She was poised and ready to be America's sweetheart and Lorde planned to ride her coattails the entire way. Making negotiations behind the scenes to secure his empire.

Fuck Jay-Z and Beyoncé. It's gonna be all about Lorde and Sahara.

He had big dreams and they couldn't wait.

His lips curled with pleasure as he drove, the weight of his plans settling comfortably into place. Sincere wasn't like the others. She was harder to break, but he knew a secret: Everyone broke eventually. All he had to do was apply the right kind of pressure. It was just a matter of time.

The thought of time made his jaw clench, because time was what he didn't have. Not with the elders getting in his business. And not with Supreme acting different.

The way Supreme had been watching him closer, the way she questioned things he used to let slide. But now it was something deeper.

Lorde had built his empire by reading people, by knowing when a man was with him or against him. And Supreme seemed to be walking close to the edge. He grabbed his phone, the glow of the screen casting a faint light over his sharp features as he scrolled through his contacts. He didn't go to Supreme. He needed something done and it could only be accomplished by someone who didn't have real power.

He had to go to someone who owed him. Someone desperate to prove his loyalty. Those were the easiest ones to use. He tapped Dre's number, bringing the phone to his ear as it rang twice before he picked up.

"Yo . . . is—is this *Lorde*?" He said it with pure shock and disbelief, like it was Jesus on the other line calling him.

Lorde kept his voice smooth, casual, like this wasn't a test. "Aye . . . you still keeping an eye on Supreme?"

Dre hesitated for a fraction of a second, just long enough for Lorde to notice, before responding. "Yeah. I mean, you told me to, right?"

Lorde smiled slightly, but there was no warmth in it. "That's right."

He drummed his fingers against the steering wheel, letting the silence stretch long enough to make Dre sweat. Then, lazily, like it was an afterthought, he began to speak. "Tell me about him."

There was a pause, but Lorde was patient because he knew he had something to say.

Dre cleared his throat. "He's been . . . talking to her a lot. Sincere, I mean."

Lorde's fingers tightened on the wheel. "That so?"

"Yeah. They got . . . close. Not like that—" Dre hurried to clarify. "I mean, not that I've seen. But they be talking like . . . like he's tryna get in her head or something. Get her to think more about what she's doing with her life. Nothing bad."

Lorde exhaled slowly, processing. Supreme wasn't the type to play hero. Never had been the type to stick his nose in shit that wasn't his business. But with Sincere? It was starting to look different and could become a problem.

"Keep watching him." Lorde's voice was easy, almost bored, but Dre wasn't stupid. He heard what wasn't being said.

"Aight. Yeah. I got you."

Lorde paused before adding, "Yeah, I know you do."

He ended the call before Dre could say anything else, his jaw tightening. Supreme was one step away from making a mistake and Lorde didn't do mistakes. He taught lessons. That said, if Supreme needed one, he'd make sure it was one he'd never forget.

Lorde pressed harder on the gas, the city around him flashing past in a blur. He wasn't going to lose control. Not of Sincere. Not of Supreme. And sure as hell not of his empire. No matter what he had to do to keep it.

Chapter 13

The silence was loud. It filled every inch of the penthouse, thick and oppressive, swallowing the space whole. The walls stretched wide, but it felt like they were closing in, pressing down on her chest, making it harder to breathe. The only sound was her own shallow, uneven breaths, breaking the stillness like fragile glass.

Just the withdrawal.

The weight of it settled deep, sinking into her bones like cement. A fever burned beneath her skin, sticky and suffocating, making her sweat through the sheets one second and shiver violently the next. Her muscles ached—no, throbbed—like they were being pulled apart from the inside out.

And the nausea. God, the nausea.

She curled into herself on the couch, knees drawn up, arms wrapped tight around her body. But it didn't help. She clenched her teeth as another spasm rippled through her, sharp and punishing, leaving her breathless.

This was hell. But she did this to herself.

No one forced her to quit cold turkey. No one dragged her into rehab or staged an intervention. She made the decision herself she was strong enough to push through it alone. Told herself she'd beat it, no matter how bad it got.

Now, she wasn't so sure.

She had done this before—fought through the brutal, ugly grips of withdrawal, clawing her way out of addiction's choke-hold. But last time, she had help: Lena, doctors—an entire team watching over her, making sure she didn't crash and burn.

This time, it was just her. And that pissed her off more than anything. She wasn't alone in this place, not really. She could feel him. Somewhere in the penthouse, lurking in the background. Supreme. Not watching her like some nurse on duty. But present.

His presence was an unspoken thing, lingering in the air like an unsaid truth, heavy and suffocating. He wasn't asking if she was okay, wasn't forcing her to drink water or eat, wasn't saying a damn thing about what she was going through.

Somehow that made it worse, because she knew he saw her suffering. She could feel his eyes on her, reading her body language the way he always did, taking in every tremor, every flinch, every slow drag of breath like he was cataloging her pain in real time.

And he wasn't stepping in.

It made her want to scream at him. To tell him to leave, to stop watching, to do something.

But she didn't.

Because deep down, a small, ugly part of her needed him here.

She forced her eyes open. The ceiling light above her cast a dim glow, flickering slightly, making the room feel like it was tilting just slightly off its axis. It wasn't, of course. The world wasn't moving. But she was.

Her head felt like it was full of sand, her body heavy, stiff, barely responding to the commands her brain tried to send. Everything hurt. Every muscle, every nerve, every cell in her body screamed in protest as she moved. She needed water.

Forcing herself upright, she moved slowly, dragging her limbs like she was made of lead. The simple act of sitting up made her head spin, her vision swimming as nausea clawed its way up her throat. And then, she saw him.

Supreme. He looked cool, relaxed, and unbothered.

He was posted up in a chair near the window, one leg stretched out, phone in hand, scrolling through something like he had all the time in the world. The soft blue glow from his screen lit up his face, casting sharp shadows over his features, making him look even more unreadable than usual.

Sincere frowned, irritation flaring through the exhaustion. "You're just gonna sit there while I suffer?"

Supreme didn't even look up. He just kept scrolling, like her pain wasn't a spectacle, like her words weren't even worth rushing for.

"Ain't like you to ask for help," he said smoothly.

Her jaw clenched. "I shouldn't have to."

Finally, that made him look up. Dark eyes met hers, sharp and knowing, cutting straight through her defenses like they always did. "You wanted to do this alone, didn't you?"

The words hit her harder than they should have, because he wasn't wrong. She had told him that she didn't need anybody watching over her, like she was some helpless, fragile little thing. She had wanted this to be her fight—her battle to win.

So why did she suddenly feel angry that he had actually listened? Her scowl deepened, fingers tightening around the edge of the counter as another wave of dizziness hit her.

"You could at least act like you give a damn," she muttered.

His expression didn't falter. "You don't want me to care, Sincere."

Her stomach twisted at the way he said her name. She turned away, pressing her palms against the cool marble surface, trying to ground herself. Trying to make sense of all of this—of him. She exhaled shakily, her fingers flexing against the counter. "This is harder than I thought," she admitted, her voice hoarse.

"I know."

Two words. That was all he gave her. No false reassurances. No sugarcoated bullshit about how strong she was, how she'd push through, how she'd be okay. And somehow, that was better than any lie he could've fed her.

Her fingers twitched. To her, it felt like the beginning of something—like her body was reaching for something familiar, something that could ground her in the middle of all this pain. Her mind grasped for it and for some reason, that comfort had a name.

Her mother.

The thought slammed into her like a punch to the chest, so unexpected, that she nearly gasped. The urge to call her, to hear her voice—even if just for a second—wrapped around her so tightly that her hands actually twitched toward her phone. It was instinct. Muscle memory. Like something inside her had cracked open, spilling out memories she had buried deep, sealed shut, told herself she didn't need anymore. But now, she needed her.

The phone was right there. She could call, maybe just to hear her voice. Maybe to apologize and say, *I need you.* Maybe to admit that she was suffering and she wasn't as strong as she had pretended to be, that she was breaking into pieces in this empty penthouse. Her fingers brushed against the edge of the phone. But she already knew how this would go. She could still hear the way her mother's voice had flattened the last time they spoke. She was cold, like she had already mourned the daughter she used to have.

Sincere's breath hitched, her stomach twisting painfully. The dial tone still lingered in her ears, pressing into her skull, ringing louder than the silence around her. She wouldn't call, because nothing had changed. And maybe it never would. Her throat burned. She pressed the heel of her palm against her chest, trying to push down the ache sitting there.

Don't think about it. Just move.

She forced herself to push off the counter, her legs trembling beneath her weight. Her body felt weak, drained, as if the mere act of standing was a battle she was losing. Water. She just needed water. She took one step toward the kitchen and—she felt it. Slowly, carefully, she lifted her head.

Supreme was seated in the chair near the window, watching her, not in a way that demanded or expected anything. He hadn't moved, but he was watching.

Sincere let out a sharp breath, the weight of his stare pressing into her like a silent challenge. "What?"

His head tilted slightly, studying her. "Who you thinkin' about calling? Your mother?"

Her stomach dropped. How the hell did he know? Her fingers curled at her sides, a sharp prickle of irritation cutting through the fog in her head.

Supreme . . . he just stared sharp-eyed, like he was already three steps ahead of her. "You got that look."

Her jaw tightened. "You don't know shit about me."

Supreme let out a low chuckle, deep and knowing. "You keep tellin' yourself that."

Her irritation flared. "You really are a smug asshole, you know that?"

"Yeah." His gaze flicked toward her shaking hands and hunched shoulders. "And you're still standing. Even though you been through hell and back. That means something. You're not that lil' girl from the hood anymore."

She blinked. He wasn't trying to comfort her or hold her hand through this. He was just stating a fact.

He gestured lazily toward the couch, where she had spent the last hours curled up, damn near broken. "You ain't over there no more. Ain't crying. Ain't folded."

Her chest tightened. He wasn't lying. She wasn't okay, not even close. But she wasn't gone. For the first time in days, she almost believed she could get through this.

She swallowed hard, straightening her spine. "I need to get through this."

His gaze darkened, something unreadable flickering behind his eyes. "Then do it."

And just like that, he pushed off the chair, stretched, and walked toward the door.

Sincere exhaled. And for the first time in forever, she felt like she might actually win.

Chapter 14

Weeks Later

Sincere fastened the diamond clasp on her necklace. It was the final touch to an outfit designed to make a statement. The mirror in front of her reflected a woman who looked eerily similar to Sahara, but this time, something was different. There was no haze behind her eyes, sluggishness in her movements, or artificial high to carry her through the night.

She looked . . . *alive*.

The realization settled like a quiet triumph in her chest, a feeling she hadn't experienced in a long time. A knock at the door interrupted her thoughts.

"Sis, you decent?" Lena's voice rang through the suite before she pushed the door open without waiting for an answer.

Sincere rolled her eyes. "Does it even matter to you whether I am?"

Lena strolled in, her sharp brown eyes scanning her from head to toe. She let out a low whistle, crossing her arms over her chest.

"Damn, girl. You're glowing! Your skin is beautiful."

Sincere turned back to the mirror, adjusting her earring. "Guess that's what getting clean does for you."

"Yeah, but what about the anxiety? You almost crashed out last time and we don't need you on the news." Lena plopped onto the bed, legs tucked under her, watching her with a scrutinizing look. "I don't know . . . sure you don't need a little bump to take the edge off?"

Sincere stilled for half a second before sighing. She grabbed a bottle of perfume from the vanity and spritzed her neck. "Not funny, Lena."

She raised her hands in defense. "Relax, damn! I'm just saying, you're about to walk into a roomful of vultures and pretenders. You really wanna go in there raw? No help at all?"

Sincere exhaled, shaking her head. "I've dealt with worse." She turned, her voice firm. "I don't need anything to get through this. I've got it."

Lena's smile faltered for a fraction of a second before she plastered on her usual easygoing grin. "Okay, boss. I hear you."

But Sincere could see the slight tension in Lena's jaw. She was brushing it off, but clearly disappointed. It made Sincere's stomach twist. She didn't want Lena to feel like she was changing up on her. The last thing she wanted was for Lena to see her sobriety as her pulling away. They could still be friends; she just wanted their friendship to be based on more than getting drunk and popping pills.

For a long time, Lena was the person who kept her afloat while she found ways to numb her pain. They bonded over trauma, but Sincere didn't want their friendship to stay that way. She reached for her clutch, straightening her posture. "Let's go. Gotta get there in time to walk the red carpet."

Lena nodded, though there was something guarded in her expression. "Yeah. Let's."

Yeah, but what about the anxiety? You almost crashed out last time and we don't need you on the news.

Lena's voice had been a ghost in Sincere's head the entire drive over, a whisper that curled around her thoughts and squeezed. She had asked that question twice before Sincere left the house. Once when she was slipping into her gown, and again when putting on the final touches of her makeup.

Both times, Sincere had ignored her. Now, as she stepped out of the car, she wished she had an answer. Because, no, she wasn't sure she wanted to do this.

But she had to.

Her heels clicked against the pavement as she walked toward the entrance of Noir, a high-end lounge in the city. Her posture flawless, her face unreadable. She was trained for this—to walk into any room like she owned it. To carry herself like she was untouchable. But tonight, she wasn't sure if she believed it. She felt it the moment she stepped inside.

The shift.

Conversations slowed and eyes turned. They weren't the usual looks of admiration or curiosity she was used to. This was something different. They were looking. Wondering. Judging.

Rocco had made sure of that.

She could feel it, the weight of his words following her like a stain she couldn't scrub off. And the worst part? On some level, she believed them. She hadn't realized how deeply his accusations had cut until now, standing in this room, surrounded by people who had probably heard it all.

Sincere uses people. She manipulates them. She takes what she wants and leaves wreckage in her wake. It wasn't just the whispers or speculation. It was the fact that maybe, just maybe . . . they weren't wrong. She had spent her life convincing herself that she was just playing the game the way men did. That she was smart, calculating, taking control of her own narrative.

But what if Rocco wasn't lying?

What if she really was just . . . hollow?

What if something was *wrong* with her?

The thought made her throat tight, her breath shallow. She straightened her shoulders, smoothing an invisible wrinkle on her gown as if brushing away the weight of their expectations. If they thought she was going to shrink under the scrutiny, they didn't know her at all.

Taking a glass of champagne from a passing waiter, she stepped into the chaos, forcing herself to believe she still belonged here.

Sincere didn't see him at first. She had been too caught up in navigating the energy of the party, trying to settle into the space. But then she felt it. That subtle shift. That unmistakable pull of eyes on her, the awareness creeping up her spine before she even turned her head. And when she did, her stomach clenched.

Rocco.

He stood across the room, draped in his usual arrogance, the center of attention, surrounded by the same brand of industry clout-chasers who had always flocked to him. But he wasn't looking at them. He was looking at her.

Sincere inhaled slowly, pressing her lips together, bracing herself. She didn't want to cause a scene or drama. But more than anything, she didn't want to deal with him.

Not tonight.

Not when she was already feeling unsteady. Still, she didn't walk away. She had no reason to. And when he started making his way toward her, she stood her ground, refusing to shrink under his gaze.

He stopped a few feet away, studying her for a beat before shaking his head slightly. "Damn," he muttered, his voice carrying just enough over the music. "I knew you'd be here, but I wasn't sure if you'd actually speak."

Sincere arched a brow, tilting her head. "Would you have?"

Rocco let out a soft chuckle, rubbing a hand over his jaw. "Fair point."

A pause.

Then, his expression shifted into something quieter, more serious. "I just wanted to say . . ." He hesitated for the briefest second before exhaling. "I know I messed up. Said some things I shouldn't have. Did a lot of shit I shouldn't have. I was a bad boyfriend, and that's on me."

Sincere blinked. She had been expecting something else. A jab. A backhanded comment. A slick remark meant to rile her up.

But instead . . . this.

An admission of guilt.

Just . . . an honest acknowledgment of his mistakes.

Sincere studied him, unsure how to respond. Because she hadn't exactly been perfect either. She had checked out of their relationship long before it ended. She hadn't been faithful. She hadn't been invested.

While she hadn't embarrassed him the way he had done to her, she had still played a role in their downfall.

So really . . .

Who was she to hold a grudge?

Her shoulders dropped slightly, the tension she was holding started to ease. "Yeah," she said quietly. "I wasn't a great girlfriend either."

Rocco's brows lifted slightly, like he hadn't been expecting that from her. A slow grin touched his lips, but it wasn't cocky, just amusement. "Damn. Look at us. Growth."

She huffed out a quiet laugh, shaking her head. They weren't right for each other. They never had been. Hurt people hurt people, and that's all they had done—found new ways to bruise each other until there was nothing left.

And now, standing here, it was painfully obvious that there was nothing left.

No anger.

No resentment.

No love.

Just two people who had outgrown whatever they once were.

"Good luck with Lorde, though," Rocco added after a beat, tilting his head slightly. "Seems like the kind of guy you needed all along."

Sincere stiffened and her stomach twisted. The moment of understanding between them snapped in half. She didn't let her face change, didn't let the reaction show, but inside? Inside, something sharp twisted in her gut.

He said it so casually, so matter-of-factly, like it was inevitable. Like she was already claimed. Like she and Lorde being together was a given. Like that's just who she was—the kind of woman who belonged to men like him.

Sincere forced her hands to stay loose at her sides, urging herself not to react. Because she knew better than anyone how much men like Rocco loved to get a reaction. Precisely why she didn't give him one.

Instead, she just nodded. "Take care of yourself, Rocco."

Something flickered in his expression, but he didn't push. He just gave her one last look before turning and walking away, his arms looping around two women who had been waiting for his attention.

Sincere watched him disappear into the crowd, exhaling sharply.

It was done and she actually felt okay about it. Because if nothing else, she knew this much:

Rocco never wanted to be monogamous.

The party continued around her, but Sincere felt like she

was floating somewhere outside of it, detached from the noise, from the energy, from all of it. She was supposed to feel relieved.

And in some ways, she did. She and Rocco had finally had their goodbye conversation. She had let go of whatever resentment she was holding.

But that last comment?

That last goddamn comment! *Seems like the kind of guy you needed all along.*

It sat heavy in her chest, curling around her ribs like something suffocating. A part of her believed it and another feared it was true. Could it be that she really was the kind of woman who found herself in the orbit of men like Lorde?

Men who took.

Men who used.

Men who didn't love the way love was supposed to feel.

And if that was true . . .

Then maybe she really wasn't built for the kind of love she claimed she didn't believe in.

Sincere swallowed hard, pressing her fingers against the smooth surface of the bar, grounding herself. She wouldn't let herself spiral.

Not over this.

Not over Rocco or Lorde.

She lifted her chin, squared her shoulders, and forced herself to let go of the weight threatening to pull her under. She wasn't about to fall apart over a man.

Not again.

Sincere forced a breath through her nose. She was done with this party. Done with the false smiles, the fake congratulations, the quiet whispers behind her back. She had faced Rocco, survived the stares, and swallowed down the gnawing insecurity clawing at her throat. That was enough.

She needed air.

She turned and wove through the party, slipping past the clusters of industry heads, influencers, and artists who had long since drowned themselves in liquor and self-importance. The music pulsed against her skin, but she barely felt it as she pushed through the heavy double doors and stepped outside. Cool air rushed against her face, crisp and clean compared to the thick, heated energy inside.

She inhaled deeply.

And then she froze.

Leaning against a sleek, black car parked at the curb, Supreme stood in the shadows, watching the party from a distance, his arms crossed, his expression unreadable.

Her brows lifted. She hadn't expected to see him here. Rolling her shoulders, she stepped forward, tilting her head slightly. "What are you doing here? Spying on me?"

Supreme exhaled a stream of smoke into the night air. "Just keeping an eye out." He took another pull from his blunt, his voice low, lazy. "Never know when things might go sideways."

Sincere folded her arms, narrowing her eyes at him. "And you assumed that I was gonna be the reason things went sideways?"

He didn't respond right away, just watched her before shaking his head. "Nah," he murmured. "But I figured if it did, I'd be close enough to step in."

Sincere let out a soft scoff, glancing away before looking back at him. "Well, you wasted your time. I handled myself just fine."

The light in Supreme's eyes faded just enough to reveal something else beneath them. "I know," he said simply.

For some reason, that hit her harder than she expected. Sincere let Supreme's words settle between them, the quiet weight of them sinking deep into her chest. She wasn't sure why it mattered so much—why *hearing* it from him meant something. But it really did.

A small, tired smile pulled at her lips. "You always gotta act like you know everything, huh?"

Supreme exhaled slowly, flicking the blunt between his fingers, a low chuckle rumbling in his throat. "Ain't about acting, ma."

Her smile widened just slightly, but she shook her head, looking away. Her body still buzzed with the lingering tension of the night—the weight of every judgmental stare, every forced interaction, every moment spent trying to convince herself that she belonged here.

But out here?

Out here, with him?

She could breathe again.

The silence between them stretched, comfortable, unforced. The sounds of the party—music, laughter, the occasional outburst—were muffled, distant.

And then, Supreme spoke again, his voice quieter this time. "You good?"

Sincere hesitated, biting the inside of her cheek before finally looking up at him. "I don't know," she admitted, her voice softer than she meant it to be.

Supreme held her gaze, something flickering in his eyes. "Yeah," he murmured. "I figured."

Something shifted in the air between them then.

They were having a moment. Sincere wasn't sure if it was the stress of the night, the exhaustion of trying to prove herself, or something deeper that had been building between them since the beginning. But she moved into him, just a little. Supreme didn't move away and didn't shut it down. He didn't do anything at all.

Sincere took that as a sign and decided to push him a little further. She leaned in . . . just enough for her lips to brush his. Just enough for the world to tilt slightly, for her pulse to stutter, for the warmth of his breath to send a shiver down her spine.

Hidden by the night, Dre stiffened as he watched them from a distance. His stomach twisted as he caught sight of the moment—Sincere standing too close. And Supreme, making no movements to push her away.

And then it happened.

The kiss was gentle and she showed more than a little hesitation, but Supreme didn't resist in any way.

Shit! Dre thought as he watched.

It wasn't much, but based on what he knew about Lorde, it was more than enough to start a war. Dre exhaled sharply, his jaw tightening. He was supposed to tell Lorde about this. That was his job and the only reason he was here. But, for the first time since he had started playing his part in this game, he wasn't sure he wanted to.

Right then, he made a different decision. Instead of putting himself in the middle of a war he knew was brewing, he turned his head, deciding to mind his business. He would leave it all up to fate.

Chapter 15

Supreme could still feel the ghost of her lips against his. Her touch was soft and hesitant.

This is a mistake. We shouldn't be doing this.

Yet, as Sincere pulled back, looking up at him with something unreadable in her eyes, he didn't move or step away. He didn't say a damn thing. For the first time in a long while, he didn't know what the right move was.

He'd been here before. He was no stranger to women looking at him like he was something to hold onto. This wasn't supposed to happen with Sincere, not when there were already a thousand ways this could go wrong. The biggest problem he had to face now was he didn't want to pull away.

That was the thing about Sincere. She was different. He reminded himself that he was only here to watch over her. In his life, it wasn't a good thing for a man in his position to second-guess himself.

He exhaled slowly, letting the moment settle between them, heavy and unspoken. And then, before either of them could say something they couldn't take back, a voice inside his head snapped him back to reality.

This can't happen.

The right thing to do would be to tell her that. To remind

her of who he was, who she was, and who the hell they were both tied to. But he couldn't do force himself to say the words when he saw the way that she was looking at him.

So instead, all he said was, "You don't want to do this. Not with me."

Sincere's lips parted slightly, hesitation passing across her face. "Maybe I do."

Supreme clenched his jaw. Her words shouldn't have made his pulse tick a little harder. Before he could figure out what to do with that, movement in the distance caught his eye. Lena was stumbling out of the party, barely able to walk straight, her head swiveling like she was searching for someone. Supreme already knew exactly who that could be.

Everything about her screamed trouble. Sincere didn't need more of that in her life. She had enough leeches around her already. Pushing the moment that he had with her—whatever it was—to the back of his mind, he brought himself back into the present moment.

"Yo, we good here?" Supreme asked, his voice steady, cutting through the tension.

Lena barely gave Sincere a chance to answer before stepping in, her arm curling around Sincere's like they were inseparable. Her nails lightly grazed Sincere's forearm. The touch was more like possession than comfort.

"Damn, we can't even have a second to ourselves before your security team steps in?" Lena teased, flashing Supreme a grin that didn't quite reach her eyes.

Supreme ignored her, his focus still on Sincere. "You ready to go?"

Sincere hesitated and Lena picked up on it instantly. So did Supreme.

Lena's grip tightened just slightly. "Come on, girl," she coaxed, gently steering her away from Supreme like he was the outsider here. "We barely even got a chance to celebrate tonight. This was a big deal for you. You faced all that bullshit head-on and still owned the room. You should feel good about that."

Sincere exhaled, her fingers tightening around her clutch. She had handled it. She was able to walk into a roomful of people who had already made up their minds about her and walked out with her head still high. But deep down, that old gnawing insecurity still whispered to her.

Lena softened her voice, as if she could hear that same whisper inside Sincere's head. "I know it doesn't always feel like it, but people see you, Sis. And not just the industry leeches. The real ones. You did that tonight."

Sincere's lips pressed together, the words sinking into her chest before she could stop them. Lena was good. Even now after everything, there was still a part of her that wanted to believe in their friendship and Lena was still looking out for her.

Supreme saw it—the way Sincere was still holding on. She was still convincing herself that Lena wasn't part of the problem. That Lena wasn't a leash.

And that was why Supreme didn't trust her.

Sincere sighed, rolling her shoulders like she could shake the weight of the night off. "Yeah . . . I guess."

Lena smiled, giving her a little shake. "Damn right. And that's why we should keep the night going. You need something that's actually gonna make you feel good."

And there it was.

The shift. Not obvious. Not pushy. Just enough to slide under Sincere's defenses.

Sincere sighed. "Lena . . ."

"I'm not talking about anything crazy," Lena said quickly, holding up her hands. "I just mean, let's go somewhere—just us. No cameras. No bullshit. No people acting like they know you when they really don't."

Supreme saw it happening. He saw how Lena was reeling

Sincere in without her even realizing it. Lena made it about comfort and safety.

And that was the real trap.

Supreme finally moved forward, stepping just a little closer, his presence enough to shift the balance. "Yeah, that sounds really nice and all," he said. "But she's done for the night."

Lena's grip on Sincere loosened slightly, but her smile didn't fade. She turned her head, flicking her gaze up to Supreme, her lashes lowering just a fraction. "Since when do you decide what she does?"

"I don't." His expression didn't change. "But I do know when someone's done for the night. And she is."

Sincere looked between them, feeling like she was caught between two invisible tugs-of- war. She wanted to believe Lena was just trying to be a friend and Supreme wasn't trying to control her. But right now, she wasn't sure who was right.

Lena sighed, giving Sincere a half-shrug. "Fine. If you really just wanna go home and be boring, I'll stop pushing."

Sincere hesitated again, her fingers twitching at her side. It wasn't just the way Lena said it—it was the tone that made her feel uneasy.

Supreme must've sensed the war still waging inside her, because he didn't give her time to question herself. "Come on," he said, softer now, but still firm. "I'll drive you."

Sincere inhaled deeply, staring at Lena for a second longer. And then, finally, she nodded.

Lena's fingers loosened slightly around Sincere's arm, but her expression didn't change. She kept smiling, still playing the role of the carefree best friend.

The moment was quiet, but it held weight. And Sincere felt it. An unspoken shift occurred between them. When she looked at Lena—really looked at her—she saw something else.

A flicker of something almost . . . sad.

Instead of pulling away completely, Sincere sighed and shook her head. "Why don't you come with me," she suggested, rubbing at her temple. "Just come back to my place. We can chill there."

Lena perked up instantly, masking whatever disappointment had just been in her eyes with an easy grin. "Now that's more like it."

Supreme's jaw ticked. This wasn't what he wanted. He wanted Lena out of the picture. But he also wasn't stupid. He knew that pushing Sincere too hard to cut her off completely would only make her hold on tighter. So instead, he kept his expression unreadable and nodded. "Fine. Let's go."

Without another word, he opened the car door and waited. Sincere slid in first, Lena right behind her. Supreme shut the door. Then, exhaling slowly, he walked around to the driver's side, slid in, and pulled off.

His hands gripped the wheel tighter than usual. Because he knew something that Sincere didn't. She thought she was keeping Lena close because they were friends. But Lena was keeping her close for an entirely different reason. And Supreme needed to figure out exactly what that was—before it was too late.

Supreme kept his hands on the wheel, his focus locked on the road ahead, but his thoughts were still tangled in the moment that had just happened.

The kiss.

He hadn't seen it coming. And yet . . . he hadn't pulled away.

Sincere sat beside him, staring out the window, her fingers tracing slow, absent-minded circles against her thigh. She hadn't said anything about it either. Maybe she was pretending it hadn't happened, and it was for the best.

Supreme knew better than to ignore the shift between them. And so did Lena. She sat in the back seat, her energy light, buzzing, like she was still soaking in the high of the night.

"So . . ." Lena dragged the word out, stretching her arms over her head like she was just making casual conversation. "You and Lorde, huh?"

Sincere rolled her eyes before glancing at Lena in the rearview mirror. "There is no me and Lorde."

Lena grinned. "That's not what the streets are saying."

Sincere sighed, rubbing her temple. "Since when do you believe what the streets say?"

"I don't." Lena shrugged. "I believe you. Tell me—what is it then? Just business?"

"Yes," Sincere said immediately.

Lena hummed, not convinced. "See . . . that's interesting."

Sincere frowned slightly. "How so?"

"Because . . ." Lena leaned forward slightly, lowering her voice like she was just two girlfriends gossiping. "You might say it's business, but he moves like it's something else. And I don't just mean how he acts when he's around you. I mean how he's handling you."

Sincere stiffened. "Lorde doesn't handle me."

Lena tilted her head. "You sure?" Lena chuckled under her breath. "I'm just saying. He's invested. And when a man like Lorde invests, it ain't just about the money."

Sincere sighed. "Lorde's invested in himself. Not me. He only cares about what I can do for his empire."

Lena nodded, like she understood. "I get it. He's strategic. But that's what makes him so valuable." She let a beat pass before adding, "He knows things, Sincere. He knows how to move, how to win. He's a mentor—he could really help you if you let him."

Sincere's patience was thinning. "I don't need a mentor."

Lena let out a small laugh. "Everybody needs a mentor."

Sincere shook her head. "I don't trust him."

Lena's expression didn't change, but there was something in her eyes that flickered. "Why not?"

Sincere turned slightly in her seat, finally facing Lena head-on. "Because I know men like Lorde."

Lena leaned back, watching her. "Men like Lorde?"

"Men who think they know what's best for me."

"You say that like it's a bad thing."

"It is a bad thing."

"Or . . ." Lena's voice was lighter, teasing. "Maybe it's exactly what you need."

Sincere shot her a dry look. "You sound like one of those 'submissive woman' podcasts."

Lena laughed. "No, they sound like me."

Sincere rolled her eyes.

Supreme kept driving. But he was listening. This wasn't Lena just running her mouth.

This was Lena planting a seed. And Supreme wasn't sure if Sincere realized it yet.

"I'm serious," Lena continued. "A strong woman with a powerful man? That's the dream, girl. You're out here trying to fight your battles alone when you could have someone who *wants* to protect you, to make sure you win."

Sincere scoffed. "You make it sound like a trade-off."

Lena didn't see the problem. To her, it was a good deal. "It *is* a trade-off. That's life. You want power, you want success? Then you need a man who's already been there. One who knows how to navigate the shit you don't."

Sincere stared at her. "A man who controls me, you mean."

Lena's expression softened slightly. "That's not what I'm saying."

"That's *exactly* what you're saying."

Lena exhaled. "Look, I get it. You don't want to be *controlled.* But men like Lorde? They don't just *control*—they *lead.*"

Sincere was silent for a long moment, digesting Lena's

words. The worst part? She knew Lena believed it. She wasn't just feeding her a line. This was something she had accepted a long time ago. That to be with a man like Lorde, to be in his orbit, to benefit from his power, meant giving something up in return.

Her freedom.

Her autonomy.

Herself.

And yet . . .

Lorde *could* make her life easier.

He *could* eliminate obstacles.

He *could* protect her from the worst of the industry's pitfalls.

But at what cost? She already owed him too much. And Sincere had never been the type to stay indebted for long. She turned back toward the window, shaking her head. "I'd rather do things my own way."

Lena sighed dramatically. "Yeah, I mean, I get that. The man is a little . . . intense."

Sincere snorted. "That's putting it lightly."

Lena shrugged. "Okay, yeah. He's a lot. But that's just a man being a man."

Sincere turned fully to face her now, her interest piqued. "Is it?"

Lena nodded, all confidence. "Yeah. He's powerful. He moves differently. He sees things from angles most people don't. And yeah, that can make him a little controlling, but . . ." She leaned in slightly, lowering her voice like they were exchanging secrets. "Men like that? They *have* to be that way. You don't get to the top by being soft. You don't hold onto power by playing nice."

Sincere was silent for a moment, turning those words over in her mind. She knew men like Lorde. She had seen what they were capable of. And part of her had always believed that strength came with a price. But at the same time . . .

"You say that like it's just something women are supposed to accept," she said finally, her tone measured.

Lena tilted her head. "I mean . . . isn't it?"

Sincere exhaled sharply, shaking her head. "No. It's not."

Throwing her hands in the air out of sheer confusion, Lena rolled her eyes. "Then what do you want, Sincere? A man who lets you run shit? A man who's soft? You really think that's what you need?"

Sincere let out a small, sharp laugh. "Why is it either-or? Why is it always *strong* or *weak*? Why can't it just be . . . *healthy*?"

Lena blinked, like the thought had never even occurred to her.

Supreme glanced at Sincere, a flicker of something unreadable in his expression.

Sincere turned back to the window. "I just think it's wild that we're expected to deal with controlling men and call it protection. Like our choices are either submission or loneliness."

Lena sucked her teeth. "Ain't nobody saying all that." It was at that moment that Lena decided to turn her attention to Supreme. "How about we get a man's opinion? You're Lorde's cousin, aren't you? What do you think?"

"I think you been confusing a lot of controlling niggas with powerful men." Supreme said, still focused on the road. "They only move like that because they think they own shit. And that's fine if we're talking about business. But a *woman*? A *person*? That ain't something you claim. That ain't something you control."

Sincere looked at him, her expression thoughtful.

Lena, on the other hand, wasn't buying it. "So what? You saying powerful men can't have strong women?"

Supreme finally glanced at her through the mirror. His eyes spoke volumes before he even said a word. "I'm saying a powerful man don't need to break a woman just to keep her."

Lena rolled her eyes, but Sincere was still watching Supreme. Something about what he said—*how* he said it—settled differently inside her.

By the time Supreme pulled up to Sincere's place, the car had fallen into an uneasy quiet. Lena had stopped talking. Sincere had stopped engaging. And Supreme had spent the last ten minutes watching how Lena's energy shifted. How her confident, almost playful approach deflated the longer the conversation went on. She was still trying, but for the first time, she didn't seem to be sure of herself.

Sincere turned in her seat, stretching slightly before glancing at Lena. "You coming in?"

It wasn't a loaded question. She wasn't testing or calling her bluff. But Lena hesitated. She glanced at Supreme. Then back at Sincere.

And something changed.

Before, she had been so comfortable in the space she had carved out in Sincere's life. But now she was seeing Sincere differently. Not as the girl she could mold, not as the artist she had been sent to watch over, not even as the same person she had been just a few months ago. She was seeing someone stronger. Someone she couldn't pull as easily. Lena wasn't sure if she liked that.

Sincere frowned slightly. "Lena?"

Lena let out a soft breath. "Actually . . . yeah. I'm not ready for the night to end."

Sincere tilted her head, studying her. "You sure?"

"Yeah, I am." She nodded quickly. "There's an after-party I heard about. Supreme, think you can drop me off?"

Supreme tapped his fingers against the steering wheel, then gave a slow nod. "Wherever you need to go."

Supreme pushed open his door and stepped out, moving around the car with an easy, unhurried stride. When he opened the back door, Sincere stepped out, adjusting her dress as she straightened. She glanced up at him, expecting a casual good night or something, but instead, Supreme nodded toward a car pulling into a parking spot a few feet away.

"Dre trailed us." His voice was low, steady. He didn't like leaving her, not with the way tonight had gone, but he had to. "He'll stay posted up, watching out for you until I get back."

Sincere followed his gaze, spotting Dre as he stepped out of his car, expression unreadable, but alert. She looked back at Supreme and nodded. "All right."

Supreme studied her for a second longer, like he wanted to say something else, but instead, he just gave a short nod before stepping away. He pulled the car door shut behind him, moving smoothly back into the driver's seat. As he shifted gears and pulled onto the road, his thoughts turned back to Lena.

Something had changed.

It wasn't just the way she had hesitated before deciding to leave. It was the look on her face when Sincere had invited her inside. That brief flicker of something—uncertainty, hesitation, conflict. Lena had always been smooth and effortless. She was good at playing her role and keeping her emotions masked beneath layers of manipulation and charm.

But tonight?

Something cracked.

He waited until they hit a red light before shifting his focus back to her, watching her reflection in the rearview mirror. She was staring out of the window, her fingers twisting in her lap, a small tension in her jaw.

"Where we going?" Supreme asked, keeping his voice casual.

Lena blinked, as if coming out of a daze. She hesitated a second before muttering an address. "Some spot in the Quarter. Supposed to be a vibe."

Supreme nodded, making the next turn. He could hear the emptiness in her voice. The drop in energy. She was trying to act unbothered, but she wasn't.

Lena let out a soft sigh, shifting in her seat. "I just need to get my mind off shit," she muttered, almost to herself.

Supreme flicked his eyes to her again in the mirror. She wasn't looking at him. "Yeah?" he said.

Lena let out a small laugh, but it was hollow. "Yeah."

He didn't say anything for a moment, letting the silence stretch between them. He had spent enough time around people like Lena to know when someone was running from something. Supreme tightened his grip on the wheel, jaw ticking slightly.

That was the difference between her and Sincere. At least Sincere was trying to crawl her way out of the wreckage.

But Lena?

She was still choosing the fire.

Still letting it burn her alive.

Supreme couldn't figure out why she was so intent on pulling Sincere back into that old life.

The next morning, Supreme found himself standing outside Sincere's door, knocking harder than necessary just to be annoying. He knew she wasn't awake yet. Which, to be fair, was part of the reason he knocked harder. He needed to see her. Not because of the kiss. Not because of the way she had looked at him afterward, waiting for him to pull away, but never moving first. Not even because of Lorde's call last night, the subtle warning laced between his words still lingering in the back of Supreme's mind.

He was here because Sincere needed better people in her life. And for some reason, he couldn't shake the feeling that he was supposed to be the one to make that happen. Suddenly, he heard slow, sluggish footsteps. His eyes narrowed.

The door yanked open and there she was—half asleep, scowling, looking like she was ready to curse him out. And yet, even in all her barely awake grumpiness, she still looked good.

Her curls were wild, spilling over one side of her face, her skin still warm from sleep. The oversized T-shirt she had on hung off her shoulder, exposing smooth skin, collarbone sharp beneath golden-brown tones.

She had no idea how beautiful she looked like this. And from the glare she was throwing his way, she wouldn't care if he told her. Her voice was hoarse with sleep, her irritation clear.

"Seriously?"

Supreme barely reacted, letting his gaze drop over her once before meeting her eyes again.

She frowned deeper. "What?"

"Damn. Good morning to you too."

Sincere crossed her arms, clearly annoyed that she was standing in front of him looking like she just rolled out of bed. "You woke me up, Supreme. The least you could do is tell me why."

He leaned against the doorframe, arms crossed. "Didn't think you slept in this late."

Her scowl deepened. "I don't. I just—" She stopped, shaking her head. "Never mind. What do you want?"

"You busy?"

She gave him a flat look, then gestured down at herself—barefoot, barely awake, still wearing some T-shirt that definitely didn't belong to her.

"Do I look busy?"

Supreme chuckled, shaking his head. "Not really. But you should be."

Sincere squinted at him. "Why?"

He pushed off the doorframe, jerking his chin toward the hallway behind her. "Go get dressed. Take a ride with me. There's someone I want you to meet."

Her suspicion was immediate. "Who?"

"You'll see."

She exhaled, crossing her arms. "See, that sounds like a setup."

He tilted his head. "Ain't no setup. Just trust me."

She hesitated, searching his face. She didn't trust easily. She kept everyone at arm's length, always questioning motives, always preparing for the worst. He could see it—hesitation warring with something else.

Finally, she let out a slow breath, tilting her head slightly. "Fine. Give me like . . . twenty minutes."

Supreme glanced at his watch. "Fifteen."

Her eyes widened. "Excuse me?"

"Fifteen minutes, ma. Clock's ticking."

She gawked at him for half a second before groaning and stomping off toward her bedroom. "I hate you," she muttered under her breath.

Supreme just chuckled, leaning against the wall as she disappeared down the hallway. He wasn't sure why this felt right—

why bringing Sincere into this next part of his life felt like the right move—but it did.

The drive was quiet.

Sincere sat in the passenger seat, arms folded, eyes flickering to the scenery outside the window. The city was giving way to something slower—streets lined with old oak trees, modest houses with well-kept lawns, the occasional group of kids riding bikes.

It was peaceful.

A world away from what she knew.

Supreme caught her sneaking a glance at him out of the corner of his eye, but she didn't say anything. And for some reason, he found it amusing. Sincere seemed to be curious about where they were going. Which was exactly why he wasn't gonna tell her just yet. Instead, he let the silence ride, his fingers drumming lightly against the steering wheel as they turned onto another quiet street.

Finally, Sincere broke first. "So . . . where exactly are we going?"

Supreme didn't take his eyes off the road. "You'll see."

Sincere exhaled, shaking her head. "I hate when you do that."

His lips twitched slightly, but he didn't respond. Minutes later, he pulled up in front of a small, but well-maintained house—a white-painted bungalow with flowerpots lining the front steps.

Sincere blinked. "This is . . . not what I was expecting."

"Yeah?" Supreme put the car in *park*, cutting the engine. "What were you expecting?"

She tilted her head, studying the place. "I don't know. You just . . . don't seem like the white picket fence type."

"I'm not." Then, after a beat, he added: "Imani is."

Sincere turned her head to him, her brow lifting. "Who's Imani?"

Supreme unbuckled his seat belt and shrugged. "Come find out. I'm thinking she will be happy to see you."

Sincere gave him one last suspicious glance before finally sighing and pushing open the car door.

She followed him up the walkway, taking in the small details—the neatly stacked books on the porch, the wind chimes swaying lazily in the breeze, the small hand-painted sign on the door that read LOVE LIVES HERE.

That made her pause. It was simple, but something about it hit her differently, as if she had stepped into a world she didn't belong in. Like this place had been made for people who grew up knowing what love felt like. That was not her.

Before she could let that thought settle too deep, Supreme knocked once. Then—without hesitation—he reached for the handle and pushed the door open, like he had done it a thousand times before.

Before Supreme could even step inside, a voice rang out from the hallway—loud, exasperated, and clearly unimpressed. "Supreme, I swear to God, if you just walked into my house without knocking like you pay rent—"

The girl who appeared in the hallway was mid-rant when she finally looked up—her eyes landing on Sincere. She froze.

Sincere blinked. Uh . . .

For a full second, the air seemed to shift, the rant completely forgotten. Then—Imani's entire expression transformed in real time. Her exasperation melted away, replaced by pure, unfiltered excitement. "Oh my God."

Sincere was still trying to figure out what was happening when—

"Oh my God!" Imani practically shrieked, her hands flying to her mouth. "Sahara? No, that can't be—shit! I can't believe you're here!"

Sincere took a half-step back, completely thrown. She . . . knew who she was?

She glanced at Supreme, who just leaned against the doorframe. "Sahara meet my little sister, Imani."

"Nice to meet you," Sincere offered her a hand and a polite smile.

Imani practically launched herself forward. Not in an overbearing way, but in a manner that was so purely excited it completely disarmed Sincere.

"Okay, first of all," Imani gushed, grabbing Sincere's hand, "you don't understand. I love you. Your music? Got me through some rough-ass nights. Like, your lyrics? The way you just say shit that people feel, but don't know how to say? That's a gift."

Sincere barely knew what to do with herself. She wasn't used to this kind of energy. She had fans—of course, she had fans.

But this?

This was different. This wasn't adoration. It wasn't the fake industry smiles or the forced, performative praise. This was real.

Raw.

Genuine.

Sincere actually felt herself blushing. "Damn," she muttered, running a hand over her head, suddenly feeling awkward. "You about to make me blush."

Imani beamed. "Nah, because for real—I've been a fan since *Poison and Honey.*"

Sincere's brows lifted. That was her first project, before she had a label or real backing. "You really go that far back?" she asked, half-intrigued, half-skeptical.

"Girl, yes!" Imani squeezed her hands. "That album? Changed my life. The way you talked about grief? About feeling lost? I felt seen."

Sincere's chest tightened. Because damn. She had fans. She

knew that. People who rocked with her music. Who played her songs on repeat. Who screamed her lyrics in concert crowds.

But this?

This was personal.

Imani had felt her. Not just as an artist—but as a person.

She cleared her throat, suddenly overwhelmed. "I—uh, wow. Thank you. That means a lot."

"Nah, thank you." Imani grinned, practically glowing. Then—her head tilted. "Wait—how do y'all even know each other?"

Supreme, who had been leaning against the doorframe, finally spoke. "I'm the one keeping her ass outta trouble."

Imani scoffed, rolling her eyes. "Oh, so now you're out here saving people?"

Sincere was unable to hold back her sarcasm. "Yeah, I was surprised too."

Supreme shot them both a look, but Imani just laughed, grabbing Sincere's hand and pulling her inside. "Well, don't just stand here like strangers. Come in, come in!"

Sincere let herself be pulled in, warmth settling in her chest at the effortless energy between them. This girl was real. She didn't seem to have any ulterior motives. Just excitement, honesty, and a love for music.

For the first time in a long time, Sincere felt like a normal girl. She glanced back at Supreme, who was watching her with that same unreadable expression he always had. This time, she thought she saw something beneath it. Something softer—understanding.

She swallowed, turning back to Imani as they settled into the small living room. This wasn't just a casual visit. And deep down, she knew—Supreme was trying to show her something about family and belonging. What life could be and maybe even about what she could still have.

Imani moved effortlessly through the cozy living room, still radiating excitement as she gestured toward the couch. “Make yourself comfortable! You want something to drink? I got sweet tea, lemonade—”

Sincere settled onto the couch, taking Imani at her offer. “Sweet tea? You really a Southern girl, huh?”

Imani gasped dramatically, placing a hand over her heart. “Ma’am. First of all, put some respect on sweet tea. It’s a staple.”

Sincere laughed, shaking her head. “Nah, see, I already know y’all drink it like it’s medicine out here.”

Imani grinned, already heading toward the kitchen. “As we should.”

The warmth of pride settled in Supreme’s chest. His gaze shifted between them before he leaned against the doorway, arms crossed. He didn’t even need to say anything. He knew this would happen.

Sincere and Imani clicked immediately.

It was easy.

Natural.

It was the kind of conversation Sincere didn’t get to have often—one without pretense, strategy, and industry bullshit. She didn’t realize how much she’d missed this.

Imani reappeared a few moments later, two glasses in hand. She handed one to Sincere and plopped down onto the couch beside her, tucking her legs under herself.

“So.” Imani grinned, eyes sparkling. “Spill it. My college girl life is nothing compared to all the things you get to do. I want to know it everything!”

Sincere raised a brow, amused. “Everything?”

“Girl, yes!” Imani waved a hand dramatically. “What’s it like? Your life? Your career? Being in the industry?” She lowered her voice into something teasing. “Do you just wake up fabulous every morning, or is it work?”

Sincere chuckled, shaking her head. "You really wanna know?"

"Duh."

Sincere exhaled, rolling the glass between her fingers. "Honestly?"

Imani nodded, leaning in.

"It's a scam."

The irony in her tone made Imani freeze. Then, she blinked before bursting out laughing. "Stop."

Sincere grinned, but shrugged. "I'm serious. Yeah, it's a dream in a lot of ways, but the part people don't see?" She exhaled. "It's exhausting."

Imani tilted her head. "Like, in what way?"

Sincere hesitated for a moment before answering. "Like . . . you don't get to just be a person. You have to be a brand. You have to be accessible, but mysterious. Relatable, but untouchable. And you're constantly surrounded by people who want something from you. Even the ones who say they don't."

Imani's expression softened. "Damn."

Sincere let out a quiet laugh, shaking her head. "I sound ungrateful, huh?"

Imani frowned. "No, not at all. You sound real."

Sincere studied her for a beat. It had been a while since someone told her that.

Imani leaned back into the couch. "What do you miss the most? About life before all of this?"

Sincere hesitated. She never let herself think about that. Now, sitting here in this quiet house, next to a girl who had a completely different life, the answer was clear.

She exhaled. "Freedom."

Imani nodded like she understood. "I get that."

Sincere gave her a dry look. "You get that? How? Girl, you're in college. You got all the freedom in the world."

Imani laughed. "That's what you think." She shrugged. "I mean, don't get me wrong—I love school. But there's pressure too, just in different ways."

Sincere tilted her head. "Like what?"

"Like . . ." Imani sighed. "Like figuring out what the hell I'm supposed to do with my life. Balancing school, family expectations, trying to keep up a social life while making sure I don't fail my damn classes. Making sure I don't let my brothers down."

Sincere frowned slightly. "They put that pressure on you?"

Imani hesitated before shaking her head. "Not like that. They just . . . look out for me. A lot." She shot Supreme a knowing look. "Like *too much*."

Supreme smirked, taking a slow sip from his drink. "You say that like it's a bad thing."

Imani gave him a pointed look. "It is when I'm trying to have a life and my overprotective brother be threatening every dude who looks at me."

Sincere snorted, turning to Supreme. "Oh, you're that type?"

Supreme gave her a look. "Damn right."

Sincere smirked, shaking her head. "Yeah, I can see that."

Imani rolled her eyes. "Exactly. He needs to chill."

Sincere laughed, but something about Imani's words stuck with her.

That protection.

That security.

Imani had someone looking out for her. Making sure she was good. Making sure she didn't get lost in the world.

Sincere never had that. She had to look out for herself. And maybe that's why being here—in this house, in this moment—felt so strange. Because this was what life could've been. She stared at Imani, taking in the small, cozy house, the framed photos on the walls, the textbooks stacked on the coffee table.

It was so simple.

So . . . normal.

And it hit her then—she never got to have this. She never got to be just a girl in her twenties, figuring shit out. She had been thrust into the world too fast, too young. She'd been thrown into survival mode before she even knew what it meant to live.

Imani was what she could've been if she had brothers like Supreme. If she had protection instead of predators. A strange tightness settled in her chest.

Maybe in another life . . . she could've had this.

Maybe in another life . . . she could've been free.

"You okay?"

Sincere blinked, snapping out of her thoughts.

Imani was watching her, brows raised in curiosity.

Sincere forced a small smile, nodding. "Yeah." She wasn't ready to admit what she was thinking. But when she looked at Imani, she felt something she hadn't let herself feel in a long time.

Hope.

That scared her more than anything.

Sincere was still laughing at something Imani had said when Supreme's phone buzzed in his pocket. He ignored it at first. His focus was on her—on the way she seemed lighter here, more at ease than he'd ever seen her. No mask, no industry politics, just existing.

Then his phone buzzed again. His gut tightened. He already knew who it was before he even looked at the screen.

Lorde.

His jaw flexed as he pulled the phone from his pocket, barely glancing at the name before swiping to answer. "Yeah."

"Damn, you been quiet lately."

At first, Supreme didn't react, but then he saw no other recourse but to respond. "Just handling things. Like always."

Lorde chuckled lowly, but there was something in the sound—something edged, like he was waiting to catch Supreme slipping. "Yeah, I figured. You been handling things really well, huh?"

Supreme knew what this was. Lorde was probing, feeling him out, trying to see how much he could get him to reveal without asking outright. So he stayed silent and waited for Lorde to talk.

"I hear she's been keeping her head up," Lorde finally said. "That's good." He continued. "She's important to the plan, you know. You keeping her out of trouble?"

Supreme let the words settle. He knew what Lorde meant. He wasn't just talking about Sincere's sobriety. He was talking about him.

Them.

Supreme took a slow breath, keeping his tone even. "She's fine. I'm making sure of it."

Lorde hummed as though he was considering that answer, trying to decide whether or not he believed it. "That right?"

Supreme said nothing.

Lorde let the silence stretch.

Then, as if to steer the conversation elsewhere, Supreme added, "She wanted to get some fresh air. Took a little ride out to the country. Caught up with a friend."

Then Lorde exhaled slowly.

Thinking.

Calculating.

Processing.

Supreme could almost hear his mind turning over the words. *What friend? Who does she have other than Lena?*

But Lorde didn't ask or challenge it. He just let it sit there, unspoken. "I been working, you know."

Supreme's eyes narrowed slightly, but he didn't respond. Lorde's voice was different now.

Lighter. Conversational. Like they were just two men talking business. But Supreme knew better. Lorde never just talked. Everything he said had intent.

"Lining up some good things," Lorde continued. "Expanding in ways that'll make us untouchable."

Supreme didn't react, he just waited.

And sure enough, Lorde chuckled, like he could feel the skepticism on the other end of the line. "I was hesitant to tell you at first. Thought you'd be stubborn about it. But I want you to hear me out. Just keep an open mind."

Supreme exhaled slowly, already not liking where this was going. "How open?" His voice carried a sharp edge of doubt.

Lorde let out a low grunt, like he was amused by Supreme's distrust. "Relax, man. I ain't on no dumb shit."

But Supreme wasn't convinced. Not after hearing what Dre told him. His grip tightened on the phone as he asked the one thing he really wanted to know. "This got anything to do with you meeting with Silvan?"

For the first time, Lorde didn't have an immediate response. Then, he exhaled. "You ever play chess?"

Supreme frowned slightly. "What?"

"Chess," Lorde repeated. "You ever play?"

Supreme's jaw ticked. "Not really," he lied. He had to know where Lorde was going with this.

Lorde made a low sound of amusement at Supreme's response. Clearly, he thought of himself as the superior one. "See, that's the problem. Everybody thinks the king is the most important piece. But me? I like the knight."

Supreme said nothing.

"The knight moves differently," Lorde mused. "Unexpected. Makes people comfortable until it don't. Most people don't even realize when it's positioned to strike."

And there it was. Lorde's barely concealed threat. "You get what I'm saying?"

Supreme flexed his fingers against the leather. "Yeah." His voice was flat and controlled, but inside he felt the board shift.

Lorde let the words settle, then exhaled, shifting back to that easy, relaxed tone like he hadn't just spent the last minute lacing his words with barely concealed threats. "Aight, then. Keep handling things."

The line clicked and then silence.

Supreme lowered the phone, staring at the darkened screen for a moment. Then he exhaled, slipping it back into his pocket. Yeah, this shit was about to get real, and he needed to be ready.

His jaw tightened as he turned back toward the house, willing his face into something neutral. He had to move carefully now, because one wrong move and the whole board would go up in flames.

Lorde was always two moves ahead and Supreme could feel the board shifting beneath him. He rolled his shoulders, pushing off the wall. He'd deal with that later. Right now, he had something else to focus on.

Inside, laughter filled the space. He followed the sound, his steps slow, his mind still halfway caught in the conversation he'd just had. But when he stepped into the doorway, he found himself pausing. Sincere and Imani were sprawled across the couch, laughing so hard they could barely breathe.

Imani was in mid-story, dramatically acting something out, her hands flying as she reenacted whatever ridiculous scenario she had been caught in. Sincere was fully invested. Her eyes were bright, her head tipped back, her arms hugging herself as she gasped for air between bouts of laughter.

Everything about her was . . . different. There was no tension in her shoulders or calculating wariness in her expression. She looked . . . genuinely happy. He just stood there, watching. *This* was exactly what he wanted. He had known this would happen because Imani needed a friend and it was clear that Sincere did. For the first time since he met her, he was seeing what she could be if she wasn't always fighting to survive. If she had people like Imani around her instead of people like Lena.

Sincere exhaled a laugh as she leaned back into the couch, shaking her head. Across from her, Imani was still animatedly reenacting some embarrassing college moment, complete with exaggerated gestures and dramatic facial expressions.

"So then," Imani continued, barely containing her own laughter, "I turn around, and this dude—this *grown* man, mind you—is there with my *entire* wig in his hands, jumping around and shouting like he just caught the Holy Ghost. I was so mortified, I damn near left my own body."

Sincere clutched her stomach, doubling over. "Stop! No, he didn't snatched your entire wig. I *know* you wanted to run away." "Ran? Girl, I teleported out of his place. I ain't never moved so fast in my life." Imani wiped at her eyes, shaking her head. "And now, every time I see him on campus, he just gives me this look, like he got dirt on me."

Sincere leaned back into the couch, her arms draped lazily over the plush cushions as laughter tumbled from her lips. She couldn't remember the last time she laughed like this—fully, freely, without thinking about *who was watching* or *what it looked like.*

Imani had the kind of energy that made you forget your worries, even if just for a little while.

"Okay, okay, but wait," Imani gasped between giggles, holding up a hand. "I didn't even get to the worst part."

Sincere wiped the corner of her eye, still catching her breath. "Sis, what could possibly be worse than your wig getting accidentally snatched mid-orgasm?"

Imani grinned, her dimples deep as she leaned forward conspiratorially. "So, fast-forward two weeks. I'm walking to class, minding my own business, and I hear someone go, '*Yo!*' I turn around, and it's him. The wig snatcher."

Sincere gasped, eyes wide. "Not *the wig snatcher*!"

"Girl, yes!" Imani smacked her thigh for emphasis. "I had no idea that we had a class together! So, anyways, that was my first and last time having a drunken one-night stand."

Sincere wiped at her eyes, still breathless from laughing. "Okay, okay, but you gotta tell me what happened after."

Imani grinned, shaking her head. "Girl, I had to transfer out of that class. You think I was about to sit across from the wig snatcher for the rest of the semester?"

Sincere let out a loud laugh. "No way you really transferred."

"Deadass," Imani confirmed. "I dropped that class so fast the professor was probably confused as hell."

Sincere shook her head, smiling. "That's tragic."

"Nah," Imani said, waving her off. "That was survival."

Their laughter filled the space, bouncing off the walls, something warm and real stretching between them.

Supreme let himself enjoy the sound and just sat back and watched. He observed how quickly they clicked, how naturally they fell into conversation, how the walls that Sincere always kept up were completely *gone* around Imani. He knew his sister. She had a way of bringing light into a room, of making people feel like they belonged, no matter who they were. And he knew how much Sincere needed this.

A *real* friend.

And that's why he brought her here. Because Imani needed this just as much. She had been through a lot—had lost people and faced her own battles. She was strong, but she didn't have many women in her life that she could be vulnerable with. She needed a friend who understood the weight of expectation, of constantly having eyes on you, of trying to find your way in a world that always wanted to put you in a box. Sincere was that friend. Watching them together now, Supreme knew he had made the right call. They were good for each other.

After what felt like hours of laughter, shared stories, and easy conversation, Sincere finally glanced at the time. Her eyes widened. "Damn, I didn't even realize how late it got."

Imani stretched, groaning. "That's how it always is when you're vibin'. Time don't exist."

"That's facts." She stood, smoothing out her outfit. "I should probably head out, though."

Imani pouted. "Ugh, fine. But don't think you're getting rid of me. I'm calling you *all the time* now."

Sincere laughed. "I'll answer."

Without hesitation, Imani pulled her into a warm hug. Sincere hesitated only for a second before hugging her back. It was rare for her to *trust* someone this quickly, but something about Imani just felt *right*.

As they pulled back, Imani beamed. "I hope I see you again soon."

Sincere nodded, her lips curling slightly. "Yeah. Me too."

As she followed Supreme toward the car, something settled in her chest. A quiet kind of hope she hadn't let herself feel in a long time.

Maybe I can have this.

Maybe I don't have to be alone.

The drive back was quiet. Sincere sat with her head against the window, fingers absently tracing patterns on the glass, lost in thought.

Supreme, on the other hand, gripped the steering wheel, his mind moving a mile a minute. Lorde was up to something. He had felt it the moment he answered that call. That pause when he mentioned Silvan. That shift in Lorde's tone, like he was working through something in real time, figuring out how much to say and how much to hold back.

It didn't sit right.

That was the thing about Lorde—when something didn't sit right, that meant it was about to get *real* uncomfortable for somebody. Supreme had spent years navigating around his mind games, never reacting too fast, never letting Lorde see when he had him figured out. Right now, that's exactly what Lorde was waiting for.

Waiting to see *if* Supreme knew. *How much* Supreme knew.

And that meant one thing:

Whatever Lorde was cooking up with Silvan?

It was deeper than business.

If Lorde was planning something reckless, something that could bring heat to the Saints, Supreme needed to know *now.*

Before things spiraled.

Before it was too late to stop it.

His eyes flicked toward Sincere in the passenger seat. She was still quiet, still lost in her own world, but there was something different about her now. For the first time since he met her, she had spent an entire day *just being* with no image to uphold or vultures circling her every move. She was just a woman, kicking back, enjoying real company.

It made him realize how much she'd been missing that. How much she *needed* it. And Lorde wasn't about to let her have it. He was always watching. Whatever game he was playing now . . . Supreme needed to be two steps ahead before the board flipped over.

Chapter 16

Lena never walked. She glided. With her shoulders back and hips swaying just enough to be noticed, she kept her eyes hidden behind designer shades as she moved down Canal Street like she owned it. And in a way, she did.

Men stared. Women whispered. The heat of the late afternoon sun kissed her skin. It felt good, but it was nothing compared to the feeling of being watched. And Lena loved being watched. She tightened her grip around the boutique shopping bags in her hand, her freshly manicured nails tapping against the glossy surface. Retail therapy always worked to fix her mood. Well, *almost.*

The high of spending money—money that wasn't even really hers—wore off quicker these days. She had picked up a few designer heels, a new handbag, and a silk dress that would probably end up in the back of her closet after one wear. She didn't need any of it, but shopping made her feel important, like she was still winning. In the world she lived in, perception was everything.

As she adjusted one of her bags, a voice cut through the street noise all around her. "Damn, ma, you really gon' act like you don't see me?"

There he was just as she remembered him: Tall, athletic, and dressed well, but not flashy. The kind of man women took home to their families. The kind who probably paid his bills on time, remembered birthdays, and planned weekend getaways instead of last-minute flights to nowhere. A good guy. The exact type of man Lena *should* want, but he did absolutely nothing for her.

Still, she pursed her lips and tilted her sunglasses down slightly as she gave him a once-over. "And what exactly do you think you got that's worth my time?"

He let out a soft laugh, shaking his head as he stepped closer. "You tell me," he said, his voice smooth. "'Cause you keep dodging me, but somehow, I always run into you."

Lena shifted the shopping bags on her arm, feigning indifference. He was persistent. She liked that.

Just . . . not enough.

"And yet," she teased, "you still ain't take the hint."

His grin widened. "I took the hint. I just don't care."

She let out a laugh, unable to help herself. He was cute and confident. But there was something about him that was just . . . *too safe.*

"You don't even know what you're chasing," she said, adjusting the strap of her bag on her shoulder.

"Maybe not," he admitted. "But I know what I want."

Lena twisted up her lips, pretending to consider his words as she reached into one of her bags, pulling out the delicate gold bracelet she had just bought. She slipped it onto her wrist, admiring the way it caught the sunlight.

"You ever think about slowing down?" he asked, his tone shifting slightly. "Actually letting someone get to know you for real?"

Lena's smile faltered for just a second. She slid her sunglasses back up her nose. "You trying to be my therapist now?"

"Nah," he said, still grinning. "Just a man who knows you gotta get tired of the game eventually."

That made her pause. Not because he was wrong . . . But because he actually thought he was right. Lena tilted her head slightly, watching him. He *really* believed that one day, a woman like her would wake up and decide she wanted the house with the white picket fence. That she'd trade late-night industry parties and expensive vacations for PTA meetings and meal prepping. Maybe for some women, that was true, but Lena craved more.

She didn't want stability. She wanted a man with power behind his name. This guy wasn't that. Lena sighed, before allowing her lips to slowly curve at the corners. "Boy, you don't want none of this trouble," she teased, slipping the bracelet back into her bag.

He chuckled, stepping closer. "That what you call it? Trouble?"

She tossed a look over her shoulder as she turned away. "Oh, baby. You have no idea."

He was still smiling when she rounded the corner. But Lena's own smile faded as soon as he was out of sight.

Dior heels clicked against the pavement as she turned the corner, her shopping bags swinging at her sides. The thrill of her encounter with her admirer had already started to wear off, replaced by the steady, nagging itch of dissatisfaction. No matter how many times she tried to convince herself otherwise, normal would never be enough for her.

The city around her was alive with the noise of cars honking, the occasional shout from street vendors, the murmur of conversation floating through the air. She barely noticed it, too lost in her thoughts. And then a shiny black car pulled up alongside her, slowing to a stop. She felt it before she saw it. The fine hairs on her arms prickled to attention the way they did when a man who made things move stepped on the scene.

The tinted window rolled down just enough to reveal a familiar face.

Lorde.

His expression was unreadable and his gaze locked onto hers.

Lena's heart stuttered before she contorted her face into something cool, forcing herself to appear unimpressed.

"How long you been entertaining that nerd-ass dude?" His voice was smooth with a hint of teasing, but there was something sharp beneath it and she definitely felt it.

Lena scoffed, rolling her eyes. "Oh, so you out here lurking now? That's cute."

With lips tugged upwards slightly, he stared at her with dead eyes. "Ain't nobody lurking. You just make it real easy to see when you on bullshit."

Lena kept walking, acting unbothered, but her pulse had picked up. He had seen the guy talking to her, which meant that he'd been watching her. Of course, he had. Lorde saw everything. That rattled her to the core.

She played it off, tossing her hair over her shoulder. "Please. That was nothing."

Lorde exhaled a quiet laugh, shaking his head. Then, suddenly, the smile was off his face and his voice dropped. "All right now. Don't get fucked up out here trying to play cute."

Lena's stomach tightened. That teasing lilt was gone. His tone had shifted, subtle but lethal. She swallowed hard, gripping the handles of her bags a little tighter.

"You know I don't like what's mine smiling in the next nigga's face."

She knew better than to argue.

She knew better than to say, *I'm not yours.*

Because they both knew that wasn't true.

Instead, she swallowed down the words, and shifted against the car door, tapping her nails against the handle. "You tryna take me somewhere, or you just stopping to check my phone records?"

Lorde's reply came fast. "Both."

Lena exhaled, then, without hesitation, yanked open the door and slid inside. The moment the door shut, the outside world disappeared. And whatever he had planned for her was set in motion. She already knew she wouldn't say no, because she never did. Lorde didn't take kindly to people rejecting him.

A chill danced up her spine as she sat down on the leather seats and his chauffeur pulled away. There it was. The fear that his presence instilled in her. The part of him that terrified and thrilled her. It made her skin prickle, made her breath hitch, made her want to run and stay all at once. And the part of her that wanted power, the part that wanted to matter, ate this up. In his world, a man like Lorde only claimed something he thought had value and, this time, that something was her.

When they got to their destination, Lorde didn't say anything for a long time after parking the car. The sound of the river filled the silence, steady and unbothered, completely indifferent to the storm building inside the vehicle. Then, finally, he moved.

With a slow, unhurried motion, he tapped on the front and the driver jumped to action to open his door. Lorde stepped out and Lena watched as he strolled toward the riverbank, his posture relaxed, his hands slipping into his pockets like he had all the time in the world. He stopped by a large rock near the edge of the water and, without looking back, gave a lazy nod.

"Come here," he called back at her.

Lena swallowed hard, her stomach tightening. It wasn't just what he said, it was *how* he said it. She hesitated only for a second before getting to it. With a heavy exhale, she steeled herself before pushing open her own door and stepping out.

The cold air hit her instantly, sending a chill down her spine as she wrapped her arms around herself and moved toward him.

She wasn't stupid.

She knew better than to test him tonight.

The second she sat down beside him on the rock, Lorde leaned back slightly, tilting his head toward her, his expression unreadable. "Now, let's kick it for a minute," he said casually, "tell me about Sincere. What happened at the party?"

Lena had known this was coming. She had prepared for this conversation all night. But now that she was here—sitting beside him, alone, with nothing but dark water and silence surrounding them—something about it felt so threatening. Her throat felt tight.

She forced herself to keep her voice even. "She was clean."

Lorde arched a brow. "Clean?"

"She didn't use. Not even a sip of liquor." Lena wet her lips, her stomach twisting as she added, "I tried. I did everything I could, but she wasn't having it."

Lorde grunted lowly, the tips of his fingers drumming lightly against his thigh as he considered her words. His gaze flashed toward the water. "That's not what I wanted to hear, Lena," he finally said, his voice smooth, but edged with steel. "I don't ask for much, but when I do, I expect results."

Lena's chest tightened. She knew that tone. She'd heard it before, just never directed at her. It was the same one he used when he was two seconds away from putting someone in the ground. She swallowed hard, her fingers twitching in her lap. "Lorde—"

"You've been slipping," he interrupted, his voice still calm. "You had one job. Keep her close. Keep her hooked. Keep her dependent. Make her trust me."

Lena's breath quickened. "I—"

"But now?" He tilted his head slightly, studying her like she was a puzzle piece that didn't quite fit. "Now she's pulling away. Maybe you weren't the person for a job like this."

Lena clenched her jaw. "I can still fix it."

Lorde was quiet for a long time. Then, in one slow motion, he reached into his pocket. Lena's entire body locked up and her breath stopped. Her heartbeat pounded in her ears, her vision narrowing as her eyes locked onto his hand.

Waiting.

Watching.

For a second, the world around her shrank. All the noise around her faded away. Her heart stilled as Lorde began to pull out his hand . . .

. . . and pulled out a cigarette.

Lena let out a shaky breath, her entire body sagging in relief as he brought it to his lips, lit the end, and took a slow drag. She thought for sure he was going to end her for good. Her relief didn't last long, however, because as soon as he exhaled, blowing a stream of smoke into the air, he turned to her and smiled. It was a slow, spine-chilling smile.

Lena's fingers curled into fists. She hated the way he purposely played with her emotions. He loved to toy with her fear like it amused him. But more than anything, she hated that it worked every time.

Lorde took another slow drag of his cigarette before speaking again, his voice softer now, more thoughtful. "You can still fix it," he repeated, nodding slightly.

"Good. I was hoping you'd say that." Lena exhaled shakily, forcing herself to nod. *This is fine. I can do this. I just need to get back in control. Get back on his good side.*

"I'll make sure she falls back in line," she promised. "Just tell me what you need me to do."

Lorde turned his head slightly, looking at her in that way that made her feel like he could see right through her. Somehow along the way she stopped being herself and became everything he needed her to be. Knowing it did nothing, because it was too late to change it. She was already in too deep.

"I've already got some ideas, but I gotta put some things in place first." Lorde flicked the ash from his cigarette, exhaling slowly. "You'll know when the time comes."

Lena forced herself to breathe, nodding once. She could do this, even though she wasn't sure she wanted to. In the end, what she wanted didn't matter, because she didn't have a choice. And as Lorde leaned back, relishing the moment, it was clear that he knew that too.

The entire way back to Lena's apartment, Lorde didn't speak. The only noise around them was the sound of the car's engine as they moved through the city. He used silence to his advantage, allowing the pressure of it to weigh on his victims like an anvil on their chest. He wasn't even looking at her anymore. It was clear that she was only valuable to him when she was doing what he needed her to do.

Lena's nerves were on edge. She knew Lorde well enough to know that silence wasn't always just silence. Sometimes, it was patience—a waiting game. She kept her eyes on the neon blur of passing streetlights, hands fidgeting in her lap. Then, just when she was beginning to convince herself that maybe he wasn't about to spring something on her, his voice finally cut through the quiet.

"I know what I'm asking you to do is hard."

Lena's stomach flipped. Her fingers curled tighter together, but she kept her expression neutral, her lips pressing together as he continued.

"But guess what?" Lorde went on. "I'm gonna give you a gift to help you get through it."

She turned her head toward him, cautious. He still wasn't looking at her, but he pulled his phone from his pocket, tapped the screen a few times, then held it out toward her. Lena frowned slightly before taking it. The moment she saw what was on the screen, the breath in her lungs vanished and her entire world tilted.

It was him . . . Her baby brother.

He was a little older than she remembered. Taller, his face much sharper, but still carrying a little baby fat. He was playing in a backyard, kicking around a small red soccer ball. Her heart clenched tight as tears came to her eyes. She had spent so long searching for him before she finally gave up and accepted that she would never see him again.

"Go to the next picture," Lorde told her.

Her fingers trembled as she swiped the screen. It was him again, this time sitting in a classroom, writing in a journal. His head was slightly tilted like he was concentrating hard.

"One more time," Lorde pushed her.

She swiped again to another picture. This one of him laughing with a friend. She covered her mouth with her hand. She hadn't seen him since the day she left New Orleans for Hollywood. She was running from her stepfather, promising herself that once she got enough money, she would come back for her brother.

Unfortunately, the day never came. In one of his drunken rages, her stepfather killed her mother before killing himself and her brother was placed in foster care. By the time Lena came back to get him, he'd been adopted by a family who wanted to keep the adoption closed.

"Oh my God," she whispered.

Tears burned at the backs of her eyes, but she blinked rapidly, refusing to let them fall.

Lorde's voice was low, soothing. "I told you I would find him."

Lena finally looked at him, all of her emotions crashing into her at once. "How?" she rasped. "Where—where is he?"

Lorde exhaled slowly, taking his phone back. "Somewhere safe."

Lena shook her head. "You don't understand. I've been looking everywhere for him. I thought—" Her voice cracked and she swallowed hard before finding her voice. "I thought I lost him forever."

Lorde tapped his fingers against his leg, pensively. "You didn't. He's been there the whole time."

Lena's breath caught in her throat. She had spent years feeling like she had failed him. Like she had allowed him to slip through the cracks of the system when she abandoned him after feeling like God had abandoned her. She wiped at her face, suddenly hyperaware of how vulnerable she was in this state. She hated this part of her. She didn't like feeling so exposed.

Lorde studied her for a beat, taking in the way that she shifted so quickly. Then, smoothly, easily, he delivered the killing blow. "I can get him back for you."

Lena froze.

The car might as well have stopped moving with the way the air in her lungs stalled.

Lorde's voice was calm and certain as he spoke again. "You two can have a nice house and a real life together. I'll take care of everything."

Lena turned toward him fully, desperation clawing its way into her throat. "How?"

Lorde leaned back slightly, tilting his head toward her, the faintest trace of a smile on his lips. "Just keep answering your phone. When I tell you the next move, I need you to do it."

Lena's stomach dropped.

There it was.

The catch.

The unspoken contract that came with anything Lorde offered.

Her mouth went dry. She already knew. But still, she asked. "What do you want?"

Lorde's smile widened, but there was no warmth behind it. "I need her broken," he said simply.

She flinched. There was no need to ask who. They both knew who he was talking about.

Lorde's gaze flickered with something darker. "Completely dependent on me. That's the only way she'll be loyal."

Lena's heart pounded.

"Once she's mine, this whole empire's locked down." He exhaled, casually, like he wasn't completely unraveling her world in real time. "You think you can do that for me?"

Lena's fingers dug into her lap, her mind screaming at her, her heart pulling in the opposite direction. She shook her head, her voice barely above a whisper. "She doesn't deserve that. She's my friend."

Lorde's expression didn't change, but something in his eyes flickered. Something cold, something dangerous. "She's not your friend. You're only there because I put you there." He leaned in slightly, his voice dropping to a near-whisper, the words curling around her like a vise. "And she only keeps you around because you make her feel good about herself. That's all. You're her little sidekick. The girl she keeps close to remind her that she's above you."

Lena shook her head, but the words dug deep.

"You think she'd pick you over her career?" Lorde pressed, his tone deceptively soft. "Over Supreme?"

Lena swallowed hard as the images of Sincere and Supreme together flashed through her mind.

"So . . . you want your brother or you gonna choose yourself over him again."

The words landed like a punch to the gut. Lena's breath shuddered out of her lips as her defenses crumbled. Her resolve was caving in under the pressure of her competing loyalties.

Lorde sat back, watching her with a patience that made her stomach twist. The fact was she already knew she'd lost. There was no choice here and there never was. She exhaled shakily and then, slowly, tears slid silently down her cheeks as she nodded.

Lorde's lips curled with satisfaction. "Good girl."

With a smooth flick of his wrist, he reached into the center console and pulled out a small bag and tossed it onto her lap. Lena's fingers clenched around it like a lifeline.

Lorde's voice was easy and smooth as he spoke next. "Keep being good to Daddy," he murmured, his dark eyes shining with amusement. "And Daddy will keep being good to you."

Lena squeezed her eyes shut. And in that moment, a sad certainty came to light.

There is no coming back from this.

The rest of the ride back was quiet. Lena sat in the passenger seat, her legs crossed tightly, fingers gripping the bag in her lap like it might disappear if she let go. She could still feel the heat of Lorde's words on her skin. The choice she had just made pressed into her chest like a fist.

I have no other option.

That was the lie she told herself.

Sincere would understand if she knew the whole story.

She had to.

It wasn't like Lena *wanted* to do this. She wasn't setting her up, not really. She was just . . . making sure she didn't stray too far away from Lorde. This wasn't bad, really. All he wanted was to give her everything.

All I'm doing is making sure she stays where she belongs until she realizes it's the best thing for her.

Lena swallowed hard. Who was she trying to convince?

Lorde had wrapped his fingers around her ribs and squeezed, using the only thing she still cared about to bend her to his will. Somewhere in the back of her mind, she heard a voice saying, *You're weak.* But that wasn't true. She was smart. This was about survival. If Sincere was really her friend, she'd get it. She'd forgive her. She always did.

Lorde's voice cut through her spiraling thoughts. "You good?"

She blinked, turning her head slightly, trying to keep her expression neutral. "Yeah. I'm straight."

He glanced at her, his gaze sharp, unreadable. "Good."

Lena exhaled slowly, looking back at the bag of pills in her lap. Her hands trembled slightly as she opened the bag. Then she thought of Sincere and the change in her since she stopped using. Her glowing skin. The way her eyes were brighter now. The way she stood taller. It really did make a big difference. And for the first time, Lena felt something unexpected.

Jealousy.

It wasn't the kind of jealousy that made her want to drag someone down just to feel better about herself. This was deeper than that and much more painful. Because while Sincere was strong enough to make hard choices, Lena had just proven that she didn't have the same kind of strength.

The car slowed as they pulled up to her place. Lorde barely looked at her as he put the car in *park*. "Handle that shit. You know what I need."

"Don't worry." Lena nodded, forcing her lips into a tight smile. "You know I got you."

She grabbed the bag and stepped out, her heels clicking against the pavement. She didn't turn around or wait for Lorde to say anything else. Once inside her apartment, she locked the door behind her, dropping the bag onto the counter and staring at it. Then, before she could give herself a chance to talk herself out of it, she grabbed the bag, walked to the bathroom, and emptied the contents into the toilet.

Her heart pounded as the pills dissolved into nothing. If Sincere could do it, so could she. Lena's jaw clenched as she hit the handle, watching it all flush away. Even after it all disappeared, her hands were still shaking. But this time it wasn't from withdrawal. It was from fear of not knowing what would come next.

Chapter 17

Sincere sat curled up on the couch, phone in hand, scrolling through a list of creative writing programs. She wasn't sure why she kept doing this to herself—reading through college websites like she was actually about to apply. But something about the idea had been tugging at her more and more lately. Perhaps it was the need for something stable that had nothing to do with the music and the expectations that came with being Sahara instead of just . . . her.

Her thumbs hovered over the screen. Supreme and Imani were supposed to be pulling up any minute now. Imani was going to bring over some of her poetry and Sincere was going to help her sharpen it, turn it into something more structured, something that could live on a beat. In exchange, Imani had agreed to answer some of Sincere's questions about college. She wanted to know more about what it was really like and what she'd have to do to get in.

A knock at the door pulled her attention. She set her phone down, stretching slightly as she padded toward the door. The moment she swung it open she was surprised about who she saw.

Lena stood there instead, propped up against the doorframe,

grinning like she'd been waiting on this moment all day. "Surprise, bitch!"

Sincere blinked. "Lena? What are you doing here?"

Lena stepped inside without waiting for an invite, kicking the door shut behind her. In one hand, she clutched a half-full bottle of 1942, and in the other, a Chanel tote dangled from her wrist, stuffed with who-knew-what. "Damn, I know you ain't forgot about me already." She spun on Sincere, eyebrows lifted. "Surprised to see me?"

Sincere exhaled, shutting the door fully before turning to face her. "I mean . . . yeah. You didn't say you were coming."

Lena waved that off like it was irrelevant. "Babe, what kinda best friend would I be if I let you sit up in here all night without a proper girl sesh?" She dropped onto the couch, kicking off her slides. "I need to talk."

Sincere studied her for a beat. "Talk about what?"

Lena huffed, setting the bottle on the coffee table. "Niggas."

Sincere's brows lifted slightly. "Which one?"

Lena paused. Her first thought was Lorde. But the one man she really loved was the one she could never tell her best friend about. She stalled, reaching for the bottle, running her fingers over the label like the words she needed were printed there.

That was all Sincere needed to fill in the silence herself. "Wait . . . is it that guy you've been seen with? The one from Lorde's crew?"

Lena exhaled dramatically. "Yeah. That's him. Milo." She felt the lie settle into place before she could think twice about it. It was easier this way.

Sincere nodded like that made sense. "What happened?"

Lena leaned back against the couch, a mischievous glint in her eyes. "Girl, I'll tell you all about it. But first, we drinking." She lifted the bottle slightly. "We need it."

Sincere hesitated. It had only been a couple weeks since she last sat in this exact spot, letting Lena convince her that one bad night wouldn't erase all the work she'd put in. She'd popped a few pills, told herself it didn't count as a real relapse, but deep down, she knew better. And now, Lena was here again, coaxing her into yet another vice.

Sincere shifted slightly. "You know I don't really drink like that anymore."

Lena scoffed. "Babe, it's tequila, not heroin. You act like I came in here with a whole damn pharmacy."

Lena watched her for a second, then smiled, reaching into her bag. "Why you look like you expecting company?"

Sincere was grateful for the change of subject. "Supreme's bringing Imani over."

Lena's expression shifted immediately. "Who the hell is Imani?"

Sincere crossed her arms loosely. "His sister. She's a friend."

Lena arched a brow. "Are you sure she's not a clout-chaser?"

Sincere laughed, shaking her head. "She's nothing like that."

Lena didn't look convinced. Sincere could already see the gears turning in her head, the way she was working through whether or not she needed to be on guard.

Sincere decided to keep going before Lena could say something else. "She's in college. I told her we could have a writing session in exchange for her helping me figure out some things about school."

"School?" Lena didn't even try to hide her reaction. She barked out a laugh, head tilting back slightly. "As in college?"

Sincere shrugged. "Yeah."

Lena let out a sharp scoff. "Babe, college is for broke people who wanna be rich. You already made it. That's hustling backwards."

Sincere felt the comment sink into her chest like a slow-moving weight. She hated that she let it get to her. But she bit her tongue, because starting something with Lena never ended the way she wanted it to.

Lena gave her a sideways look. “Tell me you’re not actually considering that shit.” Her voice was dripping with sarcasm.

Sincere’s shoulders dropped. “I don’t know. I just wanted to hear what she had to say.”

Lena shook her head, still amused. “You kill me, girl. You got money, got people waiting on your next drop, and you worried about taking fucking tests?” She tsked, reaching for the bottle again. “Sounds ridiculous.”

A sharp knock at the door cut through the moment. Sincere straightened slightly, setting the bottle down. Lena, however, leaned back, her subtle grin still lingering. “Oh, this should be fun.”

Ignoring her, Sincere rose from the couch and made her way to the door. The second she pulled it open, Supreme’s gaze locked on her first, then immediately shifted past her. His eyes landed on Lena. And just like that, the air in the room changed.

Imani, standing beside him, was the first to speak, her warmth breaking through the thickening tension. “Hey, sis.” She stepped inside, wrapping Sincere in a quick hug.

Sincere hugged her back and for a brief moment, everything felt lighter. Around Imani, she felt more like herself—less guarded and freer. Pulling back from the hug, she turned to Lena, a bright smile tugging at her lips. “Lena, this is Imani. Supreme’s sister and my new friend.” She nudged Lena playfully, like she was trying to bring her into the warmth of the moment. “She’s a poet, a college girl, and way too cool to be hanging out with us.”

Lena’s expression didn’t shift immediately. For a second, she just looked at Imani. Then, with a slow movement, she stretched and rolled her shoulders back, settling into the couch like she was getting comfortable.

Sincere felt it before she saw it—the way Lena’s posture

shifted, the way her expression flickered just slightly as her gaze landed on Imani. It was quick, almost imperceptible, but Sincere caught it. The subtle narrowing of Lena's eyes. The way her lips parted, like she was assessing, measuring.

Imani, unfazed, gave Lena a warm smile, stepping further inside. "It's nice to meet you. I've heard a lot about you."

Lena tilted her head slightly, the picture of cool curiosity. "That's nice. I heard a few things about you as well."

Imani giggled. "Oh yeah? All good things, I hope."

Lena didn't miss a beat. "Depends on who you ask," she replied with a shrug.

When Imani looked taken aback, Lena giggled. The sound of it was a bit hollow, almost mocking in a way.

"I'm just kidding," Lena told Imani with a casual flip of her hair. "Girl, you gotta relax. We joke a lot around here."

Sincere's stomach clenched. She recognized that tone in Lena's voice. Playful on the surface, but there was something else beneath it. Something sharper. Imani didn't flinch, though. She met Lena's gaze evenly, her confidence unshaken.

Lena leaned back into the couch, crossing her legs. "You're Supreme's little sister?"

Imani nodded. "That's me."

Lena studied her for a second longer as if sizing her up. "Cute."

Imani just smiled again, still unbothered. But Sincere saw it—Lena was already deciding how she felt about her. And from the way she was dragging this out, she wasn't loving what she saw.

Before the tension could settle too deep, Supreme's voice cut through it. "What's up with the bottle? We interrupt a party?"

Sincere turned her head just in time to catch his expression shift. The moment he saw the 1942 on the table, his jaw tightened, his eyes flicking to her, then back to Lena. The disappointment hit fast and hard, even before he spoke. "You drinking?"

Sincere braced herself. She'd known this was coming. She rolled her shoulders back, keeping her tone light. "It's just one drink. You can calm down, Papa Bear. We were about to have talk and tequila time, not throw a Diddy party. It's not that serious."

Supreme's expression didn't change. "Nah," he said, voice steady, firm. "It *is* that serious."

Lena exhaled loudly, dragging a hand down her face. "Oh my God."

Supreme's gaze snapped to her. "You got something to say?"

Lena sat up slightly, placing her elbow on her knee, eyes flicking between Supreme and Sincere like she was already over the conversation. "Yeah, actually, I do."

Sincere's stomach sank.

Lena gestured toward Supreme with a slow, deliberate hand. "You always act like you're the only one looking out for her. Like I'm the bad influence, when really, you just don't want her listening to nobody but you."

Sincere stiffened. "Lena—"

But Lena wasn't finished. "You act like you're her savior or some shit. Meanwhile, you don't even let her think for herself."

Supreme's tone hardened. "Sincere can think for herself just fine. The problem is that you aren't letting her."

Lena frowned. "What is that supposed to mean?"

"Tell me whose idea this was?" He motioned his head to the bottle. "Hers or yours? Because from what she told me, she wasn't drinking anymore."

Lena let out a sharp laugh, shaking her head. "Oh, so now I'm some kind of master manipulator?"

Supreme tilted his head slightly, studying her. "You said that shit. Not me."

Lena blew out a breath and waved him off with a hand. "Nigga, please. She is a *grown* woman. It's not like I'm 'round here popping pills and shoving the shit down her throat. It's a *drink* and if you have a problem with it, maybe you and Mary Poppins over here should just go home so I can spend time with my girl."

"Lena!" Sincere tried to intervene. But Lena wasn't trying to hear it. "Nah, Sincere, stop. I'm tired of him always trying to stop us from having fun. Don't you see that he's trying to come between us?" She threw her hands up in distress. "Are you really going to let a man fuck up another one of your friendships?"

Her words hit Sincere like a gut punch. Although she hadn't *let* Lorde do anything, the sentiment behind what Lena said was true. He had definitely ruined any friendship she would ever have with Aaliyah when he made the call that put an end to her life. And Sincere had stood by idly and allowed it to happen. She was helpless.

Sincere closed her eyes briefly, already exhausted. "Lena, enough."

Lena rolled her eyes, but leaned back slightly, posture relaxing just enough to make it clear she was letting it go—for now.

Imani finally spoke up, voice calm, but firm. "Sincere doesn't have to drink to have fun."

Lena's eyes flicked over to Imani, slow and deliberate, as if truly seeing her for the first time. The energy shifted again, Lena's lips pressing together in something that wasn't quite a smile, but more like a challenge. For a moment, she just studied Imani, her fingers tapping against her knee. Then she let out a short, breathy laugh, shaking her head slightly.

"That's cute."

Imani arched a brow. "What is?"

The tightness in Lena's tone matched the chill in her eyes.

"You. Speaking on shit like you part of it." She leaned forward slightly, elbow resting on her thigh. "You still gotta get in before you start talking like you're on the inside."

Sincere's stomach twisted. She glanced at Imani, who didn't even blink at the statement.

Supreme exhaled, rubbing his jaw. "Man, I ain't got time for this bullshit." He turned toward the door. "Come on, Imani. We out."

Imani hesitated, looking torn. "Sincere—"

Sincere shook her head, still feeling the pressure of the night pressing down on her chest. "I'll call you later."

Imani sighed, but nodded, following her brother out the door. The second it shut behind them, the silence stretched.

Lena exhaled, dragging her nails over her thigh like she was shaking off the energy of the moment. Then, as if the whole thing had been nothing but an inconvenience, she laughed, light and careless. "Well, that was fun."

Sincere didn't respond. She sat there, staring at the table, at the bottle that was still sitting between them. She knew what just happened. Knew the choice she had made and Supreme wouldn't forget it.

Lena nudged her knee. "Come on, don't let them ruin the night."

Sincere hesitated.

Lena tilted her head, watching her. Then, with a slow, knowing smile, she reached for the bottle, lifting it slightly. "Forget all that, babe. It's just me and you, like always. Ain't nobody else matter right now." Lena leaned in slightly, her voice softer now, almost coaxing. "You know how people get. Always tryna control you, tell you what you need, like they know you better than you know yourself. But me? I got you, always have. Ain't never switched up on you, not once."

Sincere's grip tightened on the glass, hesitation flickering in her eyes. She knew Lena cared, but something about what Supreme and Imani said . . . it stuck. They weren't wrong. They were just—not Lena. Lena and Sincere's bond was backed by history.

Lena sighed, her voice dipping lower, slower. "You remember what happened last time a man fucked with your friendship?" Her tone was light, but there was something weighted in it. "Not saying it was on you. All I'm saying is that when men come in the middle of women's business, it's always bad news."

Sincere inhaled sharply, her chest tightening at the implication. She didn't need Lena to say Aaliyah's name out loud. The wound of that loss had never fully healed, and Lena knew that as long as she pressed against it without making it too obvious, she would get the result she wanted. She just had to make sure Sincere saw her as an ally and not the enemy.

Her words softened as she continued, gently digging further into the wound. "You think I don't know how much that still affects you? And I get it. Because all you had to do was show him a little attention and Aaliyah would still be alive. You were helpless then because you didn't know any better. You're not a little girl anymore. Plus, you have me!"

Lena smiled, raising her hands up as she dramatically presented herself as a prize. Sincere giggled.

Sincere's breath caught in her throat. The guilt, always lingering beneath the surface, felt as though it would pull her under.

Lena saw it, latched onto it. "You just gotta be smart. You can't let another one do the same shit. C'mon, babe. Supreme is feeling you. That's clear. Pulling you away from me, trying to replace me with Imani?" She rolled her eyes as she said the name. "That's just his subtle way of getting close to you and getting rid of all threats."

Sincere swallowed hard, the ache in her throat nearly unbearable.

Lena saw the shift, saw the way the past curled itself around Sincere like a noose, keeping her cemented by the familiar feelings of guilt and fear. She hated using Sincere's pain against her, especially right when she'd finally trusted her enough to share the story. But this was bigger than both of them. Lorde had promised that he was going to tell her how to find her brother, and she believed him.

He said he wouldn't hurt her, she reminded herself as she tried to ignore the look on Sincere's face. *I just need to follow his instructions. Get in, get out, and that's it. He won't hurt her, so no one loses in this.*

Lena convinced herself of it again, swallowing down the sliver of guilt clawing at the edges of her mind. She lifted the bottle, watching Sincere closely. "Stop thinking so much. Just relax and let's have fun. Like always."

She could already feel it happening. The pull of Lena's words as they tangled up with her own self-doubt.

Like always, Lena had said.

The problem was how they did things in the past no longer felt like "fun" for her. This wasn't the first time that she wondered whether or not she was outgrowing Lena. The same way that she had started to think she was outgrowing Aaliyah in the time before she was killed. The things they connected on, their likes, dislikes, goals in life . . . none of it was the same anymore. But it wasn't easy to let go of someone who'd been there for you when nobody else was.

Lena leaned forward, resting an elbow on her knee, fingers drumming lightly against the marble countertop in the kitchen. "All right, first, let's pour up. Then I'll tell you what I'm going through. You are not going to believe it."

Sincere swallowed hard. She knew she shouldn't. But instead of letting herself feel the fullness of what just happened, she reached for the easiest distraction and started going through the cabinets and pulled out two glasses.

Once she placed them on the counter, she hesitated once again, staring at the bottle before pouring it in the glass. She was conflicted; she loved the freedom that came after. It made her push all of her thoughts and worries away. Helped her to relax into the moment. But . . . she also hated the way it made her fall into old patterns that she was trying to let go. The most recent one being when she ended up in the bed with Lorde.

That said, like Lena told her, it was just the two of them here. Lorde wasn't anywhere around. She could stay safely in her home and have fun with her friend. What was the harm in that?

Lena watched Sincere's fingers tighten around the glass, her hesitation hanging in the air like a held breath. She didn't push. Instead, she let the silence settle, knowing exactly what it would do. Because Sincere was never good with silence. Silence made room for thoughts, guilt and regret.

Lena couldn't have that, so she softened her tone and let the edges of her words curve into something almost affectionate. "You know, Imani and Supreme will be all right. They got each other. But me?" She tilted her head slightly. "I got you. Always."

Sincere's throat bobbed as she swallowed. Her gaze shifted toward the door, like she was still thinking heavily on something, still considering a way out.

Lena wasn't having it. She reached out, the pads of her fingers brushing against Sincere's wrist, just enough to make her look at her again. "Tell me, babe—when's the last time you did something for you? Just . . . for you? Something that just felt good?"

Sincere didn't answer. She didn't need to. Lena already knew. She saw the shift happen in real time. From the slow release of tension in Sincere's shoulders, to the way her grip around the glass loosened, and finally, the way her breathing evened out as the tension of the night finally began to slip off her.

Lena let the moment breathe, then lifted the bottle once more. "That's my girl."

And this time, when she poured, Sincere didn't hesitate. She lifted the glass, let it meet her lips, and let the warmth slide down her throat.

Lena smiled.

Just like that, she had her back.

Just like that, everything was right again.

Chapter 18

The first thing Sincere registered was the headache. It was sharp and relentless, like someone had wedged a hammer between her temples and let it sit there overnight. The second was the nausea. Her stomach twisted violently as she blinked against the daylight streaming through the curtains. Her throat was dry, her limbs were heavy. Her body felt off. Too weighed down and slow.

She inhaled deep, trying to ground herself, but the scent in the air made her stomach churn. It smelled of stale liquor, sweat, and something else. Something . . . chemical and a bit metallic.

What the hell?

She swallowed hard, wincing at the bitter taste of regret coating her tongue. Her mind was sluggish with a thick, muddy fog clouding over her thoughts. What time was it?

Hell . . . what *day* was it?

She shifted and that's when she felt it—the warmth of another body beside her.

She gasped.

No.

Panic snapped through her system like a live wire. She turned her head so fast that her vision blurred. It cleared just enough to take in the figure sprawled across her bed. It was a man.

His face was half-buried in her pillows, one arm draped lazily across his chest, his skin unnervingly pale despite his chocolate-brown complexion. Her heart slammed against her ribs.

She scrambled back, the sheets tangling around her legs, her breath stuttering as her gaze darted around the room. Pills. Bags of white powder. An uncapped syringe. Empty bottles. Her stomach lurched, bile rising in her throat.

No. No. No.

This wasn't right.

Her hands trembled as she clutched the sheets, trying to piece together something . . . anything. But her memory was an empty void, swallowing up the night before, leaving nothing but splintered flashes. She remembered Lena. Tequila. Laughing about any and everything. Then . . . nothing.

She forced herself to look back at the man, her pulse thudding wildly. He was too still. His chest wasn't moving.

Oh, God.

A strangled gasp caught in her throat. Was he . . . dead?

No.

She had to check, but she couldn't make herself move.

My phone. Where is my phone?

She shoved back the sheets, hands shaking as she scanned the room. Clothes were scattered across the floor. Her dress from the night before. A shirt and a pair of jeans she didn't recognize. Finally, she spotted it on the nightstand. She lunged for it, nearly dropping it in her frantic grip as she swiped to her call log.

She hit the call button on Lena's name with her heart hammering as the ringing started.

One ring.

Two.

Three . . .

Lena answered on the fourth, her voice bright, almost too chipper. "Bitch, you awake already?" She laughed. "I thought for sure you'd be out cold all day after last night. Especially with your new boo!"

"Lena." Her voice came out cracked and raw.

Lena's laughter faltered. "Damn, what's wrong with you? You sound like you just woke up in a horror movie."

Sincere gripped the phone tighter, chest heaving. "Lena, I don't—I don't know what happened. I don't remember anything. There are drugs everywhere. There is a *man* here!"

Silence.

Then . . . "What?"

"There are pills. A syringe. A fucking syringe, Lena! And this guy—" Her breath hitched. "I don't know him. He's in my bed and I don't think he's breathing."

Lena went quiet for half a second too long. Then, a slow inhale. "Hold up. Are you serious?"

Sincere squeezed her eyes shut, trying to steady the rapid rise and fall of her chest. "Lena, what the *fuck* happened last night?"

Another pause. Then Lena let out a nervous laugh, forced and shaky.

"Why are you laughing? This isn't funny."

"Wait, wait—so you really don't remember?"

"No, I don't fucking remember!" Sincere snapped. "I woke up and this—this—this shit is everywhere! And this man . . . I don't even know if he's alive!"

Lena cursed under her breath. "Okay, okay, chill. We'll figure this out. But you really don't remember? Babe, you were fine last night. We talked, we drank, and then you called him. You asked him to come over and he did."

Sincere's pulse skipped. "What?"

"You *called* him." Lena's voice softened, like she was reminding her of something she should already know. "That guy.

You know, the one you told me you've been low-key feeling, but didn't know how to tell him."

Sincere's breath caught. "Lena, I don't—"

"You asked me to leave," Lena cut in. "You told me you wanted some time alone with him."

Her stomach twisted. "No. No, that doesn't make sense."

"Sincere, babe, I was there. You were fine. I even asked if you needed me to stay, but you told me to go." Lena's voice was slower now. "Are you saying you think he drugged you?"

Sincere's blood turned to ice. She stared at the man's unmoving form, chest tight, mind spinning.

"Because if that's what happened . . . you need to call the police."

"I don't know, Lena. I—" Her voice cracked. "I don't know anything."

She pressed a hand to her forehead, squeezing her eyes shut.

Think, Sincere. Think.

But all she got was static.

Her fingers curled around the phone. "Should I call Stacy?"

"Hell, no." Lena's response was instant, sharp. "That bitch is only sticking around 'cause she's getting paid. You think she wouldn't use this against you? This is blackmail worthy."

Sincere's head pounded.

Fuck.

She was right. Stacy wasn't her friend. If she found out about this, she'd have something to hold over her forever.

Lena exhaled sharply. "Okay, listen. First things first—check if he's alive."

Sincere's pulse spiked. "I—Lena, I can't—"

"You have to."

Her throat closed. She forced herself to move, crawling across the mattress, her breath shaky as she reached out.

Closer . . . closer.

Her trembling fingers pressed against his neck.

A second passed.

Then another.

Then, she felt it. A faint pulse. Weak, but there. She let out a choked breath. "He's alive."

Lena exhaled, relief laced through the static of the call. "Okay. Okay. That's good. That's really good."

Sincere ran a shaking hand through her hair. "What—what do I do?"

A beat and then Lena's voice came back, lower, more serious than before. "You need to call Lorde."

Sincere's stomach dropped. "No."

"Sincere—"

"No, Lena. I am not calling him." Her voice was barely above a whisper, but the force behind it was real.

Lena sighed. "Babe. He will know how to handle this. You cannot go to anyone else. It's too risky."

Panic pressed against her ribs, threatening to crush her. She couldn't trust Lorde. She didn't even want to see him. But what other option did she have?

"I'm on my way, okay?" Lena added. "I never should've left you with him. I thought everything was cool. I didn't know! Fuck, I'm sorry."

Sincere clutched the sheets, heart hammering. Lena was sorry. But that didn't fix this. Nothing did. She sat there, staring at the unconscious man beside her, her mind racing, her body frozen. She didn't want to trust Lorde with anything. But as the walls closed in around her, the truth became undeniable.

She was trapped.

Chapter 19

The ceiling above him was cracked and he was just noticing it. Supreme had been staring at that same jagged fracture in the drywall for hours, tracing the uneven lines with his eyes, following the splintered edges that led nowhere. It mirrored the thoughts running through his mind—fractured, sharp, impossible to smooth over.

I should've stayed.

That was the thought that kept circling back. No matter how many times he tried to shut it down, no matter how much he tried to convince himself that walking away from Sincere was the right decision, he knew better. His instincts had been screaming at him. The moment he saw Lena's face, the way she had smiled just a little too wide, the way she had reached for that bottle, something had felt off. But he left anyway, because Sincere made a choice. And he had to let her.

Now, lying in bed, arms folded behind his head, body motionless, but mind on fire, he couldn't shake the feeling that he'd made a mistake. And then, his phone began to vibrate on the nightstand. He ignored it at first, assuming it was just another bullshit call about business. Another move that needed to be made. Another crisis that needed handling.

Then the screen lit up again. That's when he saw her name. It was Sincere. His jaw flexed.

For a split second, he thought about letting it ring and making her wait. If she was calling just to explain herself, to justify whatever Lena had talked her into last night, he wasn't trying to hear it. But something about the way her name looked on his screen, the way it glowed in the darkness, made his stomach twist.

He grabbed the phone, thumb swiping across the screen. Before he could say a word, her voice broke through the line, shaky, and frantic. Something was wrong.

"Supreme."

His muscles locked. Everything inside him went still. "Sincere, what's wrong?"

Her breathing was ragged, uneven, like she was struggling to hold herself together. "I—I don't know what happened. I don't know what to do. I need your help."

He sat up so fast his head spun. "Where are you?" His voice was sharp, slicing through her panic.

"Home." A choked sob cut through the speaker. "There's a guy. He's in my bed. I don't—I don't even know who he is. There's drugs everywhere and I—"

His blood ran cold. "Are you hurt?"

"I don't know!" She sounded lost, desperate. "I just—I feel off. Like I was drugged or something. I don't remember anything. I don't *fucking* remember."

His pulse hammered against his skull. His grip on the phone tightened so hard it creaked. "Relax. I'm on my way."

"What should I do? Should I call—"

"Don't call nobody. Don't move. Just sit tight. I got you."

He ended the call before she could respond, already swinging his legs out of bed. His body was moving on instinct, pulling on his jeans, grabbing his keys. This was his fault. He knew Lena was no good. He knew she had a hold on Sincere, that she was pulling her into some shit she had no business in. But he let it go, told himself. Sincere had to learn the hard way.

But now some random nigga was in her bed, and she sounded like she'd been drugged out of her mind to the point of not even knowing what happened. He flexed his jaw, fury curling in his stomach like a coiled snake. Lorde's fingerprints were all over this, but first, he needed to know exactly what he was dealing with.

He grabbed his phone and scrolled to another name.

Dre.

He had answers and Supreme was about to get every single one.

The sun had barely crested the sky, but Supreme's world was already dark. The engine of his car roared to life, a low growl matching the tension simmering through his body. He sped through the empty streets, his mind racing faster than the tires gripping the pavement.

Sincere's voice was still ringing in his ears. It was shaky and desperate, not like her at all. She wasn't the type to break easy. She didn't panic. Even at her worst, she always had a grip on herself. But this was something else. On top of all that, it felt intentional. Someone had *done* this to her. And though Supreme had a good idea of who was behind it, first—he needed confirmation.

Dre's place was on the Southside, tucked away in a quiet neighborhood that didn't match the shit he was mixed up in. Supreme pulled up, killing the engine, his eyes already scanning the house. It was early, but a light was on in the kitchen. He barely had time to knock before the door swung open.

Dre's pregnant baby mama, Keisha, stood there, rubbing sleep from her eyes, her swollen belly pressing against the oversized T-shirt she wore. Her expression softened when she saw Supreme standing there. Although she hadn't met him many times, she always made it clear how much she respected Supreme because of how much Dre admired him.

"Supreme," she greeted, surprised, but warm. "Damn, it's early as hell. What's up?"

"I hope I didn't disturb you." Supreme forced his voice to stay even. "But I need to talk to Dre."

Keisha's brows knitted together, concern creeping into her features. She glanced over her shoulder before stepping aside. "Lemme go get him."

As she turned, Supreme's gaze lingered on her for a beat. She was the kind of woman who made a man want to be better. She didn't deserve to be mixed up in any of this and Supreme hated to bring drama to her doorstep. Dre had hit the jackpot with her, as long as he didn't fuck it up.

A few seconds later, Dre appeared in the doorway. He was shirtless, his tattoos dark against his brown skin, sleep still heavy in his eyes. The second he locked eyes with Supreme, though, all of that faded. The tension wrapped around Supreme like a second skin and Dre caught on to it immediately.

"Damn, bro," Dre muttered, running a hand over his face. "What's going on?"

Supreme didn't answer. He stepped back, motioning with his head for Dre to follow.

Dre glanced back into the house, ensuring that his family was good, then exhaled sharply and stepped outside, shutting the door behind him. The air between them was heavy, charged. Supreme wasted no time getting right to business.

"What you know about Lena?"

Dre froze, the question hitting him like a bullet. His lips parted, but nothing came out. That was all the confirmation Supreme needed.

His jaw clenched. "She working for Lorde?"

Dre's throat bobbed, his hesitation stretching seconds too long.

Supreme stepped closer. "Tell me everything."

Dre sighed, his shoulders slumping, the pressure of whatever he'd been hiding catching up to him. "Look, man—"

"No bullshit, Dre. Not today."

Dre exhaled hard, hands on his hips. "I ain't wanna be in the middle of this shit. That's why I ain't say nothing. But yeah . . . yeah, she working with him."

Supreme felt the rage crack through his spine. His fingers flexed at his sides. "How long?"

Dre shook his head. "I don't know, man. A while. From what I know, she's from here. Some chick he used to fuck with back in the day. She been close to him since then."

Supreme's breath came slow, measured. "What else?"

Dre hesitated. "I ain't got all the details, but . . . whatever Lorde got going on with Sincere, it's deeper than what people think. It's not just business. It's something personal about it."

Supreme's eyes darkened. "Meaning?"

Dre exhaled sharply, rubbing his jaw. "I don't know exactly what he's playing at, but I do know this—he don't want her to be just another artist. He wants her dependent on him for some reason."

"So he can control her," Supreme completed the thought for him. "Break her. Make her see him as her only lifeline."

Dre nodded grimly. "That's what he told me."

Supreme's jaw locked, muscles coiling tight. The truth was worse than he imagined. Lorde wasn't just trying to control Sincere's career, he was trying to own her.

Dre hesitated before adding, "And it ain't just her. Lorde's working with Silvan still. He's telling the elders it's nothing, but it's definitely something."

Supreme went completely still.

Dre nodded, reading the shift in his eyes. "Yeah, nigga. He's really making moves."

Supreme exhaled slowly, his fury ice-cold now. Lorde had been lying to him. Telling him he was going legit while deepening his ties to the same motherfucker who killed his brother. The same man who had manipulated his family, destroyed what little he had left.

Dre shifted on his feet, uneasy under the fury rolling across Supreme's expression. "He told the others he's gonna dominate both sides—legit and illegal. But people are scared. He's been threatening anyone who speaks up. Especially after what happened to Bo."

After dropping that, Dre already knew what was coming next.

"Bo . . . you mean him getting killed? I thought that was over some dispute with some niggas outside the city?"

Dre nodded grimly. "Yeah. That was Lorde. He had some of Silvan's men do it to make it look like they were responsible, but everybody knows it was him. Ain't nobody willing to say it, though."

Supreme's hands curled into fists. Lorde had already started silencing people, already making sure there were no loose ends. Sincere was just another loose end to tie up.

Dre sighed. "I didn't wanna hide shit from you, but Lorde—he had me keeping secrets and keeping tabs. On you. On Sincere. I didn't feel like I had a choice." Dre shook his head, quickly trying to explain. "I never told him about anything real, though. I just said small shit to keep him from asking questions. I swear, bro. I wasn't gonna betray you like that."

Supreme didn't blink. His silence stretched long enough for Dre to start shifting on his feet.

But then, Dre's voice dropped. "He told me it was for your own good. Said you'd get too soft on her. That she'd use that to drive a wedge between y'all and fuck up the Saints. He said . . ."

Dre hesitated, swallowing hard before finishing, "He said it'd be just like what happened with Indigo."

A slow, lethal chill ran down Supreme's spine. His mind flickered back as unwanted memories slammed into him. An image came up of his brother's face. Not how Indigo always looked, but like how he looked at the end: too thin, eyes sunken, expression desperate for something. It was the last time he saw him alive. He was begging Supreme for money. He needed just enough to get high one more time.

Supreme had turned him away. He told himself it was what he had to do. That he had to let Indigo fall in order for him to stand. But he never did. The next time he saw Indigo was at his wake. He died of an overdose because of Silvan. He gave him laced drugs to get rid of him when he felt like he was no longer useful.

Supreme's chest expanded on a slow, steady inhale. His rage was quiet, but deadly. "Where's Lorde now?"

Dre looked at him warily. "Supreme, man—"

"Tell me where."

Dre hesitated, then exhaled in defeat. "He's at the club. Meeting with some suppliers."

Supreme nodded once. His decision was made. Lorde had been playing him for too long. And now it was time to end the game.

He turned to leave, but Dre grabbed his arm. "Supreme—don't do nothing reckless."

Supreme's lips curled into something that wasn't a smile. "Reckless?" He shook his head. "I've never been clearer in my life. Get dressed. You coming with me."

And with that, he walked away.

The streets were still damp from the rain the night before. The city was just starting to wake up. Supreme didn't care about the time. His thoughts were loud all morning. It didn't change until Sincere's call came through. Just like that, the noise in his head became static. Now, as he sat behind the wheel, one hand gripping it too tight, the other resting on his knee, his entire body was wired with energy that he didn't know how to deal with.

Dre sat beside him, shifting in his seat every few seconds. He wasn't talking, just rubbing his palms together like he was trying to warm himself up or bracing for whatever they were about to walk into. Before they left, Dre had kissed Keisha goodbye, his hands gentle against her pregnant belly, murmuring something Supreme couldn't hear. A man like Dre had something to lose. It made sense that he was anxious.

The second they pulled up, Supreme knew something wasn't right. He felt it from the moment he killed the engine. He felt it when he entered the building and rode up the elevator. He definitely felt it when he arrived at her door.

Dre exhaled. "Shit, man. You can smell the alcohol from out here."

Supreme didn't answer. He hadn't planned to knock and didn't even need to because the door wasn't locked. That in itself was a red flag. Once they walked inside, the smell of liquor was even stronger than before. The first thing Supreme noticed was the mess. There were empty bottles, drug residue on tables and countertops. A jacket on the floor that didn't belong to Sincere.

Then, he finally saw her. She was curled up on the couch, small in a way he wasn't used to seeing. She looked up as soon as they entered and for a second, there was nothing but pure, raw fear in her eyes.

"Supreme."

His chest went tight.

She wasn't high. He could tell that much, but she was wrecked to the core. He moved to her immediately, crouching in front of her, scanning her face, her skin. He didn't touch her. He didn't want to do anything to make her feel unsafe.

"What the fuck happened?"

She opened her mouth, but nothing came out. Then, slowly, her gaze shifted toward the hallway. It focused in on the closed bedroom door.

Supreme followed her line of sight. A beat passed and then he moved. Dre was right behind him. The second Supreme opened the bedroom door, he knew they were too late to make this end well. He'd lived enough life in the streets to pick up on the scent of death.

The curtains were drawn. The bed was a mess. And in the middle of it, there was a man. He was unmoving—practically lifeless.

Dre let out a slow, shaky breath. "Oh . . . fuck."

Sincere stepped up behind them and once she looked in, it was like she choked on air. "He's alive. I checked." Her voice was barely there. "Isn't he . . ."

Dre moved first, stepping forward, pressing two fingers to the guy's neck. He exhaled sharply. "Nah, man. He's gone."

Sincere's knees buckled and her body hit the doorframe. One hand clamped over her mouth, the other gripping her stomach.

"No, no, no, no—"

Supreme turned to her, sharp. "You know him?"

She shook her head, fast. "I don't—I don't remember ever seeing him. But Lena said . . . she said I called him. But I don't even—"

Her breathing was picking up. Supreme grabbed her wrist, steady. "Breathe."

She squeezed her eyes shut, trying to stay calm, but failing. "I looked at my phone. I did call him. But I don't even have his number saved, Supreme. I don't even know who he is."

Supreme didn't react. Instead, he reached for her phone and checked the last outgoing call.

Then, without hesitation, he dialed the number. Suddenly, there was a ringing sound coming from the dead man's pocket.

Dre stiffened. "Oh, fuck."

Supreme's jaw locked. He walked over, slipped the phone from the guy's jeans, checked the screen. Same number. No name. No saved contact. No link to Lena. But Supreme wasn't fucking stupid.

Dre looked between them, then exhaled, dragging a hand over his face. "You think this is a setup?"

Supreme nodded once. "Call for a cleanup."

Dre cursed under his breath, but nodded, stepping outside to make the call. Now it was just him and Sincere. She was still in the doorway, shaking. Supreme moved to the bedside table, picking up the empty glass sitting there. He turned it in his hand. "What were you drinking?"

"Some tequila drink." Sincere licked her lips, arms wrapping around herself. "Lena made it. She said it was something she wanted to try."

Supreme's stomach turned. "And it tasted like?"

Sincere hesitated. "I don't know. It was strong, but I didn't think—I mean, I didn't feel like it was anything weird."

Supreme set the glass down carefully. "You don't remember shit?"

Her breath shuddered. "I remember talking. I remember laughing. And then . . . then it gets fuzzy."

Supreme's fingers curled into a fist. "You feel high?"

Sincere shook her head. "I don't feel . . . like that. But I don't remember."

Her voice cracked and her hands clutched her arms tighter. She was terrified.

Supreme's chest tightened.

He was sure that this was a setup, but first, he needed proof.

The wait wasn't long before the cleaning crew arrived. Fifteen minutes after Dre made the call, the first black SUV pulled up, followed by another.

Dre exhaled low under his breath. "Shit's about to get real."

Supreme didn't answer. His eyes stayed on Sincere, watching as she sat motionless on the couch, arms wrapped around herself, her stare empty. She looked like she wanted to disappear.

The cleanup crew moved in fast. Three men, dressed in dark, practical clothing, looking more like crime-scene investigators than gangsters. They didn't ask questions, just worked.

One of them, a tall, thin man with sharp features, nodded toward Supreme as he moved toward the bedroom. "Five minutes," he murmured.

Supreme gave a short nod. "Make it three."

The man disappeared into the room.

Dre stood nearby, rubbing his jaw as he glanced around, clearly uneasy.

Sincere still hadn't moved.

Supreme crouched down in front of her, lowering his voice. "Look at me."

She didn't.

"Sincere."

Her breathing hitched slightly. Then, finally, her eyes met his.

"I need you to pull yourself together," Supreme said, steady and firm. "You hear me?"

She nodded, but it wasn't convincing.

Supreme exhaled sharply. He reached out, gripping her chin lightly, forcing her to focus. "This ain't the time to break."

Her lips parted, eyes burning, but she swallowed down whatever she wanted to say.

Supreme's jaw clenched. He released her, standing back up as the cleanup crew moved through the apartment, wiping down surfaces, packing up the body, erasing every trace of what happened here. By the time they were done, the place looked untouched. No blood. No mess.

One of the men gave Supreme a nod. "It's done."

Supreme's response was a sharp lift of his chin.

And then, like that, they were gone.

Dre exhaled heavily, running a hand over his head. "I need a fucking drink."

Sincere flinched at the word.

Supreme shot Dre a look and he muttered a quick "my bad," before shifting uncomfortably. Before anyone could speak next, there was a knock at the door. Sincere jumped and Supreme's body went still. His eyes cut to Dre, then back to the door. When he opened it, he wasn't even surprised about who he saw standing on the other side.

Lena stood there, looking casual, like she hadn't just sent Sincere into a fucking spiral the night before. "Bitch, you look like hell," she greeted, stepping forward like she belonged there.

Supreme blocked the doorway.

Lena blinked up at him, surprised. "Damn. Can I come in?"

His voice was cold. "I don't know. Can you?"

Lena frowned slightly, tilting her head. "Supreme, what the fuck—"

He cut her off. "How long you been working for Lorde?"

The second the words left his mouth, the air shifted.

Sincere stiffened on the couch.

Dre leaned back against the wall, arms crossed, watching carefully from a distance.

Lena laughed like Supreme's question was insane. She shook

her head, flicking her wrist at him like he'd just asked if she was an undercover cop.

"Boy, what?"

Supreme didn't blink. "Tell the truth."

Lena's grin faltered just slightly. "I don't know what you're talking about."

Dre pushed off the wall so that she could finally see him. He didn't say a word, because he didn't have to. The second Lena's eyes met his, she remembered. She had seen him with Lorde a few times when she was meeting with him. He knew the truth about her.

Her stomach flipped.

Supreme caught the shift in her expression.

The exact moment her lie started to crack, Lena licked her lips, stalling. "Look, I—"

"Don't lie," Supreme warned.

"I'm not lying," she snapped.

Lena sighed dramatically. "Okay, look—Lorde wanted me to keep an eye on you. That's it. I wasn't 'working for him.' He just wanted to make sure you trusted him." She looked at Sincere now, eyes wide. "I thought it was a good thing. I thought he was good for your career."

Supreme didn't react. Instead, he turned his head slightly. "Dre."

Dre moved fast. Lena barely had time to react before his hand gripped her wrist.

"What the fuck?!" she yelped, trying to pull away. "Get the fuck off me!"

Supreme took a step closer, reaching into her bag.

She jerked. "Supreme, stop!"

He ignored her, pulling out her phone. Lena froze when she saw it in his hands. Her heart pounded.

"You touch my shit and I swear to God—"

It was a wasted breath, because Supreme was already scrolling.

And then—he found what he was looking for.

The messages between her and Lorde.

Lorde: **Did you do it?**

Lena: ***Yeah.*** **Everything's done.**

Lorde: **Hold up. Let me make sure I can hear and see you. Stand in front of the TV.**

Lena: **Can you see me now? I'm waving.**

Lorde: **Yeah, I can see your big-head ass. Say something so I can test the audio.**

Lena: **Done. Did you hear me?**

Lorde: **Got you loud and clear. These should work better than the last ones. Go ahead and leave. I'll make sure ole boy gets in.**

Supreme's chest burned. His lips curled just slightly and his mind raced. Lorde could be listening and watching them right now. He quickly screenshotted the entire exchange and sent it to Sincere's phone, keeping his movements effortless and calculated. Then he deleted the messages from Lena's phone, tucking it back into her bag as if he'd found nothing. When he looked up, Lena was watching him carefully, her body rigid, and her breath shallow.

Supreme exhaled slightly. Then, suddenly, his entire demeanor shifted. "It's all good."

He turned to Dre. "Go ahead and let her go."

Dre's grip loosened immediately.

Lena stumbled back. She looked between them, confused. "What?"

Supreme handed her phone back like it wasn't evidence of her betrayal. "There's nothing there." He shrugged. "She was telling the truth."

Dre didn't react, just nodded once, playing along.

Lena was still rubbing her wrist where Dre had grabbed her, her expression carefully unreadable as she took her phone back from Supreme. His face remained neutral, but she was watching him, searching for any hint that he really knew the truth about her. She had Lorde saved under a different name.

Supreme hadn't reacted much while going through her phone, which meant either she got lucky, or he really hadn't seen shit. Either way, this was too close.

"I'm sorry about all this," Supreme said suddenly, his tone calm.

Lena blinked, caught off guard. "What?"

He exhaled like this was weighing on him. "I know I've been hard on you. But I'm just trying to look out for her." He nodded toward Sincere, who was still sitting stiffly on the couch.

"She trusts you," Supreme added, his voice dipping lower. "I see that now."

Lena swallowed. There was something about the way he said it that made her stomach twist. But she ignored it. She forced a small, exasperated smile. "That's what I been telling you this whole time, nigga. I got her."

"Yeah." Supreme nodded slowly. "I see that." He let that hang in the air for a moment before glancing back at the door. "But right now, she's still shook. Let me get her together first."

Lena's brow twitched. "You want me to leave?"

"Just for now," he said easily. "Come back later. After I handle this."

She hesitated. A part of her didn't want to leave. But something about Supreme's demeanor made her uneasy. Maybe she was just paranoid after what happened, but something felt off.

She glanced at Sincere one last time, then sighed. "All right. Just . . . tell her I'll call her later."

Supreme nodded.

Lena lingered for another second. Then, finally, she turned and walked out. The second the door shut behind her, Supreme exhaled sharply.

Dre ran a hand down his face. "Fuck."

Sincere's voice was quiet. "What now?"

Supreme looked at her, jaw tight. "We're finished here. You're all good and it's time for us to leave."

He couldn't say much to her and once she looked at her phone, she would know why. Then, without another word, he straightened and headed toward the door. Dre followed. Everything felt sharper than before when Supreme stepped outside. It was like all of his senses were on overdrive.

Dre stood beside him, shifting uncomfortably.

Supreme didn't waste time. "Lorde knows now."

Dre's whole body tensed.

Supreme didn't stop. "He can see and listen in on Sincere's place. But he doesn't know what we're planning, and we're going to keep it that way."

Dre nodded slowly, weighing his words before he answered. "Aight. What's the move?"

"You go back," Supreme said. "Act like nothing changed. Keep playing your role."

Dre frowned. "And tell him what?"

Supreme's voice was sharp, measured. "Tell him I'm compromised."

Dre blinked. "The fuck?"

"Tell him I'm soft on Sincere. That she's clouding my judgment."

Dre shifted, clearly uncomfortable. "What if he doesn't believe me? What if he thinks I'm playing him?"

Supreme's expression hardened. "He'll believe you. That's exactly what he wants to hear."

Dre hesitated.

Supreme stepped closer. "I need you to stay close to him. Feed him what he wants. Keep him thinking he's got the upper hand."

Dre studied him, tension lining his jaw. "And when the time comes?"

Supreme's expression hardened. "When the time comes," he said, "we finish this."

Dre exhaled slowly. Then, finally, he nodded.

Supreme watched him for a beat longer before looking back toward Sincere's building. He didn't trust a lot of people, but he trusted himself.

Chapter 20

The air in Lorde's penthouse was thick with cigar smoke and the scent of sweat and sex. He leaned back in his chair, exhaling slowly, watching the red glow of his cigar dim and brighten with each measured inhale. Between his legs, a girl moaned softly, taking her time, dragging her tongue along the length of his flaccid pole like she had all the patience in the world. Between her legs, another girl worked just as deliberately. Both of their muffled sounds of pleasure filled the dimly lit room, adding to the soft bass of the music thumping through the surround sound speakers.

It should've been enough to clear his mind, but it wasn't. Somehow, instead of fully enjoying himself, his jaw was tight as his mind replayed the events of the day. This wasn't how it was supposed to go. Sincere was supposed to *call him.* She was supposed to panic, run straight into his arms. He'd crafted it perfectly—the drugs and the man in her bed. The scene of destruction set up by his loyal accomplice, Lena.

But instead she called Supreme.

The realization made his fingers twitch against the armrest. She was still fighting him, choosing someone else. His grip tightened on the cigar as he brought it to his lips once more. His patience was wearing thin.

She should've known better.

His other hand slid into the girl's hair, gripping the back of her head, forcing her down harder. She moaned in surprise, but he barely heard it. His eyes flickered toward the wall where the monitors were still running. Multiple screens, multiple angles. The surveillance feeds of various properties he had under his control.

One of them being Sincere's place, which is how he saw the moment she decided to call Supreme instead of him. And less than a half hour later, guess who showed up like Captain Save-a-ho?

Lorde was seething. *I see you, nigga*, he thought the second he saw his ugly ass on the screen. But that was fine. He wasn't stupid. He always had a backup plan. He pulled his phone from the table beside him, tapping the screen with a practiced ease. Dre's name lit up and he hit *dial.*

The line rang once before Dre answered, his voice laced with hesitation. "Yo."

Lorde took another pull from his cigar, exhaling smoke as he spoke. "What the fuck happened this morning, Dre?"

The silence stretched just a little too long before Dre finally responded. "Shit got messy."

Lorde's gaze darkened. "No *shit*, it got messy. I ain't ask for the obvious. I asked what the fuck happened."

Dre exhaled like he was trying to collect himself. Then, finally: "Sincere called Supreme. She woke up freaked out, called him, and he came straight over. He was all in her ear, saying Lena set her up. Saying you had her working for you to bring Sincere down."

Lorde's jaw ticked. *Supreme, you stupid motherfucker.*

Dre hesitated before adding, "I told him he was tripping, though. Told him he couldn't let her fall apart, that he was thinking with the wrong head. That he was soft on her."

Lorde took another slow drag from his cigar, considering.

He let out a quiet laugh, low and humorless. "Soft," he repeated. "Just like I thought."

Lorde leaned forward, balancing the cigar between his fingers, staring at the embers. "You know what the problem is?" His voice was deceptively smooth. "They too fuckin' stupid to know what's good for them." Lorde let out a slow exhale, shaking his head. "That's why I do what I do. Because niggas like Supreme and bitches like Sincere don't know how to move right. They let emotions fuck up everything."

He tapped the ash into the tray. "I ain't trying to bring nobody down. I'm tryna help."

Dre stayed silent, listening.

"Sincere is poison." He let out a low chuckle. "She's gonna bring all of us down if she don't learn to play her position."

He let that sit for a moment before adding, "And Supreme is letting a bitch make him weak."

Dre cleared his throat. "I don't think he's plotting against you."

Lorde raised an eyebrow. "No?"

"Nah," Dre said quickly. "I talked to him. He's convinced he's doing the right thing. That you got nothing to do with this. That Sincere's just . . . toxic."

Lorde considered that. Then, finally, he leaned back in his chair, pulling another drag from his cigar. "Good." Because that meant Supreme wasn't ready.

Yet.

But he would be.

Lorde had been focusing too much on business with Silvan, letting Lena run shit with Sincere. That was his mistake. He needed to handle this himself. Sincere needed a reminder of who was really in control.

He stubbed out his cigar, grabbing his phone, already making moves. "Where you at?"

Dre replied. "On my way back to the block."

"Stay there," Lorde said, standing up, adjusting his pants,

pulling away from the girls like they weren't even there. "I got shit to handle."

Then he grabbed his keys and headed out. His next stop was to see Sincere. And, this time, she wasn't getting a choice.

The elevator ride up was smooth, silent, but Lorde's mind wasn't. Sincere had called *Supreme.* Not him. That fact sat bitter in his chest, wrapping around his ribs like barbed wire, a slow constriction of irritation.

She was his.

She belonged to him, whether she admitted it yet or not.

And yet, when shit hit the fan—when she was drowning—he wasn't the one she reached for.

That mistake wouldn't happen again.

By the time he reached her door, the frustration was already smoothed away, hidden beneath a blank stare—his carefully constructed armor. He knocked twice, stepping back just enough to hear the slow shuffle of movement on the other side. Then, finally, the door cracked open.

And she looked like hell.

Messy curls. Heavy, lidded eyes. Barely standing up straight, like even that was too much effort. The exhaustion wasn't just physical—it was in her shoulders, the slow way she blinked, like she was too drained to even react properly to his presence.

Lorde let his gaze drag over her. "You look like you've seen a ghost."

Sincere hesitated, gripping the edge of the door as if debating whether to shut it back in his face.

That made him chuckle.

After a few seconds, she exhaled and unlatched the chain, stepping back. He moved past her like he belonged there, scanning the space as he went. There was no evidence of the chaos from last night. Which meant Supreme had handled it.

Lorde forced himself to breathe slow, deep, exhaling as he turned back to her. She hovered near the door, arms loosely crossed, like she was unsure of how to act around him.

"I can tell you ain't slept," he murmured, watching the way her fingers twitched against her arm.

Sincere swallowed, her voice hoarse. "Not really."

Lorde nodded, stepping in closer. "Yeah, I bet."

Silence stretched between them, thick and heavy. She didn't trust him. He softened his gaze, let concern flicker through his expression, reaching for her wrist. His fingers were gentle, warm against her skin, a stark contrast to the chill in the room.

"You really thought I'd let you handle all that alone?"

Sincere's brows pulled together slightly. "What?"

Lorde chuckled, shaking his head like she was the crazy one. "Come on now, baby. You think I was just sitting back, letting you figure that shit out yourself?"

Sincere's stomach twisted.

Her mind was screaming.

He's lying.

He's testing you.

But he didn't know she knew. He didn't know she had seen the texts, that she knew he was watching her. Every move. Every breath. Every word. She had to play this carefully.

Lorde took another step forward, dipping his head slightly, lowering his voice into something warm.

"I called Supreme after you called him," he murmured, voice slow, soothing. "Told him to step in. Had to make sure my girl was straight."

Sincere's heart pounded. She kept her expression neutral, forcing her shoulders to relax.

Lie.

Lie like your life depends on it.

Because maybe it did.

She forced a breath, tilting her head slightly, feigning surprise. "You did?"

Lorde's grip tightened just a little. "Of course."

Sincere hesitated just long enough to make it seem believable, like she was processing. Then, she let her lips part, allowing a slow smile to creep up her face.

Like he had just won.

Like he had her.

"I knew it."

Lorde paused, his confidence faltering slightly as he waited with baited breath for her to continue. "You knew what?"

Sincere took a slow step closer, letting warmth creep into her voice, letting gratitude soften her edges. "I knew you wouldn't just leave me to deal with that on my own."

She reached out, fingers brushing against the collar of his shirt, her touch light. Then, she leaned in, pressing her lips against his in a soft, fleeting kiss.

Lorde's brows lifted slightly, caught off guard for half a second before he smiled against her lips, fingers curling around her waist, pulling her in. She was finally understanding who was really looking out for her. He pulled back just enough to look her in the eye, his voice dipping into something softer, something intentional.

"See?" he murmured, running his thumb across her cheek. "I told you, baby. You don't ever have to go through anything alone. I'm always here."

Sincere let her fingers trail lightly down the buttons of his shirt, her gaze flicking up at him through her lashes. "I know."

Lorde smiled. "That's my girl."

She looked up at him, her expression carefully masked, but Lorde knew he was winning. He could feel it. "You just gotta trust me, Sincere," he continued, his fingers sliding down her arm, leaving warmth in their wake. "I've been around too long, I've seen too much. I know how people move. And I know who's real and who's not."

Sincere swallowed hard.

Lorde reached down, lacing his fingers through hers, giving her hand a reassuring squeeze. "I know Supreme came running the second you called," he murmured, tilting his head slightly, reading her reaction. "I get it. He wants to be that nigga for you. But that's not real. That's emotions talking. And emotions?" He shook his head. "They get people fucked up."

Sincere's throat was dry. "You think Supreme's not real?"

Lorde endearingly rubbed his thumb over her hand. "I think Supreme wants to believe he can protect you from a world he don't even understand." His voice was gentle, like he was explaining something she should've already known. "And I think you need someone who's been in this shit long enough to know how to actually keep you safe."

Sincere felt sick because he sounded so damn convincing. And maybe if she didn't already know the truth, if she hadn't seen the texts, she would've believed him. She forced herself to lean into him just a little.

"Thank you," she whispered, her voice laced with carefully placed gratitude. "For saving me from what could've been the worst night of my life."

Lorde grinned, thumb grazing her bottom lip. "Oh, baby," he murmured, voice dripping with satisfaction. "I *always* got you."

He pushed off the counter, crossed the room, and grabbed the whiskey bottle. Pouring himself a glass, he leaned back against the counter and watched Sincere carefully. She had just kissed him like she meant it.

But Lorde didn't trust anything at face value. He knew women too well. Knew how they could make you believe anything if it meant securing a position.

And Sincere was a player just like him. She just didn't know it yet.

A cold curve tugged at his mouth as he took a slow sip, letting the warmth burn through his chest before speaking "You sure about that?"

Sincere tilted her head slightly, a silent question in her expression.

Lorde chuckled. "Thought you had a thing for Supreme."

It was a test.

Something to push, to see if she flinched.

But she didn't even blink.

Instead, she let out a soft, almost amused breath, stepping in a little closer. Close enough that her scent—vanilla, honey, something sweet and dangerous all at once—wrapped around him, making him grip the glass a little tighter.

She tilted her chin up, meeting his gaze without a single ounce of hesitation. "Supreme?" She let out a scoff, shaking her head slightly. "Nah. He's not my type."

Lorde raised a brow, his voice low and edged with hunger. "Oh yeah?"

Sincere's lips curved into something slow, something dangerous.

"He's too easy," she murmured, voice smooth as silk. Then, she let her fingers graze over his wrist, just for a second, her nails lightly dragging against his skin before pulling away. "I don't like followers."

Lorde exhaled slowly, setting his drink down, his focus fully locked on her now.

Sincere leaned in and allowed the words to roll smoothly off her tongue. "I like the man who makes shit happen."

And just like that, he felt it—the slow, creeping satisfaction of having power.

Lorde tilted his head slightly, watching her with careful amusement. "You say I'm the one in charge," he murmured, trailing a slow hand down the side of her arm, feeling the warmth of her skin. "But you hesitated just now."

Sincere arched a brow, feigning confusion.

"What's that about?" He tilted his head, watching her intensely.

Sincere exhaled, slow and measured, but didn't break eye contact. She could tell he was trying to press her, trying to see how far he could take this control. She had to play it cool.

"I'm not trying to get pregnant, Lorde," she said.

Lorde chuckled, running his tongue across his teeth. "That what you worried about?"

Sincere shrugged, stepping back slightly, keeping just enough space between them to hold onto control of the moment. "That . . . and the fact that I know you've got other bitches."

Lorde let out a loud, genuine laugh. She wasn't wrong. But hearing her say it so plainly had him grinning, shaking his head in amusement.

Sincere smiled slightly, watching his reaction. Then, she lifted a slow brow. "Men like you always do."

Lorde's laughter faded into something quieter, more intrigued. He leaned in, resting his hands on the counter behind her, caging her in. "And what?" he murmured, voice dropping an octave. "You don't like to share?"

Sincere didn't move or react the way most women did when he pressed in. Instead, she tilted her head, unbothered. "I don't do that raw shit unless I know I'm the only one."

"That right?" Lorde asked, his interest building at the hint of a challenge.

Sincere nodded, slow and steady. "Cancel all your other hos if you want to get down like that with me."

He let her words sink in. The fact that she wasn't asking was . . . different. Most women played nice. They waited for him to get bored of the others.

But Sincere was calling the shots.

And fuck, if that didn't make him want her even more.

He grinned, amused as hell. "Oh, you got rules?"

She teasingly rolled her eyes to the ceiling to think for a moment before responding. "Let's call them policies."

Lorde chuckled, dragging a slow hand down her waist. "Like, terms and conditions?"

Sincere shrugged, unbothered. "Call it what you want."

He exhaled, his fingers pressing lightly against her hip. "Damn, baby." He dragged his gaze over her, slow and deliberate, before grinning again. "You really think you special, huh?"

"I don't think." She leaned in, her voice a soft whisper against his lips. "I know."

Lorde leaned back against the counter, licking his lips as he took in every inch of her, from the confidence in her stance to the way she held his gaze without even a flicker of hesitation. Most women folded under pressure. They crumbled when he applied just enough heat.

"Consider all my other hos canceled." His voice was smooth, like the promise was already written in stone. "You're the only one I want." Sincere crossed her arms, unmoved. She tilted her head, lips twitching at the corners. "I want proof."

Lorde laughed under his breath, shaking his head. He exhaled slowly, reaching for his drink again, letting the liquor roll over his tongue before he swallowed. "Proof?" he repeated, amusement laced through his tone. "What, you want me to write a statement? Have my hos sign a release form?"

"Nah. That ain't necessary." She leaned back against the counter beside him, cool and composed. "I just need to see your phone."

Lorde damn near choked on his drink. His laughter came loud, deep, genuinely entertained.

He set the glass down, rubbing a hand over his jaw, looking at her like she had lost her damn mind. "Hell nah, you can't see my phone."

Sincere didn't even blink. "Then you can't have no pussy."

Lorde's expression went still, amusement draining.

Sincere lifted a brow, voice smooth as silk. "I'm a stingy bitch. I don't like to share."

Lorde let the words settle between them. He wasn't used to this. Most women knew who he was. They didn't question his habits or challenge him. They played their role. And that was the thing about Sincere. She wasn't playing. She was demanding.

And fuck . . . if that didn't make his blood run hot.

He exhaled, stepping closer, lowering his voice. "You really ain't gon' let me hit unless I show you my phone?"

Sincere held his gaze, steady. "That's right."

Lorde chuckled, slow, deep. Then, to her surprise, he lifted a hand, gently tucking a curl behind her ear. His voice dropped, turning almost affectionate. "All right." He held her gaze, his expression softening into something that almost felt tender. "Give me a week to settle my situations. That's all I need."

Lorde strolled out of Sincere's apartment like a king leaving his throne, shoulders loose, arrogant confidence still intact. This was how it was supposed to go.

She was his.

Just like he planned.

He slid into the driver's seat of his sleek black Benz, resting a hand lazily on the wheel.

He tapped the ignition, the soft growl of the engine rumbling beneath him as he leaned back, fingers drumming against the leather.

"She's mine," he murmured to himself.

His foot eased against the gas, pulling away from her building, pride etched across his face. *Supreme can't touch me.* The confidence stuck for a while. Then, as the city lights blurred past him, a flicker of doubt crawled up his spine.

Something about the way Sincere played the game tonight . . .

It was too good. Her words had rolled off her tongue too easily.

Lorde drummed his fingers against the steering wheel, his mind racing. The streets blurred past him, bathed in the sickly glow of streetlights, the city stretching out like a beast that never slept. His jaw worked as he clenched and unclenched it, his thoughts sharp, cutting.

She's smart. Gotta make sure she's not playing me.

His gaze flicked to his phone resting on the console beside him. Surely, he didn't get played. If there was a slight chance she was running game on him, he'd know. And then he would handle her accordingly. There was only one person he trusted to tell him exactly what he needed to hear.

Maman Clo.

It had been too long since he last let himself lean on the kind of wisdom she offered. With a sharp inhale, he reached for his phone, scrolling through his contacts before pressing the call button.

It rang once. Twice.

Then a voice, low and knowing, answered. "I was wondering when you'd finally come see me, boy."

The old woman had a way of speaking like she knew everything before it happened. It had been like that since he was young, since he'd first started running with the Saints and she took one look at him and said he had the spirit of a man who wouldn't stop until he had it all.

He shifted in his seat, but the amusement never reached his eyes. "Yeah, Maman. We need to talk."

A low hum came through the line, thoughtful, knowing. "The spirits have been restless," she mused. "And so have you, I imagine."

Lorde exhaled sharply, his frustration simmering just below

the surface. Maman Clo never asked what was wrong outright. She always made him say it out loud. That was her way.

"I got a situation I need clarity on," he said, voice steady, but edged with something colder.

"Of course you do," she replied, the faintest trace of a chuckle weaving through her words. "You wouldn't be callin' me otherwise. Come on by. I'll put the kettle on."

The line clicked dead before he could respond.

Lorde shook his head, tossing the phone onto the passenger seat.

Maman Clo never said goodbye.

The drive to her place took him out of the city into the quieter, older part of town where the houses sat farther apart, hidden behind thick iron gates and overgrown trees. Maman Clo's home had always been the same. It was small, but powerful, wrapped in creeping ivy, smelling of earth and something ancient. The kind of place that made even the hardest men hesitate before knocking.

He pulled up to the curb, stepping out and adjusting his cuff links before moving toward the front door. Before he could knock, the door creaked open. She was already waiting. Maman Clo stood in the doorway, her silver hair wrapped in deep blue fabric, her dark eyes sharp and unreadable as she took him in.

"Took you long enough."

Lorde chuckled as he stepped inside. "You always say that."

She closed the door behind him, locking it twice before leading him deeper inside. The living room was dimly lit, candles flickering along the walls, casting long, shifting shadows across the room. A faint trail of incense curled through the air, mixing with the scent of old wood and dried herbs.

On the center table, a teapot rested on a small burner, steam rising steadily from the spout. Two cups sat beside it, waiting. Maman Clo gestured for him to sit.

"Talk."

Lorde lowered himself onto the couch, leaning forward, elbows on his knees, rolling his jaw as he thought through his words. He had learned early that you didn't lie to Maman Clo. She saw right through it.

"It's about Sincere."

The old woman nodded, not looking surprised. She poured the tea, sliding a cup toward him.

"You ain't been listenin' to your gut," she said, stirring her own cup slowly. "Otherwise, you wouldn't be here."

Lorde took the cup, but didn't drink. "I need to know if she's playing me."

Maman Clo studied him for a long moment, then shook her head. "What you really need to know is if you care."

Lorde's jaw tightened. "That ain't got shit to do with it."

She lifted a single brow, unimpressed. "Don't it?"

Silence stretched between them, the weight of her words settling in the space like an uninvited guest.

Lorde exhaled sharply, rubbing a hand over his jaw. "I just need to know where she stands. If she's working against me. If I need to handle it before she becomes a problem."

Maman Clo hummed, tapping her long nails against the porcelain of her cup. "The problem ain't the girl. The problem is you."

Lorde's gaze darkened, but he stayed silent.

"You think power is about makin' people need you, makin' 'em depend on you. But power ain't control, boy. Real power is when they choose you, even when they don't have to."

Her words struck something deep, something he didn't want to name. He had built his entire life making sure people had no choice but to rely on him. That was how you won. That was how you stayed on top. But Sincere . . . she had moved different from the start.

She had looked him in the eye and told him no. And yet here she was, still in his world. Was that by her choice? Or had he just convinced himself of it?

Maman Clo leaned back, watching him. "You want me to read on it?"

Lorde's grip tightened around the cup.

He did.

And he didn't.

Because if Maman Clo gave him an answer he didn't like . . .
Then he'd have to do something about it.

And Lorde wasn't sure yet if he wanted to know.

Chapter 21

Sincere woke up with a dull ache pressing against the back of her skull, a leftover weight from everything that had unraveled the night before. She exhaled slowly, staring up at the ceiling, body still heavy with exhaustion. For a brief second, she let herself pretend it was just another day. A normal morning. No surveillance. No dead bodies. No looming presence of Lorde's control tightening like a noose around her throat.

Then she remembered.

And just like that, the illusion shattered.

She sat up, brushing her hair out of her face, glancing at her phone on the nightstand. The battery was low—she'd barely touched it after Supreme left. She needed to get out for some fresh air.

Sincere swung her legs over the edge of the bed and stood, her robe hanging loosely from her shoulders as she made her way toward the door. She wasn't expecting anyone to be waiting for her, which is why, when she pulled open her front door and stepped out into the building's small vestibule, she stopped short when she saw two men.

One was standing right outside her door, the other sitting on the bench near the elevator. Her eyes swept over them, heart thudding once, but she kept her expression smooth. “Y’all lost?”

The one standing closest to her—a tall, heavyset man with a broad chest and a shaved head—tilted his head slightly, unreadable. “No, ma’am. We’re here for you.”

Her stomach curled.

For me?

Her gaze flicked to the other guy, leaner, but just as solid, lounging comfortably like he had all the time in the world. She inhaled slowly, rolling her shoulders back before narrowing her eyes. “I don’t know you. Who sent you?”

The taller one spoke again, voice calm, but unwavering. “Mr. Lorde.”

And just like that, she understood.

This wasn’t just security. This was a message.

Her fingers twitched at her sides, but she forced a slow, measured breath. “And y’all’s names?”

The taller one nodded once. “Carl.” He motioned to the other man. “That’s Andre.”

Her lips curled into something that wasn’t quite a smile. “Cute. And what exactly are y’all here for?”

Carl’s gaze didn’t waver. “We’ve been assigned to you as your security detail. I’ll be stationed outside your residence and Andre is your new driver.”

Her stomach tightened.

Dre was gone. Supreme was gone.

And she already knew what that meant.

Sincere let out a soft, humorless chuckle. “Wow. So what, Supreme and Dre just got fired? Or did Lorde finally figure out that they don’t follow his orders the way he wants them to?”

Neither man reacted, but Sincere could see it in their posture—the unwavering steadiness of men who knew exactly what they were here for. She hated the way Lorde kept finding ways to remind her that she wasn't free. But she had to act like she wasn't fazed.

Sincere sighed dramatically, shaking her head as she adjusted the sleeve of her robe. "Well, tell Lorde I said 'thanks,' but I don't need babysitters."

She moved toward the elevator, but Carl smoothly stepped in front of her path, blocking the way with effortless precision.

He met her eyes, voice steady. "Lorde was clear. You're not to leave without us."

Her gaze narrowed, head angling slightly as if considering. "You're serious?"

Andre finally spoke from the bench, his voice quieter, but just as firm. "Lorde is concerned about your safety, Ms. Sincere."

She barked out a laugh. "Oh, is he?"

Carl nodded, completely unfazed. "After what happened with the man in your home, he doesn't feel comfortable letting you move around without protection. Especially since you don't remember exactly what happened."

Sincere's fingers curled into fists at her sides, nails biting into her palms.

There it is.

The manipulation.

The carefully placed concern.

She swallowed, shifting her weight onto one hip, keeping her tone light. "So now I'm the damsel in distress?"

Carl didn't blink. "Lorde just wants to make sure you're safe."

Sincere nearly scoffed. Safe from who? Lorde had set this whole thing up. He knew exactly what had happened. He just didn't know that *she* knew.

She lifted her chin, narrowing her eyes. "And what about Supreme?"

The moment the name left her lips, she caught the slight shift in Carl's expression.

Andre stood, stretching his arms slightly before speaking. "Lorde said he's not sure where Supreme stands anymore."

Carl hesitated, then spoke lower. "Apparently, Lena told him Supreme was acting . . . suspicious. Said he was trying to isolate you."

Sincere kept her face neutral, but inside, rage coiled like a living thing in her chest. Lorde was trying to turn her against Supreme. Trying to make her think Supreme was the one manipulating her.

And Lena—

That bitch was still feeding him information.

Sincere let out a slow breath. "Let me get this straight." She folded her arms. "You're telling me that the guy who *saved* me last night is the one I should be worried about?"

Carl didn't hesitate. "We're telling you that Lorde is the only one who's looking out for you completely."

Sincere inhaled sharply, pressing her lips together before nodding once. "Got it. Y'all got a script to stick to."

She turned on her heel, heading back inside her apartment. She wasn't going to fight them.

Because Lorde didn't know what she knew. And as long as she played along, he never would.

Sincere had always known how to adapt. It was a skill that came with survival—the ability to smile when she wanted to scream, to adjust when everything inside of her rebelled. And now, under Lorde's watchful eye, under the shadow of his paranoia, she knew she had to move carefully.

She fell into a routine that looked normal. The studio became her safe haven, the one place she could stretch time, prolonging sessions with the excuse of needing to "feel things out" before locking in a track. She took long showers, let the water run even when she wasn't in it, knowing that was one of the few places she could sit undisturbed.

She moved like she wasn't trapped. She hadn't spoken to Supreme since that morning, hadn't even tried. Lorde was too calculated, too many steps ahead, and she wasn't going to risk anything that could tip him off.

Her phone stayed on her at all times, but she never let herself get comfortable with it. She knew better. Knew that if Lorde had gone so far as to plant surveillance in her home, there was no way he wouldn't have eyes and ears on her phone too.

She decided to let it become an accessory. She texted people she was supposed to, posted things to make it seem like everything was business as usual, played the role that Lorde expected of her.

And she waited.

It wasn't until two days later, in the middle of scrolling through her notes app, that the idea finally came. It was a memory, tucked away but not forgotten, of Imani, sitting across from her, a soft glow in her eyes as she spoke about the community event she volunteered at.

Sincere had barely been listening at the time, nodding and offering half-hearted smiles, but now—now, she could hear it all clearly.

I try to make it to the park whenever I can. It's just a small event, but it's nice. You know, helping the kids, connecting with people outside of the industry.

A public community event. She could work with that. Her mind started moving, piecing it together, working out the details. She couldn't call Supreme. Couldn't text him either . . . There had to be another way to get him a message. It had to be subtle, something that wouldn't raise suspicion.

Sincere tapped her fingers against the screen, breathing in deep before exhaling. She leaned against the kitchen counter, arms folded tight across her chest, watching Carl and Andre like they were just another obstacle she had to maneuver around.

"This shit is ridiculous," she muttered, shaking her head.

Carl, who had been standing with his arms behind his back like a damn soldier, barely blinked. "What's ridiculous?"

Sincere let out a humorless laugh. "Y'all following me around like I'm some federal witness in a crime case. Since when does Lorde need me babysat twenty-four-seven?"

Andre finally really looked at her. He had barely spoken since he and Carl showed up, but his silence wasn't passive. It was calculated, measured, like he was assessing her every move.

"You got a problem with security?" he asked.

Sincere's head cocked, eyes narrowing. "I got a problem with being smothered. I got a problem with feeling like a damn hostage. I got a problem with y'all acting like I'm incapable of taking a single step without breathing down my neck."

Carl exchanged a glance with Andre before he spoke again. "Lorde said you needed extra protection. That's why we're here."

Sincere rolled her eyes. "Protection from who? I been moving just fine before y'all got here."

Carl let out a short, humorless chuckle. "Yeah? Tell that to the nigga who almost overdosed in your bed the other night."

Sincere's face went blank. Her fingers twitched at her sides, but she kept her voice steady. "I don't know what happened that night."

"Exactly," Andre cut in. "You don't know. That's the point."

Sincere opened her mouth to argue, but Carl kept going.

"Lorde told us everything. He said you were drugged and didn't remember shit. Said Supreme was acting *real* protective over you all of a sudden." Carl's eyes locked onto hers, unblinking. "Almost like he don't trust Lorde."

Sincere's stomach twisted, but her expression stayed neutral.

Of course. Of course, Lorde would spin the story to fit his own agenda.

"He's worried about you," Carl added, like that was supposed to make her feel better. "Said Supreme might be trying to use you in some way. That he might be compromised or working for someone else."

Sincere forced herself to scoff. "*Compromised*? Y'all hear how crazy that sounds?"

Andre shrugged. "We just follow orders. If Lorde says we stay on you, we stay on you."

Sincere forced down her anger. This was exactly what Lorde wanted, to make it seem like the people actually looking out for her were the ones she *shouldn't* trust.

She couldn't react and give them a reason to be suspicious. She decide to switch tactics.

"All right," she said, voice smoothing out. "I hear y'all. I get it. Lorde wants to make sure I'm safe." She allowed the faintest trace of irony to touch her lips. "But don't you think making me disappear from the public eye is gonna do more harm than good?"

Carl and Andre glanced at each other.

Sincere took that as her cue to keep going. "I'm an artist. I'm a brand. If I just stop showing up, stop being seen, people are gonna start asking questions. They are going to think that ever since signing with Crown Records, my career is going down the drain. That I might be spiraling again. And Lorde *really* don't need that kind of attention, do he?"

Carl's jaw clenched, but he said nothing.

Sincere pressed forward. "There's a community event happening at the park," she said, feigning nonchalance. "Low-key, positive, good PR. Something to remind people that I'm still here. That I'm *fine*." She met their gazes, voice laced with just enough challenge. "Unless y'all wanna be the ones to explain to Lorde why my public image is slipping because *you* couldn't figure out how to keep me safe in a crowd?"

Carl's expression twitched. "You're not going alone," Carl finally said.

Sincere smiled, slow and knowing. "Of course not. That would be *unsafe.*"

Andre still didn't look convinced, but Carl was already resigning himself to the decision.

"We'll take you," Andre finally said. "But you stay where we can see you. No disappearing, no slipping off. We move when you move."

Sincere lifted her hands in mock surrender. "Wouldn't dream of it."

They didn't look convinced. She didn't care. Step one was complete. Now, she just had to get to the park.

They hadn't even fully parked before Carl was already talking. "You already know the deal, right?" His deep voice carried the weight of authority. "Ain't no slippin' off, no disappearances, and no talkin' to nobody we ain't approve of first."

From the passenger seat, Andre snorted, his tone sharper, less patient. "And don't try that slick shit neither. We move when you move. We blink when you blink. If you so much as sneeze wrong, we on your ass."

Sincere pressed her lips together, suppressing the urge to roll her eyes. They'd barely come to a stop, and she already felt the weight of their paranoia pressing against her. She turned to them, voice light, measured. "Y'all got it. I swear. I just wanna do my little community service, smile at some people, and go home. Ain't that what Lorde wants? Good PR?"

Carl gave a slow, skeptical grunt, his sharp eyes scanning the scene. "You play it right, yeah."

Andre, on the other hand, wasn't buying it. He twisted in his seat, his stare sharp. "You wanna keep up that public image so bad, then do what you came here to do and keep your ass where we can see it. Ain't no reason for you to be makin' rounds like you runnin' for office."

Sincere sighed, gripping the strap of her bag. "I got it. Damn. Y'all act like I got a history of pulling magic tricks or something."

Carl gave a small, knowing shake of his head. "Nah, but you got a history of not listenin'."

She shot him a look, but didn't argue. No use pushing too hard—at least, not yet.

Andre cracked his neck, his expression like a loaded gun. "And don't be gettin' all social with folks. Lorde don't want no new influences fuckin' with your head."

Sincere let out a short, humorless laugh, shaking her head. "You mean he don't want me talkin' to Supreme."

Andre's silence was answer enough.

Carl let out a breath like he was already tired. "Just do what you gotta do, shorty. And don't do nothin' stupid."

Sincere pasted on her most dazzling smile and swung the car door open. "Wouldn't dream of it."

The park was alive. Music was playing from nearby speakers, the scent of fried food thick in the air, kids sprinting across the grass while parents trailed behind them. Volunteers moved between tables, handing out supplies and directing people toward different booths. The noise, the movement, the sheer energy of it all should have been overwhelming.

But for Sincere, it was a cover. She stepped out of the car, adjusting her hoodie, keeping her face angled slightly downward. Carl and Andre flanked her instantly, their presence heavy at her sides.

Sincere pressed her lips together, forcing herself not to roll her eyes. They hadn't even made it five steps from the car, and she was already over it. She let them talk and let them feel like they had the upper hand. Meanwhile, her eyes scanned the park, tracking the faces in the crowd.

A sudden burst of excitement cut through the noise.

"Oh my God—Sahara?"

Sincere barely had time to register the voice before a group of teenage girls swarmed her, eyes wide, phones already out.

She turned on the charm instantly, offering a small smile. "Hey, y'all."

The girls squealed, moving in closer. "Can we get a picture?"

"I love you!" one of them said. "You're even prettier in person!"

Sincere let out a soft laugh, slipping into the role effortlessly. "Of course, of course."

She posed for a few quick photos, keeping her expression easy. But as the girls snapped their selfies, she lowered her voice just enough for them to hear. "I'm keeping a low profile today, all right? Just enjoying the event. Keep it between us?"

The girls nodded eagerly, whispering among themselves like they were in on a secret.

Carl and Andre stood a few feet away, watching the whole thing unfold.

Satisfied that she'd handled it, Sincere offered one last smile before gently extracting herself from the group and easing back toward the crowd. She needed to find Imani. It didn't take long to spot her. She was standing near a volunteer booth, handing out school supplies, her face warm and relaxed as she spoke with someone beside her.

But she didn't look over.

Didn't react to seeing Sincere.

That was . . . strange.

Sincere took a step closer, watching the way Imani's body language stayed closed off. Not cold exactly, but not open either.

And then it clicked.

The last time they spoke, the tension had been thick.

Sincere frowned slightly, an odd feeling settling in her stomach. She hadn't heard from Imani at all. No calls or texts. But then, realization dawned. The phone. Lorde had given it to her. And now, standing here, looking at Imani's unreadable expression, she wondered—had he blocked her from reaching out? Had he filtered who could contact her, who she could hear from?

Her grip on her hoodie tightened, but she kept her face neutral as she walked toward Imani.

At first, Imani kept her stance guarded, but when Sincere got close enough, her composure broke. Her face lit up, relief crashing through her features as she launched forward and hugged her tight.

Sincere barely had time to react before Imani squeezed her. "You just went ghost on me!" Imani said, pulling back slightly. "Girl, I been calling you, texting you—I thought something happened to you!"

Sincere inhaled sharply, her arms still wrapped around Imani.

She *had* tried to reach her.

Lorde must've blocked it.

"I didn't get anything," Sincere murmured, keeping her voice low.

Before Imani could press further, Andre's voice cut through the moment. "Aight, that's enough of all that," he grumbled, stepping closer. "You doin' too much."

Sincere let out a slow breath and waved them off. "Relax. She's my friend."

Imani took a step back, eyes flicking to the men at her sides. "Who are they?"

Sincere exhaled, keeping her tone casual, but her words deliberate. "They are the reason I can't text you or your brother." She lifted her chin slightly. "They're watching my every move."

Imani's face darkened. "Sincere . . ."

"I don't have time to explain," Sincere cut in quickly, tilting her head like she was just chatting. "I need you to do something for me."

Imani's jaw tightened, but she nodded. "What is it?"

"I need you to get a message to Supreme. I need to see him."

Imani's brows pulled together. "Where?"

Sincere hesitated, scanning the crowd, making sure no one was too close. Then, her voice barely above a whisper, she said, "My old house." Sincere pressed forward. "No one lives there now, but I still own the place. I'll send you the information on how to get inside." She gave her a specific time. "Tell him to be there. I'll make sure I show up hours later so they don't see him go in."

Imani nodded slowly. "Okay. I got it."

Before Sincere could turn to leave, Imani grabbed her wrist, stopping her. Sincere looked up, startled, as Imani reached behind her, grabbing something from the table. She turned back around and pressed a small, spiral-bound journal into Sincere's hands.

"For you," Imani said softly. "A new book for you to fill with all the beautiful songs you're gonna write about how you survived this."

Sincere's throat tightened. She looked down at the journal, her fingers running over the smooth cover. A lump formed in her throat as she nodded, swallowing hard. "Thank you," she whispered.

Imani smiled, squeezing her hand once before stepping back.

Sincere turned, mask slipping back into place as she walked toward Carl and Andre. For the first time in a long time, she didn't just feel like she had a friend. She felt like she had family.

Sincere barely had time to shut the door behind her before she caught the scent of expensive cologne and burnt tobacco curling through the air. The combination was familiar. She turned her head, gaze sweeping across the room, and there he was.

Lorde.

He was sprawled across her couch, one arm draped lazily over the backrest, fingers tapping a slow rhythm against the cushions. His jacket was gone, leaving him in a sleek black dress shirt, the top buttons undone like he hadn't planned to stay long.

But he had been waiting.

That much was obvious.

Sincere forced a warm smile, tilting her head. "Didn't know I was expecting company."

Lorde tapped ash from his cigar into the tray beside him. "Didn't know I needed an invite."

Her heart pounded in her chest, but she kept her expression light, moving toward the kitchen, her every step controlled. She reached for a bottle of water, twisting the cap off with ease, buying herself a moment.

"Well, now that you're here," she said lightly, twisting the cap off. "You want something to drink? Or are you just here to do a home invasion in peace?"

Lorde chuckled, low and amused. "Nah. Just checking in."

Sincere took a sip of water, tilting her head slightly as she turned back toward him. "I'm good," she said, her tone deliberately warm. "You got my new security detail watching me like I'm the damn president."

Lorde's gaze sharpened slightly. "That little park event," he murmured, "seemed really last-minute."

Her heart clenched, but she let out a soft laugh. "I just needed some fresh air, babe. Had to remind the world I'm still one of them, you know? The people love me and they love you *with* me."

She crossed the room toward him, her movements fluid, controlled. He watched her the entire way, taking in the way she moved, the easy confidence in her voice. But something about it made him pause. This wasn't the same Sincere who had pulled away from him just days ago, who had looked at him with uncertainty and hesitation.

This was different.

His fingers tapped against the couch, slow and deliberate. "You're in a good mood."

Sincere perched on the armrest beside him, her nails idly dragging across his sleeve. "Shouldn't I be?" she asked, letting her voice dip just enough to sound teasing. "My man just told me he's been looking out for me. That he handled things."

Lorde's eyes flickered. His instincts kicked in, coiling low in his stomach, but he kept his expression smooth. "Funny," he mused. "Couple days ago, you were moving different, looking at me like you ain't know whether to trust me or not."

Sincere inhaled slowly, keeping her mask in place. "I had a rough night. You saw how shaken up I was. But then I thought about it," she said, tilting her head slightly. "And I realized—I was never alone in that."

Lorde leaned back slightly, studying her. She was saying all the right things. Stroking his ego just right. But was it *real*? Or was she just telling him what he wanted to hear? His gut told him to test it, to push a little further.

"You sure about that?" he murmured, dragging the back of his fingers across her jaw, tilting her chin up slightly. "Ain't no part of you still wondering what my motives are?"

Sincere let a smile play on her lips, shifting closer. "Lorde," she said, voice soft. "You think too much."

Lorde's eyes widened slightly. "That right?"

She let her nails scrape lightly against the fabric of his sleeve, her touch light, but deliberate. "I know what kind of man you are," she whispered. "And I know you don't do anything without a reason."

His gaze darkened, locking onto hers. "And that don't bother you?"

Sincere tilted her head, dragging a slow, lazy fingertip across his collar. "Why would it?" she murmured. "As long as I'm on your side."

Lorde's grip tightened slightly against her hip, his body reacting to her words in a way that made his pulse slow, steady. Maybe he had been overthinking it and she was finally seeing that she belonged to him.

"That's my girl," he murmured, tapping her thigh lightly before shifting her off his lap and standing with smooth ease. "I got some shit to handle," he said, adjusting his watch. "But I'll be back."

Sincere nodded, keeping her expression warm, her movements relaxed as she leaned back against the couch.

Lorde took a step toward the door, but paused, glancing over his shoulder one last time. "Stay close, Sincere."

The words settled in the air between them, a quiet command wrapped in something that almost sounded like care. But Sincere knew better. "Actually," she said, shifting in her seat, "before you go, there's something I wanted to run by you."

Lorde turned back, brow lifting slightly. "Yeah?"

She nodded, leaning forward like she was letting him in on something private. "I want to take some time to write. Get back to the music properly."

Lorde's gaze sharpened, but he didn't interrupt. She took that as her cue to keep going.

"I was thinking about heading over to my old place—the childhood home," she continued. "There's something about being in that space that gets me to that deep place I need for writing."

Lorde's expression stayed unreadable, but Sincere saw the flicker of hesitation. "You wanna go *back* there?" he asked, tilting his head slightly.

She gave a soft, almost nostalgic smile. "Yeah. That house holds a lot of memories. Some I need to face. You know how it is—you gotta dig deep to pull out the real shit."

Lorde's jaw rolled, a flicker of resistance tightening his features.

Sincere pressed forward. "I want to stay there overnight at least. Get lost in it. No distractions, no noise."

That made him pause. "Overnight?"

She nodded. "It's just for the creative process. You know how I am when I get in my zone."

Lorde rubbed his chin, contemplating. He didn't like the idea of her being somewhere outside of his control, not for that long. But this was about her music. If there was one thing Lorde could respect, it was the hustle.

He sighed, nodding once. "Fine. But Carl and Andre are going with you."

Sincere didn't let her relief show. She just gave a small shrug, standing up to stretch. "That's fine. But they stay outside. I don't need their bad attitudes messing up my energy, especially *Andre*."

That made Lorde laugh, a real, low chuckle. "Yeah, that nigga's an asshole."

Sincere shook her head, a trace of humor slipping through. "Tell me about it."

Lorde studied her for a second, his mood lighter now. Then he nodded toward the chessboard sitting in the corner.

"You play?"

Sincere followed his gaze, then let out a soft laugh. "Not at all."

Lorde leaned back, his voice dripping with confidence. "Good. I'll teach you."

She arched a brow. "You tryna hustle me?"

He leaned in slightly, his voice dipping. "You know I always play to win, ma."

Sincere met his gaze, keeping her expression open, her voice soft. "Then show me how."

Lorde grinned, gesturing toward the board. "Come on, then."

She took a seat across from him, letting the moment play out. The pieces sat between them, an intricate battlefield of carved wood and strategy. Lorde's fingers hovered over the board, his touch deliberate as he moved a pawn forward.

"Chess is a game of power," he murmured, watching her as she studied the board. "Every piece got a role to play. The pawns? Disposable. They move forward, never back, always sacrificing. The knights? They move different—unexpected, catching niggas off guard. But the king?" He tapped the black king piece lightly. "The king don't do much, but everything revolves around him. You protect the king at all costs. 'Cause when he falls, the game is over."

His voice was so smooth, so deliberate, that Sincere almost forgot what she was doing. It was rare to hear him like this—calm, patient, even *gentle*. He was actually teaching her, not just playing with her.

For a moment, she let herself forget what he was. She picked up a piece, hesitant. "And the queen?"

Lorde leaned back slightly. "The most powerful piece on the board."

Sincere's brow lifted. "Why?"

He chuckled. "'Cause she can do anything. Move however she wants, go as far as she needs. But she gotta play smart. If she moves reckless, she gets taken out—and the king? He's fucked."

Sincere rolled her knight between her fingers. She wasn't sure if they were still talking about chess anymore.

Lorde gave a lazy wave toward the board. "Go 'head. You make the first move."

Sincere glanced at him, then back at the pieces, fingers tightening around the knight she had been rolling between her fingers. She didn't know much about chess, but she knew enough to not want to embarrass herself. She slid a pawn forward, slow and deliberate, watching for his reaction.

Lorde hummed, amused. "Safe move." He reached for his own piece, shifting his knight into position effortlessly. "But safe don't win wars."

Sincere scoffed lightly, tilting her head. "Not everybody likes going to war."

Lorde propped his elbow on the table, leaning his chin into his hand. "Everybody *in* one, whether they like it or not. Life's a constant battle. The difference is whether you fight back or sit still and wait to get got."

Sincere made another move, letting his words sink in. "You always been like this?"

Lorde lifted a brow. "Like what?"

She gestured vaguely. "So damn intense. You talk like every step in life is some kind of battlefield."

He chuckled low. "'Cause it is." He nodded toward the board. "You playing chess right now, but you ain't really *playing* yet. You moving pieces 'cause you feel like you supposed to. Not 'cause you got a real strategy."

Sincere frowned, glancing at the board. "That's 'cause I don't know how to play."

Lorde's gaze lingered on her before he reached forward and slid one of her pieces back a space. "Then let me teach you."

His voice was softer now. Not demanding. Just . . . guiding.

Sincere watched as he pointed at the different pieces, explaining their movements, their strengths, their weaknesses. He was patient, surprisingly so, and for the first time since she met him, she saw something other than control in his eyes.

"Why do you wear those beads?" she asked after a beat, nodding toward his wrist. The obsidian beads were smooth, polished, threaded together like a quiet shield around him.

Lorde glanced down at them, rubbing his thumb over one of the stones. "Protection."

"Protection from what?"

His voice carried a teasing lilt. "You don't believe in all that, do you?"

She shrugged. "I don't know what I believe in."

He tapped the beads absently. "Maman Clo gave 'em to me. Said they keep the bad spirits away."

Sincere studied him. "Who is she?"

"My grandmother," he answered, shifting a piece on the board without looking. "Raised me after my pops got killed. She's a *mambo*, a real one. People come to her when they need guidance. Protection. Answers."

Sincere hesitated before making her next move. "You believe in all that?"

Lorde chuckled. "Shit, I *know* it's real. You can't grow up in New Orleans and not know. This city is built on spirits and debts."

She tilted her head. "Debts?"

Lorde flicked his gaze up to her, eyes dark and unreadable. "Everybody owe somebody somethin'."

Something about the way he said it sent a shiver down her spine. But she pushed past it.

Sincere studied him for a moment, then nodded toward the board. "You move like somebody who's always thinking five steps ahead."

Lorde angled his head, voice edged with dry humor. "That supposed to be a compliment?"

"An observation," she corrected. "Like you've always known exactly what you wanted."

His voice dropped, but his tone stayed certain. "I have."

Sincere hesitated before making her next move. "And what's that?"

Lorde sat back, fingers drumming against his knee. "You ever thought about what you really want?"

Sincere frowned slightly. "What do you mean?"

Lorde leaned in just a fraction. "I mean beyond the music. Beyond the career. What's it all leading to?"

Sincere hesitated. No one had ever asked her that before.

The edge in his face eased, revealing something quieter. "Me? I want a family. A real one. A woman I can love. A house. Maybe even a dog." He chuckled slightly. "Shit, I don't know. Never had none of that. But Maman said I could. Said *we* could. She's the one who told me you were part of my destiny that night at the carnival."

Sincere's breath caught in her throat. Any reminder of the night Aaliyah was killed made her feel like she was living the night all over again. "She did?" Her breath hitched slightly, but she masked it. "What exactly did she say?"

"That you were the one I was looking for." His voice dropped slightly. "That you had what it took to be a queen. She told me that she saw it in your cards when she gave you a reading. She said our destinies were connected."

That's when she put it all together. Lorde's Maman Clo was the woman who had given her the tarot reading. The one that had ended with the *Death* card.

Sincere swallowed, forcing herself to stay composed. "You really believe that?"

Lorde's gaze never wavered. "I *know* it."

For a moment, she wasn't sure what to say. The intensity in his words, the conviction she saw there . . . It was overwhelming.

She glanced up at him, at the way he watched her so intently, and before she could stop herself, she asked, "Where'd you learn to play?"

"My pops taught me," he said, his tone casual but distant. "Used to say it was a game for kings."

She hesitated, then pushed further. "Was he a king?"

His jaw tightened as he gave a short shake of his head. "Nah. But he wanted to be."

She took her time with her next move, trying to navigate both the board and the conversation. "What happened to him?"

For the first time, Lorde didn't answer right away. He sat back, eyes flickering toward the ceiling, the tension in his jaw subtle, but there. "He trusted the wrong nigga," he said finally. "One of his own. A Saint, just like him. Thought he was building something good. Thought he could change shit. But greed makes niggas stupid. His own *friend* took him out."

Sincere swallowed, feeling the weight in his words. *That's what made him like this.*

She saw it now—the reason behind the cruelty, the hunger for control. It wasn't just about power. It was about never being vulnerable. Never letting someone close enough to take him down the way his father was taken down.

"Lorde—"

"Don't," he cut in, shaking his head slightly. "I already know what you gon' say. That I shouldn't be mad. That I shouldn't let that shit define me. That hate ain't the way."

The curve of his mouth carried only bitterness. "You still don't get it, do you?" He gestured toward the board. "This world ain't about love. It's about strategy, control, and power. You think you can change people? That shit gets you killed. The world is the devil's playground, and if you wanna survive, you gotta learn how to *play*."

His words sat between them as they continued to play.

For the first time, Sincere saw him—not as the villain in her story, or the monster she had made him out to be, but as a man who had been hurt.

With that, he slid his rook across the board, knocking her king over. "Checkmate."

Sincere barely looked at the board. Her stomach felt tight, like she'd lost more than just a game.

Lorde studied her for a moment, then leaned forward. His hand grazed her cheek, his touch soft, almost reverent. Then, before she could move, before she could even *think*, his lips brushed against hers. His touch was cool, firm, and lingering just long enough to send a shiver down her spine.

And then, just as quickly, he pulled back. "Get some rest," he murmured, standing. "You gotta make sure your mind is right to write them hits. Gotta get some Grammys out of you." He winked an eye at her and Sincere couldn't ignore the butterflies she felt in her stomach. And with that, he was gone, leaving her sitting there, staring at the board.

The kiss still tingled against her lips.

And the worst part of it all was that, for a split second, she had forgotten to hate him.

Chapter 22

"I got you locked in for a sit-down with *Vibe* next week," Stacy rattled off, her voice brisk and businesslike. "*Complex* is interested in an exclusive about the album, but they want visuals to go with it, and *Essence* is still waiting on you to confirm that cover shoot. Oh, and let's not even talk about the brand deals sitting in my inbox."

Sincere shifted the phone to her other ear, rubbing at her temple. "*Essence*? Damn. I forgot about that one."

"I know," Stacy replied pointedly. "You keep forgetting and they keep circling back. They want you bad. And honestly? You need to take it. That cover would solidify you as more than just a streaming artist—it puts you on a whole new level."

Sincere sighed, letting her eyes flick toward the window, where the city lights blinked back at her. "I hear you."

"I hope so," Stacy said dryly. "Because I've been trying to drill this into your head for months. This is your first solo project under a label. They're watching your every move, waiting to see if you can carry this shit on your own. You can't afford to get distracted right now."

Sincere's stomach twisted. That was the problem, wasn't it? She was distracted. Every time she tried to refocus, some new piece of the mess Lorde had created pulled her back under.

But still . . .

She was different now.

A few months ago, she would've rolled her eyes, made some sarcastic remark about Stacy nagging her to death. She would've brushed her off with a "Damn, you talk too much, Stace," before hanging up.

Now she could hear the truth in Stacy's words, the value in her expertise. And she hated that it had taken her this long to appreciate it. "I'll lock in the *Essence* cover," Sincere said finally, voice softer. "And the *Vibe* sit-down too."

For a second, all Sincere could hear was the faint sound of papers shuffling on the other end. When Stacy finally spoke, her tone had shifted—something carefully creeping into her words. ". . . You serious?"

Sincere smiled slightly. "Yeah. I mean . . . you're right. About all of it."

Stacy let out a laugh. "Damn. Maybe you really are growing up."

Sincere chuckled. "Yeah, well. Shit changes."

Stacy exhaled and for the first time in a while, the weight between them didn't feel so heavy. Then she spoke again and just like that, the moment shattered. "Anyway, none of this is my problem anymore."

Sincere blinked. "What?"

Stacy sighed, like she had been preparing for this. "This is me officially handing in my resignation."

A sharp silence settled over the call.

Sincere swallowed. "You're quitting?"

Stacy let out a short, humorless laugh. "Girl, you say that like you're surprised."

"I knew it was coming," Sincere admitted, voice quiet. "Just figured you'd at least finish out the year first."

"Yeah, well," Stacy said. "My sanity wouldn't have lasted that long."

Sincere stared at the ceiling. "Who's replacing you?"

"No idea," Stacy replied. "But according to Lorde, you'll get whoever you want. No questions asked."

That made Sincere pause. "He said that?"

Stacy's tone turned wry. "Mm-hmm. I swear, I don't know how you do it. You got all these men wrapped around your damn finger, giving you whatever you ask for. Even my own damn husband. Maybe I need to take notes."

Sincere didn't bother arguing. What was the point?

Stacy sighed, her voice softening. "Look, for what it's worth, I hope this whole thing works out for you. Whatever this is."

Sincere stayed quiet.

"You good?" Stacy asked after a beat.

"Yeah," Sincere murmured. "I'm good."

"All right, then. Guess this is it." Stacy hesitated. "I'll see you around, Sincere."

And then she was gone.

Sincere lowered the phone slowly, staring at the blank screen. She hovered over her recent calls. Lena's name sat there—unanswered. Sincere chewed the inside of her cheek. Lena wasn't answering and it had to be because she knew that Sincere had found her out. That was the only explanation.

Sincere stared at the unanswered calls, the texts sitting on *delivered* but never *read.* The silence was deafening, but it wasn't empty. It was full of guilt and the weight of truth. Lena knew she had been caught and knew there was no talking her way out of this one.

Sincere exhaled slowly, pressing her phone against her thigh. It was almost funny in a twisted way. Lena had always been the one with the silver tongue, able to spin a lie so well that even she believed it. She could talk her way into and out of anything. Except this time. There was nothing to say.

Sincere had given her chances, ignored the red flags, let

Lena drag her down time and time again under the excuse of *loyalty*. But now that Sincere *knew* for a fact Lena had been feeding Lorde information, that she'd been a snake in the grass this whole time—Lena didn't even have the decency to answer her phone and own up to it.

Sincere clenched her jaw, tossing her phone onto the bed beside her. It didn't matter. She didn't need Lena anymore. She didn't need her excuses, her fake friendship, her ability to make every betrayal sound like an act of love. Lena had made her choice. Sincere had bigger things to focus on.

With that thought in mind, she grabbed her phone again. She needed to get a discreet message to Imani. After a moment, she typed: **The writing process always starts at 8:00 pm. Creative flow is everything. I can't wait to get started writing tonight.**

She stared at the message for a moment before pressing *post*.

Seconds later, Imani liked it.

Sincere let out a slow breath, relief washing over her. *She got it.*

Now, all she had to do was set the rest of her plan in motion.

Sincere pushed open the door and stepped into the vestibule where Andre and Carl were posted up, their focus locked onto a battered deck of cards spread across the small table between them. A nearly empty bag of chips lay crumpled to the side, and the air was thick with the scent of their cologne, mixed with the faint trace of cigarettes from earlier.

Andre had a card in his hand, ready to play, but when he spotted Sincere, he glanced up, eyes narrowing.

"I need y'all to take me somewhere," she said, folding her arms as she leaned against the doorway. "Tonight."

Carl exhaled, already bracing for whatever was about to come. "Where to?"

"Seventh ward to my childhood home. I need space to write, and that's the place I do my best thinking."

Carl nodded, but Andre was still watching her with that lazy, suspicious stare. "How long?"

"Overnight."

That made both of them pause.

Sincere clocked the way their postures shifted, how Andre sat back in his chair like he was already preparing to shut that down.

Before he could, she cut him off. "I already told Lorde," she said smoothly. "He's good with it."

That was enough to make Carl glance at Andre, waiting to see how he'd react.

Andre let out a deep, dramatic sigh, shaking his head before finally speaking. "*Man*, I knew your ass was gonna pull some shit like this as soon as we got started with this game. And why you had to go over our head and talk to Lorde about it?"

Sincere leaned back, voice dry. "Because I didn't feel like arguing with *your* mouthy ass."

Carl exhaled a quiet laugh, but Andre just stared at her, unimpressed.

"You sure Lorde cool with this?" Carl asked with an arched brow.

Sincere nodded. "He is. He knows I need the space to write."

Andre scoffed. "And it *just so happens* that the only place you can write is some run-down house in the middle of the fuckin' hood?"

Sincere narrowed her eyes. "It's not run-down. And it's *mine.*"

Carl sighed. "You do realize we gotta stay out there all night now, right?"

Sincere shrugged. "Not my problem."

Andre shook his head. "Nah, 'cause I *know* your ass gon' be complainin' if somethin' happen."

"Nothing's gonna happen," she countered smoothly. "Not with two *big, bad Saints* watching me, right?"

Carl pressed his lips together, clearly holding back a laugh.

Andre glared. "Ain't nobody laughin'."

Sincere's grin was quick and cutting. "I am."

"You know what? You *always* got some shit to say," he muttered.

She arched a brow. "And? Stop actin' like you don't like it."

Andre squinted at her, like he was trying to decide whether to cuss her out or let it slide. Then, after a beat, he let out a low chuckle, shaking his head.

"Aight, you got it," he admitted, pushing his cards aside. "I *do* kinda be feelin' it when a woman pop her shit. But don't tell nobody."

Sincere tapped her temple, grinning. "Your secret's safe with me."

She turned to head back inside, but before she could close the door, she heard Andre's voice again. "What you lookin' at, you soft-ass nigga?" He barked at Carl, who had been grinning at the exchange. "Stop all that cheesin' and play your card so I can win my money back."

She stepped back inside, satisfaction warming her chest.

Carl chuckled, shaking his head, and slapped a card down. "Come on, man. Let's just get this over with."

Andre grumbled under his breath, but finally gave in.

Sincere was completely satisfied as she closed the door behind her.

As the night sky began to cloak the city, Sincere sat on the windowsill of her bedroom, staring out into the darkness. Her fingers drummed against her thigh, thoughts racing. She was anxious. Time felt like it was moving at a snail's pace. *Lorde thinks he's untouchable. That he can do what he wants with me. I can't keep living like this. I want nothing to do with him.*

And yet . . .

She exhaled slowly, pressing her forehead against the glass. She had spent so much time hating Lorde, but now that she had seen more of him—seen the *man* beneath the monster—she couldn't shake the feeling that he wasn't beyond redemption. *Stop it*, she told herself. *He can't be saved.* Not after what he did. He *killed* Aaliyah like she was nothing. He wasn't a good man and never would be. Lorde had taken so much from her. Not just her friend. He'd taken her freedom, her career . . . her life. She couldn't continue to live a life where he got to dictate all the moves she made. He wanted her to love him and she never would.

She grabbed her bag, slipped her phone inside, and rose to her feet. She had a lot of things she needed to consider, but all of that had to wait until later.

Right now, it was time to meet Supreme.

Chapter 23

The ride home was a quiet one. Sincere sat in the back seat, staring out the window as familiar streets blurred past. She felt like she was watching a memory instead of the present.

The house wasn't far from the heart of the city, but it was tucked in a part of New Orleans East that had changed a lot over the years. Some of the houses were newer, rebuilt and remodeled since the time she last was there, while others had greatly changed. Of course, Sincere's home was still standing strong. She had made sure of that over the years. It was different, but almost completely the same.

As they pulled up, she felt her heart tighten. The last time she'd been here, she was just a girl, allowing herself to have dreams that felt impossible back then. Now, she had made something real from what was once a fantasy.

Both Andre and Carl jumped out of the SUV before she could even reach for the door. Carl scanned the surroundings like they had just entered enemy territory. Andre stretched as he stood back, cracking his neck like he was getting ready for a fight.

Sincere sighed, stepping out of the car. "Y'all are a little dramatic, don't you think?"

"We get paid to do a job," Carl replied smoothly, heading toward the house. "And we don't do it halfway."

Andre didn't bother responding. He just walked straight to the door, checking the locks, before turning to her expectantly.

Sincere fought back the irritation bubbling in her chest. She needed them to leave. The second she pulled out her keys and unlocked the door, they pushed past her, stepping inside like they owned the place.

"What the hell?" she snapped.

Andre was already heading toward the hallway, gun in hand. "Checking the house."

Sincere folded her arms, her tone edged with mockery. "What do you think, I'm hiding a fugitive? This is my place."

Carl stayed near the door. "You know the drill. Lorde wants to make sure you're safe. We ain't leaving you alone without clearing the place first."

Sincere exhaled, keeping her expression bored even though her heart was hammering against her ribs. They couldn't find Supreme. He was supposed to be here already. Where was he? The search didn't take long. She only had to endure just a few minutes of doors creaking open and Andre's heavy boots thudding against the floors.

"All clear," he finally announced, reappearing in the hallway.

Carl gave her a once-over, as if deciding whether she was planning something. "We'll be out front. Don't try nothing stupid."

Sincere gave him a dry smile. "Wouldn't dream of it."

Andre scoffed. "Yeah, we heard that shit before."

With that, they stepped outside, locking the door behind them. Then, just as she let out a shaky breath, she heard it. It was the smallest sound, but enough to let her know she wasn't alone. She spun toward the hallway.

Supreme stepped forward from the darkness, moving with the kind of quiet control that had always set him apart from any other man she'd ever met. Her breath caught as she watched him. It had only been a few weeks since she last saw him, but standing in front of him now, it felt like years had passed. Her entire world had shifted in such a short amount of time, and yet he was still him. He was the one steady thing in the middle of all the chaos.

He was dressed in all black, his fitted tee stretching over the kind of body that was built to protect, to shield, to take hits so others wouldn't have to. He had the body of a soldier. But it wasn't just his presence that made her feel safer. It was the way he looked at her. He didn't say anything at first. He just took his time reading her. His deep, steady gaze skimming over every inch of her like he was checking for unseen wounds.

Sincere felt exposed beneath his gaze, but nothing like the way Lorde made her feel when he was trying to find her weaknesses so he could exploit them. Supreme's gaze wasn't hunting for vulnerabilities. He was making sure she was okay.

She had spent so long convincing herself that no man would ever truly put her first. That love, in any form, was transactional. But Supreme had never asked for anything. Yet, he had always been watching over her and keeping her safe.

Her throat went dry and suddenly she felt it—the pull in the center of her chest. It was deeper than attraction. It was much deeper than any desire she had ever felt. This wasn't the feeling she had felt for Lorde the other night. Supreme didn't need fixing. Being around him didn't drain her. Being around him felt like breathing.

His eyes softened slightly. "You okay?"

She tried to answer, but for a moment, all she could do was look at him. And in that moment, she knew it was *him*. The one man who had ever made her feel safe. The one man who was meant to be hers.

"Yeah," she finally managed, her voice quieter than she meant for it to be. "I'm okay."

Supreme's gaze lingered on her, like he wasn't sure if he believed her. But then he nodded once, stepping closer. "Good."

The space between them felt too small. Too much was stirring inside of her from him being so close. Turning around, she walked to the living room and took a seat. Supreme followed suit. Sincere swallowed hard and took a slow breath, trying to shake off the effect he had on her. She couldn't afford to get caught up in this.

"I need you to listen," she said, her voice lower, more urgent. "I need to tell you everything about what happened in the past. I need you to know the real story between me and Lorde."

Supreme didn't move a muscle. He sat as still as a statue, and she told him everything. Then she told him about Lena.

"She won't answer my calls," Sincere admitted. "I've called. I've texted. Nothing. I'm worried about her."

"Nothing happened to her." Supreme's jaw tightened. "The only reason she's staying away is because she knows you know."

Sincere swallowed hard. "Yeah. That's what I'm afraid of. She was the only person I had."

"Not anymore," Supreme spoke up. "You have Imani. And you have me."

As if he had spoken a spell, Sincere instantly felt something change. She suddenly felt safe enough to breathe and say the things she hadn't dared to let pass her lips. She was sitting on the couch in the house she grew up in, the worn fabric familiar beneath her fingertips. Supreme sat across from her, his broad frame taking up space in a way that should have made her feel smaller, but instead, it made her feel steadier.

He was watching her carefully, his dark eyes locked onto hers, waiting. Like he knew there was more she needed to say.

She exhaled slowly, running her fingers through her hair before finally speaking. "I need to tell you something else."

Supreme's posture didn't change, but his gaze sharpened, his focus narrowing in on her. "I'm listening."

She swallowed hard. How could she say this? How could she make him understand without breaking herself apart in the process? "It's Lorde." She looked down at her hands. "I'm losing control."

Sincere pressed forward before she lost her nerve. "He's watching everything. Controlling everything. Stopping by whenever he wants to." Her voice was barely above a whisper now. "And I'm running out of ways to keep him at arm's length."

Supreme's entire body went rigid. His hands curled into fists against his thighs, but he didn't interrupt her.

"I can't keep pushing him off forever. Eventually, he's going to expect more. He's going to demand it." She let out a shaky breath. "And if I don't give him what he wants, he's going to figure out that I've been playing him. I'm afraid of what will happen then."

Supreme's silence was louder than anything he could have said. She lifted her gaze, searching his face, trying to find some kind of reassurance in his expression. But what she saw there wasn't comfort. It looked like rage.

Sincere shook her head quickly, trying to backpedal. "I'm not saying I'll let it happen. I'm saying that—"

"That you feel like you have no choice." Supreme's voice was rough, edged with something dangerous. "You don't need to explain."

For a long moment, Supreme didn't say anything. That was worse than whatever she expected. She could handle yelling. She could handle frustration, but this silent, contained fury made her chest tighten. It made her stomach twist with something she couldn't name.

Finally, he leaned forward, his elbows resting on his knees. "Sincere." His voice was lower now, steady but intense. "Look at me. I need you to hear me when I say this. You are not alone in this." His eyes locked onto hers, and she felt those words settle into her bones. "You don't have to do anything you don't want to do."

Her breath hitched. "But what if I do?" she whispered. "What if it's the only way to keep him from figuring me out? What if I have to—"

Supreme was shaking his head before she even finished. "No. I will never let that happen."

She swallowed, her hands curling into the fabric of her jeans. "I just don't want you to look at me differently . . ." Her voice was small, fragile in a way she hated.

Supreme's brows pulled together. "You really think that would change the way I see you?"

She looked away. "I don't know."

His fingers brushed against her chin, tilting her face back up to his. "Sincere, listen to me." His tone was firm but gentle, each word sinking into her skin like an oath. "There is nothing you could do to change how I see you. Nothing."

She exhaled shakily, searching his face, and found nothing but sincerity.

"I'll do everything I can to make sure it doesn't come to that," he continued. "But let's say we were in some imaginary universe, and it came to that. You don't owe anyone an explanation for doing what you have to do to survive."

Her chest ached, because she believed him. For the first time in her life, it made her wonder if the feeling that she felt for him was love. It could be and *that* was terrifying. She let out a short, breathless laugh, trying to lighten the heavy emotion pressing against her ribs. "When did you get so damn wise?"

Supreme leaned back against the couch, his amusement shimmering in his eyes. "Always been wise, ma."

Sincere rolled her eyes, a real smile ghosting over her lips. "Oh yeah? What's the plan then, Mr. Wise?"

His expression sobered, the levity fading. "I'm going to handle everything, but I have to move carefully." His gaze flicked toward the door, as if making sure they were still alone. "I can't rush this. I have to move on logic, not emotion."

Sincere nodded slowly, understanding his words. This wasn't just about her. This was about survival. Supreme was all about playing the long game.

"You have to trust me," Supreme added.

"I do." Her voice was quiet but firm.

The air in the room had changed. Sincere could feel it. It was a slow, simmering tension pressing against her skin, thickening the air, pulling her deeper into the moment. It wasn't lust. She knew lust. She had drowned in it before. This was something else.

It was built in the way Supreme looked at her, like she was something rare and he saw her in ways no man ever had. She had spent so long being wanted for her body, her name, her image. But Supreme wanted all of her. And when he stood up, he reached for her—slowly, carefully, giving her time to pull away if she wanted.

He pulled her up and she stepped forward, closing the space between them. Supreme's fingers flexed at his sides before he lifted them, skimming the bare skin of her arms, like he was savoring the moment. "C'mere," he murmured.

Her breath caught. She had known this man for some time. But she had never known him like this. She moved closer, her hands instinctively curling into the fabric of his shirt. He let out a slow exhale, his fingers tightening slightly on her waist.

"Damn, ma," he murmured.

She swallowed, her heart hammering. "What?"

His expression turned languid, threaded with heat. "I was tryna be cool about this, but you makin' it real hard for me."

Heat flushed through her, deep and sudden. A rush of warmth pooled low in her stomach as his hands slid down to her hips, holding her there, firm but not forceful.

"I'm not stoppin' you," she whispered, voice almost shaky.

Supreme exhaled slowly, his forehead tipping forward until it rested against hers. His voice was lower now, softer. "I need you to be sure, baby."

She closed her eyes for a second. Then she lifted her head, her lips brushing against his. "I am."

That was all it took. Supreme kissed her—slow, deep, and unhurried. Not like a man who was just trying to have her, but like one who had been waiting.

Sincere sank into it, her body molding against his like she'd always been meant to be there. His hands slid up her back, fingertips dragging along her spine, memorizing her. The kiss was a slow-burning unraveling, deep and deliberate, his tongue sliding against hers in a way that had her knees weakening beneath her.

She had kissed so many men before, but never with this kind of care and intensity. He was reading her with every touch, learning her reactions, adjusting his movements, mapping out every single thing that made her melt.

And *God*, she was melting.

Her fingers slid into the short curls at the back of his head, tugging slightly, and he groaned against her mouth. That sound sent a fresh rush of warmth pooling through her veins. She needed more of him. He was taking his time like he was anticipating her, but she didn't feel like she could wait. The urgency that she felt messed with her mind—it was another new feeling. She pulled back slightly, her breath unsteady.

Supreme's gaze washed over her face, his pupils blown wide, his lips slightly parted. "You good?" he murmured again, voice thick with restraint.

Sincere licked her lips, nodding. "Yeah."

Supreme's jaw ticked. He held her gaze for a moment, then nodded once. "Aight."

Then, with the kind of careful ease that sent a shiver down her spine, he lifted her into his arms, making her wrap her legs around his body. She gasped slightly, but he held her steady, one arm beneath her thighs as his fingers slipped past her panties, the other wrapped securely around her back to hold her in place. Sincere let out a soft moan, her body responding to the hardness of his desire pressing against her.

"You good?"

She nodded against his neck, already breathless.

And then he carried her to the bed.

She had never felt anything like this before.

Supreme moved like a man who had been holding himself back for too long. He was gentle, but still in control. Every touch was measured and intentional. His lips moved over hers, slow and deep, as his hands explored her body like he was trying to commit every detail to memory. He worshipped her. Every curve. Every breath. He read her like she was the only thing in the world that mattered. And when she finally let herself completely unravel beneath him, Supreme held her through every moment of it.

His name fell from her lips like a prayer, and he groaned against her skin, pressing his forehead against hers, breathing her in as he dove in deep. It was then that Sincere realized . . . she had never really made love before. Sure, she'd had *sex*. She'd lost herself in the haze of lusty desire, reveling in the fleeting euphoria of bodies colliding, and the mindless pursuit of pleasure. But this was love.

Supreme had been waiting for this, but he wasn't the only one. She had been as well. She had been waiting her entire life for the moment when she would finally make love.

"What if I told you I loved you?" Supreme whispered in her ear.

Her stomach did a flip as that thought popped into her mind. The main reason being because she knew it was true. She could feel it in the way he held her, the way he whispered her name against her skin, the way he moved inside her like he was afraid to break her, but desperate to keep her.

And she gave in to him completely.

When Supreme entered her from behind, he began to massage her shoulders, helping her body to relax and adjust to his massive size. Once he was in, he lowered his hands, gripping her hips. He began moving, slowly at first, and then switched up the motion, sliding out slowly before slamming right back in. The contrast of the movement nearly drove Sincere crazy. She had to bite down hard on her bottom lip to stop herself from screaming aloud.

He pounded into her, his thrusts becoming more urgent. Sincere rode the tempo like a professional, making her ass quake. The vision of it sent all the blood in Supreme's body rushing to his dick. He reached his hand around her body and pinched her nipple.

She moaned, her pussy clenching around him as her sweet nectar dripped down her thighs.

"Tell me who this belongs to?"

The answer spilled right out of her lips. She didn't even have to think about it. The words came out naturally. "You, Daddy . . . all of this belongs to you," she purred. She'd said that line before, but this was the first time that she actually meant it.

Wanting to take it up a notch, Supreme reached around, his fingers finding her clit. He rubbed it in time with his thrusts, sending waves of pleasure through her body. Sincere felt herself getting closer and closer to the edge, but when he used his other hand to grip her ponytail, snapping her head back, she lost it.

She cried out, her orgasm hitting her like a freight train. The sight of her bucking her ass to the shock waves coursing through her body, was what did it for Supreme. He let out a low growl, his dick pulsing inside of her as he followed her right into bliss.

Later, when the storm of their emotions subsided, Supreme pulled her close. His hand slid over her back as he pulled her close to him, his lips brushing against her forehead. Neither of them spoke for a while. They didn't need to. Everything between them was felt. It didn't need to be explained.

Sincere's fingers traced small patterns against his chest. Her heart was still pounding, but in a different way now. For once, she felt like sticking around after the sex was over. It was a new feeling and it almost made her nervous. Instead of fighting the urge, she closed her eyes and decided to relax into it. She had never felt safe enough around a man to do this. It was new territory, but she was ready to explore.

Supreme pressed a soft kiss to her temple. "You good?"

Sincere nodded against his chest, closing her eyes.

Yes, I'm good. More than good.

Chapter 24

The entire inside of Lena's apartment smelled like takeout and body odor. She sat on the couch, a half-eaten box of lo mein balanced on one knee, the TV playing some reality show she wasn't even watching. Her phone sat on the table, untouched for hours. She wasn't in the mood to scroll or text. She was just waiting.

She hadn't left in days, maybe even weeks. The days bled together in a haze of sleepless nights and days of way too much thinking. She was still telling herself it would all be fine, that Lorde would come through soon. But the longer the silence stretched, the harder it was to believe it.

The lo mein tasted like cardboard. At this point, she was just shoving it in her mouth to distract herself from the pain. She set the box aside, rubbing her hands down her face.

Even though she did everything he told her to do, she couldn't make herself believe that it was enough. Because she knew how Lorde worked. She spent years witnessing the way he thought.

If something went wrong, it was *never* his fault. It was always yours.

And a *lot* had gone wrong. Even though Lena did what he told her, things had still gone wrong.

Sincere was supposed to call Lorde that night, not Supreme. She was supposed to surrender to him, throw herself at his feet and prove that he was the only one who could save her from anything. But that didn't happen and the reason was because of him. His treatment of her was why she didn't trust him. But Lorde would never look in the mirror and see where he had gone wrong. He would only see that Lena failed at making Sincere trust him.

Knowing that is what had her scared. There was no way that Sincere would trust her again. And, even if she did, Lena didn't feel like she could ever look her in the eyes again, knowing what she did. If Lorde didn't come through on his promise, then she would have nothing to gain from betraying a friend.

Lena shook her head, tension coiling in her chest. She had been waiting for this call. And then finally, when she least expected it, the phone began to vibrate. Her breath caught. She grabbed it so fast she almost dropped it.

Her stomach twisted, her fingers tightening around the device. She could feel the one thing that she'd been trying so hard to ignore. That creeping sensation in her gut she'd been shoving down and refusing to acknowledge. She hesitated for half a second, then forced herself to take a breath.

She swiped to answer. "Damn," she said, her voice light, playful. "Took you long enough to hit me up."

There was a pause, just long enough for the hairs on the back of her neck to stand up.

And then, with a voice as calm as the eye of a category 5 hurricane, he spoke.

"Been lookin' for you, ma. You ain't been on the block in a minute." Lorde's voice was smooth. "You good?"

Lena forced a laugh. "Damn, I can't take a break without you sending out a search party?"

Lorde chuckled, but there was no warmth in it. "I was expecting you to report back to me by now. You know I don't like being ignored."

"I haven't been ignoring you. I know I didn't reach out, but . . ." She shifted, forcing herself to sound unbothered. "I've been waiting on you, actually. Figured you'd call once you handled things with Sincere."

A beat of silence followed, and she sat on the edge of it, not breathing.

Then—"Let's link."

Her throat went dry. "Right now?"

"Yeah." His tone was deathly flat. "You know the spot."

That was when she knew and the floor tilted under her. Finally, the truth stopped playing hide-and-seek in her mind.

She knew *the spot.* It was where Lorde took people who didn't come back—the bayou—the same place he'd taken her before when he told her all about his plan.

Lena licked her lips, her mind racing. She did everything he asked. Hadn't she? Her voice came out steady, but she could hear the thin layer of fear beneath it. She knew that he could too.

"What's going on, Lorde?"

"C'mon, ma. Just pull up. Ain't 'bout nothing. I just wanna talk to you. I'll send a driver to scoop you."

Lena's stomach churned. She knew better than to go. Her mind spun through excuses, through escape plans, but she knew Lorde. There was nowhere to run. His reach extended everywhere. She could hear him waiting on the other end for her to make a choice, either come voluntarily or be taken against her will. She had made plenty of mistakes in her life, but going out scared wasn't about to be one of them.

She sat up straighter, gripping the phone just a little tighter. "Aight," she said, her voice even. "I'm getting ready." She hung up before he could respond.

For the first time in weeks, she got up to take a shower, get dressed, and face whatever was waiting for her. Even if she already knew how this story ended.

Lorde stood by the water's edge, inhaling the damp, humid air of the Louisiana swamps. The murky surface stretched before him, rippling as something unseen moved beneath it. Gators, probably. He exhaled slow, rolling his cigar between his fingers, watching as the thick mist hung low over the cypress trees, curling like ghostly fingers through the Spanish moss.

This was a place of death, where secrets sank deep into the black water and never surfaced again. The perfect place for him. His phone buzzed in his pocket, breaking the heavy silence. He frowned, glancing down at the screen.

It was Maman Clo.

Lorde answered immediately, pressing the phone to his ear. "Maman."

The old woman's voice drifted through the receiver, low and heavy with something he didn't like—worry. "I had a dream about you, boy."

Lorde closed his eyes briefly, tipping his head back toward the sky. He didn't want to hear this. Not now, when he was about to tie up another loose end.

"Maman, I don't got time—"

"You need to listen." Her voice cut through his protest, firm and unwavering. "You on the wrong path, Laurent. You need to turn back while you still can."

Lorde's jaw clenched at the use of his full name. "I'm doin' exactly what needs to be done," he muttered. "Some things got in the way of what's supposed to be mine. I'm just setting it right."

She spoke after a long pause. “This ain’t the way.”

Lorde shook his head, pacing a few steps along the swamp’s edge. The crunch of gravel beneath his feet was the only sound besides the occasional croak of a frog in the distance. “I trusted the wrong people, Maman. You saw what was supposed to be mine, the future you told me I was promised. You think I’m about to let anybody take that from me? Hell, no. I’m cleaning house.”

“You are your father,” she said to him after another long pause. “He was a good man. He saw the good in people. *You are him.* Or at least, you can choose to be.”

“Nah.” Heat burned through his chest, but his voice was ice when he spoke. “My father was a *simp*.” Lorde pressed on. “He trusted the wrong people. That’s what got him killed. You think I’m about to make the same mistake?” He let out a short, humorless laugh. “Nah. I’m smarter than that.”

Maman Clo sighed, the sound heavy, full of something Lorde couldn’t, or wouldn’t, name. “You keep thinkin’ that, boy. One day, you gon’ see.”

Lorde’s gaze flicked up just in time to see headlights approaching through the dense trees. The car rolled to a stop, dust settling in the humid air. It was Lena.

He straightened, rolling his shoulders back. “I gotta go, Maman,” he said smoothly, already moving toward the car.

“Laurent, wai—”

Click.

He ended the call. And just like that, any lingering uncertainty drowned beneath the stillness of the swamp.

Lorde rolled his neck, letting the tension settle deep in his shoulders as he stepped out of his car. The bass from inside the club rumbled through the pavement, vibrating up his legs like a living thing. Neon lights flickered, flashing with the words

GIRLS, DRINKS, SIN in gaudy colors, painted the cracked sidewalk in electric red and blue.

He inhaled, taking in the scent of liquor, sweat, and perfume. This was the pungent mix of indulgence and corruption that defined this place. Women draped themselves over plush VIP booths, their bodies adorned in barely-there dresses. Tables overflowed with bottles of champagne, gold-plated hookahs billowing fragrant smoke into the air. Cocaine was out in the open and pills were being passed around like candy. Men in designer suits leaned in to take their hits off the dusty glass in front of them like it was nothing.

Lorde walked through it like he owned the place. But—he didn't. *Silvan* did and that fact sat like a thorn in the back of Lorde's mind, pricking at his pride every time he stepped foot in one of these establishments. It was the most popular club in the city.

He wanted to own clubs like this, but the elders of the Saints, the old heads, wouldn't allow it. They said that places like these represented their past. They wanted the Saints to keep their hands clean. Go legit with legitimate businesses. For Lorde, going legitimate meant going broke. Until he could get the elders out of the way permanently, the only way he could do business like this was to partner with men like Silvan.

Silvan had a presence that unsettled even the most ruthless men. He didn't have to flaunt his power . . . it just was. His movements were slow and calculated, like a king lounging on his throne, with full confidence that no man around could unseat him.

Lorde spotted him in the VIP lounge, surrounded by two women draped over his shoulders, their long nails tracing the tattoos on his dark skin. His signature gold teeth flashed as he grinned at Lorde's entrance, tapping his fingers against the table in a lazy rhythm.

"Look who finally decided to check in," Silvan drawled, his

voice smooth and amused. "I heard you startin' to clean up your mess so you can finally focus on business. About damn time."

Lorde's steps faltered for just a second—quick enough that most wouldn't notice. But Silvan did. "Always hearing 'bout me, huh?" Lorde schooled his face, lowering himself into the seat across from him. "You keep my name in your mouth like I'm your woman."

Silvan chuckled, dismissing the girls at his side with a lazy wave of his hand. They pouted but didn't protest, slinking away as he leaned forward, arms resting on his knees. "You know how it is, bruh. I got ears everywhere."

Lorde took a slow sip of the drink a waitress had just set down in front of him. He made a mental note: Silvan's men weren't just working with him. They were reporting back to Silvan too. The realization didn't sit well with him.

Silvan reclined in his seat, watching Lorde like he was a chess piece he'd already moved into position. "See, this why you my dog, Lorde." He gestured lazily, the ice in his drink clinking against the glass. "You don't hesitate to eliminate obstacles that stand in the way of your goal. That's why you gon' run this city."

Lorde paused to let his ego absorb the words. He took another sip, letting them settle. But then, Silvan flipped the conversation. "Check this, brother. I'ma keep it real wit' you," he said, swirling his drink. "Supreme is gonna be a problem."

Lorde remained composed, but his grip tightened around his glass. "Man, Supreme ain't built like that."

Silvan tilted his head, pretending to consider it. "You sure?" He let the question hang, waiting for Lorde to really think about it. "You need to make sure you ain't underestimating your enemy."

Lorde exhaled then rolled his shoulders back. "Supreme ain't my enemy."

Silvan studied him for a beat. Then he leaned in, lowering his voice. "That's how your pops got got, ain't it?"

A muscle feathered in Lorde's jaw, but he didn't speak.

Silvan tapped his ring against his glass. "Didn't his friend turn on him? You can't let that shit happen to you. You gotta be more vigilant. When you find a snake in your circle, gotta cut that shit off at the head." He tilted his glass toward Lorde, as if making a toast. "Ain't no point in eliminating the lil' garden snakes when you still got the king cobra runnin' loose."

Lorde had spent his whole life thinking about his father's death. He had replayed it a thousand times in his mind. His father had been betrayed. By someone he trusted. And now, Silvan was planting the same idea in his head.

Silvan sat back, letting it sink in. "I got eyes everywhere, bruh. And what I see is Supreme actin' real reckless. He don't respect you no more. Plotting to turn you into the elders. Get you replaced."

Lorde's fingers twitched. "You don't know what the fuck you talkin' about."

Silvan laughed, shaking his head. "You think that nigga still riding for you? When the last time you even heard from him? I'm tellin' you, he movin' like he planning somethin'. And you sittin' here waitin' on it . . ." He let the words hang before delivering the final blow. "Just like your pops did."

Lorde's grip on his glass was so tight, he thought it might shatter. He didn't trust Silvan. He wasn't a fool. But, at the same time, he couldn't help but think . . . what if he was right? What if Supreme *was* playing him?

Silvan watched him closely, saw the seed take root. He grinned, satisfied. "Think about it, big dog. Don't let history repeat itself."

Lorde exhaled slowly, setting his glass down. His mind was already turning.

And that's when Silvan knew he'd won.

He poured another drink, the liquid sloshing smoothly into the crystal glass before he slid it across the table to Lorde. It was a slow, intentional gesture meant to look like an offering, but Lorde knew better. This wasn't generosity. It was a transaction.

Silvan leaned back, gold teeth flashing as he spoke, voice smooth like syrup. "You want my advice?" He tapped the side of his own glass, making a dull *clink* against the table. "Handle Supreme before he handle you."

Lorde stared at the drink, his fingers twitching, but he didn't pick it up. Not yet.

"And if you need help?" Silvan grinned, lazy and smug. "You know I got you."

The weight of the offer sat between them.

Lorde finally wrapped his fingers around the glass, lifting it, but instead of drinking, he turned it in his hand, watching the way the liquid moved. It was all a game to Silvan. Lorde had always known he couldn't fully trust him, but this was the moment that solidified it. Silvan wasn't just an ally; he was a puppet master. He was the one moving pieces and manipulating the board.

And for the first time in a long time, Lorde wondered if *he* was the one being played. Still, he couldn't afford to show doubt. He lifted the glass in a slow toast before knocking back a sip. "I don't need help," he said, voice even and controlled.

Lorde set the glass down with a soft *clink*, his mind already moving at a hundred miles per hour. Silvan had planted a seed. Now, it was up to him to decide whether or not to let it grow.

Chapter 25

I keep runnin' to the wrong ones,
Lookin' for the right love . . .
Keep breakin' my own heart,
Don't know how to find trust . . .
Maybe I was never meant to make it out alive . . .

Sincere exhaled, shaking her head. The words felt flat and empty. She leaned back in her chair, staring down at the notebook on her desk, the lyrics staring back at her like they were taunting her. The melody had come to her easily, drifting in and out of her mind all morning, but the *feeling* wasn't there.

And without the feeling, the words were just words.

She picked up the pencil, tapping it against the desk as she tried to pull something *real* from herself. But it was like there was a block inside of her—some invisible object pressing against her chest, keeping her from going too deep. Lorde's control was fucking with her head. Her mind, her heart, her creativity . . . it all felt *trapped*.

Sincere closed her eyes and took in a deep breath. She needed something *real* to anchor her. And then, without thinking, she reached for her phone. Her thumb hovered over the name that had been sitting there, untouched, for months.

Mama.

The last time they spoke, it had ended with a slammed phone and words neither of them could take back. She could still hear the hurt in her mother's voice, the disappointment laced through every syllable. It had cut *deep.*

Sincere clenched her jaw, willing herself not let the pain take root again. But the truth was, she *missed* her mother. She missed *home.* Maybe she wasn't ready to hear her voice yet. But she *had* to see her. If she showed up in person, maybe her mother wouldn't turn her away.

She set the phone down and took a deep breath. She already knew where her mother lived. She always had. Her mother thought she had given her forwarding information to the people who bought the house Sincere grew up in, but what she didn't know was that *Sincere* was the buyer. She had paid for the house in full through a third party, not because she planned on living there, but because she couldn't stomach the idea of another family making memories in a place that held so many of her own.

When her mother had provided her new address, she had unknowingly given it to her daughter. Sincere pressed her lips together. It was time. She needed someone she could trust. Someone who *knew* her, not the version of her that Lorde had crafted. And if her mother still had love for her—if she could still *see* her beneath all of this—then maybe she wouldn't feel so alone.

The sound of men laughing greeted her the moment she stepped outside her apartment door. Carl and Andre were exactly where she expected them to be posted up in the vestibule, killing time with a deck of cards spread between them. Carl was leaning back in his chair, arms crossed over his chest, while Andre squinted down at the cards in his hand like they had personally disrespected him.

"Bro, *ain't no way* you got everything you pretending to have in your hands."

"Man, hurry up and play," Carl groaned, shaking his head. "We both know you 'bout to fold."

Sincere cleared her throat. "I need y'all to take me somewhere."

Both men looked up.

Carl set his cards down lazily, lifting an eyebrow. "You call Lorde yet?"

Sincere rolled her eyes. "It ain't about Lorde. Plus, I don't need to. He already told me I can go wherever I want as long as y'all are there."

Andre squinted, slightly amused. "Damn. Shorty get a little freedom and start feelin' herself."

Carl ignored him, leaning forward slightly. "Where we goin'?"

Sincere hesitated. All of a sudden she was second-guessing her decision. "I'm going to see family," she said simply. "My mother."

Andre whistled low. "Huh? You got family?"

Carl cut him a look. "Man, shut up."

Sincere crossed her arms, staring down Andre until he held up his hands in mock surrender.

"I just need to visit my mom. Now," she continued. "That a problem?"

Carl and Andre exchanged a look.

"Nah," Carl said slowly. "Just didn't expect it."

"Shit, I'm surprised too," Andre added. "Figured you was one of them Hollywood types. Folks dead to you soon as you touch money."

Sincere scoffed and rolled her eyes. "Yeah, 'cause y'all really know me like that."

Carl sighed, pushing his chair back. "All right. Let's get it done. But don't take too long."

Andre grumbled as he gathered up the cards. "Man, this is some bullshit. Right when I was 'bout to win."

Carl barked out a laugh. "Yeah right."

Sincere didn't say anything as she followed them to the car, sliding into the back seat as Carl got behind the wheel. The moment the door shut, she exhaled, pressing her head against the window, watching the city pass by.

Carl kept his focus on the road, but Andre, of course, had to run his mouth. "What's the occasion?" he asked, glancing at her through the rearview mirror. "Ain't talked to her in a minute, huh?"

Sincere shrugged, not taking her eyes off the window. "Something like that."

"Damn. What she do to you? It's that bad?"

"Did I say that?"

"Nah, but you ain't say it wasn't either."

She sighed, shifting in her seat. "I just . . . need to see her, all right?"

Andre held up his hands. "Aight, aight. I'm just sayin'. Don't let her hit you with that 'I told you so' too hard. Mamas love that shit."

Carl snorted. "You would know."

Andre shot him a look. "Nigga, shut up."

Sincere ignored them, gripping her phone in her lap. She didn't know what she was expecting when she got there. All she knew was that she needed to do this, no matter how much it hurt.

The car rolled to a slow stop in front of a small, modest home nestled between two others just like it. An old brick house with faded shutters, a tiny front porch, and a few potted plants that had seen better days. Sincere sat still, staring at it. It wasn't the house she grew up in. It was the one her mother had chosen for herself after washing her hands of everything that came before.

Carl and Andre didn't say anything, but she felt their eyes on her.

"Damn," Andre finally said, speaking up first. "You makin' all that money and didn't even bother to take care of ya moms? Now I *know* somethin' happened."

She swallowed. "I sent her money, but she always sent it back. No matter how I tried to get it to her."

Carl's brows shot up to his forehead. "Moms refusing money? That's crazy."

"She said 'money earned through evil deeds was the devil's poison'," Sincere continued, repeating the words that stung her when she heard her mother say them. "When I became an entertainer, my life became chaotic. My songs were 'worldly' and 'sinful'. She wanted her peace, even if it meant keeping me at arm's length."

"Oh." Andre nodded his head slowly. "She's a Holy Roller."

Sincere let out a sigh as she nodded. "Yeah, to the extreme. I guess she feels the harder she goes for Jesus, the more likely he is to save me." Her hand found the door handle, fingers gripping it tightly for a second before she forced herself to move.

"No turning back now," Carl told her before pulling a book out from somewhere he had it stashed. "Let us know if you need us to pull her off you if she tries to beat the devil out ya' ass."

Just as he opened the book, Andre slapped it out of his hands. "Nigga, put that fuckin' book down! You ain't gettin' paid to read."

Sincere was too nervous to find humor in their ridiculousness today. She stepped out of the car, taking slow, measured steps toward the front porch. The sun was still setting, the sky a soft blend of purple and gold, but something about the quiet made her uneasy. She lifted her hand and knocked. A few seconds passed, then she heard movement.

The door cracked open just enough for a familiar face to appear. She was older now, but still beautiful in such a striking way. Dark eyes, tired but sharp, taking her in like she wasn't sure she was real. Her mother didn't open the door fully. She didn't step out or even smile. Instead, she leaned against the frame, arms crossed, gaze unreadable.

"Well, look who decided to remember where she came from." She looked her over, scrutinizing her cautiously. "What are you doing in New Orleans again, Sincere? Or should I say . . . 'Sahara'?

Sincere forced a smile, masking the sting of her mother's tone. "Hi, Mama. Can I come in?"

The entire living room smelled like lavender. It was subtle, but unmistakable. The scent was woven into the fabric of the couch cushions, clinging to the air like a memory that refused to fade.

Sincere sat stiffly on the edge of the couch, hands folded in her lap, scanning the space. True to her profession as a nurse, her mother's home was completely free of clutter, mess, or even a hint of dust. Everything was meticulously kept, down to the perfectly arranged throw pillows. A bookshelf stood in the corner, the same one from her childhood, filled with worn-out novels and old family pictures that hadn't been updated since she left.

Her mother moved silently in the background, the soft *clink* of ceramic filling the quiet as she set two cups of tea on the coffee table. She took her time, slowly lowering herself into the chair across from Sincere, as if neither of them was in a hurry to start whatever this was.

She studied her for a long moment, gaze sharp despite the fatigue lining her face. Then, finally, she decided to speak. "You look thinner. Are you eating?"

Sincere blinked. Of all the things she thought her mother might say first, that wasn't one of them.

A small, breathy laugh escaped her. "I'm fine, Mama. Really."

Her mother didn't look convinced, but she didn't press the issue either. Instead, she picked up her tea, taking a slow sip as the quiet stretched between them.

Sincere wrapped her hands around her own cup, letting the warmth seep into her palms. She wasn't sure how to do this. How to talk to her mother after so much time had passed and everything that had happened.

Thankfully, it was her mother who finally broke the silence. "I saw you on TV a few months back on that award show."

Sincere tensed up. She had a feeling she knew where this was going. "Yeah?"

Her mother set her cup down. "Yeah." She tilted her head slightly, studying her. "You looked . . . different."

"It's been a long time, Mom. People change."

"Yes, especially when they are told to. When they belong to the public, the public has *all* the say." Her mother's lips pressed together, a quiet disapproval settling into the fine lines of her face. "I didn't raise you to live in a world where people own you, Sincere. But that's what you let them do. Got you up there butt naked selling sex like a common whore."

The words landed like a gut punch, quiet but heavy. Sincere stiffened, her fingers tightening around the teacup. She wanted to say it wasn't like that, but she couldn't help wondering if she traded one cage for another.

She swallowed down the bitter lump in her throat, forcing

herself to meet her mother's eyes. "I make my own choices. I've been an independent artist for a long time, making my own decisions about myself and my brand. I only *just* signed to a label. I've been making my own decisions about my career, and I still do."

"You *just* signed, huh?" Her mother sighed, shaking her head slightly. "Is that true?"

Sincere looked away. For all her mother's coldness, she had always seen right through her. The tension sat thick between them.

And then—

"I don't know what made you this way. I never raised you to bow down under the pressure of a powerful person. But I wonder if this all started with Aaliyah."

The name cut through the air like a blade, sharp and drawing blood immediately. Sincere's stomach clenched. She forced herself to breathe. "What about her?"

Her mother's expression darkened, pain building behind her gaze. "I begged you not to go out that night." Her voice was quiet, but firm. "You didn't listen. You never listened to anything once Aaliyah got to you."

Sincere's throat tightened. "I know, Mama. I know I should've listened." Her voice barely made it past her lips. "And I've paid for it every day since."

Her mother's gaze didn't soften. She didn't offer comfort. Sincere bit the inside of her cheek, swallowing down the emotion creeping up her throat. Maybe she had been stupid for coming here. For thinking things could ever be different.

"Lorde came back. He—he took me from my home in Atlanta."

Her mother straightened at the name. The shift was immediate. Her expression didn't just harden; it sharpened. "Lorde?"

Sincere hesitated, but there was no point in lying. "Yeah."

Her mother inhaled slowly, setting her cup down with an eerie calm. "He's back?"

Sincere nodded. "And he's controlling everything. My career, my life—everything. He won't let me go."

A beat of silence stretched between them. Then, for the first time since she'd stepped foot in the house, her mother looked shaken. "And you let it get this far?"

Sincere bristled. "You think I had a choice?"

Her mother shook her head, pushing herself up from the chair. She walked over to the window, staring out like she was expecting to see Lorde himself pulling up outside. "I told you to stay away from that world. Told you that power like his don't come without a price. But you never listen."

"Mama, I didn't ask for this," Sincere snapped. "I didn't even know my music would take off. And when it did, I thought for sure it would keep him away from me! I didn't want him back in my life. I didn't—" She exhaled sharply, raking a hand through her hair. "I'm trying to fix it. I just—I don't know how."

Her mother turned to face her, arms crossed over her chest, her voice quieter, but no less firm. "You can't fix a man like that, Sincere. He's not built to be changed."

Sincere swallowed hard. "I don't wanna fix him."

Her mother studied her for a long moment, her eyes searching, reading her the way only a mother could. "You're scared." She shook her head. "If he's back, you're already in too deep." She crossed the room, standing directly in front of her now. "Tell me the truth. Has he hurt you?"

Sincere hesitated. It wasn't an easy question to answer. Although not physically, he was hurting her in every way that mattered. "He's breaking me." Her voice was barely above a whisper.

For the first time, something softened in her mother's face. It wasn't exactly warmth, but it was something.

Her mother sighed, rubbing a slow hand over her face. "You know what's gonna happen if you stay under him, right?"

Sincere nodded. "That's why I'm trying to get out."

Her mother sat down beside her. "You know he ain't gonna let you just walk away."

"Yeah. I got that part."

Her mother was quiet for a long time, staring at her like she was thinking something over. "What do you need?"

Sincere hadn't expected anything other than a lecture, disappointment—maybe even blame. She swallowed past the lump forming in her throat. "I—I don't know."

Her mother exhaled. "Figure it out. Fast. 'Cause whatever's coming next? You need to be ready."

For the first time since stepping foot in the house, Sincere felt something close to relief. The tension in the room shifted. It wasn't gone, but it was softer, less sharp-edged. Her mother sat back in her chair, looking Sincere over like she was trying to reconcile the grown woman in front of her with the little girl she used to be.

"You still writing?"

Sincere blinked at the unexpected question. "Yeah." She nodded. "Still writing. Still making music."

Her mother hummed, reaching for her cup again. "I listen, you know."

That caught her off guard. "You do?"

Her mother took a slow sip of tea before setting the cup down. "'Course, I do. It's the only way I know what's going on with you." She exhaled, glancing at the bookshelf across the room. "I hear you, baby. Even when you don't call, even when you don't come around. I hear you."

Sincere swallowed past the sudden lump in her throat. "I didn't think you'd want to."

Her mother's eyes met hers, unreadable but steady. "I don't always want to. Sometimes it hurts. I hear the pain in your voice, the way you carry things you don't ever say out loud." She shook her head. "You've been through a lot. More than I wanted for you. But you're still here. That means something."

The warmth in her mother's voice cracked something inside Sincere, something she hadn't even realized was locked away. And suddenly, she wasn't just the artist, the brand, the woman trapped in a world too big for her to control. She was just Sincere, her mother's daughter.

She inhaled deeply, letting the moment settle before hesitating. "Can I ask you something?"

Her mother raised an eyebrow. "Since when you need permission to run your mouth?"

Sincere let out a soft, breathy laugh before shaking her head. "If someone was trying to control everything about your life," she started carefully, keeping her voice measured, "how would you handle it?"

Her mother didn't hesitate. "You remind them who you are."

Sincere sat back slightly, processing that. "And if they don't respect that?"

Her mother leaned forward, elbows on her knees, voice quiet but firm. "Then you take back what's yours. No matter what it costs."

Sincere felt those words settle into her bones. She wanted to believe it was that simple and she had the power to just take back her life. But Lorde . . . he wasn't some ordinary man. He was a monster, a master at making people believe they had control when he was the one pulling the strings.

Her mother watched her carefully. "This about Lorde?"

Sincere looked down at her hands, debating for a moment. Then, softly, she said, "Yeah."

"That boy ain't never been nothing but trouble."

"He has me trapped, Mama. I can't just leave, I can't just walk away. He—he owns too much of me. My career, my public image, everything."

Her mother's face hardened. "He own you, or he just think he do?"

Sincere hesitated. Because that was the real question, wasn't it? Did Lorde own her or did he just convince her that he did?

Her mother sighed. "You're smart, Sincere. Smarter than I think even you realize. If you want out, you'll find a way. But that's on you."

Sincere swallowed. "It's not just him."

Her mother tilted her head slightly. "So, it's someone else then. What's his name?"

Sincere blinked. "How you—"

Her mother stared into her eyes, reading her completely. "Baby, you my child. You think I don't know when you got a man on your mind?"

Sincere let out a soft groan, pressing her fingers to her temple. "I don't got a man on my mind."

Her mother gave her a knowing look. "Mm-hmm. And I'm the pope."

Sincere rolled her eyes, but didn't argue. Because the truth was . . . yeah. She had a man on her mind constantly. That was part of the problem.

"What's his name?"

Sincere paused for a moment, unsure about whether she was ready to share. "Supreme."

"Supreme." Her mother watched her for a beat before shaking her head. "You love him?"

The question sent a shock wave through her chest. Sincere hesitated, because the answer was obvious, but saying it out loud made it real.

Her mother must've seen it on her face, because she sighed. "Then be smart about it. You already got one man who thinks he got ownership over you. Be damn sure you don't let another one."

Sincere frowned. "Supreme ain't like that."

Her mother hummed like she wasn't completely convinced, but didn't argue. "I just want you to have peace, Sincere." She met her eyes. "I didn't raise you to be anybody's prisoner. Not mine. Not his. Not nobody's."

Something shifted in Sincere at those words, because for the first time, her mother was acknowledging it. The way *she* had controlled her too. Maybe she had always meant well. Maybe it had been her way of keeping her safe. But control was still control. Even if it was done with loving intentions.

Her mother sighed, rubbing her palms against her thighs before standing up. "You was a little girl to a single mother. It was just me, baby. Nobody else to help, nobody else to guide you but me. And I needed you to listen. I needed you to trust me. I had to keep a firm grip on you. Sometimes I went overboard, I know, but you were my baby." She exhaled. "But you ain't a little girl no more. You a grown-ass woman. You gotta speak up for yourself. You gotta make your own rules. And if a man don't like it?" She shrugged. "That's his problem to deal with."

Sincere felt something in her chest loosen. For the first time in years, she felt like she could breathe around her mother. She nodded slowly. "Yeah. You right."

Her mother eyed her. "Damn right, I'm right."

Sincere laughed. And just like that, something between them started to heal. They talked for what felt like hours, catching up on all the moments that were missed between them. When the sun began to set, it was time to go and Sincere felt like she had gotten everything she ever needed from this visit.

"Don't make this the last time you come to see me," her mother said, wringing her hands together. It was a show of anxiety. She cared so much about her daughter, she just didn't know how to be there for her in a way that mattered. She wasn't sure how to give to Sincere without compromising her own mental health and need for a quiet, uneventful life.

"It won't be," Sincere told her. "I promise."

She stood, smoothing out her clothes as she prepared to leave. The air between her and her mother had shifted. Everything wasn't completely mended, but it was stitched enough that the wound didn't feel so raw anymore.

She expected a simple farewell, a nod maybe, or some last lingering words of caution. But instead, her mother stepped forward and wrapped her arms around her. It took Sincere a moment to react to it. Her mother was not a woman who gave hugs easily. The embrace was firm and solid. It made Sincere felt like a daughter again.

Her mother exhaled, her voice softer than it had been all night. "You're stronger than you think, Sincere. Don't let anyone make you forget that."

Sincere squeezed her eyes shut, pressing her face into her mother's shoulder, breathing her in—the scent of lavender, the smell of home. It was something she had almost forgotten. She wanted to stay like this. To hold on to the feeling of safety, but she couldn't.

She pulled back, forcing herself to smile, even as her chest ached. "I won't."

Her mother gave her a final searching look before stepping back. "Good."

Sincere swallowed hard, nodded, and turned toward the door. She walked out, not looking back, afraid that if she did, she might not leave at all.

Chapter 26

The air inside the safe house felt different tonight, not heavy or tense, but crackling with energy. Supreme sat at the old wooden table, eyes on the cards spread in front of him, but he wasn't playing or thinking about the game. His mind was on the bodies.

He'd heard about a few men disappearing, but he didn't really pay it that much attention. Disappearances and death came with the street life. The next day was promised to no one. Anyone's number could be pulled at any time. Not once, not until Dre mentioned it, had he ever considered that Lorde may have been behind it.

Across from him, Dre exhaled slow with a blunt pinched between his fingers, watching Supreme like he was trying to decide if this was even a conversation they needed to have.

Supreme turned a card over between his fingers. The slow drag of it against the table was the only sound in the room. "I need to know everything. It's hard for me to process that Lorde would go this far just because he wants to work with Silvan. That he would *murder* any of our brothers without cause. Is that what everyone really thinks?"

"Ain't no thinking about it." Dre scoffed, shaking his head. "We *know* it's Lorde."

Supreme finally looked up.

Dre met his gaze, eyes sharp, jaw tight. "Bruh, he think he slick, movin' in silence, but the streets been talkin'. When Rell got shot, his brother said it was one of Silvan's boys. He *told* Lorde about it. And now, Rell's brother is missing too and Silvan's people been showin' up more and more in our hood. You think that's a coincidence?"

"But why would he have Rell killed?"

Dre blew out a long chain of black smoke. "Because Rell is loyal to you. He refused to work with Silvan. Lorde ordered him to supply Silvan's clubs with some of our product. When he told Lorde he wasn't going to give them shit, Lorde sent Silvan's men after him. Made it look like he was a random casualty of war instead of an inside job."

Supreme shook his head. "Damn."

"Exactly," Dre replied, patting the top of his blunt to drop the ash. "He is moving under the radar because he's not ready to go public yet. He didn't want news of what he was doing getting back to the elders or to you. Had to do the groundwork first."

Supreme didn't ask what Dre meant because he didn't have to. Deep down, he already knew. Lorde wasn't just getting rid of threats—making sure there was nobody left who could challenge him once he was ready to make his move.

Dre sat back, exhaling a slow stream of smoke. "I ain't tell you this before 'cause Lorde made it seem like he was protectin' you. Said he didn't want you caught up in Silvan's bullshit. Didn't want you gettin' in the way, endin' up on the wrong side of it before he got a chance to talk to you."

Supreme stayed quiet and let him talk.

"But that was some bullshit." Dre shook his head. "He ain't protectin' you, bruh. He been keepin' you occupied, makin' sure you too busy dealin' with Sincere to see what he really been on."

Supreme felt something tighten in his chest. Lorde had played it well, sending him to handle Sincere's contract, then making sure he was locked onto her every move, like he was the only one who could keep her in check. He'd known exactly what he was doing, keeping his right hand busy so it didn't know what the left was doing.

Dre rubbed a hand over his face. "Lorde been playin' you. He runnin' with Silvan, feedin' dope through his clubs, movin' girls. And he usin' some of the Saints to do it."

Supreme went still. This wasn't just about power or control. Lorde was turning the Saints into something they were never meant to be.

Dre kept going. "The worst part about it is, it ain't even like they got a choice. He tellin' 'em this is how we level up. That we gotta come up with different ways to make money.' And anybody who got a problem with it"—he met Supreme's gaze—"they don't last too long."

Supreme exhaled a long, slow breath as he set the card down on the table. "Who else knows?"

Dre let out a breath. "Ain't nobody sayin' it out loud, but everybody know. The ones still around? Either they scared, or they gettin' paid too good to care."

That's what Lorde was banking on: That nobody had the heart to stand up to him. That fear would keep the right ones in check and their greed would do the rest.

Supreme leaned back, rolling his shoulders like he was settling into something. Then, finally, he spoke. "Then it's time to remind 'em who the fuck they really supposed to be loyal to."

Dre's eyes sharpened. "Say less."

"You sure that *this* is the way you wanna do this?" Dre muttered under his breath as they stepped into the warehouse, his gaze shooting around like he expected a trap.

Supreme didn't answer right away. He didn't need to. If they weren't sure about it by now, they had no business walking in here in the first place.

The air inside was thick with dust, the scent of oil and rust lingering from when this place had been something more than a forgotten storage space. A single, flickering bulb overhead cast long, distorted shadows against the metal walls. The Saints gathered inside weren't just anybody—they were the ones Lorde had overlooked. The ones he assumed would always stay in line, no matter what.

He underestimated them.

Milo sat on the edge of a rusted table, arms crossed, one knee bouncing slightly. He wasn't nervous, but he wasn't relaxed either. Tay stood by the door, like he was debating whether or not he should even be here. The others—Jace, Trey, and a handful more who had been watching Lorde's moves with suspicion—stood nearby, waiting.

This was the moment of truth.

Milo was the first to speak. "This a setup?"

Supreme took a slow step forward. "If it was, you'd already be dead."

That got a reaction. Tay shifted uncomfortably, while Jace let out a quiet chuckle, shaking his head like he appreciated the boldness.

Milo exhaled, looking unimpressed. "What is this, Supreme? Some kinda intervention?"

Supreme took his time, letting the moment settle over them. "This ain't no intervention," he said finally. "This is a reality check."

His gaze moved slowly across the room, locking eyes with each of them, making sure they *felt* what he was saying. "Lorde got y'all thinkin' he still runnin' shit in a way that benefits us all. That the Saints are under control. But tell me—when's the last time y'all felt like we was actually in control of anything?"

Nobody answered because they didn't need to.

Supreme continued, stepping further into the space, making himself impossible to ignore. "He makin' moves outta fear. He lettin' Silvan in, cuttin' deals in the dark. You know what that mean?" He let the question hang for a second before answering it himself. "It means that he's making moves that only benefits him. It mean we just another piece on somebody else's board. We have to put a stop to what Lorde is doing."

"I don't know about that, bruh." Tay frowned. "Lorde put us on."

Supreme turned his attention to him, voice sharp. "Nah. He put *himself* on. And now he sellin' us out."

Tay flinched slightly, but he held his ground. "He just doin' what he gotta do. Expandin' our reach."

Supreme scoffed, shaking his head. "Expandin'? We ain't expandin', bruh. We bein' swallowed whole."

The room stayed silent. He stepped closer to Milo, watching the way the older man studied him. Supreme knew him. Milo wasn't stupid. He was old enough to see the shift, young enough to still want more than what Lorde was offering. *This* was the moment to push.

"You think Lorde ain't lost control?" Supreme asked him. "Look at the bodies droppin'. How many of our own ain't here no more? How many gone *missing*?"

Milo didn't look away, but he wasn't arguing either.

Supreme nodded. "That's what I thought."

Jace ran a hand over his face, exhaling slowly. "Damn."

Supreme let the weight settle before he spoke again, his voice quieter now, but no less commanding. "We all know how this ends. If we let Lorde keep runnin' things, we either fall in line under Silvan—or we die." He tilted his head slightly. "So y'all tell me. Which one sound like a win?"

Nobody spoke.

Milo decided to speak next. "You got a plan?"

Supreme's gaze didn't waver. "Yeah. But it ain't just about takin' Lorde down." He leaned in slightly. "We gotta go about it the way the bylaws say we gotta do it and bring it to a vote. If a majority vote says that we pull out of all deals with Silvan, then Lorde gotta do it."

"Wait . . . you not trying to take over?"

Supreme frowned. "*Hell* no. Lorde was made for what he's doing. I only want to redirect him. A long time ago the elders told us what the vision was for us. Working with Silvan is not going to allow it."

Tay hesitated. "How not? If we makin' more money with Silvan, won't that just give us what we need to start more legitimate businesses? Then we can pull out from the partnership."

Supreme shook his head. "Silvan don't work that way. He would never allow it. He's counting on us to let him in so that he can see how to take over. Think about it."

Supreme let the silence linger, watching the men in front of him carefully. The ones who had spoken up had already made their choice, but there were still a few who hadn't moved, who kept their hands in their pockets and their eyes darting around like they were weighing their options.

He leaned back against the stack of crates behind him, crossing his arms over his chest. His voice, when he spoke, was steady but sharp. "Ain't nobody walkin' outta here neutral," he said, his gaze sweeping across the group. "I need the vote on record so we can move forward. If you want to pull out of the deal with Silvan, stay so we can discuss next steps. If you don't want to be part of this, no pressure. You can go."

The room stayed quiet.

Supreme took a slow breath. "I ain't Lorde and I'm not the type to run y'all on fear. I expect you to be real with me and I'll be real with you." His voice dropped lower. "But if you stay, be prepared to stand on that. If not, you need to get out the way."

One of the younger soldiers, Kev, hesitated before finally

stepping forward. He looked nervous as hell, but there was determination in his voice when he said, "I'm with you, Supreme."

Another followed. Then another. Slowly, it was happening. Hands were lifting everywhere.

Supreme nodded once, pushing off the crates. He didn't thank them. He didn't celebrate. He just accepted it. Dre stood next to him, calculating the votes.

"Good."

He let his gaze settle on the last two men who hadn't moved, the brothers: Milo and Juno.

Milo licked his lips, glancing at Juno like he wanted backup before finally clearing his throat. "Look, you know I got love for you, but . . ." He hesitated, eyes shifting toward the door. "I just—I need time to think 'bout this shit."

"Nah," Supreme said smoothly, shaking his head. "Ain't no time left."

Juno straightened his posture, shoulders squaring up. "What you sayin', then? That we gotta pick sides right now?"

Supreme stepped toward them, slow and controlled. "That's exactly what I'm sayin'."

Juno scoffed, shaking his head. "Man, that's crazy. I done put in years wit' y'all. I ain't 'bout to stand here and act like I don't respect what you doin'. But Lorde—" He exhaled sharply. "He still got control, man. This ain't gon' be as easy as y'all think."

Dre laughed under his breath. "If you scared, just say that."

Juno's jaw tightened. "I ain't scared. I'm smart."

Supreme studied him. He was too defensive and had too much hesitation. That told him everything. Juno was gonna fold. Maybe not today, maybe not tomorrow—but the second the pressure hit, he'd flip. And Milo was just waiting for somebody else to decide for him. It was better for them to leave now.

Supreme nodded slowly. "Aight." He kept his voice neutral.

"I hear you." He waited for them to leave before turning back to the others. "Meeting's done. I'm going to tell the elders that we have a majority vote so I can get their approval and blessing before I talk to Lorde. I hope that he'll go with what the brotherhood has decided is best for everyone involved."

The group murmured in agreement, breaking off into smaller conversations as they all started to leave.

"And do not speak to anyone who wasn't in this room about what just happened," Supreme added as he watched them leave.

Dre waited until everyone was out of earshot before side-eyeing Supreme. "Man, I don't like this shit. If you know Milo and Juno gon' run back to Lorde, why let 'em walk outta here?"

"I can't stop them from doing anything." Supreme didn't look away from the door. "And I ain't got what I need yet."

Dre scoffed. "We got a majority vote. That's all we needed, right? Why we waitin' to talk to Lorde? We can't let him get the jump on us."

Supreme exhaled, running a hand over his beard. "I can't make no moves without word from the elders."

Dre's expression darkened. "You think they gon' back this?"

"They don't got a choice." Supreme finally turned to him, his voice firm. "Unless Lorde stops what he's doing, we are already at war."

Dre studied him for a second, then shook his head. "You know Lorde better than I do. He's not going to back down from this."

Supreme's jaw tightened. "Maybe not. But I can't move forward unless I'm sure about that."

Chapter 27

"So why the fuck y'all got me way out here?"

Lorde's voice was sharp, cutting through the thick humidity hanging heavy in the air. The scent of damp earth and swamp rot clung to the back of his throat. Insects buzzed in the distance, but besides that, everything was still. It would have been serene had it not been for the menacing glare on Lorde's face. He was practically baring his teeth.

Milo and Juno stood a few feet away, shuffling slightly. Their restless energy signaled to Lorde that they were about to say some shit he wasn't gonna like.

"We couldn't meet in the city," Milo muttered, his voice low.

Lorde's brow furrowed, irritation burning beneath his skin. "Why?"

Juno exhaled sharply, rubbing a hand over the back of his neck. "'Cause we ain't tryna be seen talkin' to you."

Lorde gave him a slow blink as he processed the words. Then he tilted his head, as the meaning completely settled in. "You ain't tryna be seen . . . talkin' to me?"

Juno shifted uncomfortably. "Look, man, it ain't like that. We just—"

Lorde held up a hand, silencing him before he could finish. "Nah. Say what you came to say."

The tension crackled. Milo inhaled sharply, as if bracing himself. "Supreme held a vote, man."

Lorde's brows lifted slightly, though his expression didn't change. "A vote?"

"Yeah," Juno cut in. "Brought the Saints together, had 'em decide whether or not to force you to cut ties with Silvan."

Milo shifted again, clearly uncomfortable. "Look, man—he ain't trying to strip your power. He just wants you to stop fuckin' with Silvan. To get back focused on what we was supposed to be about."

Juno nodded quickly. "It ain't personal, Lorde. He just tryna keep shit tight. Keep us clean."

Lorde chuckled. It was a low, quiet sound, but there was nothing humorous about it. "Y'all niggas stupid."

Milo and Juno both stiffened.

Lorde leaned forward slightly, forearms resting on his knees, his tone deceptively smooth. "How the fuck am I supposed to be king if another nigga is out here tellin' me what I can and can't do. Y'all don't see how that's stripping me of power? What kinda king gotta answer to somebody else?"

Neither of them answered.

"If he can make 'em vote on me once, he can do it again." Lorde's eyes flickered, sharp with something unreadable. "And next time, it won't just be about Silvan."

Juno licked his lips like he wanted to argue, but thought better of it.

Milo sighed, shaking his head. "We just tryna keep the Saints solid, man. We ain't tryna pick sides."

Lorde arched a brow. "Not tryna pick sides?" He scoffed. "Just by showin' up to Supreme's little meeting, y'all already picked one."

Juno lifted his chin slightly, like he was trying to reclaim some control. "We still ten toes down for you, Lorde. That's why Supreme kicked us out. We ain't let nothing he said sway us."

Milo nodded. "Yeah, we told him we was ridin' with you. No question."

Lorde said nothing. Instead, he studied them. Then . . . he began to laugh. It wasn't a laugh that signaled relief. It was a laugh that basically said, "Y'all just fucked up."

At the sound of it, both Juno and Milo stiffened.

Lorde sighed, shaking his head as he pulled his gun from his waistband, so fast neither of them had time to react. He quickly squeezed the trigger, letting out two shots.

Milo and Juno hit the ground before their brains could even register what had happened.

The sound of the gunfire faded, swallowed up by the vast emptiness of the swamp. Their bodies lay still, eyes wide open, faces frozen in shock.

"Dumb-ass niggas," he muttered. "Would've made more sense to play along. You get more information then."

Lorde barely spared them another glance as he exhaled, rolling his shoulders like he was just shaking off a bad mood. Weak links had no place in his kingdom. Monk, who had been standing near the car, barely flinched. The man was used to this, especially these days.

"Clean this shit up," Lorde muttered, tossing him a glance before snatching the keys from his hand. "And make sure they ain't found. Come up with something to make it look like they ran away."

Monk hesitated but nodded quickly. "Got it, boss."

Lorde didn't wait for a response. He slid into the driver's seat, gripping the wheel so hard his knuckles turned white. His mind was moving too fast. He needed something to calm him.

No—not something. *Someone.*

His phone was in his hand before he even thought about it.

What you doing, ma?

A few seconds later, his phone vibrated.

Working on a new song. What's good, Daddy?

His grip loosened. Sincere was talking to him differently lately, like she knew who she belonged to. It was like she was getting comfortable under his thumb, which was exactly where she needed to be.

Lorde tossed his phone onto the passenger seat. He could've texted back and told her to be ready for him . . . But why ask for what was already his? He didn't need an invitation. He was just gonna pull up and remind her exactly who she belonged to.

When Lorde arrived at Sincere's place, he didn't knock or ring the doorbell. He just let himself in. The door swung open without resistance, and Carl and Andre didn't even question him as he stepped inside. However, he did pick up on the silence that fell around them as soon as he stepped on the scene.

Sincere's apartment was quiet, dimly lit. It had a relaxing vibe that bred creativity. He paused for a moment and just stood there, taking in the space, wondering where he should start looking for Sincere. Then he heard the sound of soft music, drifting in from somewhere near the back.

A sinister grin tugged at his lips. He moved through the apartment like she was beckoning to him. His fingers flexed at his sides as he turned the corner, walking toward the sound of the music. When he finally saw her, his steps slowed to a halt. She hadn't noticed him yet. He stood there for a moment, enjoying the luxury of watching her in her element.

She was standing by the window, her back to him, with the gentle lights of the city spilling in, painting her skin gold. She had on some little satin gown that clung to her curves, something simple, but so seductive at the same time.

And, *fuck*, she looked good.

Sincere knew he was there long before she let him know that

she did. She needed a chance to adjust her mind, to calm it in preparation for whatever he was going to make her do. She had to take some time to settle her heartbeat. Soothe her fear.

Lorde's presence was impossible to ignore. It pressed against every one of her senses. Everything about him was so intrusive. She didn't even need to turn around to know when he entered her space. Sincere inhaled slowly, steeling herself, before forcing a neutral expression onto her face and turning to face him.

"So . . . you don't knock now?"

Lorde's lips slowly crept up his face, slow and lazy, like he had all the time in the world. "Didn't think I needed to."

His gaze roamed over her, not in a way that showed appreciation, but like a man looking at something he owned. Sincere fought the urge to cross her arms. Her natural reaction was to create space between them, to protect herself from whatever expectation was simmering in his eyes.

"You good?" she asked, tilting her head, keeping her tone light.

Lorde chuckled, stepping closer. "Yeah. I'm good."

His eyes never left her, his presence swallowing up the space around her. "You been real good to me, ma." His voice dipped lower, softer. "Doin' exactly what I need, letting me guide you. Keepin' me updated. That's how it should be."

She nodded, trying to keep her breathing even. "Of course."

"You don't even know how much I appreciate that."

Sincere knew where this was going.

Lorde reached out, fingers grazing the curve of her waist before settling there, his grip warm and firm. His touch wasn't forceful, but it also wasn't asking for permission. "Now," he murmured, pulling her flush against him, "let me show you how much I appreciate you."

His lips hovered close to her ear. His breath was hot against her skin. Sincere's heart pounded against her ribs. She forced a smile, keeping her posture loose and casual, like she wasn't internally screaming for an escape.

"You don't have to do all that," she teased, tapping his chest lightly. "I know you appreciate me."

Lorde chuckled. He looked at her like she was playing a game he was amused by. "That ain't enough."

His hands slid lower, his grip tightening. Sincere's mind raced when he pushed his hands under her dress. She needed a way out. A distraction . . . *anything.*

Lorde's fingers ghosted over the edge of her panties, his touch lingering. Her pulse stuttered when he began pulling them down. Hesitantly, she stepped out of them, forcing herself to play along.

Suddenly, his grip on her waist tensed, and then it vanished entirely when he stepped back from her. Sincere barely had a second to process the sudden change before Lorde yanked his hand away like she had burned him.

She frowned. *What?* She looked down at the seat of the satin panties that he was now holding in his hands and that's when she saw it—a faint streak of red. Lorde stared down at his hand like it had betrayed him. Then, like something *disgusting* had just crawled onto his skin, he flung her shorts away from him, stepping back fast.

"The *fuck*?" His voice was sharp, almost startled. "You're bleeding?"

Sincere blinked. She looked down, realization settling in. Her period was on. She hadn't even realized it. With a tilt of her head, she schooled her expression into something unreadable. "I guess so." She shrugged. "Is that a big deal?"

Lorde's expression twisted. He didn't speak, but the discomfort was clear. He stepped back again, shaking his head like he needed to clear his thoughts.

Sincere stilled, watching him closely. This was *different*. She had never seen him look like this before. The man who had walked in with all the confidence in the world was suddenly . . . unsettled.

He exhaled sharply, eyes cutting to her before darting away. "*Ou ta dwe di m sa*!" His voice was sharp and edged with something she couldn't place.

Sincere raised a brow. "Huh? What does that mean?"

His jaw clenched as he stepped back again. "You should've told me," he muttered in English this time, his voice tight, like even speaking was grating against his nerves.

Sincere scoffed. "Told you what? I didn't even know myself! What's the big deal anyways?"

Lorde ignored her. His fingers flexed at his sides, shaking out his hands like something invisible had latched onto him. "*Pa gen jwèt ak san.*" His voice was lower now, more to himself than to her. "*Sa se pouvwa. Yon fi ka mare yon nèg ak san li. Kontwole li.*" He looked distressed. "I need to call Maman."

Sincere frowned slightly, catching enough of the words to get the meaning.

Blood is power. A woman can bind a man with her blood. Control him.

Ohh!

He wasn't just disgusted. He was *scared.*

Sincere blinked, something cold settling in her stomach. "You actually believe that?"

Lorde shot her a sharp look. "You think this shit is a joke?"

Sincere held his gaze, studying him. The fact that this terrified him was fascinating. Lorde, the man who moved through the world like a king, like nothing and no one could touch him, was unraveling over a little bit of pussy blood.

She lowered her head slightly, watching as he continued to put space between them, shaking his hands out like he could rid himself of whatever energy he thought had touched him.

"*Gade sa ou fè*!"

Look at what you've done.

He muttered the words under his breath, shaking his head like he was trying to rid himself of something unseen.

Sincere almost laughed. Not because it was funny, but because . . . It was pathetic.

He had no problem forcing himself into her space, no problem controlling people, forcing them into submission or even killing them. But he was scared of her body? Scared of *blood*?

She inhaled, a slow, careful breath, and suddenly . . . she felt the change. She wasn't scared of him anymore. He wasn't some big, bad god of a man. He was *human*.

Sincere took a step forward and Lorde tensed. It made her feel so powerful. "Relax, baby," she murmured, lifting her hands. "I'm not going to hurt you. What's going on?"

Lorde scoffed, but he didn't step closer. He was still rattled and very much on edge.

Sincere bit her bottom lip to hide her smile. "Maybe you should go so I can clean myself up," she said, voice light, almost teasing.

Lorde's eyes snapped to hers. For a second, she thought he might argue. That pride would force him to push through whatever fear was gripping him. He exhaled sharply, stepping back again. "*Mwen pa ka rete isit la.*" His voice was clipped, his jaw tight.

Sincere didn't know what he said, but she could tell he was getting the hell out of her place. That was all she wanted. "Yeah." She nodded, suppressing her amusement.

Lorde didn't respond or linger. He didn't try to reclaim the power in the moment. He just turned and left. For the first time since he had entered her world, she felt like she had won. Once he was gone, Sincere sat cross-legged on her bed, fingers running absentmindedly over the sheets, her mind still tangled in what had just happened.

Her lips pressed into something halfway between a laugh and a smile. The man who walked around like a king and demanded obedience, who pulled strings behind the scenes to control her—was still just a man. Her fingers traced slow patterns against her thighs as she let the realization settle in.

Chapter 28

Supreme sat on the hood of his car, parked under the shade of an old oak tree, rolling a purple Skittle between his fingers before tossing it into his mouth. He chewed slowly, watching the gravel road in front of Maman Clo's house, waiting. He'd been out here for an hour now, waiting. A light breeze rustled the trees overhead, carrying the familiar, heavy scent of the swamp, but Supreme barely noticed it. His focus was locked on the long, winding driveway leading up to the house, waiting for the moment he already knew was coming.

When Lorde's car finally pulled up, he reached into the bag of Skittles, digging out a red one—then tossing it aside onto the dirt. The dye in the red ones caused cancer. At least, that's what he heard, so he didn't eat them. He wasn't about to risk it. He grabbed a green one, popped it into his mouth, and sat up a little straighter, watching as Lorde climbed out of the car.

He had been waiting for over an hour, knowing his cousin would show up sooner or later. Lorde was the type to act like he didn't need nobody, like he was above it all, but when shit got heavy, he always came here. Whether he needed guidance, reassurance, or a blessing before making a major move, Maman Clo's house was his place of absolution.

Tonight was no different.

Supreme crushed another Skittle between his teeth, then rolled up the bag and tucked it into his pocket. When he hopped off the hood, Lorde still hadn't seen him. His head was down, fingers flying over his phone—probably texting some chick to ease his nerves. It was probably Sincere.

By the time he looked up, he was halfway to Maman Clo's front steps. That's when Supreme decided to make his presence known. "Long day?"

Lorde froze. His whole body tensed for half a second before he turned slowly, his expression sliding into something dark. But Supreme knew that look. It was the same one he always had when he felt backed into a corner. He was already calculating how to flip the situation in his favor. It wouldn't happen this time.

Supreme took a few steps forward, forcing Lorde to acknowledge him, to stand still and listen. Lorde's lips twitched, but the smile didn't fully form. His voice was smooth, but Supreme caught the tightness underneath.

"What you doin' out here, cuz?"

Supreme tilted his head slightly. "Could ask you the same thing."

Lorde exhaled sharply, shaking his head. "Man, I ain't got time for this."

He started to turn, to walk past him like this was nothing. Supreme stepped into his path and blocked him. Lorde stilled. The air between them began to charge with tense energy.

Supreme's voice dropped. "We need to talk."

Lorde lifted a brow. "Oh, we talkin' now? You mean like you and the Saints was talkin' about me behind my back?"

Supreme ignored the bait. "You know what this is about. I ain't here to play games with you, bruh."

Lorde studied him for a long second, then stepping back. "Aight." He motioned toward the side of the house. "Let's talk."

As they stood in the dim light from the porch, crickets, frogs, and all the other sounds of the swamp surrounded them. Supreme was the first to speak. He crossed his arms over his chest, eyes locked onto Lorde. "You got a lot of things being said in the streets about you."

Lorde let out a short laugh, shaking his head. "The fuck that mean?"

Supreme's jaw tightened. "It means people are watchin' you, Lorde. And they don't like what they see."

The hint of smugness dulled in Lorde's features.

"We built this together," Supreme continued. "We had a vision based on what the elders put in place and we acted on it. Together, we started building a legacy. Restaurants, clubs, the music business . . . next, we were about to start managing athletes. We were supposed to take the Saints to another level, clean up our business, make it so that nobody could touch us." Supreme shook his head, somberly. "These dealings you got going on with Silvan is some backwards shit. You can't do this."

"Ain't nobody taking shit from me, Supreme." Lorde's voice had a subtle sharpness to it. "This empire I built is *mine*. While everyone was talkin' about it, I *did* it! And I'll run it how I see fit."

Supreme exhaled slowly. "At what cost?"

Lorde's gaze flickered, just for a second, before he masked it.

"You don't have to throw it all away chasing somethin' that'll only bring more destruction," Supreme pressed further. "Don't you want more for your son?"

Lorde's entire body went still. His jaw locked, his hands curling into loose fists at his sides. Then, with a slow, deliberate inhale, he shook his head. "You don't know shit about what I want for my son."

Supreme didn't back down. "I know you ain't tryin' to leave him nothin' but a grave. I know you want him to be proud of the man you are. You keep him hidden in the suburbs not just to protect him from our world. You want to protect him from hearing about the real you."

Lorde's eyes darkened. That hit him deep. The only thing that mattered in the world more than money, power, or anything else was his son. But what would become of his son if he yielded to Supreme? Would he even be able to take care of him the way he needed to if he wasn't in charge? Of course not, because Supreme was trying to take everything from him.

Instead of giving in to his cousin's reasoning, Lorde took a step back. He let out a short, humorless laugh, shaking his head. "I knew this was comin'. I knew you was waitin' for your moment to take it all from me."

Supreme clenched his jaw. "Man, it ain't like that."

"Ain't it?" Lorde sneered, taking a slow step closer. "You got the Saints votin' like this some democracy. Tryin' to tell me what I can and can't do. But you?" He exhaled sharply. "You ain't got no claim here, Supreme. You ain't got no seat at my table. I barely made room for Silvan, but he was right. He *told* me I shouldn't trust you."

Supreme's stomach twisted, frustration bubbling to the surface. "He's using you, Lorde. You think Silvan respects you? He's playing you against me because he knows I'd never work with him."

Lorde chuckled lowly, shaking his head. "Man, you sound real jealous right now."

Supreme stepped forward. "I sound like a man who knows when a snake is whisperin' in his brother's ear."

Lorde went still, but Supreme didn't break eye contact with him. The arrogance slid back into his features, sharp and merciless. "There's no vote. I don't give a fuck what y'all niggas say. And there's no us. From here on out, you're dead to me."

His voice was calm when he said it. The words hit harder than Supreme expected. Even though he knew this was where things were headed, hearing it was different. He couldn't help feeling like the man he was talking to was no longer his cousin. He was someone else.

As Supreme turned back toward his car, something made him pause. It was a flash of movement coming from the window ahead. He stilled, eyes narrowing as he glanced up at the house. For a brief second, he thought he saw someone watching from behind the curtain.

Maman Clo.

She didn't step outside. Didn't make her presence known. But Supreme knew she saw and heard everything. He exhaled slowly, shaking his head. Maybe she could talk some sense into Lorde. Deep down, Supreme wasn't sure if even she could pull him back from this. Lorde wasn't listening to reason. If Maman Clo couldn't reach him either . . . Then it was over. Without so much as another glance back, he got in his car and pulled off.

At 2:34 a.m., the gym was completely quiet . . . except for the dull thud of fists slamming into leather.

Thud. Thud. Thud.

Sweat dripped from Supreme's temples, rolling down the ridge of his nose before hitting the mat beneath his feet. His muscles burned, his breath came heavy, but he didn't stop. He couldn't, not with Lorde's words still ringing in his ears.

There's no vote. There's no us. You're dead to me.

His fists slammed into the heavy bag again, sending it jerking backward. He caught it mid-swing, fingers gripping the fabric so tightly his knuckles turned white.

Dead to me.

Lorde meant that. He wasn't just talking out the side of his mouth, throwing empty threats into the air. Lorde didn't say shit he wasn't ready to act on. And Supreme knew exactly what that meant. He inhaled sharply, rolling his shoulders, trying to shake the feeling crawling up his spine. Lorde wasn't just drawing battle lines—he was already moving pieces. Supreme wasn't ready to go to war with his family.

Lorde was unpredictable on a good day. Now he was spiraling. Silvan had his claws in him and Lorde had turned his back on the Saints. The people closest to him weren't his brothers anymore. They were just bodies to be used, moved, and disposed of as he decided. That's what Lorde did with people who went against him.

Supreme's phone rang and he frowned. It wasn't often that he got a call at this hour. His breathing slowed, his fist still clenched midair and he stared at the number that flashed across the screen. It wasn't saved and didn't look familiar. But it was local. Something cold settled in his gut.

He wiped his hands on his shorts, exhaling once before swiping to answer. "Yeah."

A second of silence. Then—a gut-wrenching scream. It was more than a cry. It was a pain-filled wail. His shoulders went rigid, his stomach twisting. Then came the voice and that's when Supreme almost lost it. It was Dre's baby mother.

He frowned into the phone. "Keisha?"

"You motherfucker!" she shrieked, her words high-pitched and wild as she wielded them like a weapon. "You got him killed!"

Supreme blinked, his pulse spiking. "What?"

Her breathing was erratic, choppy, like she was trying and failing to hold herself together. But she wasn't here to cry. She was in so much pain and rather than deal with that, it was much easier to cut Supreme with her rage.

"It's your fault, Supreme!" Her voice cracked, her fury vibrating through the line. "You did this! You might as well have put the rope around his fucking neck yourself!"

The words hit him like a sledgehammer to the chest. He felt

them in his ribs, in his bones, and in the back of his throat. His grip on the phone tightened. "What the fuck are you talking about?"

"He's dead. Dre—he's *dead!*"

The world tilted.

The gym disappeared.

Nothing existed except those two words.

Dre. Dead.

His stomach lurched, but his voice stayed steady, sharp. "How?"

Another ragged breath came across the line. Then her next words ripped the air from his lungs. "They hung him! They hung him from a tree!"

The *world* went silent. Supreme couldn't hear his own breathing or even feel his heart beating. The ground beneath his feet didn't feel real anymore.

No. No. No!

The words didn't make sense. Hung? Not shot. Not stabbed. *Hung.* His jaw locked, his throat burning as the rage started to spread. He felt something hot, toxic, and dark slithering into his bloodstream.

"They strung him up like a fucking animal," she spat, her voice dripping with hatred. "I woke up and saw him hanging there. His feet weren't even touching the ground, Supreme! He—" Her voice cracked again, breaking into sobs.

Supreme's entire body coiled tight, like a bomb about to go off. His free hand curled into a fist at his side, but inside he was raging. Lorde was behind this; only he would take it this far.

"*You* killed him," she choked out, still blaming him. "You put him in this position. You started all this shit, and now my kids don't have a father! And for *what*?"

Supreme couldn't respond because deep down, he couldn't say she was wrong. He knew who was behind this and why.

Lorde wanted to send a message. He decided that leaving Dre swinging from a tree like they were back in the Jim Crow era was the way to do it.

His stomach turned, a slow breath hissing out between his teeth. His entire body locked. This wasn't a quiet hit. It was a *statement.* Lorde wanted this to be seen. He wanted niggas to talk about this.

Supreme's voice was low when he finally spoke—borderline deadly. "Where is he?"

"He's still here," she spoke, her voice much quieter now. "The police said they can't remove his body because it's a crime scene. They have him still hanging there!"

Supreme didn't even realize he was moving until he grabbed his keys, snatched his jacket, and stormed toward the door.

Dre was gone and Lorde was going to pay for it.

The drive to Dre's house was nothing but a blur.

Supreme barely registered the roads as the streetlights strobed by him. The city was still in that eerie quiet before dawn, but everything inside of him was screaming. His grip on the steering wheel was iron-tight, as his foot mashed heavy on the gas. Dre's voice still echoed in his head—laughing, talking shit, calling him *bro* like it was second nature. Now all that was left of him was a body.

His jaw clenched as he turned the corner onto Dre's block, his stomach coiling the second he saw the blue and red lights flashing against the trees. The street was lined with people—neighbors standing in their doorways, some whispering to each other, others just staring, faces grim.

Then, his gaze locked onto the tree. The one right in front of Dre's house. It was empty now, just swaying slightly in the wind, but Supreme could still see it. He could still picture him there, his body hanging like a fucking trophy.

His breath shuddered through his nose as he parked, pushing open the door with a controlled slowness that belied the rage simmering beneath his skin. He was mad at Lorde, but he was also furious at himself. Because Keisha was right; *he* was the one responsible for this.

Supreme barely got two steps toward the house before a voice cut through the night.

"'Bout time you got here."

He turned his head.

Whispers stood near the curb, his tall, lanky frame barely visible in the dim light. His hoodie was pulled low over his forehead, his hands shoved deep into his pockets. But it was his face, the hard, unreadable expression, that made Supreme pause. He knew Whispers. Knew that no matter how bad shit got, the man never lost his composure. But tonight, he looked *sick*.

Supreme exhaled slowly, steadying himself before walking over. "Talk."

Whispers glanced back toward the house, then shook his head. "Ain't nothin' to say that you don't already know." His voice was low, flat. "Keisha said he went to bed with her, but must've gotten up sometime throughout the night. She woke up and found him on that tree right there. Strung up." His jaw twitched. "Like a fucking animal."

Supreme swallowed hard, his hands flexing at his sides. He didn't need to ask Whispers anything else because he already knew who did it and why.

"He had a note in his mouth," Whispers continued, voice dropping even lower.

Supreme's stomach twisted. "What it say?"

Whispers's expression darkened. "Same thing the other three had. It said, *What's your vote, now?*"

Supreme frowned. "What you mean 'the other three'?"

Whispers's jaw clenched and that's when Supreme noticed

the way his hands were still buried deep in his pockets, like he was holding something back.

Supreme took a step closer, his voice dropping. "Whispers. Explain."

Whispers exhaled, slow and heavy. He turned his head slightly, scanning the street, making sure no one was close enough to overhear. Then, finally, he spoke. "Dre ain't the only one, Supreme."

Supreme's chest tightened. "What?"

Whispers nodded toward the far end of the block, where a blacked-out SUV was parked near the coroner's van. "They found three more bodies. Same shit. Hung with notes in their mouths. Dre was the only one hung outside of his own home."

The words slammed into Supreme's chest like a sledgehammer. His breath came in slow, jagged pulls, his fists curling at his sides.

Four?

Supreme forced out a breath, working to keep his voice steady. "Who?"

Whispers hesitated. "Kev. Gutta. And Smoke."

Supreme's teeth clenched so hard his jaw ached.

Kev was the youngest of them, always eager, always tryna prove himself. Gutta was a seasoned soldier, not the smartest, but loyal as hell. And Smoke was one of the oldest Saints still standing, been rocking with them since Supreme and Lorde were teenagers being trained for their roles. All hung with notes in their mouths, like they were nothing. As if their *lives* meant nothing.

The street around him seemed to disappear, his vision tunneling as rage threatened to swallow him whole. Supreme felt a muscle in his jaw twitch, his hands shaking as he forced himself to breathe.

Whispers watched him carefully. "I know what you thinking, but don't do nothin' reckless."

Supreme barely heard him. His mind was already moving.

Lorde planned this and he didn't just act out of paranoia. This was strategic and calculated. This wasn't just about punishing Supreme. This was about maintaining complete control. Lorde wanted to scare the others into submission. He wanted them to see those bodies swaying in the wind and understand what happened when you defied him.

Supreme let out a slow, shaky breath. "Where were they found?"

Whispers licked his lips, shaking his head. "Spread out. Different spots in the city. But same MO. Somebody—maybe Lorde, maybe Silvan's people—wanted this shit to be seen. And it worked."

Supreme exhaled sharply, dragging a hand down his face. His head was spinning, his stomach in knots. Dre. Kev. Gutta. Smoke. They weren't just *bodies*. They were family.

"Where's the rest of the crew?" Supreme asked, his voice coming out rough, strained.

Whispers glanced a little further down the street, where a few familiar figures stood, lingering in the distance. "They watchin'. Listenin'. And scared as fuck. I'm trying to keep all this quiet, but news is spreading fast."

Supreme already knew what was coming when Whispers continued speaking.

"If anybody votes after this, I'd be surprised."

And that was Lorde's goal. It wasn't enough just to kill. His aim was to paralyze. To make sure no one dared to stand against him again. Supreme swallowed back the molten rage bubbling in his chest. He couldn't afford to lose it here. He had to think and move smarter, because there was only one path forward.

If Lorde wanted war . . . Fine. He was about to get it.

Chapter 29

Sincere tapped her pen against the notebook in front of her, frowning at the empty page. After sitting in the same exact spot for hours, she had made zero progress. She had the exact same thing on the page now as she had before she began—nothing.

She sighed, dragging her fingers through her hair before tossing the pen down in frustration. It wasn't that she didn't have ideas. She did. The words were there, lurking in the back of her mind, almost teasing her, but every time she tried to pull them forward, they faded like smoke.

Pushing back from the desk, she rolled her neck, stretched her arms, and stood up. A jog always helped when she got like this. It was the perfect remedy when her creativity felt muted.

Grabbing her hoodie from the back of the chair, she slipped it on and headed toward the door. She didn't get more than two steps out the door before Carl and Andre spotted her and started complaining.

"Ah *hell* nah! I know yo' ass not about to do what I *think* you're doing," Andre said.

"Nah. We ain't doin' this again." Carl's voice rang out behind her, exasperation already settling into his tone as he stood to his feet.

Sincere turned, raising a brow as she tugged her ponytail tighter. "Do *what* again?"

"You know what it is!" Andre pointed at her like she was personally responsible for his last near-death experience. "This whole 'Sincere goes on a nice, relaxing jog, and Andre and Carl almost burst a fuckin' lung' thing."

Carl grunted, rubbing his chest as if the memory physically pained him. "We damn near had to call for backup the last time we ran behind your ass."

"It's just a quick workout." Sincere laughed, shaking her head. "Y'all are dramatic as hell."

Carl folded his arms. "Nah, ma. We realistic. We runnin' security, not no damn track team. So, this time, nah." He made a swiping motion in front of his neck to dramatize his words. "We tailin' you in the car. You need us, we'll be right there. You get tired, we'll be right there. But we ain't runnin' behind your ass this time." Andre sucked his teeth. "Not ever again."

"Poor babies." Sincere grinned. "Y'all really that out of shape?"

"Don't try me like that, Sahara! You know I been workin' on this physique."

Sincere rolled her eyes. "Yeah, like yesterday when I came out here and caught y'all eating doughnuts from Krispy Kreme."

"What?"

Carl put a hand up, stopping himself before he said something out of pocket. He took a breath instead, shaking his head. "Let's just hurry up and get this shit done."

Still grinning, Sincere tugged her AirPods into place, zipped up her hoodie, and jogged out of the building, stepping into the crisp early morning air.

About an hour later, Sincere wiped sweat from her brow as she rounded the last block toward her building, her breathing steady, but her legs burning in the best way. That was exactly what she needed. She felt good. The creative block from earlier was gone. Her mind was rippling with ideas.

Carl and Andre were still posted in the car as promised. Carl rolled down the window as she passed, squinting at her. "How you still got energy left?"

Sincere grinned, walking backward as she shot him a wink. "Guess I'm built different."

Andre groaned. "Man, get inside before you jinx yourself. I'm not about to mess up my fit if you faint and I have to carry your ass back in there."

Still laughing, she jogged back inside the building and took the elevator up to her floor, peeling off her hoodie as she made her way to her bathroom. The shower was already running, steam curling around the room, when her phone started to vibrate against the counter.

Glancing at the screen, her breath caught in her throat. It was Stacy. Her fingers hesitated over the phone before swiping to answer. She hadn't heard from Stacy since she quit.

Sincere pressed the phone to her ear, forcing her voice to stay light. "Um . . . hey, Stacy. What's up?"

There was a pause. Sincere's breath caught in her throat. Something was wrong. "Sincere . . . are you alone?"

Something about Stacy's voice made her stomach tighten. It was off.

Sincere frowned, her earlier ease disappearing. "Yeah. I'm good. What's going on?"

"It's Lena."

Sincere's pulse stuttered. "What about her?"

Stacy exhaled, her voice dropping even lower. "She's dead."

Sincere's entire body locked up. ". . . What?"

Stacy exhaled. "They found a body in the swamp. Someone reported it a few days ago, but they only just confirmed through the autopsy. It's her."

No.

This wasn't real.

Lena wasn't dead.

She *couldn't* be.

Sincere shook her head as if that would make it not true. "That doesn't—" Her voice caught, her chest tightening. "That doesn't make sense. She was just—she was just—" She couldn't even finish the sentence. Lena was *just* here. That's what she wanted to say. But she couldn't . . . because Lena wasn't just there. She hadn't seen or spoken to her in weeks. Not since the day she found out that she was working for Lorde.

"I know," Stacy said quietly. "I know, Sincere."

Sincere's head spun, thoughts crashing into each other, unable to form anything cohesive.

Stacy's voice cut through the fog. "She doesn't have any family. No next of kin to get her things."

Sincere's stomach churned. She had always known that Lena had no family, but hearing it now—hearing it like this—made her feel sick.

Lena had *nobody*.

Stacy hesitated before adding, "I can fly back. Handle it for her. But I didn't want to do it without asking you first."

Sincere's throat burned. The guilt hit her so hard she nearly doubled over. Lena was dead.

And the last words Sincere ever said to her weren't kind. After she saw the texts Supreme sent from her phone, she had sent her the nastiest messages. She told her not to ever contact her again. Called her a snake. A user. A groupie bitch.

She had been angry, hurt, and disgusted. And now, she would never get the chance to fix it. The sob broke free before she could stop it. Sincere didn't even have the strength to be embarrassed.

"Yes." Her voice came out shaky and utterly wrecked. "Yes, please. I—I can't do it. I can't—" She covered her mouth, trying to silence the gasping sobs that were already coming too fast and strong.

Stacy let out a breath. "Okay."

Sincere barely registered the sound of her voice. She wasn't there anymore. She was back in her home in Atlanta, drinking wine and laughing with Lena until their stomachs hurt. She was walking off the stage after her last show, watching Lena off to the side, jumping up and down and squealing as she clapped her hands. She was in the back of a car, feeling Lena's hand squeezing hers, giving her strength when her nerves were an absolute mess.

That was the Lena she knew. There was no way that all of that could have been fake. No way that she was acting the entire time just to keep tabs on her for Lorde. Lena was her *best* friend and, as soon as Sincere calmed down enough to go see her, she would hear her explanation. Because, deep down, she knew that Lena didn't want to betray her. She knew that Lorde had to be behind it.

But now she would never get the chance.

Her best friend was gone.

Forever.

"I'm booking my flight now." Stacy's voice was softer now, like she wasn't sure what to say. "I'll text you when I land."

Sincere nodded, even though she knew Stacy couldn't see her. "All right."

"Take care of yourself, Sincere," Stacy finally said.

The call ended and Sincere sat there, phone still pressed to her ear, staring blankly at nothing. Her chest felt tight. The walls of her apartment felt too close. The silence was suffocating. She needed something to help her through this. No . . . someone. She didn't trust herself to be alone.

Her fingers were already moving before she could think. She barely even registered what she was doing until she heard the familiar ringing.

One ring. Two. Three.

"Hello?"

Sincere opened her mouth, but nothing came out. She clenched her jaw, forcing down the sob threatening to break free. "Mama." That one word was all she could manage.

Her mother's voice changed instantly, the sharp edge in her tone softening instantly. "Baby? What's wrong?"

Sincere swallowed hard. "I need you. Here."

There was no hesitation. "Send me the address. I'm on my way."

That was it. No questions and no lecture.

Sincere did as she asked and then dropped the phone onto the bed beside her. She curled into herself, collapsing under the weight of her many emotions.

Sincere didn't remember how she ended up on the floor. She felt hollow. The words were still ringing in her ears.

She's dead.

Lena was gone.

Her mind kept replaying it, twisting it, refusing to let it settle. Her hands shook as she reached for her phone. With numb fingers, she swiped through old photos—images of Lena laughing, videos of them doing TikTok dances. She paused on a picture Lena had sent her of Sincere standing with Lena's arm draped over her shoulder. It was a paparazzi photo of them laughing after a fun night of partying and dancing. Lena sent a message along with it: *Me and my twin.*

Squinting, Sincere stared at the photo centering on the expression on Lena's face as she looked at her. There was pure love and adoration in her eyes. It was something that couldn't possibly be faked. Sincere swallowed hard, her vision blurring. She didn't have proof, but something told her that Lorde was behind this. It only made sense.

How did it come to this? How had she lost another friend? Lorde was taking *everything* from her. Sincere exhaled shakily, pressing the phone to her forehead, squeezing her eyes shut. Her chest felt tight, like her ribs were caving in.

Her fingers hovered over Supreme's number before she could stop herself. She hesitated, her pulse hammering. He had told her before that they had to be careful. That Lorde was watching everything, and it wasn't safe for him to be close to her right now. But . . . she just needed to hear his voice.

Before she could talk herself out of it, she hit the call button.

The line rang.

And rang.

And rang.

Then—voicemail.

Sincere's throat clenched. She pulled the phone away, staring at the screen as the call disconnected. Of course, he couldn't pick up. He had to stay away because of Lorde. The loneliness she felt pressed in deeper. It was suffocating. Her heartbeat pounded in her ears. She began to second-guess if calling her mother was the right move.

She's just going to say this is my punishment. That I brought this on myself.

But what other choice did she have? She couldn't be alone. Feeling like this for too long without support would force her to relapse. She swallowed hard as she held her phone tightly in her hand, realizing that she had no one else. For the last two years, Lena *was* her someone else.

Sincere choked on a sob as her grip on the phone loosened, and then she was collapsing, pressing her face into her arms, tears spilling freely. For once, she didn't fight it. She just let it come.

When her mother finally arrived, Sincere felt like it was right on time. She couldn't wait a second longer for her to come. They sat on the couch, the lamp next to her casting soft figures on the wall around them as Sincere tried to find her words. She had so much to say, but her words were failing her.

Before long, her mother started humming a tune. She pulled Sincere close to her and laid her head on her lap. Next thing Sincere knew, her mother's hands were in her hair, running through her curly strands with slow, practiced motions, gently massaging her scalp. The familiar rhythm took her back to long nights when she was a little girl, curled up in her mother's lap after a bad dream or a long day, feeling her mother's fingers comb through her curls.

Sincere let out a shaky breath. "I used to hate this when I was a kid. I hated lying still, but after a while, it always calmed me down."

Her mother's hands didn't pause. "I remember."

Sincere swallowed. "It's crazy how things change. Right now, I feel like lying here is the only thing keeping me together."

Her mother sighed softly, continuing her slow movements. "You always tried to hold everything in. Even when you were little, you'd sit in that bed, quiet as a mouse, thinkin' if you didn't say nothin', the bad things wouldn't be real."

"Sometimes I still think that way."

Her mother's fingers paused just briefly before she resumed. "That's not livin', baby. You can't try to bottle things up until they go away. That never works."

Sincere's breath hitched. She blinked, staring at the ceiling, trying to hold back the words she had been swallowing down. But in the moment she felt too raw, too exposed, and too safe for her to keep it all in.

"Lena's gone. Another one of my best friends was murdered."

Sincere exhaled shakily, blinking through the blur in her eyes. "I can't stop thinking about how it all ended. She was my best friend. She betrayed me and I didn't get a chance to make things right."

Her mother stayed quiet, waiting, and listening.

Sincere clenched her jaw, staring down at her hands. "I keep wondering if I pushed her to it. If I made her hate me somehow."

Her mother's sigh was soft but heavy, like she was carrying her own regrets. "You can't make anyone do anything. People do things for their own reasons and, sometimes, it has nothing to do with you."

Sincere shook her head. "But she said she loved me. I just can't see her doing this to me without a reason. Unless she really just didn't care about me."

Her mother exhaled, her fingers continuing their slow movements in her hair. "Maybe she did love you. And maybe that still wasn't enough. Love doesn't always take precedence over everything else."

Sincere's breath stilled.

Her mother's voice was gentle, steady. "You didn't make her betray you, baby. She did it for her own reasons. Whatever reason she did it is on her, not you."

Sincere's throat burned. "I just don't understand how you can love somebody and still hurt them like that. She pretended to be someone she wasn't. Made me trust her, but she was only getting close to me for other reasons."

Her mother sighed. "Because people are selfish! They love you how they know how. And some people never had anyone around who genuinely cared for them, so they don't know how to do that for anyone else. Some people couldn't tell real, unconditional love if it popped them in the face. They can't trust it."

Sincere sucked in a shaky breath. "I just feel so stupid. I was so open with Lena about everything. I feel like I should've known."

Her mother's hands slid down to cup the side of her face, forcing Sincere to look at her. "It wasn't your job to predict betrayal. It was her job to be loyal."

Sincere searched her mother's face, looking for the usual judgment, the usual "this is what happens when you live wrong" expression. But it wasn't there. There was only understanding. And maybe . . . a sliver of regret.

Her mother exhaled. "You didn't deserve this. But you gotta let all the guilt and shame go." Her mother's voice softened even more. "And you don't gotta carry it no more."

Sincere let out a choked sob, feeling like her heart was being ripped from her chest. Her mother just held her, letting her cry, rubbing slow, soothing circles against her back.

"I know how you feel about the 'Jesus stuff' as you call it. But I just want to remind you that Judas betrayed Jesus, you know."

Sincere blinked, taken off guard. "What?"

Her mother's expression didn't waver. "Judas betrayed Jesus, and Jesus was the perfect friend. Stop pretending you have to be perfect to earn true friendship. Even the one perfect person who walked on Earth still couldn't get it to work."

Sincere took a long breath. "Maybe."

"Ain't no maybe in it." Her mother shook her head. "Not everybody who is friendly is meant to be your friend. And yes, that hurts, but it's the world we live in."

Her mother exhaled. "Anybody who will turn their back on someone who is good to them has something truly ugly inside. And that ain't got nothin' to do with you. You just gotta pray for those people and move on."

Sincere bit her lip, her vision blurring again. "I don't know how to do that."

Her mother's voice softened. "Yes, you do."

She let the words sit for a moment, brushing Sincere's damp cheek with her thumb. "You just gotta stop trying to make sense of nonsense. Some people are just broken. And you can't fix 'em."

As her mother's words settled in, Sincere's phone began to vibrate against the couch cushion beside her. The sound barely registered at first, but when she glanced down and saw the name on the screen, her breath caught in her chest. It was Supreme.

Her fingers hesitated before swiping to open the message.

Just saw your call. You good?

Sincere exhaled slowly, a small smile tugging at her lips before she could stop it.

Her mother, always observant, didn't miss the shift in her expression. "Who's that?"

Sincere shook her head, brushing her thumb lightly over the screen. "Nobody."

"Supreme, huh?" Her mother lifted an eyebrow. "Mmhmm. That don't look like 'nobody' to me."

Sincere sighed, rolling her eyes. "It's just a friend, Mama."

A knowing look softened her mother's face. "A friend that just made you smile like that?"

Sincere hesitated, glancing down at the message again, warmth spreading through her chest. "Yeah . . . and I think he's a real one. At least, I hope so."

Her mother studied her for a moment before nodding, her expression softening. "Real ones are hard to find, Sincere." She reached out, tucking a curl behind her daughter's ear. "Don't push them away."

Sincere swallowed, the weight of her mother's words settling deep. She glanced down at Supreme's message one last time before typing out a simple response.

I'm good now. My mom's here.

She hesitated. Then, after a moment, she added to it.

Thank you.

He might not have been sure what she was thanking him for exactly, but she did.

For checking on her.

For being there even when he wasn't.

For just being real when everything else in her life felt like a lie.

Chapter 30

Supreme pulled out his phone, thumbs moving over the screen as he sent a quick message to Imani.

Check on Sincere when you get a chance.

He didn't wait for a response. He knew his sister—if he asked her to do something, she would. And, right now, he needed to focus. Sliding the phone back into his pocket, Supreme lifted his gaze to the men gathered around him—the elders.

They stood in a semicircle, their faces shadowed under the dim warehouse lighting. All of them had aged out of the game gracefully, their hands clean of blood for years, while still holding the sharpness in their eyes that only came from living a life where power was held and never given away.

Most of the youngest Saints had no idea these men even existed. That was intentional. Their identities were protected so they could live in peace after laying the foundation that held the entire organization together. But they weren't just ghosts from the past. They were the true decision-makers, and that's why Supreme called for this meeting.

Tension sat heavy in the room, thick enough to cut. Whispers moved methodically, bringing each man inside one by one, ensuring that weapons were collected, pockets were emptied, and any recording devices or communication tools were confiscated before entry. The elders weren't new to the process, but they didn't like it either.

One of them—Bishop, an older man with salt-and-pepper hair and a permanent scowl—watched Supreme closely as Whispers finished the last search. "All this necessary?"

Supreme met his gaze without hesitation. "I know it feels extreme, but I can't be too careful. Lorde has a way of making people do things they wouldn't normally do, especially when family is on the line."

Another man scoffed under his breath. "You questioning our loyalty now?"

Supreme shook his head. "This isn't about trust. It's about survival."

That shut them up.

He stepped forward, planting his feet shoulder-width apart, his stance firm. "I need your advice."

The room stayed silent, waiting for him to continue.

"Dre is dead."

A murmur of acknowledgment passed between them. None of them looked surprised. Supreme didn't expect them to react much. Men like these didn't flinch at death, but he wasn't done.

"Three other Saints gone too. Killed the same way."

That got their attention.

Supreme's voice was steady, even as his jaw clenched. "We know what's happening. We know Lorde's making these calls. What I need to know is . . . how do we move forward?"

A hush fell over the room. One of the quieter elders, Mathis, decided to finally speak up. He shifted in his seat and let out a slow, unimpressed breath. "You already know what to do. Why are you asking us?"

Supreme didn't respond immediately. His fingers flexed slightly, his gaze flickering to the ground before meeting theirs again.

Bishop saw the hesitation for what it was. "Oh." He leaned forward, resting his elbows on his knees. "You don't want to make the decision because he's your cousin." His voice was calm, almost amused. "You're hoping for some leniency."

He took a breath before adding, "Unfortunately, my son, that's something we cannot give."

Supreme's stomach twisted. He already knew this. Hell, he had known the second he called this meeting what the answer would be. But hearing it and having them lay it out so plainly was something else entirely.

Supreme's mind raced back to when they were kids. Back when Lorde wasn't Lorde. He was Laurent, a boy with a mean streak and something to prove. They weren't friends, not really, but they were family. And even in a world as ruthless as theirs, family was supposed to mean something. But did it really?

"I didn't want this," Supreme said finally, his voice quieter, but rougher than before. "I wanted him to step back. I wanted him to see reason."

Bishop nodded like he understood. "And yet, here we are."

Another elder, a broad-shouldered man named Clive, leaned forward. "What did you expect, Supreme? That he'd roll over because you asked nicely? That he'd hear reason? That's bullshit. He's gon' rogue, but he's still a Saint. We were bred to fall on the sword for what we believe in."

"Even so." Supreme exhaled sharply. "I was hoping."

Bishop chuckled. "That was your first mistake. Hope don't hold no weight here."

A heavy silence fell over them.

Then Bishop spoke again, voice firm. "Lorde is too dangerous to keep alive. We've given you our judgment. It's time to move."

Supreme clenched his jaw. "We don't have another way?"

Clive shook his head. "No."

Mathis leaned back. "If we let him live, what happens next? He falls back in line? He takes his punishment like a man?" He scoffed. "You know better than that."

Supreme did. Lorde would never stop. He would never bow his head. The second they showed even an inch of mercy, he'd use it against them. That's who he was. That's who he had always been.

Supreme forced the weight into a single nod. "Then it's done."

Bishop studied him. "Are you ready to do what needs to be done?"

Supreme held his gaze for a long moment. Then, finally—he nodded.

Bishop smiled faintly, satisfied. "Good."

The rest of the plan unfolded quickly.

Step one: Strip Lorde's resources. The Saints had ties to law enforcement, government officials, and people who could pull strings without leaving fingerprints. One call and Lorde's assets would start slipping through his fingers like sand.

Step two: Cut his connections to the organization. No more protection. No more security. No more Saints backing him in the streets.

Step three: Let the walls close in.

They didn't need to hunt Lorde down. He would come to them. When a man like Lorde lost control, he got desperate. And desperation made people reckless.

"What about Silvan?" Supreme asked, feeling utterly exasperated.

Bishop's gaze was steady as he gave Supreme one last directive. "Once Silvan sees Lorde is no longer useful, he'll handle himself."

Supreme's brows lifted slightly. "You think so?"

Bishop shook his head. "Silvan ain't loyal to nobody but Silvan. When he sees Lorde has nothing left to offer, he'll drop him like deadweight. He might even do the work for us."

Supreme considered that. It was a valid point. But he didn't want to wait for Silvan to move first. He wanted this shit over. *Now.* "What do we do in the meantime?"

Bishop's gaze met his, sharp and knowing. "We wait."

Supreme clenched his jaw. He hated waiting, but he also knew that it was the smart move. Lorde thought he was the one making the calls. That he was the one playing the game, but in reality, the board was already shifting.

Soon enough—he'd realize it was already checkmate.

In New Orleans, the night's humidity clung to your skin in a way that made the air feel heavier than it was. Supreme sat in the driver's seat of a blacked-out SUV, gripping the wheel as he watched the house in front of him. He was posted up in front of Lorde's mansion, or what *used* to be. The estate sat on a massive plot of land, set back from the main road, shielded by iron gates and towering hedges grown for privacy. It had always felt like a fortress, but tonight, it was about to fall.

One by one, cars pulled up behind him—SUVs, bikes, a blacked-out van—all full of Saints. The ones who had voted and made their choice. They were eager to get things back on track. Supreme let out a slow breath, rolling his shoulders. He stepped out, the others following suit.

Whispers came up beside him, adjusting his gloves as he gave the place a long, slow once-over. "You sure 'bout this?" he asked.

Supreme didn't answer right away. "Yeah." His voice was firm. "This ain't personal. It's protocol."

Whispers scoffed. "Shit feels personal to me."

Supreme didn't argue. Maybe it was. He motioned to the men behind him. "Let's move."

The house was too quiet as they approached. Supreme had already made sure Lorde wasn't here. He was probably holed up somewhere, trying to figure out his next move. But by the time he did, he wouldn't have a home to return to.

They entered fast and then moved faster. Every room was checked, secured, and emptied.

The first priority was the weapons. Guns, ammo—all confiscated. The Saints weren't leaving Lorde with anything he could use to stage a comeback. Next came the valuables—jewelry, watches, cash stashes, anything with resale value. Lorde's closet alone held enough designer fits to stock an entire boutique. But it all got stripped—boxed, bagged, and loaded into the vans outside.

One of the men, Tate, whistled as he held up a thick Cuban link chain. "Damn. Nigga really thought he was royalty."

Whispers chuckled, shaking his head. "Nigga damn near was. But kings only rule 'til the people say otherwise. And, clearly, the people have spoken."

Supreme kept moving, overseeing the process, making sure no detail got overlooked. Out in the driveway, the real work began. Two men worked to hot-wire Lorde's prized car—a matte black Maybach—while others secured the rest of his fleet. By the time Lorde got word of this, his entire driveway would be empty.

One of the younger Saints, Kilo, watched the scene with wide eyes. "Damn, y'all really takin' everything?"

Supreme turned to him, his voice steady. "Leaders can't own property or independent assets. Everything belongs to the Saints, and it isn't signed over to them until they retire. When someone goes rogue, it all comes back to us."

Kilo absorbed that, nodding slowly. "Shit. So basically . . . this is what happens when you forget the code."

His gaze hardened, tone cutting like ice. "This is what happens when you think you're bigger than the code."

Kilo didn't ask any more questions.

As the last of the valuables were packed away, chains were looped around the iron gates, locked tight. Lorde wasn't just losing his home—he was losing access. Supreme took a step back, watching as the final locks were secured. The house wasn't his anymore.

Whispers stood beside him, arms crossed. "So, what now?"

Supreme exhaled slowly, staring up at the house. The walls that had once made Lorde untouchable were now just a prison he didn't even own.

"Now he learns."

Whispers raised a brow. "Learns what?"

Supreme's gaze was cold. "What it feels like to have nothing."

Whispers let out a low whistle, shaking his head. "This nigga finna lose his mind."

Supreme's jaw tightened, his voice quiet but firm. "That's the point."

Chapter 31

Lorde was in the middle of the perfect dream . . . that suddenly turned into the most horrific nightmare. It was one that felt too real, a dream that pulled him in until he got lost in it. It felt like it meant something. He was standing at the top of the city, looking down at everything he built. The skyline stretched before him, endless and powerful. He could see everything, everyone, all moving under his rule.

A throne sat behind him. It was ornate, gold, and made for a king. It was his throne. He reached for it, his fingers grazing the cold surface of the armrest—then it crumbled beneath his touch. The ground split open, his empire turning to ash, the city beneath him swallowing itself whole. He tried to move, tried to stop it, but his feet were sinking, dragging him down. Just before he sunk into a deep hole, the sound of shouting jolted him awake.

"Lorde, wake your ass up!"

His eyes flew open just in time for the bedroom door to slam against the wall, rattling the whole damn room. His heart was pounding, disoriented from the dream, his mind still caught between reality and the ruins of his kingdom.

Nia was standing in front of him. And she was *pissed.*

"Nigga . . . why you trying me? You got me out here looking stupid in front of my friends!"

Lorde groaned, dragging a hand down his face. The dream was already fading, but that feeling was still there. It felt like something had gripped his chest and squeezed. "What the hell are you yelling about?" he muttered, his voice heavy with sleep.

She stood at the foot of the bed, arms crossed tight, nails tapping against her bicep like she was holding herself back from throwing something. "My card declined," she snapped. "All of them."

Lorde blinked, still piecing himself together. "And?" he said lazily. "Just use another one."

"I *did*, nigga. Every single one."

Now he was awake. He sat up slowly, the sleep leaving his body fast. "What you mean, 'every single one'?"

"Exactly what the hell I said." Her voice was sharper this time, cutting through the last of his grogginess. "I was out with my girls, we ate, had a couple drinks, I pulled out my card like I always do. It declined! Tried another one. That one declined too! The fuck is going on, Lorde?"

That unease in his chest tightened. This wasn't normal. His money didn't move like that. Lorde swung his legs over the side of the bed, reaching for his phone. He swiped through notifications, expecting something—a fraud alert, a banking issue, any sign of what the hell was happening. But there was nothing.

His frown deepened. He tapped into his banking app, waited for it to load . . . error. He tried again. Error. His jaw clenched. "What bank bullshit they on now?" he muttered, exiting the app and going straight to his messages. Nothing unusual. Unread texts from his crew. Some notifications about Sincere. And also, a message from Silvan.

Your lil Saints problem gettin' out of hand, bruh. If you need my help, you know where to find me.

His stomach dropped.

His Saints problem? Something must've happened.

His chest tightened.

No way. No fucking way.

He got up, fast, grabbing his pants off the chair and yanking them on.

Nia was watching him, her glare still cutting. "Lorde, you better not be playing with my money. I don't care what you got going on with Sahara, it better not affect me."

He shot her a look. "Why the fuck would I do that?"

"Because niggas like you only loyal to power. And when power shifts, the ones closest to you always get burned first."

Lorde's nostrils flared. "I don't know what the fuck you talking about, but you need to calm all that down."

She scoffed, shaking her head. "I just need to know if I need to start making different plans. Because if your shit is crumbling, I'm not about to go down with you."

His chest burned, his pride bristling. She thought he was losing. She thought he was done. The one loyal person he thought he had was letting him know that if he went down, she wasn't riding with him.

He reached into his pocket, pulled out a thick roll of cash, peeled off a few hundreds, and threw them on the bed. "Here. I'll hit the bank later and fix this shit."

Nia took the money, but her expression didn't change. She didn't believe him, but Lorde wasn't even thinking about her anymore. He needed to get home now so he could figure out what was going on.

Lorde's fingers gripped the steering wheel so tight his nails dug into his palm. The closer he got to the house, the heavier that feeling in his gut became. Something wasn't right. The air felt off. His nerves were unsettled, a signal that something wasn't right. Then, as he turned the final corner and the house came into view, he felt his breath catch in his throat.

The gates were chained shut.

What. The. Fuck.

He blinked, his grip on the wheel tightening. He had never seen that before. His mind immediately started working. This had to be some kind of mistake. Maybe one of his guys locked it up after a delivery. Maybe his security had updated the system without letting him know. But even as he tried to convince himself, he knew the truth. Something was very, very wrong.

He shoved the car into *park* and jumped out, marching toward the gate. The heavy-duty chain looped through the iron bars, secured with a thick industrial lock. He was locked out of his own house. His chest tightened. He pulled out his phone, fingers tapping out his access code. The screen blinked, *ACCESS DENIED.*

His stomach dropped. Lorde tried again, punching the numbers in with a little more force.

ACCESS DENIED.

His jaw clenched so hard it ached. His pulse pounded, a slow, steady drumbeat of anger swelling in his veins.

He tried one last time.

ACCESS DENIED.

His hands shook. His nostrils flared. This was Supreme. *That nigga really had the balls to pull this?* He took a slow, loaded breath, forcing his emotions back down. If the front door wouldn't let him in, he'd find another way.

His eyes shot across the property. Something had to be open. After checking and finding nothing, he decided desperate measures had to be taken. Without hesitation, he picked up a brick from the garden bed and hurled it.

CRASH.

The glass shattered, spilling onto the hardwood floors inside. The sound echoed across the empty driveway, cutting through the silence like a knife. He was too far from the neighboring houses for anyone to notice. He reached in, unlatched the window, and hauled himself inside. His boots hit the floor with a crunch, broken shards splintering beneath his weight. Then, he looked up—and his breath caught in his throat.

The house was empty—stripped, completely gutted. Lorde's pulse thundered, a slow, rolling heat building in his chest. The living room was cleared out. His artwork was gone. His Persian rugs, his imported liquor, the grand piano . . . all gone. Even the goddamn curtains had been ripped from the rods. It looked like the ghost of his life, like nothing had ever been here at all.

He took a staggered breath, his body stiff with disbelief.

They really did this.

His mind was racing, flipping through every possibility, every explanation. Then, it hit him—the stash. His heart slammed against his ribs as he moved, his steps sharp, calculated. He headed straight for the study, where his most secure safe was hidden behind the bookshelf. He dropped to his knees, running his hand along the baseboard. His fingers found the latch. He yanked it open . . .

Empty.

His emergency cash reserves were gone. His gold bars had disappeared. He swallowed hard, a slow, vicious fury building in his chest. Then, he reached for his next line of defense, his guns. But the hidden compartment beneath the desk was empty. His weapon stash behind the liquor cabinet was completely wiped out. His final gun, the one under his bed for emergencies? That was gone too.

Lorde staggered backward, his breath coming short and hard. The walls felt smaller, like they were closing in on him.

This was not just a robbery. It was a message. His fingers curled into fists, his jaw clenching so tight his teeth ached. Supreme—this was all him.

That traitorous-ass nigga.

Lorde felt something cold and ugly settle in his stomach. He had heard whispers that Supreme was making moves and even suspected he was lining people up against him. But this was war. His head pounded, his breath coming faster.

Supreme thought he could cut him off, take everything he had built, and just walk away unscathed. Nah, this wasn't over. Not by a long shot. Lorde took a slow step forward, his mind sharpening. His resources might be gone, but he wasn't out of the game. He still had Silvan and other connections. And most importantly—he had an undying thirst for revenge.

His hands shook, not from fear, but from pure, unfiltered rage. Supreme thought he won, but this was far from over. Lorde stormed out of the empty house, fists clenched so tight his knuckles turned white.

His rage was so heavy that he could barely breathe. His car sat where he left it, untouched. The fact that he still had this was a small mercy throughout a day full of losses. He climbed inside, slamming the door shut, the silence of the cabin only amplifying the rage roaring inside his chest. His hands shook as he pulled out his phone. He had one move left.

Lorde knew the risks, knew that dealing with Silvan had always been a delicate game. But he also knew that in a world like this, power recognized power. And no matter what Supreme had done, no matter how deep he'd cut, Lorde was still a power to be reckoned with. He just needed to reload.

He pressed the call button.

It rang once.

Twice.

Three times.

Then, suddenly, he heard a sound on the other line.

"Well, well, well. Look who decided to check in." Silvan's voice oozed amusement.

Lorde's jaw ticked. He could already hear the condescension in his tone. He didn't have time for this. "I need you to front me some hardware and cash," Lorde said, his tone clipped and controlled. "I'll pay you back double."

A slow exhale from the other end of the line. Then . . . laughter. Gut-deep, full-bodied laughter, as if something was completely and utterly hilarious. It made Lorde's vision pulse red.

"Damn, Lorde. You really got your ass put out on the curb, huh?"

Lorde's grip on the phone tightened. "Nigga, I ain't got time for this shit."

"No, you really don't." Silvan's tone shifted, still amused, but now carrying something menacing beneath it.

Lorde forced himself to keep his voice level. "You got it or not?"

Silvan was silent for a second. "How you gon' pay me when you're not king anymore?"

The words landed like a punch to the chest. Lorde's body went rigid, his heartbeat a steady hammer against his ribs. "The fuck you talking about?" His voice dropped lower, more lethal. "I'm still running this shit."

"Nah, Lorde. You're out. I heard all about it. Everybody taking orders now from Supreme."

Lorde's breath stalled. He blinked. For the first time since everything crumbled, he felt something close to disbelief.

Silvan's voice came smooth and unbothered, like he was talking about the weather. "And don't confuse this for friendship. We were never friends. You just didn't see it."

Lorde's mind spun. This wasn't just about Supreme. Silvan knew everything. He knew about the coup and that Lorde was done before he even realized it himself. Silvan had been watching and waiting. Letting him dig his own grave. And now he was standing over it, tossing in dirt.

Lorde swallowed hard, a sick, ugly feeling unfurling in his gut. "Silvan." His voice came out low, sharp with warning. "Don't play with me."

Silvan clicked his tongue. "That's the thing, Lorde. I never was. You just thought you were untouchable. Now you know you're not."

Click.

The line went dead and Lorde froze, the silence ringing in his ears. His fingers slowly curled around the phone, his knuckles going bone-white. He stared at the screen for a long moment, his breathing slow, measured. And then, he lost it.

With a roar of fury, he hurled his phone across the car, the screen shattering against the dashboard. His chest heaved, rage boiling so hot he could feel it in his veins, thick and scalding. Everything. Every-fucking-thing he had built was gone. And now, even Silvan had cut him loose. He was alone. Completely, utterly alone.

He had nothing.

Lorde stumbled back into the house, into the kitchen, his body moving on autopilot, his mind a storm of rage and disbelief. His footsteps echoed in the emptiness. His once-pristine home was nothing but a hollowed-out shell now. His fingers twitched, his jaw locked. His mind was moving too fast, spiraling in a thousand directions—plotting, raging, sinking.

And then he saw it.

A small plastic baggie sat dead center on the bare kitchen counter. Lorde froze. The house had been wiped clean, stripped of everything valuable, yet someone had left this. A single baggie of cocaine.

He stepped closer, his chest rising and falling heavily, his pulse a dull, pounding drum in his ears. The baggie was sealed tight, the powder inside white as bone, the plastic crinkling slightly as he lifted it. His eyes narrowed. Scrawled across the plastic in bold red marker was one word.

Mercy.

His stomach twisted. *Mercy.* Yeah, right. They were mocking him. Leaving him scraps like he was some stray nigga, some corner fiend, some desperate junkie who needed a little extra to cope. His grip tightened on the bag. Maybe they weren't wrong.

His breath came heavy as he ripped the bag open, the familiar, bitter scent of the powder hitting his nostrils immediately. His heart pounded, his thoughts snarled together in a tangled, chaotic mess. He needed to shut it all up and stop feeling.

He grabbed an old credit card from the counter, one that had been declined at the gas station just an hour ago, and raked it through the powder in a quick, practiced motion. He leaned down, pressing one nostril closed, and snorted the line in one harsh inhale.

The burn was instant. A white-hot sting up his sinuses, sharp and biting, setting his nerves on fire. He exhaled hard, his head jerking slightly as the drug rushed through him, spreading in waves, a sick mix of relief and electricity seeping into his bloodstream.

He fell back into a chair, his head lolling slightly as his limbs tingled, the tension melting away. The rage, the humiliation, the loss—all of it dulled. And then there was a voice. Soft and sweet, coated in venom.

It was Lena.

You be good to Daddy and Daddy will be good to you.

Lorde's body jerked, his eyes snapping open.

She's not here.

But her voice whispered through the room, curling around him like a ghostly caress, threading through his mind with a mocking lilt.

You be good to Daddy and Daddy will be good to you.

His fingers dug into the armrests.

His breathing hitched.

He closed his eyes, pressing his palms against them, willing her away.

You be good to Daddy—

"Shut up," he rasped. But the words looped in his head.

Again. Again. Again.

He shook his head violently, his teeth gritting as he pressed his hands harder into his face. But the cocaine had opened a door and now Lena was inside. Her laugh. Her smile The way she had kissed up to him when it suited her, only to whisper secrets behind his back. The way she had played him. Just like Supreme. Just like everyone else.

He shot back up to his feet, his chair scraping hard against the tile. He needed more to drown her out. Lorde leaned down, cutting another line, his movements quick, frantic, sloppy.

You be good to Daddy—

Another sharp inhale.

Another burning rush.

Another layer of numbness settling in.

But the voice didn't leave because, deep down, he knew what he had done, and it was going to haunt him forever.

The room was dark, except for the faint lighting from the streetlights leaking through the half-closed blinds. Lorde sat slumped in his chair, elbows braced on the table, staring at the empty space in front of him. The cocaine had settled into his veins, but it hadn't done what he needed it to do. The high felt shallow and the numbness was hollow. His mind was still spinning, still racing, still clawing for a solution that was evading him.

His phone sat beside him, screen black, like it was waiting for something. Without even thinking or questioning it, he picked it up and dialed Maman Clo.

The phone only rang once before she picked up the line. "Boy, what did you do?"

Lorde's breath caught in his chest. His grip tightened around the phone, his jaw clenching. "I didn't do nothin'," he snapped. "Things were done to me, Maman. And I'm about to make everybody pay for it."

A long, heavy silence stretched between them. So long that Lorde pulled the phone from his ear, frowning at the screen. "What the fuck?" he muttered. "Did these motherfuckers cut my phone off too?"

"The problem isn't anybody else, Laurent," Maman Clo finally said, her voice steady, but heavy with an emotion he couldn't place. "The problem is you."

Lorde's frown deepened. "Me?" he repeated. "I'm the problem?"

"You have to let the hate go, boy," she continued, like she hadn't heard him. "Hate is a disease. It don't want justice. It don't want peace. It only got *one* goal—to eat you alive until there's nothing left of you but an empty shell. If you keep holding onto it, thinking it will protect you, that's what will happen."

Lorde laughed. It came out like a short, bitter chuckle. "Let it go? You tellin' me to just let people walk all over me?" His voice rose, incredulous. "You tellin' me to lay down and take it? That ain't what you taught me, Maman! You taught me to stand up. You taught me to be a man, to fight back. And now you want me to roll over like a fuckin' dog?"

Not once in his life had Lorde ever talked to Maman Clo this way, but this was the first time he ever felt like she wasn't in his corner. He never once doubted her loyalty, but right now she was sounding more like his enemies.

"I want you to see the truth," she said, voice calm but firm. "I want you to stop lettin' that anger blind you."

"Blind me?" Lorde shot back, pushing up from his chair. "I

see clearer than I ever have. Supreme played me from the start! He been plottin' this from the beginning. He wanted what I had, and he waited 'til the time was right to take it. He turned everybody against me and you think I'm just supposed to accept that?"

Maman Clo sighed, long and tired. "It ain't about acceptin' it," she said. "It's about knowin' when a war ain't worth fightin'. It's about knowing whether your real enemy is someone else or if it's inside of you."

Lorde shook his head, pacing now, his blood boiling. "You don't get it," he muttered. "You don't understand what they did to me. They trying to ruin me! After all I've done for them. They used me just to fill up their pockets so they could replace me with Supreme. They probably been plotting this shit from the beginning."

"Oh, I understand," she said. "I understand better than you do. I understand that you lettin' your ego make your decisions for you. And that's gon' be your downfall, boy."

Lorde's teeth gritted. "I ain't got time for this," he said sharply.

More silence.

Then, finally, Maman Clo spoke again. "I love you, boy," she said softly. "I promise I raised you the best I could, using all the strength the ancestors gave me. I wanted you to be better than all the ones who came before you. Better than your father. Better than me."

Lorde swallowed hard. Something deep twinged in his chest, but he forced it down. "And you did a good fuckin' job," he said, his voice tight, emotions held back by sheer force of will. "Nobody could've done better, Maman. You did everything they wanted you to do."

In that moment, Lorde swore that he could almost hear the beating of her heart. Then, barely above a whisper, he heard her say, "I hope so."

Lorde closed his eyes.

"You take care of yourself, boy."

He forced out a breath. "I will."

The line went dead.

Lorde sat there in the silence, phone still in his hand, but his mind miles away. He had never defied her advice before. Not even once. Something deep inside him whispered that he should listen. That he should just let it all go and give in to Supreme. Just take whatever they left him and rebuild. They would punish him, but he was still a Saint. They would still look out for him as long as he showed humility.

But then, a darker voice rose up inside him. This voice was louder, much stronger, and definitely meaner.

Give in to that nigga? For what? He set you up. He stole from you! He got you out here lookin' weak as shit! And you just gon' roll over and let him do this shit?

Lorde's eyes flickered open. His chest tightened, his nails biting into his palms. Supreme always acted like the level-headed one. The *reasonable* one. The one who always stood on principle and talked about loyalty. But *this* was the truth of it all. *This* was the real him.

Supreme had always wanted to take over. He was just waiting for his moment. He played the long game with patience and now, he had everybody fooled. Lorde's jaw locked as he gritted his teeth. And then, another thought came to mind as he began laying the foundation of his plan.

Sincere had been acting differently lately. A little too accommodating and a little less defiant. If Supreme was really playing him like this, if he had gone behind his back, then . . . could he have gotten to her too?

Lorde's stomach tightened.

No fuckin' way.

Sincere needed him. She *owed* him. He had done too much for her. Not only that, but he also knew things about her that she didn't want the world to know. He could use that to remind her who she belonged to. If she helped him, it was all good. He would protect her for the show of loyalty. But if she didn't . . .

Time to move.

Lorde pushed up from his seat, his heart pounding, his mind clearer than it had been all night.

It's time to see where her loyalty lies.

Without another thought, he turned and walked out the door.

Behind him, the room plunged deeper into darkness.

Chapter 32

The melody was haunting.

Sincere's fingers drifted over the piano keys. Each note she played reflected the storm of emotions raging inside her. She wasn't just writing a song. She was unearthing something buried down inside of her. Something she wasn't sure she wanted to look at too closely.

Her voice was soft as she murmured the lyrics under her breath, testing them against the melody.

"I've lost too many people . . . Maybe it's my fault . . ."

She exhaled, her hands pausing on the keys.

"Maybe I just don't deserve to keep anyone close."

The words lingered in the air, heavy and unspoken. A part of her hated how much she believed them. She pressed her fingers into the ivory, leaning into the music, trying to drown out the ache pulling at her chest.

Then, suddenly, there was a knock at the door. Her hands froze mid-chord. Sincere glanced at the clock: 10:47 p.m. A sinking feeling settled in her stomach. Nobody visited this late, not without calling first. Her heart began to pound, but she pushed the feeling down, standing slowly. Carl and Andre wouldn't have let someone up without telling her, but they weren't there.

She approached the door cautiously, peeking through the peephole. Her breath caught. Lorde was standing right outside. A wave of dread crashed into her so hard it almost knocked her off balance. Her fingers tightened around the doorknob. Every instinct in her body told her not to open it. But she knew him—if she didn't, he'd keep knocking. He'd make a scene. And she didn't need that right now.

She took a slow, steadying breath before unlocking the door and pulling it open. Lorde stood in the dim hallway, his frame backlit by the overhead light glowing above. But it wasn't his presence alone that sent chills through her. It was his eyes. They were wild, glassy, and burning with dark intensity. His shirt was slightly wrinkled like he had been gripping at it, and his breathing was uneven, sending a subtle tremor in his chest.

Sincere knew that look. She'd seen it in too many men before him. He was high and spiraling. Her pulse spiked, but she kept her face unreadable, her voice smooth. "Lorde . . . what are you doing here?"

He exhaled a slow chuckle, running a hand over his beard. "Damn, baby, that's how you greet me?"

Her stomach turned. That voice. Its slow, almost teasing cadence. It was Lorde trying to act like himself, like the man who still had control, but she could hear the edges fraying beneath it.

Sincere forced a small, measured smile. "It's late," she said simply. "You should've called first."

His lips twitched. "Didn't think I needed to call my girl before stopping by."

Her skin crawled at the possessiveness in his tone, but she didn't flinch, trying her hardest not to react. That was the key to getting through moments like this. Never show your fear. Instead, she tilted her head slightly, playing along just enough to keep things from escalating too soon.

"You been drinking?" she asked, her voice light, like she was making an observation.

His eyes narrowed as he stepped closer. "Nah. Just thinking. A lot."

Sincere held her ground. She could smell it now—the mix of liquor and other things. A chemical scent was clinging to him. She took a slow breath, keeping her posture relaxed, her tone even. "What's on your mind?"

For a moment, he just stared at her. Then, without warning, he reached out. His fingers grazed her jaw. His touch was too aggressive. She resisted the urge to recoil. Instead, she stayed perfectly still, letting him believe she wasn't rattled.

His voice dropped lower, almost affectionate. "You been really good to me lately."

Her stomach pulled into tight knots. She knew what he meant. He'd been enjoying the way she played along. The way she sent texts that felt like submission, the way she let him believe he was reeling her back in. She was only doing what she needed to do to survive. But Lorde wasn't fooled. He knew she wasn't all the way his. He was only here to test her. He wanted to see how far she would let him go.

She forced a small smile. "I've just been focused on my music, trying to stay out the way."

Lorde nodded, his thumb lightly tracing her chin. "Good," he murmured. "I need you to keep doing that."

His eyes locked onto hers. They were dark and unreadable. "Because you and me? We got unfinished business."

Sincere's pulse thundered, but she didn't show it. She simply nodded. Lorde, on the other hand, pulled his lips into a slow and satisfied smile, as if he had just won something. Her stomach churned. She knew, without a doubt—this was only the beginning. Lorde wasn't here to talk. He was here to claim what he thought was his and she needed to find a way to survive it. The second she moved aside, he pushed past her. No hesitation, no waiting for an invitation—like he had the right.

Sincere swallowed back the surge of unease creeping up her spine as Lorde moved through her space like he owned it. The air around her instantly felt tighter, like the walls were closing in.

He didn't stop until he reached the center of the living room, where he turned, dark eyes locking onto her like a target. His chest rose and fell unevenly, his fingers twitching at his sides. Cocaine, liquor, and rage were all swimming beneath his skin, practically boiling over.

He turned toward her and his lips curled into a bitter, humorless smile. "You know what happened to me?"

Sincere inhaled carefully, keeping her expression neutral. She had to play this right. She stepped forward, closing the door behind her with quiet precision. "I heard a little bit."

Lorde's eyes flickered, narrowing slightly as he searched her face for a lie. "How'd you hear?" His voice had an edge now.

Sincere crossed her arms, lifting a brow. "The men you had watching me told me they didn't need to anymore." She let the words settle before delivering the final blow. "Said you weren't king of the Saints anymore."

For the first time, Lorde flinched, just slightly and only for a second. But she saw it. His jaw locked. His fingers flexed. His whole body tensed like a coiled screw wound up too tight. And then, he dropped his head, not in shame, but in pure, suffocating realization.

The silence stretched between them so long it was suffocating. And then, just when she thought he wouldn't say anything—he did. "Oh." It wasn't loud or angry. It was just . . . empty, like the words had knocked the breath out of him.

Sincere's chest tightened. For the first time, Lorde actually looked . . . defeated. He moved, slow and unsteady, sinking onto the nearest chair like the truth of his situation had finally settled onto his shoulders. She didn't move or dare step closer or try to comfort him. A caged animal was the most dangerous when it realized it had nowhere left to go.

After a long pause, he lifted his head, studying her with something almost like curiosity. "So, why'd you let me in?" His voice was lower now, rough around the edges. "Thought you hated me."

Sincere kept her tone cool. "Why wouldn't I?" She could've left it there, but she wanted to see his face when she twisted the knife. "You looked like you needed someone."

Something flickered behind his eyes. It was something he was trying to bury beneath bravado and bitterness. For a split second, he looked like a man who didn't know where to go next. But the moment was gone just as fast as it came and the mask slid back into place.

Lorde scoffed. "I would think you wouldn't want shit to do with me."

Sincere tilted her head slightly, her voice even. "I don't."

And then, she let her lips curl into the faintest hint of a smile. "But you knew *that* from the beginning."

His face twisted at her honesty. She held on as long as she could, but she couldn't play this game with him anymore. The moment Lorde's expression hardened, Sincere knew she had struck a nerve. His hands curled into fists on his thighs, his body rigid, but the tension didn't fully explode just yet. Instead, his voice came out smoothly and deceptively calm.

"You know what's funny?" he said, his gaze locked on the floor like he was trying to suppress something dark from spilling over.

Sincere stayed silent. She wasn't here to play his games.

Lorde let out a low chuckle, shaking his head before finally looking at her. "I spent years building this empire. Years making sure everyone ate, keeping everything balanced. And you know who I did all that with? Supreme."

His jaw tensed, his voice thick with resentment, betrayal, and fury. "That was my brother. My blood in everything except name. And this is how he repays me? Can you believe that? The one person I thought had my back—"

"Honestly?" Sincere cut in, tilting her head.

Lorde's eyes lit up, eager, like he had finally gotten someone to understand.

"No." She exhaled sharply, letting the weight of her words drop between them. "I can't believe Supreme would treat anyone like that. Doesn't seem like his character."

The flash of relief that passed over Lorde's face was almost sad. For half a second, he thought she was on his side. Then, she forced a knife into the wound.

"But it seems like yours."

The entire room shifted. Lorde blinked. His expression froze. Like his mind had short-circuited trying to process what she had just said. Then, his features twisted, rage curling at the edges of his face.

"The fuck does that mean?" His voice was quieter now, but there was no mistaking the danger simmering beneath it.

Sincere kept her posture relaxed, but her heart was pounding. She had already pushed him over the edge, might as well make sure he drowned. "You really don't know?" she asked, lifting an eyebrow. "The cameras. Lena. Dre. The way you kill your own people when they don't obey you. You're out here asking me how Supreme could do you dirty like this, but if you really think about it, shouldn't you be asking yourself why everybody wants you gone?"

Lorde sat up straighter, his breathing heavier. His eyes darted around the room as paranoia slid into his bones. "How do you know that?"

"Because you're predictable." Her delivery was flat and unbothered.

That set him off. Lorde surged to his feet, his chair screeching against the hardwood. The air in the room grew thick. He was stinking it up with his bad energy, trying to intimidate her by allowing his towering presence to loom over her. Sincere didn't move. She just watched him, waiting for whatever was coming next.

His jaw clenched so hard it looked like it might snap. His breathing was uneven, his eyes wild. "You think you know me, huh?" he spat. "You think you got me all figured out?"

Sincere lifted her chin slightly. "I think you're a man who never learned how to do anything but react to being afraid."

Lorde laughed out a short, humorless thing that was closer to a snarl. "Afraid?" he repeated, stepping toward her. "You think I'm afraid?"

Sincere held his gaze. "Yes."

"Of what?" His voice was sharp, clipped.

"Losing control. You're afraid of letting someone else get the best of you."

Lorde let out another dark chuckle, but there was no humor in it. He exhaled, dragging a hand down his face, before shaking his head. "You really think Supreme's the hero in all this?"

Sincere tilted her head. "I don't think Supreme is perfect. But I do know he's *not* you."

Lorde's expression flickered. For a brief second, she saw a flash of something buried deep beneath his anger. It was raw, wounded, and scary. "You have no idea what I've been through."

Sincere sighed. "Then tell me."

Lorde hesitated. His tongue darted out, running over his bottom lip as he inhaled slowly. Then, his shoulders slumped just a little. For the first time since he walked in, his voice wasn't laced with rage or arrogance or entitlement.

Just pain.

"My father was killed by the one person he trusted."

Sincere stiffened.

Lorde's gaze grew distant, like he was being pulled back into the past. "His own brother. Best fuckin' friend," he murmured. "Gunned him down right in front of me. And you know what that taught me? That you can't trust nobody. Not even family."

Sincere felt something twist inside her. She could see it now. The small boy inside Lorde, watching the only person he trusted get taken away. The part of him that never healed. But she wasn't about to let that be an excuse.

"Then you learned the wrong lesson."

Lorde's eyes snapped back to hers.

Sincere's voice was calm, but there was steel beneath it. "Your father was killed because he wanted to make things better." She let the words hang in the air before delivering the final blow. "The man who killed him was greedy and selfish. Out of those two characters, which one do you think is being played by you?"

The moment almost suffocated him. Sincere's words pressed down on the room like an iron hand. Lorde just stared at her. Then, something inside him broke. His breathing turned ragged. His nostrils flared, his chest rising and falling like a storm building inside of him. And then . . . he laughed. It was a cruel, hollow sound that didn't reach his eyes or sound human.

"You stank-ass bitch." His voice was sharp, dripping with venom, but his expression looked like she had just cracked something deep inside him.

Lorde's upper lip curled into a sneer as he took a step closer. "Can't even sing. Pussy is trash. Lena's was tighter. Probably because it's all loose from fuckin' Supreme."

The words should have stung. And . . . maybe once upon a time, they would have. But not now. In fact, Lorde just looked pathetic.

Sincere didn't blink or flinch. She simply tilted her head, watching him. And then, in the calmest, most bored voice she could muster, she said, "Oh, so you admit his dick is bigger than yours?"

The silence was instant. Lorde froze. His jaw clenched, his hands twitched, his face twisted into something unrecognizable. And then . . . he lost it. With a guttural, animalistic roar, he lunged. His hands wrapped around her throat before she could even react. The impact knocked her backward, her head hitting the edge of the couch as his grip tightened like a vise.

Sincere's hands flew up, instinctively clawing at his fingers, her nails digging into his skin, but he didn't let go. He squeezed harder. His face was a mask of pure hatred, his teeth gritted, his body trembling as his fingers crushed down on her windpipe.

"You think you're funny?" he snarled, spit flying from his lips. His grip tightened again, and black spots exploded behind her eyes.

Panic set in. She kicked, trying to buck him off, but his weight pinned her down. Her lungs burned. Her vision blurred. Her thoughts scattered. That's when she knew it. This was it. This was the end.

If it's up to him, I'm dying tonight.

Chapter 33

Sincere's vision tunneled, the world closing in as Lorde's grip crushed down on her throat. Her lungs screamed for air. Her hands clawed weakly at his wrists, but the strength in her arms was fading fast. Everything was slipping. Her body. Her breath. Her life . . . It was all fading away.

She barely heard the crash of the front door and registered the blur of motion that stormed inside. She was too busy fading into whatever life was waiting for her after this one. And then—the pressure was gone. Her body collapsed to the floor as she gasped, sucking in jagged, desperate breaths. Her chest heaved. Her throat burned. She coughed violently, her fingers trembling as they clutched at the tender skin of her neck.

Lorde wasn't touching her anymore. He couldn't, not with Supreme's arm locked around his throat, yanking him backward into a headlock with unforgiving force. Lorde choked out a curse, his hands clawing at Supreme's arm, but Supreme was unmoved. His grip was steel. His face, murderous. Behind them, the door swung open wider, and Sincere barely lifted her head in time to see Andre and Carl step inside, their faces like carved stone.

Carl's jaw clenched, his eyes dropping to her gasping form.

The way his expression twisted, Sincere didn't even want to know what she looked like.

Andre, however, was already focused on Lorde, his lip curled in disgust.

"You sick motherfucker," he muttered, stepping forward, his fists clenched.

Lorde gasped for air, struggling in Supreme's unrelenting hold. "Let me go, nigga!"

Supreme wrenched him harder, forcing him toward the nearest chair and slamming him into it. Lorde barely had time to recover before Supreme was on him again, pressing down on his shoulder with one heavy, unmovable hand.

"Don't move," Supreme warned, his voice calm, yet brimming with violence.

Lorde lifted his head, wild eyes darting from Supreme to Andre to Carl. Then, they landed on Sincere. The venom in them was instant.

"You little bitch," he rasped, his voice hoarse, but filled with hate. "You called him?"

Sincere barely had enough breath to speak. She didn't even have the energy to laugh in his face. But before she could say anything, Andre's voice cut through the thick, suffocating air.

"No. We did."

Sincere's head snapped toward him, surprise shining through the exhaustion in her body. Andre's expression was unreadable. His arms were crossed and his mouth set in a tight line.

When she hesitated, still breathing hard, he added, "Just because you sent us away didn't mean that we stopped looking after you."

She stared at him with gratitude shining in her eyes. She looked at Carl, who was standing beside him, nodding in silent agreement. Then at Supreme, whose grip on Lorde never wavered.

Something inside of her shifted when she realized that Lorde was wrong. She hadn't lost everyone and he was about to find out exactly what that meant.

"You were working with them," he spat, his voice raspy but dripping with accusation. "Should've known you ain't got no loyalty. Just like your dead friends."

Sincere stilled. The words landed like a slap.

Aaliyah.

Lena.

Both gone, because of him. And now he wanted to throw them in *her* face?

She tilted her chin up, her voice hoarse, but steady. "You should be the last person to talk about loyalty."

Lorde's eye twitched. For a second, she thought she saw something behind his rage. He looked uncertain and exposed, but it disappeared as quickly as it came. Before he could retaliate, Supreme finally spoke. His voice was measured, but there was a finality to it that left no room for doubt.

"The elders have ordered an execution for your crimes."

Lorde stared at him, his chest rising and falling with slow, unsteady breaths. Then—he laughed. He leaned forward slightly, looking at Supreme like he'd lost his mind. "The weak leading the weak," he scoffed, shaking his head. Mockery bled into every word. "Y'all really think you can replace me?"

Nobody said anything, but Supreme's jaw clenched. His hands balled into tight fists. Sincere could see it now. Lorde didn't think he was losing. He thought this was temporary. He thought he could claw his way back into his position. Even now, when the walls had already collapsed around him.

Supreme exhaled, his shoulders tight with restraint as he stared at the man he had once called family. "Unc called you Lorde for a reason," he said, his voice quiet, but firm. "You were supposed to be a messiah for the Saints. Build something bigger than all of us."

Lorde tilted his head. For a second, it almost looked like he was considering the words, like some part of him remembered what they used to talk about—before power, before greed, before blood.

But then, his eyes darkened. His mouth curled into something bitter and when he spoke, his words dripped with mockery. "A messiah?" he repeated, letting out a humorless laugh. "Like *Jesus*?" He looked Supreme dead in the eyes. "Man, fuck that."

He wasn't done. "Maybe I am like him," Lorde said, his voice low, simmering with venom. "Got betrayed by all my friends, just like he did."

The room was still. Sincere stared at him, disgust curling through her gut. "That's sacrilegious," she muttered under her breath, shaking her head.

Lorde's head snapped toward her so fast, she barely had time to react. "Bitch, shut your ho ass up," he spat, pure filth coating every word. "You ain't even worth this conversation."

Sincere didn't flinch. She just stared at him, because now she saw it for what it was. This wasn't a man trying to hold onto power. This was a man trying to hold onto the lie that he was still in control. But he wasn't and Supreme was done wasting time.

He lifted his chin, a silent signal to the men surrounding them. Andre and Carl stepped forward. Whispers moved in behind Lorde, his movements slow, calculated.

Lorde saw it, *felt it*, and he tensed. Realization finally settled in that this was it. There was no talking his way out, no escaping, and no second chances. He was no longer Lorde of the Saints. He was just a man. And men can be *replaced*.

"Fuck nah. It ain't going down like this."

The next few moments happened in a blur. One second, Supreme was motioning for his men to restrain Lorde. The next, Lorde was on the move. *Fast.* His body lunged forward, his hand reaching for Supreme's gun. Sincere saw it happen before anyone else. Her breath hitched and her instincts took over. Before she could even think, her hand flew to her thigh, gripping the cold metal of the gun Andre and Carl had left when she sent them away. She had no idea about the situation that was brewing because they couldn't speak on it. She had no idea that her life might be in danger, but clearly, they had.

She didn't hesitate and didn't stop to question herself. She just pulled the trigger.

Bang!

The sound was deafening.

The gun kicked back against her palm, the force sending a jolt through her body. Lorde staggered as the first shot ripped through him. His face twisted in shock as the bullet slammed into his chest. For a split second, his body froze.

Then . . . *Bang!*

He fired the gun in his hand. The sound tore through the air, sending a cold spike of fear through Sincere's chest. Her stomach dropped and she barely had time to register what happened before she saw Supreme stumble back. A dark stain spread across his side, his face tightening as pain ripped through him. Sincere's heart slammed against her ribs. but she quickly regained her focus. This time, she didn't stop.

Lorde was still standing. And even though he looked just as shocked as she did at the fact that he'd just shot his cousin, he was still holding the gun. And if he was breathing, that meant he could still kill them.

Her fingers tightened around the gun just as he lifted his as well. And before he could react, before he could take another shot . . . She fired again.

Bang!

The air was thick with gunpowder and blood, an acrid mix that clung to Sincere's senses like a brand, like something permanent that would never wash away. The weight of the gun in her hand felt foreign, heavy with finality, but she wasn't trembling. She wasn't hesitating. She wasn't stopping.

Bang!

It hit him lower, tearing through flesh and bone, and this time, Lorde collapsed. His knees buckled beneath him, sending him crashing down onto the cold hardwood floor, but even then—he wasn't done. His body writhed, his fingers flexing weakly, as if trying to fight against the inevitable. A sharp gasp rattled through him, a wet, choking sound that clawed its way out of his throat. Blood bubbled up at his lips, staining his teeth and yet, he still looked up at her with deep-seated hatred.

Sincere saw it in his eyes, the disbelief and pure rage. The refusal to accept that this was how it ended. He thought he was invincible. He thought she'd never have the strength to pull the trigger. He was *wrong*.

But still, she gave him a chance.

Her voice came out steady. "Drop the gun, Lorde."

Lorde coughed, a wet, guttural sound, but that menacing smirk still curled at his bloodstained lips. He was mocking her and the very idea of surrender. His fingers twitched around the gun, gripping it like a lifeline, like he'd rather die than let it go.

Andre took a step forward, his hands up. "Man, just put the gun down," he urged, voice tight with warning. "This don't gotta end like this."

Lorde laughed—or at least, he tried to. The sound was broken, shattered, thick with blood. His eyes shot back to Sincere, and with one last, desperate breath, he moved. The gun in his grasp lurched upward just as Andre lunged.

"Stop—"

Too late.

Sincere fired again.

Bang!

The gunshot cracked through the room, sharp and final. Lorde jerked violently, his body slamming back against the floor. This time, he didn't move. Blood pooled rapidly beneath him, dark and endless, seeping into the floorboards like a stain that could never be erased. Sincere stood over him, breath coming hard, gun still raised.

Lorde's lips parted slightly, the smug expression finally wiped clean off his face. But even now as his body twitched with the last shreds of life, there was something in his eyes. Something inside of him still held hate. It refused to die quietly. His mouth trembled. Blood bubbled past his lips, coating his teeth as he forced out a single, rasping breath.

"I hate you. You *fuckin'* bitch."

Sincere didn't even flinch at his words. She just stood there, watching as the life drained from his eyes until his body went still. She didn't turn away. She stood quietly and watched as the past, the monster that had haunted her for so long, finally ceased to exist.

Then, there was silence and the world around her stilled. The air seemed to shift, the thickness it held suddenly lifting. Sincere let out a slow breath, finally lowering the weapon. Behind her, Supreme groaned in pain, shifting slightly where he stood, but she couldn't look at him yet. She was too busy getting used to this new feeling. It was novel. One that she hadn't experienced in so long that it felt peculiar.

It was the feeling . . . of being free.

Epilogue

The sun stretched lazily across the horizon, spilling golden light through the windows of Sincere's home. It was a place that finally felt like hers. The scent of fresh wood polish lingered in the air, mixing with the faint aroma of vanilla candles burning on the mantle. She had spent years in so many different spaces that never truly belonged to her, moving like a visitor in her own life, never quite feeling like she truly belonged. Now, as she stood barefoot on the cool hardwood floors, surveying the place she created for herself, she began to relax into a new feeling that she was slowly getting used to.

Peace.

"You put that mirror too high," her mother called from across the room, hands on her hips as she squinted up at the grand, gold-framed mirror Sincere had just mounted in the foyer.

"What do you mean?" Sincere asked, wiping her hands on her leggings. "It's perfect."

Her mother scoffed. "For who? A basketball player?"

Sincere rolled her eyes, but grabbed the drill to adjust it anyway. The past few days had been unexpectedly healing. Her mother had insisted on helping her settle into the new house. Scratch that . . . it was *their* house. The decor style was a mix between Sincere's love for extravagance and her mother's deep-rooted love for the country.

The living room was dripping in chandeliers and velvet furniture, but the back porch opened up to sprawling acres of green land. Her mother had already started mapping out where she wanted to put the garden, talking about raising chickens, hogs, and even making homemade wine.

Sincere had eyed her from across the room when she first mentioned it. She held a teasing shimmer in her eyes. "So let me get this straight. The same woman who made me throw out my R and B albums in high school because they were 'worldly' . . . is talking about making her own wine now?"

Her mother didn't miss a beat. "If Jesus turned water into wine at the wedding, how come I can't have some every now and then?"

Sincere snorted, shaking her head. "You are something else."

Her mother smiled, wiping dust off a wooden rocking chair she had dragged in from the truck earlier. "You said this house was for both of us, right? That means I get my dream too. I've always wanted a farm. And you get your . . . fancy chandeliers."

Sincere bit back a smile as she looked around. The house was beautiful, warm and regal at the same time. It was the perfect mix of the two of them. Before she could say anything, a sharp knock at the front door echoed through the space.

Her mother wiped her hands on her apron, glancing toward the entrance. "That your lil' boyfriend?"

Sincere's heart skipped the way it always did when she thought about Supreme. She wasn't about to let her mother have that satisfaction, though. "No," she said quickly. "He's *just* a friend."

Her mother arched a knowing brow. "Mm-hmm."

Ignoring her, Sincere hurried to the door, smoothing her curls down before pulling it open. And just like that, her entire world softened. Standing on her porch, dressed down in sweats and a fitted tee, but still he was commanding every inch of space around him. Supreme's presence was effortless, like he belonged wherever he went. And beside him, Imani was beaming as she held up a housewarming gift bag, its golden ribbon catching the sunlight.

Sincere's lips parted in surprise. She barely had time to react before Imani let out an excited squeal and launched herself forward, wrapping Sincere in a hug that felt like home.

"Girl, do you know how hard it was for me not to pop up on you sooner?" Imani laughed, rocking them both side to side as she squeezed tighter. "I missed you!"

Sincere chuckled, hugging her back just as tight. It had been too long since she felt something this easy.

"Missed you too," she admitted, shaking her head as they finally pulled back. "But you act like I was dodging you or something. I was gonna hit you up soon."

Imani narrowed her eyes, lips twitching. "Mm-hmm. You were 'gon hit me up soon.' Lying already?"

Sincere gasped, hand over her heart. "I would never."

"Oh, so I guess my phone was broken?" Imani put her hands on her hips, grinning. "Or did you just forget about me now that you out here being all grown and mysterious?"

A guilty grin tugged at Sincere's lips. "I wasn't being mysterious. I was getting myself together. But if it makes you feel better, I thought about texting you plenty of times."

Imani sniffed dramatically. "You *thought* about texting me? Damn, that's crazy. You used to be real."

Sincere laughed harder, playfully shoving her shoulder. "I hate you."

"Nah, you love me," Imani corrected with a wink. "But it's okay. I understand that you went through a lot and had to deal with that. Just don't let it happen again."

Just like that, the weight on Sincere's chest felt lighter. Then, her gaze flickered past Imani and landed on Supreme. He stood leaning in the doorway, arms crossed, a teasing glint in his eyes. "Damn," he said, his voice low, teasing. "You this happy to see my sister, but I don't even get a hello?"

Sincere tilted her head, pretending to think. "Hmm. I don't know. Do you really deserve a hello, stranger?"

Imani cackled. "Ohhh, she got you."

His expression sharpened with quiet amusement as he pushed off the frame, taking his time walking toward her.

"Just like you said . . . I had to heal. Not in the same way, but . . ." He shrugged off the rest.

He looked good in a way that made something in her chest tighten. Healed and whole. Still him, but somehow more of a man than he'd ever been. When he finally stopped in front of her, his presence settled around her like something tangible. His eyes showered over her, that same unreadable look he always had, and for a brief second, something passed between them. There were no words, but it was felt.

Sincere exhaled, forcing herself to stay cool. "Okay, okay. I'll be nice. Hey, Supreme."

Supreme quirked a brow. "That's better."

Then, without breaking eye contact, he pulled a manila envelope from his back pocket and held it out. "I wanted to give you this," he said, his voice still steady. "It's the paperwork giving you back the rights to all your songs."

Sincere froze.

"I sent an electronic version," he continued, watching her reaction carefully, "but I figured having you sign the papers in person would make it feel more official."

Her heart thudded, her breath catching as she stared at the envelope in his hand. This was it. This was the last chain link breaking. She had freedom. He was giving her back everything. She launched herself at him, wrapping her arms around his neck, holding on tight.

Supreme let out a gruff chuckle, stumbling back half a step before steadying himself. "Damn, woman. I'm not a hundred percent yet."

Sincere laughed against his chest, shaking her head. "You're ridiculous."

Imani snickered in the background. "Aww, y'all cute."

Sincere pulled back, narrowing her eyes while trying to bite down her grin. "Don't do that."

Imani grinned. "I just be stating facts, baby."

Supreme smiled, but his gaze stayed on Sincere.

"Mama, you don't have to tell the rest of this story. I'm sure they don't want to hear it."

"Yes, we do, Mama," Imani chimed in. "Please go ahead and tell it!"

The sound of clinking silverware and quiet laughter filled the dining room as Sincere shook her head. She was not trying to take this trip down memory lane. Her mother sat at the head of the table, effortlessly holding court as she recounted the old story about Sincere's childhood, not caring even a bit about her protests.

". . . And I'm telling you," her mother continued, wiping tears of laughter from her eyes, "this child was *determined* to outsing the entire choir! She stepped right up in front of the microphone, didn't even wait for Sister Jenkins to finish leading the song, and belted out 'His Eye Is on the Sparrow' like she was about to get a record deal that Sunday."

Imani gasped dramatically, her eyes wide with delight. "Not you hijacking the solo!"

Supreme chuckled, shaking his head. "So, you've *been* bold."

Sincere groaned, dropping her head into her hands. "Can we *not* do this?"

Her mother ignored her, waving a dismissive hand. "Girl, hush. Anyway, Sister Jenkins was so stunned she just stepped back and let her have it. Pastor tried to be nice about it afterward, but I *know* they talked about us at Bible study that week."

Imani was *howling*.

Supreme nodded, his lips edging into a smile. "Sounds about right. That moment right there was the birth of Sahara."

Sincere sighed, shaking her head. "See, this is why I should've let y'all starve instead of cooking."

Her mother gave her a knowing look. "You ain't 'bout to let nobody starve. You get that from me."

Pure love filled every space in the room. Sincere glanced around the table, taking it all in. She was sitting in a roomful of people who felt like home. For so long, she thought she was destined to be alone. She was afraid that everyone she let close would either betray her or leave. Tonight felt like proof that maybe, just maybe, she had been wrong.

She inhaled deeply, letting the moment settle inside her, before pushing her chair back. "I need some air."

Supreme eyed her, reading between the lines. "I'll come with you."

She didn't argue. She didn't want to. Of all things she wanted in that moment, she wanted him close to her.

The night air was cool when they stepped outside. It was crisp with the scent of freshly turned soil and hay. A sky full of stars stretched above them, untouched by the lights of the city. Sincere's home was so far from the city's center that it felt like it was on an island all by itself.

Supreme stuffed his hands in his pockets, glancing around at the land. "I still can't believe this is where you live now."

Sincere smiled. "Didn't think I had it in me?"

"Nah," he mused, stepping over a wooden fence. "I just thought you were more . . . city."

She nudged him playfully. "You mean you thought I was too bougie to be country."

He chuckled. "I *know* you're bougie. I just ain't know you had this in you."

She waved a hand at the stretch of land before them. "Well, believe it. This is home now."

Supreme scanned the open fields, taking it in. It was such a different world from what he was used to. A better one, though. He couldn't complain.

"Not bayou enough for you?" Sincere teased, leading him toward the barn.

Supreme's brows bunched and he shook his head. "This is country as hell."

Sincere laughed, reaching out to pet one of the goats as they passed. "You're acting like I got you milking cows and making butter from scratch."

He raised a brow. "You *do* got cows, though."

She grinned. "And if I handed you a bucket, what would you do?"

Supreme gave her a deadpan look. "Hand that shit right back. Ain't 'bout to ruin this outfit."

She burst out laughing. But after a moment, the laughter faded into something quieter, something unspoken. They stood there, side by side, watching the animals, listening to the night. Supreme provided the kind of comfort that didn't need words to make it feel deep.

Supreme exhaled. "Can I ask you something?"

Sincere turned to him, tilting her head. "What?"

His gaze was steady as his question hung in the air. "You seeing anybody?"

Sincere's breath caught for a second, but she kept her voice light. "You really think I got time for that?"

He nodded slowly, like he was considering that. "So that means no."

"It means I'm minding my business," she replied, setting the record straight.

Supreme licked his lips, his voice dropping just a fraction. "And while you tending to your business, you think you got time to go on a date, though . . . with me?"

The question lingered between them. Sincere's heart thudded against her ribs. She thought about everything they'd been through. And then, slowly—she smiled. Something was being set into motion right then, something neither of them could stop even if they wanted to.

Sincere's smile lingered. Behind it was thoughtfulness and curiosity. She studied Supreme, tilting her head slightly. "Before I answer that, I got questions."

Supreme raised an eyebrow, biting back a grin. "Oh yeah?"

She nodded. "Yeah. My grandfather used to say that a woman should always know what kind of man she's dealing with before she gives him her heart."

Supreme chuckled, folding his arms across his chest. "Smart man. What kind of questions are we talking about?"

Sincere's expression turned playful, but her voice held weight. "The only card suitable for a queen is her king. Are you a king, or are you a joker?"

Something flickered in Supreme's eyes. It wasn't amusement, though, it was understanding. Slowly, he rolled up his sleeve, revealing the fresh ink on his forearm. It was a chess king piece—very bold and defined. The ink was still deep against his skin like it hadn't fully healed yet.

Sincere's heart skipped a beat. Without thinking, she yanked up her own sleeve, revealing the matching queen piece on her wrist. For a moment, neither of them spoke until Sincere decided to. "Did you know I had this done?" she asked, her voice barely above a whisper.

Supreme shook his head, eyes locked on the matching ink, a

flicker of surprise breaking into a smile. "Nope. I had no idea. When'd you get yours?"

"Two weeks ago."

"I was first, so you copied me." His smile deepened. "I got mine a month back."

Sincere let out a half-laugh. She glanced down at their arms, their matching ink etched in fate. Two pieces of the same board. Two forces that had always been meant to move together.

"Well, look at that." Supreme chuckled under his breath, shaking his head. "A match made in heaven."

Sincere met his eyes and felt completely at peace. She smiled, brushing her fingers over the ink on his arm before lifting her gaze back to his. "And now, a match made on Earth," she added.

The night was warm, filled with the scent of wild magnolias, her favorite flower. The stars stretched wide above, glimmering like they were watching them. Sincere walked beside Supreme, their hands threaded together, fingers locked in something neither of them had to question anymore. There was no rush in their steps. No urgency. Just being.

For the first time in a long time, she wasn't moving toward something she had to prove. She wasn't running from pain, or from herself. She wasn't a woman searching for the pieces of herself anymore, because she had already found them.

She glanced up at Supreme, watching the way the moonlight cut across his sharp jawline, the way he walked with the kind of ease only a man with nothing to prove could carry. It made her think of the first time they had been together. How his breath had felt against her skin, the way he had looked at her, touched her, and whispered into her ear.

You feel like home.

She hadn't believed it then.

Back then, she had been too used to people breaking her down into pieces they could carry before leaving her behind.

Back then, she had been a woman fighting to exist outside of the wreckage. But now she understood. She believed it, not because Supreme had said it, but because she knew it to be true.

She squeezed his hand, smiling to herself.

He looked down at her, brow lifting slightly. "What?"

Sincere exhaled a quiet laugh, shaking her head. "Nothing."

His eyes lingered on her, studying her like he already knew whatever she was thinking, before he pulled her closer.

She sighed, resting her head against his arm as they continued walking, letting the moment settle into her bones, letting the peace of it curl around her like something permanent.

"I love you, Sincere," Supreme said, whispering the words right into her ear.

She lifted her gaze, meeting Supreme's eyes as he looked at her like he already knew what she was about to say.

"I love you too, Supreme."

And in that moment, she understood something even deeper. She was no longer a graveyard. No longer the place where boys came to die.

No.

Now, she was the place where a king could live.